ROISIN MEANEY

After the Wedding

HACHETTE
BOOKS
IRELAND

First published in Ireland in 2014 by HACHETTE BOOKS IRELAND
First published in paperback in Ireland in 2014 by
HACHETTE BOOKS IRELAND

Cataloguing in Publication Data is available from the British Library.

ISBN 978 1444 743 579

Typeset in Apple Garamond by Bookends Publishing Services.
Printed and bound in Great Britain by Clays Ltd, St Ives plc.

Hachette Books Ireland policy is to use papers that are natural,
renewable and recyclable products and made from wood grown
in sustainable forests. The logging and manufacturing processes
are expected to conform to the environmental regulations
of the country of origin.

Hachette Books Ireland
8 Castlecourt Centre, Castleknock, Dublin 15, Ireland

A division of Hachette UK Ltd
338 Euston Road, London NW1 3BH
www.hachette.ie

For Maureen, Tony and Tess

MONDAY, 6 MAY

The grass darkens the pink of her sandals as she crosses the little patch of lawn between their pretend house and the path. Her toes get wet and slippery; she stoops to dry them with the front of her cardigan, and lingers to examine a furry black caterpillar as it pleats its way across the path in front of her.

'Where are you going?' she asks, but it doesn't tell her because it can't talk. She lays her finger on the ground before it and it clambers all the way over, tickling her with its little legs. She wishes she had some food for it. Mrs Carmody read them a story about a very hungry caterpillar that kept eating stuff. He had a red face, and one bit of him got ripped off by Brian, and Mrs Carmody had to put Sellotape on it.

She says goodbye to the caterpillar and walks on, past the house with the man who was sitting on his garden seat yesterday when she was going to the beach with Mammy. He wore giant blue shorts and no top and his tummy was pink and fat and he had a can of beer on it, like it was a table. When they passed him he said, *Hello, ladies*, and Mammy squeezed her hand too tight and made her walk faster. She's glad he's not there now.

All the curtains are closed in all the windows she sees. Everyone must still be asleep. She keeps walking until she gets to the last one. There's a white ribbon tied on the silver car parked outside. Granddad put a white ribbon on his car when Auntie Nuala was getting married. She was a flower girl, she wore a pink dress and sparkly shoes that she was allowed to keep, but they're too small for her now.

Mammy and Daddy got married too. Mammy told her she was there, but she doesn't remember because she was just a baby. Mammy showed her a book with all photos of the wedding, and in the photos she's got a white dress and a white hairband although she has hardly any hair, and Gary is small and has clothes like Daddy, even a tie. Ruairi isn't in any photo: he was still in Heaven.

She runs a finger along the ribbon on the car. It feels slippery. She looks at the house and sees someone opening curtains. It's a big boy in a blue T-shirt who looks out and waves at her. She waves back and then skips off in case she gets in trouble for touching the ribbon. She sings a song Mrs Carmody taught them about a butterfly, but she can't remember all the words so she sings *la la la*.

She's almost at the end of their road when she remembers Baba. She thinks she left him on a chair in the kitchen. She wants to go back and get him but Gary is there, and Gary is mean. He put all the Frosties from the box into his bowl so there were none left for her, and when she said she was going to tell

Mammy he twisted her arm and made it hurt, so she ran out. Now he'll be in big trouble because it's his job to mind her when they get up before Mammy and Daddy.

She'll go down to the beach and look at the sea. She won't stay for a long time because she's hungry and her toes are a bit cold and she misses Baba; she'll just stay long enough to get Gary in trouble. She remembers the way to the beach from yesterday with Mammy. Daddy took the boys to see the lighthouse and Mammy said they'd have a ladies day instead, just the two of them. They had crisps and lemonade, and she had two paddles, even though the water was freezing, and she built a sandcastle and buried Mammy's feet.

She reaches the big road. The beach is down a lane on the other side. She looks the two ways before crossing the road, just like Mammy told her.

A red car is coming. She stands still and watches it getting bigger.

✳

Standing by the window, sixteen-year-old Andy Baker yawns and pushes a hand under his blue T-shirt to scratch absently at his stomach as he listens to the intermittent slosh of his father's razor in the bathroom sink next door. If he put his ear to the wall he'd probably be able to make out the whispery rasp of the blade scraping its way along his father's chin. Like paper the walls are in this house. He won't be sorry to leave it.

He remembers the first time he set eyes on it, eleven years old and hunched heartbroken in his seat, barely looking up when Dad stopped the car and told him they'd arrived. Not interested in looking at a stupid house on a stupid island – who cared where they lived, when Mam wasn't going to be there with them?

The scooped-out feeling she left inside him is still there. The loss of her still makes him sad, but it's a blurrier-edged sadness now, like a softer echo of the sharp pain he felt right after she died. He wonders if it'll ever completely go away, or if he'll still feel something's missing when he's much older than Mam got to be, and his teeth live in a glass of water at night.

Nearly six years on, he can't conjure up her voice in his head any more, can't hear her calling up the stairs to him, telling him to hurry up or he'll be late for school. But he recalls how she would stick out her bottom lip and blow her fringe from her eyes, and he remembers that she loved Turkish Delight, and that she baked a coconut cake with fluffy white icing for every one of his birthdays, until she was too sick to bake anything.

He remembers how embarrassed he used to get when she'd sit on his dad's lap, and how she used to laugh at him for that, but not in a mean way. And when he smells the perfume she used to wear, even now, it summons such a lonesomeness in him that he has to fight the urge to cry.

He remembers things he wishes he didn't, like how horrible it was when she was sick, when she wrapped her bald head in brightly coloured scarves and drew eyebrows on her forehead with a black pencil, and how she looked like a ghost of someone he didn't recognise, with hollowed-out cheeks and eyes that had no light in them, eyes that seemed already dead. He remembers how bad her breath smelt near the end, as if the cancer – which he pictured as a lumpy brownish treacly gloop – was inching up through her, clogging all her pipes and tubes, pushing its stench ahead of it.

'You're my star,' she'd whisper, drawing him close with the claw her hand had become, 'my precious star,' and he would breathe through his mouth and do his best not to pull away from her.

He watches a gull wheel high in the sky, which looks whiter than it was yesterday. Yesterday was one of those unexpectedly wonderful days that you find dropped into a bunch of ordinary ones. From early morning the sun shone out of a perfectly cloudless sky. People who'd come to spend the bank holiday weekend on Roone gathered towels and buckets and headed for the beach, wanting to grab the good weather, wanting to stretch out their winter-white bodies for the sun to pink up.

Andy and his dad had been busy packing, piling up boxes and cases in the hall and ferrying them to Nell's. Late in the afternoon, when all they could do had been done, they'd washed the car and tied the ribbon on it, and afterwards they'd cooked a pizza and eaten it on the patio. *The last supper*, his dad said, catching a droop of melted cheese and folding it over his slice. Giving Andy half a glass of wine so they could toast the last supper.

He hears water gurgling from the sink. In a minute his dad will come out and it'll be his turn to make himself ready for the day. He glances at the bed where he's laid out the navy suit he got in Tralee three weeks ago. His first proper suit, bought for his dad's second wedding.

His dad's second wedding. Today Andy is becoming a stepson, and gaining a stepmother. He isn't quite sure how all that stuff makes him feel.

'Stepmothers get a bad press,' Laura had told him about a week ago. 'I was terrified of the ones in *Snow White* and *Cinderella*, and when my dad remarried – I was about your age, actually – I was all set to hate her, but she turned out to be impossible to hate. In fact, she ended up becoming my best pal.'

Andy's met Laura's stepmother. She came to Roone last autumn when Laura and Gavin were in the middle of turning Mr Thompson's house into a B&B. When Andy was introduced to her he thought Laura must be pulling his leg. They looked about the same age: how could she be Laura's stepmother? But nobody's leg was being pulled – and anyone could see they liked one another a lot.

Nell is about the right age to be his stepmother. If Mam hadn't died she'd be forty now, just five years older than Nell. And he and Nell have always got on – right from the start, when he didn't want to talk to anyone on Roone, she knew how to leave him alone until he was ready. If he had to choose a stepmother he'd probably choose her. It's just a bit weird to be getting one at all.

And another kind of weird thing is that Nell was engaged to his uncle Tim first, before they broke it off and she switched to Dad. And Uncle Tim will be at the wedding today, and so will his wife Katy, who was Nell's penfriend for years. All a bit of a muddle.

He takes his new white shirt from the wardrobe and lays it

on the bed next to the suit. He opens a drawer and takes out the skinny green tie he found in a Tralee charity shop, the same day he got the suit. He bought the tie for a laugh; it was only twenty cents, and he was going to show it to his dad and tell him he'd got it for the wedding, just to see the look on his face – but when Nell saw it she'd loved it, and begged him to wear it.

He's looking forward to moving into Nell's house. It's bigger than this one – well, most houses are – and it's closer to his favourite beach. And John Silver lives there too, of course, which is a big plus. For the first time in his life he'll be living in a house with a dog. He and his dad looked after John Silver while Nell's house was let out two years ago, but knowing you were going to have to give him back eventually was a bit of a bummer.

He hears the bathroom door opening. He goes out to the corridor and there's his father, standing with a red towel around his waist, hair in a tumble.

'All yours.'

There's a bit of toilet paper stuck to one side of his chin. Andy grins at it.

'What's so funny?'

'You got paper on your face,' he replies, walking into the bathroom, which is full of steam and smells like he's just walked into a forest.

✳

In his bedroom James Baker pats himself dry. He's been awake since just after five, lying open-eyed as the dawn slithered in through the window and picked out of the darkness the wardrobe, the chest of drawers, his wedding suit hanging in its grey nylon carrier on the back of the door.

His bedroom window was open, like it was all year round. He heard the first birds, and later a distant barking dog, and just before he got up the cheery clatter of a tractor in some field not too far away. Jim Barnes maybe, getting a good run at the day.

As he lay there waiting for eight o'clock to arrive he found himself thinking of Karen – inevitable, maybe, on this particular day. The first woman who'd walked up an aisle to him was bound to be called into being as he was about to stand at the top of another aisle to receive his second bride. He and Karen had had a dozen years together, which was a lot more than some people got – but surely this time round Fate would be more generous to him.

At half past six he pushed back the duvet, too full of nervous energy to stay where he was. He pulled on his painting jeans and T-shirt and tiptoed barefoot to the kitchen and made coffee. He took it out to the patio, where the easel Nell had given him for Christmas held his half-finished painting of *Jupiter*, the small yellow rowboat she'd inherited from her grandfather. He picked up a brush.

So much inspiration here on Roone, so much he wanted to capture on canvas, a small group of galleries around the country willing to display what he produced. Someone happy to buy one, every now and again. Money, or the lack of it, didn't bother James – he earned enough from the day job in Fitz's bar to support himself and Andy. He painted because he loved it.

At ten to eight he cleaned his brushes and stripped off his

clothes in the bathroom and scrubbed himself shiny in the shower, thinking about the day ahead, about the years that were waiting to be lived with Nell and Andy, and maybe more children. He felt light-headed with happiness at the thought of it all. He rinsed shampoo from his hair and wrapped a towel around his waist and filled the sink.

As he scraped the last of the night's stubble from his chin he fancied he heard a small child outside, singing in a high voice – something about a butterfly? – just before he cut himself.

He eases the scrap of toilet paper away now, swabs the tiny red mark underneath with antiseptic. They've hardly taken the straightforward route, he and Nell. Oh, he fell in love quickly enough: within a few months of their arrival on Roone he realised to his utter disbelief – still grieving for Karen, not looking for anyone to replace her – how important Nell was becoming to him. He held back, unsure of how she felt, afraid to trust being in love again – and while he was dithering, his brother came to Roone on holidays, and James in his innocence introduced him to Nell.

They became an item almost at once, with Tim making the journey from Dublin to the island every weekend to be with her. James stood miserably by as his younger brother wooed and won her. He heard with despair of their engagement, he witnessed Nell's happiness as she prepared for her wedding day. He suffered the torment of imagining her and Tim together, once Tim had moved his weekend things from James's house to Nell's.

And then it was all called off – Nell called it off – and James didn't dare hope that his chance might have come. He waited for a reconciliation, convincing himself it was inevitable, so afraid was he of playing his hand and being rejected. But there was no reconciliation. Tim didn't reappear on Roone, no attempt was made to resurrect the relationship, and James saw little evidence that Nell was pining for his brother. She was sad, undoubtedly, that her plans with Tim had come to nothing, but as far as he could see, not heartbroken.

Her friendship with James seemed as strong as ever; indeed, there were times when he imagined he detected something more, a new softness in her glances, a tenderness in her voice – but as the weeks turned into months, he struggled to find the courage to tell her how he felt. And in the end, it was Nell who did the telling.

'He was the wrong brother,' she murmured, one unforgettable afternoon as they tramped across the damp sand near the water's edge of Roone's longest beach. Both of them scarved and overcoated, their boots sucked into the sand with every step. It was November, three months after her broken engagement. It was freezing, dusk was already falling at four o'clock, and nobody else had been foolish enough to go near the beach.

'I knew that day you came to see me in the hospital,' she went on, 'the day after my house went on fire. You brought marshmallows, remember? You pulled the bag out of your pocket and put them into my hand, and I realised then that I'd picked the wrong brother.'

And right after saying it she'd stopped walking and turned to look at him, searching his face for his reaction.

'I'm not making a fool of myself here, am I?' she asked – and he kissed the tip of her frozen pink nose, and he enfolded all the layers of her in his arms and tried to contain his overflowing heart. And as they stood entwined, he whispered at last the words of love that had stayed so long unspoken.

Telling Tim wasn't something he relished. He decided to wait until they were face to face, which didn't happen until Christmas. James and Andy had travelled to Dublin to spend the few days as they always did with Andy's grandmother, and Tim arrived at noon on Christmas Day to join them for the festivities.

James's news didn't appear to come as a surprise. He chewed his lip as he digested it.

'Always knew you had a soft spot for her. Used to think she had one for you sometimes.'

'She didn't,' James replied, 'not until after you split up.' She picked the wrong brother first, which took a bit of the sting out of James coming second.

'You did for her though, didn't you?'

'I did.' Nothing to be gained now with lies, and his conscience was clear: he'd never tried to change her mind, much as he'd wanted to.

The afternoon was crisp, the sky full of unshed snow. The brothers sat in the little gazebo at the back of the house they'd grown up in, waiting to be summoned to the dinner Andy and his grandmother were preparing.

Tim stretched out his legs, crossed one ankle over the other, straightened the crease in his grey trousers. 'You must have been happy when we split.' The words said without rancour; he might have been remarking on the long-range weather forecast. But James, who'd grown up with him, heard the steel at the edge.

He regarded his brother's shoes, which had probably cost more than James's entire range of footwear. 'I wasn't happy. I thought you'd probably get back together.'

'But when we didn't, you saw your chance and jumped at it.'

James made no response, knowing that whatever he said would be wrong now. Tim's resentment was to be expected: he would have to ride it out, and hope that time would wear it down. They sat side by side on the wrought-iron bench, the smell of roasting turkey drifting out from the house, Chris Rea driving home for Christmas on somebody's radio.

'As it happens,' Tim said, uncrossing and recrossing his legs, 'I've met someone myself.'

James looked at him. 'You have?'

'From Donegal. Early days.'

And before James could ask any more, Andy had appeared to call them in, and that was the end of that, until a letter to Nell in February revealed that the Donegal someone was her long-term penfriend Katy. And a few months later, while they were all still getting used to the notion of Tim being with someone who wasn't Nell, he and Katy went on holidays to Italy and came home married, just like that.

And in September Katy announced that she was pregnant, a week after James had got down on one knee in Nell's hair salon – empty of customers at the time – and asked her to marry him.

And today it's going to happen: today he and Nell will become husband and wife. They're not having anything like the big splash-out wedding Nell and Tim were going to have. And they're not getting married on Roone, as they had planned to do last December.

Today they'll make their vows in a little church on the side of a hill that overlooks the Atlantic in County Clare, about three hours' drive from Roone. The wedding party, all ten of them, will make their way there in three cars, and will fit around a single table in the Ennistymon restaurant where a meal has been booked for after the ceremony.

He begins to dress. The day will be bittersweet, and there is nothing he can do about that. Nell will do her best to hide her grief, and he will try to make it easy for her. The wedding is happening because they both want it to, but December's tragedy will soak into every minute of it.

He slips on his shirt, still creased from its packaging, and does up the buttons. Andy is going to wear the hideous green tie he bought as a joke, because for some unknown reason Nell had taken a fancy to it and asked him to wear it. Any worries James might have had about his son accepting Nell as a stepmother had melted away when he heard that.

He's getting married. He and Nell are getting married. Again he feels a flip of happiness as his mouth curves into a smile. Still half dressed, he takes his phone from the bedside locker and places a call.

Laura answers on the second ring. 'What's wrong?'

'Nothing is wrong. I just wanted to touch base with someone, and I'm not allowed to call the bride.'

'Getting jittery?'

He grins. 'Not a bit. Happy as Larry.'

'Good. Now I have to fly – I'm in the middle of three breakfasts, and Ben has just spilt the milk. Touch base with Hugh if you need someone to talk to. See you in Clare – don't be late.'

She hangs up before he can reply. Living on Roone for less than a year, and already she's become as much a part of the island as James and Andy. Nell's next-door neighbour – theirs too after today. Walter's old house turned into a bed and breakfast; the scattiest on the island, he's sure.

'Can't cook to save my life,' Laura admits to anyone who enquires, but so disarmingly that people forgive her anything. James wouldn't be surprised to hear she had the guests making their own full Irish, and feeling they'd been specially chosen to do it.

He throws his phone onto the bed and finishes dressing.

❋

Once upon a time Nell Mulcahy fell in love with James Baker.

They're made for one another, everyone says it. Much more suited than Nell and Tim ever were, it's obvious now. He'd never have settled on Roone, that fellow. Never tried to get to know anyone, back to Dublin in his fancy car every Sunday night. Just as well it didn't work out with him and Nell.

Funny that she moved from one brother to the other, though, wasn't it? Funny that she didn't go for James in the first place, seeing as how they were friends ever before she met Tim. Everyone already matching the two of them up, then along comes Tim and sweeps her off her feet. And now look at her, settling on James after all. Better, though. Much better.

They don't say all that to Nell's face, of course. They say it to Laura's face – or rather, Maisie Kiely did, about a month ago.

'Don't get me wrong,' she said, holding out her sherry glass for Laura to refill, 'we all think the world of Nell, we'd love to see her settled down. But there's been so much upset, hasn't there? Her father leaving out of the blue like that, whatever was wrong with him, and then the whole business with Tim, and right after that her lovely little house burning down. And when she was all set to marry James, everything cancelled again with what happened to poor Moira, God love her. You'd wonder will things ever go right for her.'

'They didn't cancel. They're still getting married.'

Maisie looked offended. 'But not on *Roone*. Not *here*, where all her friends are. They're going to *Clare*, and only having their families there. What kind of a wedding is that going to be?'

Laura thought it best not to mention that she'd been invited, the only non-family guest. 'The main thing is they'll be married – and they can always have a bit of a party here later on.'

'They can, I suppose.' Maisie pursed her lips and sipped her sherry. 'And what about yourself?' She searched the sitting room and found Gavin going from group to group with a bottle of red wine in one hand and a teapot in the other. 'Has he any notion of making an honest woman of you?'

'Any day now,' Laura told her. No need to mention that she'd already turned poor Gav down twice: Maisie would have it around the island before teatime.

It was just before Easter. It was the official opening of Walter's Place, which was what Laura and Gavin had decided to call the B&B, seeing as how everyone still referred to the house as precisely that, even though poor Walter would have been gone two years in July, and Laura and Gavin had moved in last August. It would probably be known as Walter's place long after she and Gav – and possibly the twins – were pushing up daisies in Roone's quaint little graveyard, or wherever they all ended up.

'We're bowing to the inevitable,' Laura said to Nell, who agreed that they might as well.

Poor Nell, so shaken by her mother's death, so quiet and sad for weeks afterwards, her wedding plans with James put on hold until she could find the will to move forward with them. The second time something had happened to mess with her dream of walking down the aisle.

And poor Moira, who had simply been in the wrong place at the wrong time. Crossing a street in Tralee just before Christmas, mown down by a car that had skidded on black ice and rammed straight into her. Gone to Tralee to choose a birthday present for Nell, not realising as she went across on the ferry that morning that she was travelling to her death.

But that's in the past, and they all have to look to the future now. Laura spoons scrambled eggs onto toast and remembers the night she did her level best to seduce the man who is marrying Nell today, when she and the boys had rented Nell's house for a fortnight, two summers ago.

Stripping off for him in Nell's sitting room while the twins were asleep, dying for the feel of a man's hands on her body, and widowed James Baker with his tragic blue eyes had seemed the ideal candidate for the job.

His heart hadn't been in it. She'd known that, and had been willing to overlook it. She wasn't asking him to put a ring on her finger, just to make her happy for an hour. But then Seamus had woken up, and by the time Laura had quietened him and come back to the sitting room, James had thought better of the whole thing, had buttoned himself up again and was ready to go home.

Just as well, seeing how things had worked out with him and Nell. Bit awkward now maybe, if he and Laura had had a fling. And she'd ended up meeting Gav anyway, as soon as she and the boys had gone back to Dublin.

She fishes a poached egg out of its saucepan and plops it onto a plate as the kettle comes to the boil and clicks off. 'Ben, elbows down,' she says, pouring water into the waiting teapot, lifting the egg again to slide a slice of toast beneath it.

'How can you *see*?'

'Mammy eyes,' she tells him, 'in the back of my head.'

No pair of Mammy eyes needed to know his elbows are on the table. Ten times a meal she has to remind him, and Seamus not once. They never cease to amaze her, these two miracles of hers.

She delivers the breakfasts – mushrooms forgotten on the full Irish, third time this week, but her offer to provide them is brushed aside, thanks be to God: barely enough time as it is to get herself ready for the wedding. She checks her watch on the way back to the kitchen. Gav due home from his rounds any minute, three-quarters of an hour tops before Hugh and Imelda arrive to pick her up.

'Schoolbags,' she says, elbowing open the door, hands full with cereal bowls and juice glasses. 'Seamus, did you feed the hens?'

'It's Ben's turn.'

'Is *not*. I did it the last day.'

And while she's sorting that out Gav arrives, and she hands over to him and heads upstairs, praying for no interruptions. Amazing how indispensable she becomes the minute she disappears.

In the bedroom she pulls her T-shirt over her head and steps out of her size-eighteen skirt. She takes the bright pink dress from the wardrobe and holds it up before the mirror. Is the colour a bit daring, considering her current shape? Will she look like a giant ball of candy floss?

Probably, but at this stage she has no choice. She steps into the dress and eases it up over her bump. She's not looking forward to the journey in the back of Imelda's car – for the past few months she's been useless in any kind of vehicle – but she's impatient to see the church again, to sit within its thick walls and feel its serenity.

The church had been her idea. She'd told Nell about it back in March.

'It's on the coast road between Liscannor and Doolin, halfway up a little hill. Aaron and I found it when we spent a week driving around Clare, the summer before the boys were born. We didn't expect it to be open but it was. It was deserted except for a little black kitten fast asleep on a pew near the door. We sat there for about twenty minutes.'

Nell flicked a pebble from the stone wall. They stood on either side of it, huddled into jackets. 'What was it like?'

'Well, it wasn't in the least bit fancy. No padding on the kneelers, plain whitewashed walls, very few statues. I remember the sun coming out from behind a cloud and lighting up the stained glass in the windows. The colours were so vivid, they splashed onto the altar and the walls. I could smell flowers, even though there weren't any that I could see. And we could hear the sea quite clearly, although it was some distance away. There was something incredibly peaceful about the place, and Aaron felt it too. I think you'd like it.'

'How long ago?'

'About eight years.'

'Is it still there?'

'I have no idea – but it would be easy enough to find out. I just thought it might suit, you know. Close to the sea, not a million miles away. It might be what you're looking for.'

Nell didn't answer. Look at her, Laura thought, still so fragile. Eyes brimming at the smallest thing. She needed the comfort of a wedding, needed James to be moved in, and Andy. Let normal life resume with a husband to look after her, and a stepson for her to nurture.

'Would I see if I can find it again?' Laura asked. 'I could hunt around on the internet.'

'Do.'

'And if you wanted to see it I could go with you, if James wasn't free.'

And when Laura had managed to track it down, and Nell had phoned the parish priest and made an appointment to visit, that was exactly what they had done the following Monday.

'You won't feel it till the B&B is open,' Nell said, as she drove them to the ferry. 'Are you looking forward to running it?'

'Well, I'm not looking forward to the toilet-scrubbing or the bed-making, not to mention the hoovering and dusting and washing and ironing, but it'll be nice to be earning something again. The only part I'm really dreading is the breakfast.'

'Is it? But you're well able to fry a sausage.'

'I am – even I couldn't really cock that up – but it's the thought of the smell of it every morning. I'm nearly gagging just talking about it now.'

'Really? But you love fry-ups.'

'I do – when I'm not pregnant … Mind the ditch there.'

'You're *pregnant*? Since when?'

'I think about the middle of November. I haven't done a test but I'm four months late, and I can't look at food till noon – and I've already put on nearly a stone. I'm pregnant alright.'

'Laura, that's wonderful, congratulations – but four *months*? You really should have gone to Dr Jack by now.'

'I will, when I get around to it. Not that he'll tell me anything I don't already know, apart from a more accurate due date.'

'But he still needs to check you out and make sure everything's OK. Have you told Gavin?'

'I have. He's over the moon.'

He'd cried when she'd broken the news – first time she'd seen him in tears. Big baby tears, his whole face dissolving, bless him. She'd felt like holding a tissue to his nose and telling him to blow, like she'd do with the boys.

'Aisling didn't want kids,' he wept. 'At least, that's what she told me.' Aisling is his ex. She's had two children with Roy, whom she was seeing – and doing a lot more than seeing – while she was still married to Gavin. Poor old softie Gav.

'It's a girl, by the way,' she said to Nell.

'A girl? How can you know? You haven't had a scan.'

'No, but it feels like a girl.'

'Oh, come on – you can't possibly tell.'

'Wait and see.'

And as it turns out, Laura was half right. She smooths the pink dress down over her mountain of a stomach. What she knows now, after finally getting around to seeing Dr Jack, is that she isn't having a girl, she's having two. Twins again – and with a little over three months still to go, she's well on the way to the hippopotamus look she wore so well when she was expecting the boys.

It was planned. They wanted a baby – Gav *really* wanted one, and Laura had no objection. Of course, they could have planned it a bit better, arranged for the baby to arrive around Christmas when things were quiet, rather than in the middle of the tourist season.

No matter: she'll manage, like she always does. She managed when her opera-singer mother moved to Australia with Trudi, her voice coach, leaving twelve-year-old Laura to take her chances with Luke, who was always more interested in making art than looking after his daughter. She'd coped when he disowned her for marrying Aaron, a penniless unemployed bricklayer, a month after her nineteenth birthday.

The only time she almost fell apart was when Aaron was found swinging from the end of a rope a week before his twin sons were born, depression finally proving that Laura was no match for it. She'd been tossed into a nightmare of black days and endless nights, sleep a distant memory. Tears beyond her, so mired in shock and grief she was.

Thank God for her stepmother Susan, who had taken over the babies, practically becoming their surrogate mother until Laura eventually crawled out of Hell and found a way to carry on without Aaron. The wound he left inside her will always be there, but eight years on she and the boys have Gav, and they've begun a new life on Roone, and the future is showing distinct signs of turning out well.

She unpins and reassembles her hair, anchoring it with several clips to the top of her head. Poor Nell, dying to get her scissors to it, but Laura is hanging on to her Meg Ryan tumble of curls until she hits forty at least. She pats on foundation, adds a smudge of blusher, a slick of mascara, a stroke of lip gloss.

She eyes the face in the mirror, sticking out her chin to make the second one disappear. Only thing about a bit of fat, it keeps the wrinkles away. She'd pass for twenty-three, which is probably as much as an overworked twenty-seven-year-old mother of two can hope for.

Mother of four soon. The thought excites and unnerves her in roughly equal parts. Think positive, she tells herself.

Two sweet little girls to dress in shocking pink and lime green, and teach how to handle boys. That, or two hungry squalling creatures to keep her and Gav up half the night. Maybe Nell and James would like to adopt one. Or maybe she'll persuade Susan to abandon Luke and move in with them for the first six months.

She crosses to the window and looks out at the view that was Walter's all his life. A field across the road dotted with Michael Brown's sheep and beyond it the sea, the sight of it never failing to make her breathe easier. She pushes up the sash window and sticks her head out, inhaling the glorious seaweed-scented air. Better than any perfume, and free to anyone who wants it.

A good enough day to get married, not as fine as yesterday but not bad. The sun trying to find a way out through the clouds, a bit of a breeze blowing but no sign of rain. Hopefully the same in Clare. She turns her head to look down the road, and makes out what is probably Hugh and Imelda's maroon car making its way towards her. On the dot, as usual.

Imelda doesn't approve of her. Oh, they get on fine when they meet – she suspects Imelda is amused by her – but the fact that Laura and Gav aren't married wouldn't go down well there. And Laura hasn't missed the glances when she wears her low-cut tops – she can hear Imelda tut-tutting in her head. Pity about her: Laura was blessed with generous curves, and sees no harm at all in showing them off. Might be a bit of jealousy there too, Imelda not being what anyone would call well endowed.

She and Nell's uncle are a match made in Heaven. Hugh is

lovely, but a bit prim and proper like Imelda. Bet she's glad she bumped into him, at the ripe old age of fifty-whatever-she-was. Probably given up hope, probably reading convent brochures and wondering which one to book into.

Laura squeezes her swollen feet into shoes that will be kicked off as soon as she gets into the car. She puts lip gloss, purse, compact, confetti and camera into Nell's little sequined grey bag. No phone: let her have a proper day off for the first time in nine months. Whatever emergency happens can wait till she gets back.

As she walks downstairs the front doorbell rings, and she makes out Hugh's shape behind the frosted glass.

✳

'Lovely bright dress,' Imelda says, as Laura gets in. Maybe slightly too bright for her current size – so big already, and still a few months to go – and a bit indecent on top, as usual, but the pink colour suits her, and her face is really pretty. Pity she wouldn't get Nell to take a bit off her hair, though: there's just so much of it, and always half tumbling down.

'Did you talk to Nell this morning?' Imelda asks.

Laura shakes her head, dislodging a hair clip. 'I meant to ring her,' she says, pushing it more or less back into place, 'but I was up to my eyes.'

'I tried her about an hour ago but got no answer – she must have been in the shower.'

'James rang. He says he's fine, but I think he might have a bit of stage fright.'

'Oh, poor thing.' Imelda meets Hugh's eye in the rear-view mirror. 'You thought he was nervous when you talked to him yesterday, didn't you?'

'Just a bit. You girls don't realise what we go through when we get married.'

Imelda smiles as she turns the key, remembering Hugh's white face on the day of their wedding. Not that she hadn't been terrified herself, shaking like a leaf as she'd walked up the aisle on her brother-in-law's arm. A bride at last at fifty-four, too sick with nerves to enjoy the experience until it was over and she was sitting beside Hugh at the top table in Manning's reception room.

She drives the fifty yards to Nell's gate and Hugh gets out again. 'I should have phoned,' Laura murmurs, as they watch him walk up the path to the red front door.

Imelda thinks of Moira, and how much she would have loved to be here on her daughter's wedding day. 'I'm delighted it's James,' she'd confided to Imelda, the very last time they talked. 'Tim was lovely, but I couldn't see him settling on Roone, and Nell would never have been happy living in Dublin. And I'm so glad that James found someone else after his wife died. I always hoped that he would.'

It was December. They were drinking coffee in Lelia's, like they often did, and Moira was telling her about the shopping trip to Tralee she was taking the following day to find a birthday present for Nell. Imelda can still see Moira pulling on her grey winter coat and easing her hands into black leather gloves. The last living image of her.

''Bye for the present,' she'd said, leaning over to brush her cheek against Imelda's. 'I'll give you a ring tomorrow evening, let you know how I get on.' But the phone call had never happened, and the next time Imelda had seen her, Moira was lying under a sheet on a slab in a Tralee hospital morgue.

'You don't have to come with me,' Hugh had said, his face destroyed by the news they'd just got – but of course Imelda had gone with him. She'd driven him to the ferry, she'd held his hand as they crossed the steel-grey sea. She'd listened to him weeping quietly as she'd crawled every icy mile of the horrendous road to Tralee, and she'd thought of Moira making her way carefully along the same road that very morning, never to come home again.

She pushes aside the bleak memory as Nell's front door opens and she emerges, pulling it closed behind her. Imelda watches as she embraces Hugh, arms wrapped tightly around her uncle for several seconds. She sees her drawing back, pulling a tissue from the little cream-coloured bag slung on her shoulder, dabbing briefly at her eyes, shaking her head at some remark of Hugh's.

Poor creature, preparing for her wedding day all alone, her mother's loss still so acutely felt. Imelda kicks herself for not having thought to spend the previous night in Nell's house: she should have had some company this morning.

Laura opens her car door. 'I'll sit in the back with Nell,' she says, clambering out. The same thought in her head probably, not that she could have stayed at Nell's, with her two little boys and a house full of guests to look after. But Imelda has no such distractions, just her and Hugh, who could easily have been left on his own. How could she have been so thoughtless?

Nell is dressed in sky blue, a simple sleeveless shift dress in linen that stops just above the knee. She carries a cream jacket slung over one arm. Her shoulder-length brown hair is parted to one side and held off her face with a small tortoiseshell slide. Her eyes are red-rimmed, her cheeks flushed, but she's smiling as she approaches the car.

'Morning,' she says, reaching in through Imelda's open window to kiss her cheek. She smells of soap.

Imelda puts a hand on her arm. 'How are you, darling?'

'Oh, you know, a bit of a mess.' The query causing her eyes to fill again, reaching into her bag to retrieve the tissue. 'I knew it would be like this – but I'm happy, honestly. I'm finally getting married!' A small laugh, damp with tears.

Imelda squeezes her arm. 'You look beautiful.' And heartbroken. 'I have the flowers in the boot. They're in a cool box.'

'Thanks.'

The car's rear door opens. 'Come in here,' Laura instructs. 'I have to tell you about the pair from Oklahoma who stayed last night – he's a faith healer, and she had demons coming out her ears until she met him. Mad as coots.'

Doing her best to distract. Nell climbs in as Hugh takes his seat beside Imelda, and they set off for Clare. The waistband of Imelda's wine trouser suit is snugger than she remembers: serves her right for not checking to see if it still fitted. The last time she wore it was for Marian and Vernon's thirtieth wedding anniversary last August – she must have put on a few pounds since then. Better cut out the bread for a while, and the butter.

As they approach the pier the eleven o'clock ferry is docking. James and Andy will have taken the earlier one, by prior arrangement: wouldn't do for the bride to arrive before the groom. They wait as the cars drive off the ferry, every one of them with a licence plate from a different Irish county, except one that has come all the way from France. It's the May bank holiday, the proper start of the tourist season on Roone.

Imelda enjoys the island in summer, full of colour and bustle. It was the time of year she saw it first, when she came with Marian and Vernon to stay in Nell's house for a fortnight. They didn't get great weather – she remembers coming home from a walk more than once like a drowned rat – but rain has never bothered her. And of course she'd met Hugh on one of those rainy days.

As they wait to board, Sergeant Fox drives past in his squad car. 'Going a bit fast,' Hugh remarks. 'Must be an emergency.'

Imelda smiles. The biggest emergency since she's come to live on the island was one of Jack Flaherty's cows out on the road, up by the creamery. Sergeant Fox must have the easiest job in Ireland, stationed on Roone for the past twenty-odd years. No need at all for a guard most of the time, thankfully.

She finds Nell in her rear-view mirror. She watches her checking her face in a little compact, dabbing her nose and cheeks with a sponge. Her wedding day at last, after two false starts. Unable to celebrate it on her beloved island without her mother there to see her, but marrying the man she loves with her father waiting to walk her up the aisle, and if anyone deserves her story to have a happy ending, it's Nell Mulcahy.

The last car drives off the ferry and Leo Considine beckons them on. Imelda starts the engine and they leave the island behind them.

✳

All morning she's been fighting tears, or giving in to them. Couldn't answer the phone to Imelda earlier, couldn't talk to anyone just then, the grief pouring out of her.

'I'm off to Tralee in the morning,' Mam had told her on the phone, 'need to pick up a few things' – and Nell hadn't tried to dissuade her from travelling on the icy roads, knowing she'd be wasting her time. Mam always listened to what you had to say, then quietly did whatever she'd been planning to do.

'Be careful,' Nell said instead, her head full of the wedding that was happening in ten days' time, no room for anything else. Her thirty-fifth birthday, just two days away, hardly thought of in the excitement. 'Go easy on the roads, sounds like they're treacherous.'

'Oh, you needn't worry – I'll crawl all the way.'

But crawling all the way hadn't saved her, and in the end the wedding plans had come to nothing, and Nell had spent her birthday putting her mother into the ground.

Her eyes are burning. She looks nothing like a radiant bride. Poor John Silver mustn't have known what to think, putting a paw into her lap as she sat bawling at the table in her pink dressing gown, toast untouched, tea getting cold. *I'm OK*, she'd told him, cradling his paw in her hands, but he'd known she wasn't.

Getting into the blue dress afterwards, she was reminded of the very different one she'd got when she was engaged to Tim. Cost a fortune but so beautiful, a proper wedding dress in the palest sea green, handmade silk flowers trailing across its off-the-shoulder neckline, tiny mother-of-pearl triangular buttons dotting their way down the bodice.

She remembered trying it on for the first time, how fluidly it draped itself over her body, nestling up against her curves as if it had been waiting for her. She remembered its softness against her skin, how transformed she looked in the bridal-shop mirror. She remembered thinking, *This is the one.*

Such plans she'd had, over two hundred and fifty on her guest list, practically the whole adult population of Roone. Poor Henry Manning nearly having a canary when she went to the hotel to book the reception and told him how many he was going to have to feed.

Laura talks away beside her, doing her best to keep Nell from brooding. Funny to think that the two women in the car would hardly be with her today if they hadn't each decided to book a stay in her house two summers ago. Imelda married to Hugh now, Laura living on the island with Gavin, Nell's third tenant. You couldn't make it up.

Two years ago Nell was engaged to Tim – and now look at her, on the way to marry his brother. Two years ago her parents were still together, and Mam was still alive. The tears threaten again. She blinks hard and turns to Laura.

'Did you remember the camera?'

'Of course I remembered the camera. Some official photographer I'd be if I forgot it.'

'You don't have to spend your day taking photos. A few is all I want.'

'Don't you worry about that, I love it.'

'Pity Gavin couldn't come, and the boys.'

'Are you kidding me? The best thing about today – apart from you getting married, obviously – is that I've escaped on my own. Fond as I am of the men in my life, you have no idea how happy that makes me.'

'Well, I'd have liked them to be here.' Nell winds the window down an inch. 'I'm really glad you suggested that church – have I told you that?'

'Once or twice.'

'It's always open,' the priest had told her, 'on the owner's instructions. Just turn the handle and walk in, and then come and see me after' – and as soon as she'd entered the stone church, Nell knew she'd found the place she was to be married in.

It was simply laid out, as Laura had said. Roughly finished whitewashed walls, plain wooden seats, a small unadorned altar over which a little softly glowing red lamp was suspended on a chain from the ceiling.

Four square stained-glass windows on each side wall, fourteen mounted line drawings depicting the Stations of the Cross running beneath the windows. A statue of the Madonna and Child to the left of the altar, a plain crucifix to the right, a single confessional box by the door.

A faint smell of incense hung in the still air. The sea could be heard rumbling distantly through the door they left ajar. Nell slipped into a pew across the aisle from Laura and they sat in silence for several minutes. Here, Nell thought. This is the place, right here. She closed her eyes and listened to the sea and gave herself up to the serenity of the building and tried to think about nothing.

Eventually she heard Laura getting to her feet. She opened her eyes.

'Let's go and meet this priest,' Laura said. 'I could kill for a cuppa.'

They found his house as he had described it, tucked into the lee of the six-foot-high stone wall that separated it from the church.

'Hello,' he said, smiling. 'Which one of you is Nell?'

His breath smelt of coffee. His head was completely bald, bushy eyebrows compensating, freckly skin around his grey eyes splitting into creases. The backs of his hands sprinkled with sandy hairs and mottled with pale brown daubs, the left sleeve of his dark green jumper unravelling at the cuff. Grey sneakers under black trousers.

They shook hands: his was warm, despite the biting cold of the day. No sign yet of summer in the first week of April, no hint of the lengthening of the days that was to come.

He showed them into the sitting room, whose every horizontal surface – coffee table, mantelpiece, shelves and much of the floor – was hidden under framed photos, mismatched table lamps, glass bowls full of shells and pebbles, a clutch of peacock feathers poking from a big green bottle, several pots of houseplants in dubious health, a handle-less cup of cocktail sticks, a brown teapot missing its lid and holding a clutch of biros, unstable-looking towers of books, stacked boxes of Monopoly and chess, Cluedo and Scrabble (a little rubber mouse perching on top), precarious pillars of CDs, bundles of ruffle-edged magazines.

There was a musty feel to the room, as if its single window was rarely opened, but the creamy-yellow walls lent a homely air. The big wooden fireplace inset with dark green tiles was filled with reddened coals, and the couch he cleared of newspapers for them was deeply comfortable.

'Griffin,' he'd told them, as they'd shaken hands, 'but Noel is fine.' He made a pot of tea, and produced fig rolls to go with it.

'You don't mind if he stays?' he enquired, gesturing at the kitten – tabby, not black, but maybe a descendant of the one Laura had seen years earlier – that had followed him in from the kitchen and leapt onto his lap as soon as he sat down. They assured him they didn't.

'I love a good wedding,' he told them.

'There won't be many of us,' Nell said. 'Ten altogether.'

'Small,' he agreed, scratching absently under the kitten's chin with his index finger as it nestled into him, purring loudly. 'No matter: it's quality that counts, not quantity. Do please have some of the biscuits.'

'It's Monday of the May bank holiday we were thinking of – would that suit?'

'Should be fine. I don't think there's anything booked. What time had you in mind?'

'Maybe early afternoon. We'll be coming up from Roone – most of us will.'

'Ah, Roone. I spent a week there a good few years back. A lovely spot.'

'Yes … So, around half past two?'

'That sounds fine.' He rummaged on the chock-full mantelpiece and found a pair of glasses. He perched them on his nose and leafed through a big leather-bound notebook he took from the top drawer of a bureau in the corner. 'Yes, Monday the sixth is free. I'll pencil you in right now.'

'Thank you.'

He looked at Nell over the glasses. 'I'll need a letter from each of your parish priests, just to make sure you're not secretly married to other people. And you'll want to think about any readings you'd like, and music too – or maybe you have all that sorted already.'

'No … I'll get back to you on those, if that's alright.'

'That's fine.'

Laura left the room then to use the loo – 'first door at the top of the stairs' – and there was a small pause, during which Nell watched the kitten, playing now with the loose thread on the priest's sleeve, quite possibly, she thought, the cause of it in the first place. They'd always had a cat at home. Mam loved them. She felt her throat becoming tight, and lifted her mug quickly.

'Nell, I hope you'll forgive me,' the priest said then, taking off the glasses and pushing both his sleeves to the elbow, 'but it strikes me that there's something saddening you. Feel free to tell me to mind my own business – but if you want to talk about anything, I'm a good listener.'

Lord, he'd noticed. She couldn't pretend everything was fine. 'We had a … family tragedy,' she began, 'a few months ago, just before Christmas.' Blinking rapidly as she watched the kitten, curled up now, head tucked into its little ball of a body. 'My mother—' She broke off, unable to get the words past the hot lump in her throat.

The priest was instantly contrite, setting the kitten on the arm of his chair as he got to his feet, offering tissues from a box he conjured out of the room's clutter, suggesting a little drop of brandy.

'I wonder if he'll bring the kitten to the wedding,' Laura says.

Nell turns, surprised at the parallel tracks their thoughts have been running along. Or not so surprising, given the day that's in it.

Ferry operator Leo Considine appears at Imelda's open window, brushes aside the money Hugh offers him. 'On the house today,' he says, winking at Nell. 'All the best to you now.' The whole of Roone aware that it's her wedding day.

She thanks Leo, sits back and looks at the patchwork of grey and blue and white sky above her. She's on her way to marry James. In a few hours she'll be his wife. The happiness sits quietly within her, side by side with the sadness.

✳

She grips his arm tightly all the way up the aisle. Thirty feet, forty at the most. He takes it slowly, wanting to make it last, wanting to hang on to her for as long as possible. The symbolism of the act isn't lost on him – the ancient ritual of a woman being surrendered by one man to another – and as they continue their measured procession he wonders if other fathers feel the resistance he's aware of, a reluctance that might even be a sort of jealousy.

He's acutely aware of the sound of his footsteps on the tiled floor of the aisle. He wishes the organist, some local woman he presumes, would raise the volume a little, but her rendition of the tune he recognises but can't place remains subdued. He does his best to smile at the faces turned towards them, even though he's not the one they're all watching.

Nell is battling tears. He knows this without looking at her. The person she most wants to be there is absent, snatched abruptly from them, and there isn't a thing Denis can do to stop that hurting her today.

He hasn't seen the blue dress before – but of course she'll have bought it specially. He hopes she didn't go alone to find it. The father of the bride isn't privy to such information, even when the mother is no longer around. Maybe Imelda accompanied her: he's seen how protective of Nell she's become since December, and is grateful.

As they approach the top pew Laura steps into the aisle and clicks her camera twice at them. Nell's designated wedding photographer, in keeping with the no-fuss feel of the day, wearing a dress the rather alarming colour of the strawberry

Angel Delight he remembers Moira making for dessert when Nell was young. Pretty face though, nice and round and soft-looking.

And as she steps out of their way here is James, waiting at the altar to receive his bride. Beside him stands Andy, an inch or two taller than his father, an odd tie the colour of marrowfat peas under his navy suit. Some kind of fashion statement, no doubt. His father's best man, but no after-dinner speech on the agenda. 'He'd die of embarrassment,' Nell reported, 'so we told him there was no need.'

Denis turns and embraces her now, presses his cheek to hers. 'Be happy, my darling,' he whispers, feeling her tremble against him. He releases her and takes his seat next to Laura, fishing in his trouser pocket for a handkerchief and blowing his nose, looking at his polished shoes until he feels the possibility of displaying far too much emotion has passed. Laura squeezes his arm, grins at him when he raises his head.

He glances across the aisle to where the small Baker family contingent is sitting. Just three of them: mother of the groom Colette, Tim, and Katy, the woman he married instead of Nell.

'They're married,' Nell told her father last July. 'Tim and Katy. They got married in Italy, told nobody. James had no idea, and neither did Colette.'

Denis could see why Tim might have done it that way, given the history. What were the chances though, that he'd end up married to Nell's penfriend? After sixty-three years, the world hadn't finished astonishing Denis Mulcahy. He worried that Nell might be upset by the turn of events, until it became apparent that she was more than happy with her change of romantic partner.

And presumably Tim was happy too, a husband and father within two years of his split from Nell. Some might say his marriage had come about too hastily, but having himself experienced the startling joy of falling in love at first sight – two hands reaching for the same cup, that was all it had taken – Denis knows it's possible. Fortunate for Tim that Katy hadn't already said yes to another man.

Shame Colette had been done out of her younger son's wedding all the same: women seem to love the occasion. On the other hand, James was giving her a second day out today. And Tim and Katy had provided her with her first grandchild in February.

Denis had met Katy for the first time a few minutes before today's wedding, while they were waiting for the bridal party to arrive. Tall, with poker-straight glossy black hair, like Uma Thurman's in that Tarantino film. High cheekbones, dark-fringed eyes, a soft northern lilt to her voice. Just about as different from Nell as you could get: if Tim had been trying to find her polar opposite, he'd done it.

The strangest thing has happened, Katy had written in the one and only proper letter Nell had received from her, which Denis had been shown. *I don't know how you'll feel about it. I know you've said things are well over between you and Tim, but I'm still not sure how this news will go down. Just before Christmas, purely by chance . . .*

She hadn't used the word 'love', nothing so specific, but you could tell by the carefully guarded phrases that the relationship was significant.

'How *do* you feel about it?' Denis had asked.

Nell didn't answer right away. She turned the letter over in her hands, an expression on her face that Denis couldn't define.

'It's … a little strange,' she said then. 'Just the thought of him with someone else, I mean. Oh, I know that's silly, it's completely over between us, but just … and I suppose it's a bit weird that it's Katy.'

They met, the two women, not long afterwards. Nell's idea. 'I just think we should. We always said we would, and maybe now is the time.'

She hadn't said a whole lot about it afterwards, but Denis could gather, more from what she didn't report, that the encounter in a Limerick hotel lobby had been awkward. He imagined the strained conversation, the polite phrases stuttering between them despite the hundreds of postcards they'd exchanged over the years.

Small wonder the correspondence had faltered and died soon after that, Tim's migration from one to the other proving too disconcerting for what was, after all, just an on-paper relationship.

Sitting in his good suit in this charmingly simple church, watching as his daughter waits for the bald priest to pronounce her a wife, Denis longs for Claire to be there. Impossible, of course. Even if she wasn't married to another man, Denis couldn't present her to this assembled gathering, with the sense of Moira's absence almost a physical thing – worse, he suspects, than if Claire had walked in on his arm when Moira was still alive to witness it.

He sees in his mind's eye the face of the wife he abandoned. The grey eyes that Nell had inherited, the light-coloured hair, somewhere between fair and biscuit, the placid expression that was her default one. Poor Moira, married for more than thirty years to a man who didn't love her. The object of silent pity, no doubt, when he'd walked away from their marriage. The scandal he'd caused is a source of continuing shame for him – the respected principal of Roone's primary school leaving his wife for another woman. Rightly or wrongly, when presented with a choice, Denis had opted for love.

He shifts his focus to Andy, remembering the withdrawn, lost boy of eleven or twelve who'd moved to Roone with his father. Scarcely able to look anyone in the eye, let alone string a coherent sentence together. Small wonder, given what he'd gone through. Walloped sideways by his mother's death, too young to properly articulate his grief, too old, maybe, to cry in front of his father.

Nell had been good for him, undoubtedly. She'd befriended him and James; she'd brought the two of them, and sometimes just Andy, out in her boat when she could; she'd coaxed smiles from him. And look at him now, sixteen since March and a changed person, still quiet but much more at peace.

'He writes poems,' Nell told her father. 'James has shown me some. They're lovely.' Denis hopes the boy appreciates getting Nell for a stepmother.

And now she's Nell Baker, the words *man and wife* finally

uttered by a broadly smiling Father Griffin. Denis watches his daughter lift her face to receive her new husband's kiss, conscious no doubt of the eight pairs of eyes that are fixed on them. Nine if you count the priest's, who must have seen his share of just-married kisses.

They leave the church, pausing outside just long enough for Laura to take a few more snaps. The day is dry but breezy, the patchy sky hinting at showers to come, the gusts ruffling hair, causing skirts to billow and sending Imelda's confetti flying in the wrong direction to spatter itself over the furze bushes that fringe the church grounds.

Denis shakes the priest's hand. 'I take it you're coming to the meal?'

'I am. Delighted to have been asked.' The priest's grip is strong. 'I understand you were widowed not so long ago. Allow me to offer my condolences. It must be difficult today.'

Unaware, it sounds like, that Moira and Denis had separated. No need to enlighten him, no point in complicating things. Denis thanks him and accepts his offer of a lift to the restaurant in Ennistymon, a dozen miles or so back along the undulating coast road.

They pile into the respective cars, the configuration changed slightly. Nell sits in with James and Andy, leaving Laura to travel with Hugh and Imelda. The Baker group remains intact, no cause for change there. They've journeyed in Tim's black BMW from Dublin, leaving Lily in the care of her maternal grandparents, summoned from Donegal for the occasion.

'They were delighted,' Katy had told Denis before the

wedding. 'They're wild about her, love any excuse to get a go of her.' The first grandchild, it turns out, on the maternal side too.

Katy and Tim had bought a house, according to Nell, somewhere in the Dublin mountains when Lily was on the way. Money, or lack of it, not an issue in that household, with Tim a full partner in his computer-programming workplace and Katy some kind of a solicitor as far as Denis remembers.

'I take it Nell is an only child?' the priest asks, as they drive off in his rather battered Fiesta, the last car of the convoy.

'Yes, we just had the one.'

'And what's this she told me she did again?'

'She's a hairdresser. She has the only salon on Roone.'

The priest gives a startling bark of laughter. 'Not much good to me then,' he says, patting his bald head.

'Are you a Clare man yourself?' Denis enquires.

'I'm not. I'm Galway. I was born and bred just outside Clifden, so I haven't come too far.'

'And how big would this parish be?'

With such small talk they stitch the ends of their journey together, as Denis does his best to ignore the fact that the car smells strongly of cat.

❋

The restaurant is tucked into a side street, small and family-run, a corner table reserved for them, as Nell had requested. No fuss, no drama, the usual menu and a modest, carefully iced cake to follow that Imelda has made.

'She didn't ask, I offered,' she told Hugh. 'I wanted to do something concrete for her.'

'You didn't think she'd rather something a bit lighter?' he asked, and she called him foolish and sent him to Gavin and Laura's for eggs. It touched Hugh to see how she'd instinctively drawn closer to Nell in the awful days and weeks following Moira's death. Not trying to replace her mother, just letting it be known that she was there when Nell needed the comfort of an older female companion.

Across the table Hugh sees James leaning towards his new wife to whisper something in her ear, bending his head to brush the back of her neck with his lips before drawing away. He catches the blush in his niece's cheeks, the fond smile she gives her husband before returning to pick at her grilled rainbow trout.

She's lost weight since Moira's death, the bones in her face more prominent, the few extra pounds she always carried fallen away. He knows this spare, lean frame is considered a good thing among women, but he never saw the point of it. He prefers a more rounded, softer-looking figure in a woman. Maybe living with James will coax Nell's curves back; maybe their marriage will give her fresh heart and fill her out again.

He regards James, in conversation now with Andy on his left. He thinks today must have put James's first wife back into his thoughts; she must have crossed his mind as he was putting on his suit this morning, as he was saying, 'I do,' to Nell just over an hour ago.

The wedding has reminded Hugh of his own marriage, not yet

past its second anniversary. He recalls his anxiety as he waited for Imelda in the church on Roone, where all the significant religious episodes of his life – baptism, first confession, first communion, confirmation – had taken place. Crowded the day he married Imelda, all the people he'd grown up with there to witness the occasion, the big gathering Nell had planned for her wedding to Tim.

What if she doesn't come? was all he could think of, standing in the new grey suit he'd bought, sick with nerves, the boiled egg he'd forced down at Moira's house sitting like a stone inside him. *What if she changes her mind? What if she decides she doesn't want to spend the rest of her life married to an incomplete man?*

He pictured the faces of his friends and neighbours, the pity he'd see in them when it became apparent that he'd been abandoned. Maybe none of them really believing that it could ever have happened. Poor deluded Hugh, they'd be thinking, to imagine that anyone would want him.

But he wasn't abandoned. He'd sensed a rustle in the crowd behind him, he'd heard Peggy Reilly starting the opening bars of the 'Bridal Chorus'. He'd got to his feet, heart in his mouth, and dared to look around – and there Imelda had been, walking towards him on her brother-in-law's arm, looking every bit as terrified as Hugh had felt.

He catches her eye now across the table. He winks at her, and she smiles back, the simple upward tilt of her mouth making his insides dissolve. *For every old foot there's an old boot*, his grandmother would tell him, as he sat on her knee as a young boy. It had taken Hugh fifty-one years to find her, but Imelda has been well worth the wait.

After the meal James thanks everyone for coming, and the little assembly begins pulling on jackets. Outside the rain is starting, tiny dots speckling the path. Hugh sees Katy hugging Nell briefly in farewell, saying something that makes Nell nod and smile.

Small talk: 'Thanks for the dinner', 'All the best'. The kind of things you'd say to the most casual acquaintance, someone you meet now and again at other people's dinner parties, or an opponent, a friend of a friend maybe, in an occasional game of doubles on the tennis court.

Katy gets into the car and Hugh watches Tim approach Nell to say goodbye. No embrace there, not so much as a handshake, Nell's hands holding the edges of her jacket closed as they speak, Tim's hand hovering close to, but not touching, her upper arm. 'Hug Lily for me,' he hears her say. Lily, her niece by marriage, the child of the man she'd thought would father her babies.

And there is Nell's new mother-in-law taking leave of her now, elegantly turned out in a pale green jacket and skirt, pearls at her throat and ears, lilac shawl draped gracefully across her shoulders. Tim's green eyes, fringed with darkened lashes. Neat ankles above shiny shoes the colour of pale skin. Surprisingly few pure white strands threaded through the brown hair. Dyed, he assumes. Colette must be in her mid-sixties at least, with James in his early forties.

See her kissing Nell on both cheeks with what appears to be genuine affection. Reconciled, by the look of it, to the musical-chairs love lives of her sons. Relieved, no doubt, that both seem happily settled now with their respective partners.

The shiny black car pulls away smoothly, Colette seated in the front beside her son. *Won't see them again for a while*, Hugh thinks as he waves them off with the others.

Father Griffin is next to leave. 'Thank you so much for taking us in,' Nell tells him.

'My pleasure. Every good wish to you both. You make a delightful couple.'

The homeliness of his car – pocked with mud splashes, dented and dusty, front number plate askew – provides a striking contrast with the BMW. He toots the horn as he drives off, back to his little church on the hillside. Not a bad life, Hugh reckons, if a lonely one at times. He knows all about loneliness – or he did.

The two remaining cars start for home, Denis travelling now with Andy and the newly-weds, Laura staying with Hugh and Imelda. Both cars are rust-spotted, like all the island vehicles; one of the side-effects of living in a place surrounded by salt water. Not that anyone is particularly bothered: on Roone a car is no more than something to get you from A to B until it wears itself out, or disintegrates from the rust.

No honeymoon has been planned for the newly-weds. 'We might ask Colette to come and stay on Roone for a week with Andy in the autumn,' Nell said when Hugh asked. 'We're thinking of France, but I don't really mind where we go.'

Imelda and Hugh flew to Scotland after their wedding, to a little family-run hotel outside Edinburgh that Hugh had found on the internet. There was a working fireplace in the low-ceilinged bedroom, full of a blazing coal fire when they arrived.

The sprung mattress on the big ancient bed creaked loudly when either of them moved a muscle, banishing the awkwardness of their first night together and filling it instead with merriment as they pictured their jovial host and hostess listening to the performance from their own bedroom. In the end they abandoned the bed in favour of the more discreet hearth, and Imelda was successfully deflowered by the light of the dying embers.

Their porridge in the morning had come with a jug of thick cream, and they'd detected no knowing looks in the countenance of Mrs Thompson – no sign of the husband – as she told them about buses into Edinburgh, and the opening times of the castle and the museums.

'I might grab a nap,' Laura announces from the back seat. 'Can hardly keep my eyes open after that dinner.'

Within minutes Hugh hears the soft drag of her exhalations. He turns to Imelda. 'You enjoyed the meal?'

'I certainly did. Nell told me the priest recommended the restaurant.'

Hugh looks out at the hedges and the sheep-dotted fields and intermittent houses. A tractor waits in a gateway for them to pass, the driver lifting a finger off the steering wheel to them. White sheets flap and billow on a clothes line. A few more drops tap on the car window as they approach the first of their ferry ports at Killimer.

Nell married, the sixth of May a new date for them to mark each year. Hugh stretches his legs as much as the car will allow, and lets his own eyes close.

※

They drop Nell's father in Tralee, at the railway station car park where James picked him up that morning. Andy watches him hugging Nell before getting into his Ford Mondeo.

Andy wonders if he misses Roone, after spending most of his life living there. He doesn't know Mr Mulcahy well, has never had much contact with him. He was principal of the school when Andy moved to the island and joined the sixth class there, but Andy hadn't been interested in making friends with anyone then, least of all his school principal.

It suddenly occurs to him that Mr Mulcahy might be his step-grandfather now – does getting a stepmother mean you inherit all of her family too?

Andy hadn't known about the other woman for ages. Nobody had said anything to him. It hadn't occurred to him that a man as old as Nell's father would still be interested in sex. He did think it strange that someone would just leave his family and his job out of the blue like that, but it hadn't interested him enough to pursue it.

And then he'd overheard Nell and his dad talking about it one day – he was in his room, they were out on the patio – and he was shocked and slightly nauseated at the thought of old people still doing it, still *wanting* to do it. Even now he prefers not to think about it.

He's seen no sign of the other woman – anytime Nell's father comes to the island he's alone – but she's out there somewhere. He thought she might be brought to the wedding, now that Nell's mother isn't around any more, but she didn't appear.

When Andy thinks about sex, which is most of the time, he pictures girls he knows from school, or those he hangs around with on the island. He takes their clothes off in his head: he unbuttons their dresses, unhooks their bras, slides down their panties. He takes his time with the underwear (which is always lacy, and either black or red).

He imagines them undressing him: pulling his T-shirt over his head, unbuckling his belt, unzipping the fly of his jeans, hooking their thumbs into the waistband of his boxers to push them out of the way. By the time they're both completely naked he's usually achieved what he set out to achieve, so he rarely travels further than that in his imaginings.

The thought of actually having sex with a girl, any girl, is exciting almost beyond the point of endurance – but he can't imagine wrinkled bodies coming together, can't stomach the thought of Mr Mulcahy in bed with a woman. And the idea of his father doing it with Nell isn't any less off-putting – they're not exactly old but they're getting there – so he denies those thoughts any space in his head.

'He's coming to dinner on Friday,' Nell announces, when she gets back into the car, turning her head to watch her father drive away.

Andy wonders where he'll sleep. Since Nell's mother died

her father has been returning to Roone roughly every other weekend, spending one or two nights in Nell's only spare room. But this evening the spare room is officially becoming Andy's bedroom, and her father will be left without a place to sleep next Friday.

He still has his own house on the island, of course, but he might feel a bit funny going back there, seeing as how his wife went on living in it after he left, and now she's dead. He might be afraid her ghost would come back to haunt him for what he did, or something.

It's five to eight and still broad daylight by the time they get to the ferry terminal for Roone. Somewhere between Farranfore and Dingle they'd lost Laura and the Fitzpatricks, the Ring of Kerry clogged with tour buses and rental cars and groups of brightly coloured cyclists. They have to sit in a queue for the Roone ferry, even this late in the day. Two vehicles ahead of them is a silver minivan with some radio-station logo painted on the rear.

'Must be doing a programme on Roone,' Andy's father remarks.

As they wait, Nell turns in her seat. 'I was wondering if you'd fancy painting your room. The wallpaper might be a bit girly for you.'

Andy can't remember what the wallpaper in her spare room looks like. He was shown around like everyone else when she moved into the house, the one she'd got built to replace the house that had burnt down, but that was well over a year ago. Since then he's only been in the kitchen, or on the patio.

'You can have a look,' she tells him, 'and see what you want to do. As long as you don't go for black with silver skulls.'

He smiles. 'OK.'

He remembers her trying to persuade him to let her cut his hair in the weeks and months after he and Dad had moved to Roone, when having hair long enough to hide behind had seemed pretty important. In the few photos he has of that time he looks like a freak, a time-warp hippie with a sullen face you can barely make out behind the lank brown curtain.

And then he decided to get it cut, out of the blue. Except that it wasn't out of the blue, it was around the time Mr Thompson had been looking for someone to clear out his attic. Andy had taken on the task to shut his dad up, and because it seemed as good a way as any to earn a bit of cash.

And over the course of the couple of weeks he'd spent on the job, Andy had warmed to Mr Thompson, whom he'd hardly ever spoken to before, but who had seemed interested in what Andy had to say, and offered him books of poetry to read.

Andy had taken them out of politeness – but to his surprise he'd found himself enchanted by the richness and imagery and rhythms of the verses, and as he read, he felt a tightness within him begin to uncurl and loosen.

And eventually he risked telling Mr Thompson about Mum, and how she'd written poetry, and how he thought he might try writing a poem for her. And Mr Thompson didn't laugh, and the tight place inside Andy loosened a little more, and he thought that maybe it was time to stop blaming everyone for Mum dying of cancer. And as he tried to figure how exactly someone stopped being unhappy, it occurred to him that he might try cutting his hair and see how that felt.

And so he went to Nell's salon of his own accord one day after leaving Mr Thompson's, and he asked Nell to take it all off, to shave it so short you could see his skull underneath. Talk about a change. His dad nearly hit the roof when he saw it, and Andy overheard him giving out to Nell on the phone afterwards. His dad rarely lost his temper, but when he did it was pretty impressive.

The ferry arrives and empties its cargo of eight cars, and eight more drive on to take their places, and they move up the queue to fourth position. Twenty past eight; after nine by the time they'll reach Nell's house. Not Nell's house any more, he reminds himself, their house now. Cool.

He hopes the walls are thicker than in the old house. He'd rather not hear anything that goes on in the other bedroom.

✳

'Something is wrong,' she says to James.

She can tell by the increased activity in the harbour: far too many boats for this time of the day, even on the May bank holiday. Her fingers tighten on the ferry's rail as she hears the distant *put-put* of the coastguard helicopter, over by the north face of the island. Let it not be a drowning, she prays, let it be a rescue. A German tourist had drowned last summer, a woman fallen overboard from a yacht. Islanders and visitors huddled silently by the pier to see her being hauled, inert, from the water.

'Leo,' she calls to the operator, walking among the parked cars, issuing tickets. 'What's up?'

He crosses the deck to them. 'A child went missing on the island this morning. There's been no sign of her all day.'

'Who?'

'Nobody from here, a family on holidays.'

'Were they on the beach?'

He shakes his head. 'Don't think so – I heard she just disappeared from the house they were renting.'

'Dear God.'

Nell slips her hand into James's as she turns to look out to sea again. A missing child, every parent's worst nightmare. She sees the boats searching the water, a mix of trawlers, lifeboats and pleasure craft; everyone praying, no doubt, that they'll find nothing, that the girl will be discovered safe and well on land somewhere.

'We'll call to Manning's,' she says to James, 'and hear more.' The hotel has always been the designated centre of operations for any island gathering: whatever activity is being carried out, apart from the annual beach barbecue, will be steered from there.

The ferry docks and they drive off, and as they make their way towards the hotel they spot Lelia Doherty on the path.

'The family are staying in Bayview Cottages,' she tells them. 'They must be near you, James. The little girl just walked out of the house this morning, they're not sure what time exactly. The parents were still in bed.'

'How old is she?'

'Four or five, we think. I've been dropping food down to the pier – some of the fishermen have been out there for hours. There are search parties going around the island too.' She turns her face towards the sky, smudged now with pink and purple and grey-blue, and pierced with the first stars. 'Dark soon.'

A lost child, a family beside themselves, everyone racing to find her before the night comes.

'We'll get changed,' Nell says, 'and come back.'

'Lord,' Lelia says, looking at them properly, 'it's your wedding day – I completely forgot.'

And while Nell and James have been getting married, quietly and without fuss in Clare, Roone has been thrown into turmoil.

THE AFTERMATH

Everything has changed; everything has been turned the wrong way around.

It began with a phone call to Sergeant Fox, some ten minutes before Imelda and her party drove onto the ferry on their way to Clare. An agitated female voice reported that her five-year-old daughter had left their holiday home some time earlier, and was now nowhere to be found.

A lost child: an instant priority. Within a quarter of an hour the incident was a newsflash on Roone's local radio, with listeners being asked to keep eyes peeled for a fair-haired child in a blue dress, white cardigan and pink sandals.

Long before the bridal party arrived at the church in Clare, a poster had been hurriedly fashioned. Have you seen Ellie? it asked, above a smiling, chubby-faced, curly-headed girl, pudgy fingers wrapped around an ice-cream cone that dribbled onto her hand. Copies of the poster were taped to Roone's shop windows, and tacked onto telegraph poles and tree trunks throughout the island.

By the time Nell was walking up the aisle on her father's arm, a photo of five-year-old Ellie Ryan was being shown on national television screens, along with library footage of Roone. Before the wedding guests had taken their seats in the Ennistymon restaurant, the queue for the island ferry had backed up further than anyone could remember, and the tarred car park of Manning's, Roone's only hotel, had begun filling with vans displaying the logos of TV and radio stations from all around the country.

Social media soon became involved. The word flew across Facebook and Twitter, the news of a little Irish girl's disappearance being passed from account to account, an image of the poster travelling around the world within minutes, comparisons with other vanished children inevitably being made.

At that stage Sergeant Fox, Roone's single law enforcer, had been joined by several police officers from the mainland. Since the island didn't possess a police station, Manning's Hotel, by virtue of its size and central location, became their impromptu headquarters, with plain-clothed and uniformed personnel travelling to and from a room at the rear of the reception area that was made available to them.

As newly married Nell Baker journeyed home from Clare with her husband and stepson, as various details of the morning's incident were still being broadcast throughout the island population, a hastily convened press conference took place in a reception room at Manning's. Ellie's bewildered parents were summoned and positioned side by side behind a table, along with the detective who had been assigned to lead the investigation.

The mother, blonde and dazed in a crumpled blue dress, cheeks and throat a mottled pink and white, remained silent throughout the ten minutes or so, both hands clutching a little cream-coloured cardigan as she ignored the questions of the reporters, gaze focused somewhere beyond them, white lips moving silently. Her daughter missing more than nine hours.

The father looked equally disoriented, pinpricks of stubble emphasising the chalky pallor of his terrified face, the hand he raised to push back his dark hair trembling visibly. 'We just want her back,' he said, voice catching as cameras flashed so repeatedly that they lent a marionette jerkiness to his movements. 'We just want our little girl back. Please, if anyone has … taken Ellie, please give her back to us. You can have everything we have – we'll give you anything you want. Please.'

That he was capable of talking at all, that he could string words together in any kind of coherent way, was incomprehensible to the island parents, who had gathered around televisions to watch the report, which was screened live. The thought of any of their children going missing was too horrible to contemplate.

The searches of the island on the first day continued into the night, nobody wanting to give up and go home. Those forced to remain indoors – mothers of youngsters, teens not old enough to participate, pensioners too infirm – lay awake, listening to the piteous sound, every so often, of the little girl's name being called outside, Ellie … Ellie … a heartbreaking chorus that echoed throughout the island until the first grey light nudged its way past bedroom curtains.

And now it's morning, and James returns to the house after

spending his wedding night searching with other island men, Nell and Andy having been persuaded to return home some hours earlier. He walks into the kitchen to find a wide-awake Andy waiting for him.

'I saw her,' Andy says right away, before James can ask why he isn't in bed. 'It must have been her. Yesterday morning, she was standing by the car. I was in my room, I opened the curtains and—'

He breaks off, and James sees that he's close to tears.

'Hey,' he says, pulling out a chair, 'you weren't to know, don't worry.'

'But she was on her own, and she's only five – I waved to her.' Biting down on his bottom lip to stop it trembling.

'You remember what time it was?'

'I think … about twenty past nine, or a bit earlier.'

'We'll go to the hotel,' James tells him, 'and let the guards know. It'll help them with the investigation. I'll have a shower and we'll go down.' Not imagining the information will be of much help at this stage to anyone apart from Andy, who might feel less guilty for having waved the little girl on her way.

Later that morning Father William is interviewed in the church grounds.

'It's just terrible,' he says, his round face uncharacteristically sombre when it appears on television screens. 'Nothing like this has ever happened on Roone before. Nobody knows what to make of it. We're all in shock.'

A vigil is held in the church that same evening, word spreading rapidly throughout the day. Islanders and tourists alike turn up, crowding into the pews, standing in the aisles. Only at Christmas, or for a wedding, is the church so full. Candles are lit as dusk falls; prayers are offered for Ellie's safe return. In the third pew from the back Laura Dolittle holds tightly to Ben and Seamus's hands as Father William urges carers of young children to be vigilant.

For much of the week following Ellie's disappearance the sea around Roone remains filled with familiar and unfamiliar craft, the pier scattered with vehicles, varying clutches of locals and tourists milling about, waiting for news. The coastguard helicopter hovers and swoops overhead, like an anxious observer of the activity below.

The searches on land also continue, steps being retraced when searchers run out of new territory. Police dogs strain on leashes, nosing through thickets and burrowing into ditches and panting across sand dunes and pattering into caves. The holy well is investigated, along with all the other island wells. Shed and barn doors are thrown open, haylofts and milking parlours and farm buildings of every kind explored.

Houses are investigated too, of course. Police work in groups of two or three, working their way around the island, ringing doorbells, rapping on knockers. Crouching to peer under beds, opening wardrobes and piano lids and chest freezers, climbing attic stairs while householders and holidaymakers stand about with folded arms, shaking heads and murmuring with whoever is close enough to murmur back.

The lobby of Manning's Hotel has never been busier. Henry Manning moves silently among the various men and women scattered about – media, police, search parties – repositioning seating as needed, ordering tables to be cleared, sandwiches to be replenished, another round of coffee provided by his harried staff.

Vehicles come and go in a constant stream from the hotel car park, more media vans arriving daily, the story gaining rather than losing momentum as the week passes.

The island's bed and breakfast premises are unexpectedly inundated. At Walter's Place Laura's four guest rooms are filled to capacity, and she loses count of the callers she's forced to turn away. The island's two campsites become dotted overnight with tents.

On the day of the disappearance Ellie's family is moved discreetly out of their rented holiday home – just four doors down, it turns out, from the house James and Andy have vacated – and taken to an undisclosed location. By the following morning every Roone local knows that they've been put into a similar holiday home on the far side of the island. This information is not shared with a single reporter.

The media isn't idle though, far from it. Residents are ambushed coming out of their driveways, or standing behind the counters of their various business premises. On Wednesday, two days after her wedding, Nell Baker is visited by a woman who asks for a wash and blow-dry – and who reveals, mid-shampoo, that she works for a national newspaper.

'Tell me what the real Roone is like,' she says. 'There must be a dark side to it. I just want to paint a picture for our readers. You'll be an anonymous source, of course.'

Nell rinses off the shampoo and sends her packing with dripping hair. Locals in Fitz's pub downstairs from the salon are equally tight-lipped, limiting their comments to the mundane until hovering strangers are well out of earshot.

Lelia in her café across the road is more forthcoming, providing any enquiring reporters with colourful accounts of pagan rituals, grave-robbing, drug smuggling and demonic possessions on the island until they leave her alone.

There are mixed opinions among the islanders about Ellie's fate. Some insist that nothing sinister can possibly have occurred, that whatever has befallen the child must be considered a tragic accident. Others concede that darker forces may have played a part in her disappearance, however incredible the notion seems of a child being taken, or worse, by someone on Roone.

The possibility of the child having been taken off the island is of course also taken into account, although Leo Considine, who operates Roone's only ferry to the mainland, recalls no suspicious activity on the day in question. Nonetheless, Ellie's poster becomes a common sight throughout Kerry and beyond, and police all over Ireland are briefed on the case.

While uncertainty remains, nobody on Roone is taking a chance. Mothers wait each weekday at the school bus stop and bring their offspring straight home, along roads that a week before were deemed perfectly safe. Younger children are no longer allowed out on their own; bedroom windows are locked tightly at night.

Everyone prays for a happy outcome. But with each day that passes, fewer believe it can possibly happen.

FRIDAY, 10 MAY

Laura rushes into the kitchen carrying a stack of cereal bowls. 'Two full Irish,' she mutters, clattering the bowls onto the draining board. 'One soft poached egg, no runny white, one scrambled egg on brown toast.'

Ben looks up from his breakfast. 'Mum.'

'Don't talk to me.' She pulls sausages and rashers from the fridge. 'Two full Irish, one soft poached egg – Seamus, take those shoes off the table. Whose turn is it to feed the hens?'

No response.

'Whose?' Glugging sunflower oil onto the warm pan, jabbing at the sausages with a fork. 'Answer me.'

'You said don't talk.'

'Give me patience. Two full Irish, one soft poached, one scrambled. Please feed the hens before the bus comes, one of you, I don't care which one.'

She tosses the sausages onto the pan, her stomach churning gently as it's been doing every morning since Walter's Place opened for business. She grabs an egg and cracks it into a bowl.

'Mum, I need a kiwi for school,' Ben says.

In the act of reaching for a second egg Laura turns to stare at him. 'A kiwi?'

'Yeah. I have to bring it for drawing.'

'We don't have any kiwis. Why didn't you tell me this yesterday?'

'I did, but you didn't hear me.'

'An' I need a bucket,' Seamus says.

'*What?* Lord almighty.' She cracks the second egg into the bowl, flings in salt and pepper. 'Ben, you can bring a tomato – tell Miss Barnes it's the closest we had.' She shakes the pan, making the sausages hop. 'Seamus, there's a bucket in the back shed – and if you don't take down those shoes right now they're going in the bin.'

'That's Caesar's bucket. It's smelly.'

'Rinse it out with the hose, it'll be fine – and if you get wet you'll stay wet for the day.' She tumbles the egg mixture into a small saucepan, splashes water from the kettle into another. 'Soft poached egg on brown toast – or was it the scrambled on brown? Ben, knock on the dining-room door and ask is the brown toast for poached or scrambled eggs.'

'Why can't he do it?'

'Ben,' she repeats – and the tone of her voice has him scrambling down from his chair. 'Get the bucket,' she orders Seamus, 'and do it without one more word, or there'll be trouble. And hand me those shoes so I can put them in the bin.'

Ten minutes later the kitchen is empty, the school bus having mercifully whisked away her sons, the breakfast orders having been delivered, more or less accurately, to the group in the dining room. As Laura wearily runs water into the sink to wash the saucepans, the back door opens and Gavin appears, home from his morning deliveries.

He kisses her cheek, wraps an arm around her waist to press her briefly to him. 'How're you feeling?'

'I'll live.'

He takes a half-eaten piece of buttered toast from a plate on the table and bites into it. 'What was Caesar's bucket doing at the gate?'

She groans. 'Seamus was bringing it to school for art.'

'I'll run it down in a while.'

'Thanks ... Any news?'

He shakes his head, holding the remainder of the toast between his teeth as he takes off his jacket and drapes it over the back of a chair, on top of a small pair of navy tracksuit bottoms. 'Nope. Not a thing.'

And even though it's the answer she was expecting, Laura feels the awfulness of it bearing down on her, sapping her remaining energy as she pulls on rubber gloves and watches the gushing water making bubbles dance in the sink.

No news. No sign. It's been four days since Ellie Ryan has been seen. Of all the places in the world, how in God's name could it have happened on Roone?

From her first glimpse of the island two summers ago, Laura had felt a connection with it. Before that, even: from the minute she typed her holiday-home requirements into the website's search engine – last two weeks in July, three people, two bedrooms, by the sea – and Nell's house had popped up, the only one offered to her out of a database of at least a thousand. A white one-storey house whose front door and windowsills were painted red. Two bedrooms, adjacent to beaches, close to village.

She clicked on *more details* and discovered one double room, one twin. A twin room for the twins, a double for her. A little paved patio to the rear, a lawn in front. Kitchen, sitting room, bathroom. Nothing fancy, but all they needed. And the only one on offer, although there must surely have been many more houses that fitted her requirements. Fate, or a computer glitch.

The house was located on a small offshore island that she'd never even heard of. She typed *Roone* into Google images and her computer screen filled with a view of the island's harbour, dotted with colourful boats sailing under an improbably blue sky, a row of pastel-painted houses behind it, gently undulating hills providing the backdrop. Pure tourist fare but still beautiful, and tempting enough for her to make the booking.

She remembers standing at the ferry rail two months later with the twins, seeing the reality of the harbour and the houses and the hills, and knowing she'd made no mistake in choosing the island. She recalls driving off the ferry and making her way past the landmarks she'd memorised from Nell's directions, steering them towards the house with the red door – and thinking, *That was no computer glitch*.

And wasn't she right? Didn't she find the book that Gav had left behind when he'd stayed in Nell's house the fortnight before them? She'd taken his address from Nell and returned it to him when she and the boys had got back to Dublin – and look at them now, living all together in the house that had belonged to Walter.

'Let's buy it and move here,' Gav had said, when the four of them returned that winter to spend Christmas on the island. 'Let's sell my house and buy Walter's.'

Laura was amused and alarmed in pretty much equal measure. They'd been a couple for less than half a year. They didn't live together, although he'd been spending Friday nights under Laura's rented roof from the time he'd made it plain that he had no intention of doing a runner.

And while the prospect of moving to Roone made perfect sense to her – and she was fairly sure the boys wouldn't object – the thought of taking this giant step with Gav wasn't something she was entirely sure she was ready to do.

'It needn't be for good,' he said. 'It could be just an adventure. A year or two, see how it goes. Dublin will still be there.' Scaling back, because he had seen her uncertainty. He might be happy to think about forever, but he understood that maybe she wasn't. Not yet.

An adventure, though: she liked the sound of that. She had no house to sell in Dublin, only a lease that ran till May. And the crèche she owned and ran could be wound up in June, when she'd be taking summer holidays anyway. She could easily cut ties with Dublin.

Leaving her father wouldn't be a problem: he'd scarcely notice if they went to Australia, like her mother had. The only person who might miss them – who *would* miss them – would be Laura's stepmother, Susan. But Roone wasn't the other side of the world: she could visit them easily.

So Laura agreed to go and see the house, which wouldn't tie her to anything. They made an appointment with Conor Heath, who was part farmer, part fisherman, part auctioneer, and he showed them around the property that had been Walter's.

It was a mess. Wallpaper peeled from walls, damp patches bloomed on ceilings, floorboards creaked, doors stuck, taps dripped into stained sinks. But the rooms were spacious, and its marble fireplaces were intact and beautiful. The view of the sea from the front bedroom windows was breathtaking, the wide curving staircase magnificent. It must have been a splendid house once, and it could be again.

Laura stood alone in the kitchen while the boys roamed upstairs and Gavin talked football with Conor in the room Walter had called 'the drawing room', and she recalled the evening she and the boys had sat at the kitchen table with James and Andy, and Walter had fed them fish pie and bread-and-butter pudding. She closed her eyes and heard the tin-whistle tunes he'd played for them afterwards, just a few days before they'd left Roone and Walter had died.

She imagined them living there. Eating at the same kitchen table, sitting in front of the fire on winter evenings. The boys playing football in the field by the side of the house, picking apples to put into tarts. She imagined living in a house with a drawing room, right next door to Nell.

Yes, she could see it happening. What was more, it made perfect sense.

The asking price wasn't too horrendous. They made an offer a bit below it there and then, before Gav had even put his Dublin house on the market, and were told that it would be passed on to the distant relative of Walter's, now living in Newfoundland, who had inherited. Three days later they went back to Dublin – and over the following few months they'd made it happen.

'I couldn't be more delighted,' Susan said, when Laura broke the news. 'About time you had a bit of excitement.'

'It's not forever,' Laura told her. 'Just a trial run. Nothing's set in stone. You'll come and see us often, won't you?'

'Far too often.'

Laura's father wasn't mentioned: neither of them suggested that he visit Roone too. Some stories were never going to have a happy ending.

They packed up in August and moved to the island, a little over a year since they'd first laid eyes on Roone on their separate holidays. To Laura's relief, Gav seemed happy to defer his dream of opening a small zoo on the property in favour of her plan.

'We could turn the house into a B&B. It's plenty big enough, and Roone is full of tourists in the summer. I could manage that side of things and you could resurrect Walter's organic-vegetable business, and we could restock the henhouse and sell the eggs. And you could get a little secondhand van and do a delivery service around the island.'

And that was precisely what they had done – and over the following months Laura discovered, among other things, that renovating a house with two small boys underfoot is something best undertaken just once in a lifetime, and that running a B&B is harder than it looks, and requires the kind of stamina pregnant-with-twins women aren't generally noted for, and that hens are unbelievably messy creatures.

Money is uncertain. The last of the proceeds from Gav's Dublin home went on the renovations, and sometime around the middle of August there will be two more mouths to feed. But the vegetables seem to grow of their own accord, and the hens lay big brown eggs in return for their bed and board, and the apple juice practically sells itself.

And money has never mattered a scrap to Laura, as long as they have enough to eat, and halfway decent clothes, and a fairly regular supply of wine in the fridge – not that she's been able to have much of that lately.

And on the first of August last year, which was her twenty-seventh birthday, and four days before they were due to move to Roone, Gav had asked her to marry him and she had said no. He'd asked her again at Christmas, and she'd given him the same answer. 'We're fine as we are,' she'd told him. 'It ain't broke, no need to fix it.' And she saw the hurt in his eyes and tried to take it away by assuring him that she was happier now than before they'd met, and delighted that they'd decided to take this chance together, and thrilled that he was in the boys' lives, which was all perfectly true. He was as good a father to Ben and Seamus as any man could be.

70

AFTER THE WEDDING

But he's not Aaron. He doesn't remotely resemble the man with the pure black hair and lean, beloved face and haunted grey eyes that (thankfully) neither Ben nor Seamus inherited. He's not Aaron, and she can't imagine ever being married to any man but Aaron.

Roone is special, though. There's something intrinsically good about the island, she's convinced of that. Not that bad things don't happen here – people die on Roone, just as they do anywhere else. Fine people like Walter, who walked upstairs one afternoon and collapsed on his landing, and never woke up.

And there are drownings too, of course: the sea claims as many victims off Roone's coast as it does in any other waters. Nell's grandfather and Walter's father drowned together, both fishing from a trawler that was dashed to smithereens on the rocks in a sudden storm. Accidents happen, people get sick, hearts get broken on Roone, the same as they do the world over.

But there's another level to the island, a sort of benign, quirky undercurrent that permeates daily life so gently that none of the locals pay it any heed at all, and most tourists remain completely unaware of it.

Certain apple trees bear fruit out of season – there's one in their very own little orchard – whose juice lifts moods and cures insomnia. A sign that nobody claims to have erected stands on the island's westernmost cliffs and points out to sea, informing anyone who reads it that the Statue of Liberty is three thousand miles in that direction.

People often smell chocolate, or oranges, at the cemetery, though no plants with those scents grow anywhere on the island. Every so often Willie Buckley sets down his usual fifteen lobster pots and finds sixteen waiting for him when he goes back – and the extra one, invariably, will have vanished by the time he's setting them again.

Acknowledge it or not, there's a benevolent force at work on the island that Laura prays will somehow bring about Ellie's safe return – although with each passing day the fear is growing in every island heart, hers included, that nothing short of a miracle will be needed for that to happen. But miracles *do* happen – and what better place than on Roone?

She must tell Walter about it, next time he shows up.

✳

She is woken this morning, as always, by the soft rattle of a cup against its saucer. She opens her eyes and watches her husband placing the tea on the locker. Up before her every day, one of those people who can't stay in bed once he wakes. Slipping quietly out, careful not to disturb her. Not that she'd object to being disturbed, once in a while.

'Thank you,' she murmurs.

He sits on the side of the bed, lays a hand on the blankets above the curve of her hip. 'I'll head out for a few hours, if you don't need me for anything.'

'I don't.'

When he's gone she raises herself up on an elbow and reaches for the cup. Every inch of the island must have been thoroughly combed by now: with so many people involved, four days is more than enough time to search a place the size of

Roone. But a sizeable crowd of locals, Hugh included, still turns up every morning at the hotel, splitting into groups of five or six to inch their way across waste ground that's already been gone over more than once, or to shove sticks into the same ditches as the day before.

Of course she understands why they do it. They have to keep doing something, however fruitless it seems, because doing anything is better than doing nothing. Doing nothing means acknowledging that you've given up hope, and nobody is ready to do that. Not yet.

She finishes her tea, listening to the buzz of Jim Barnes's tractor in the field beyond their garden wall as she runs through the tasks that are waiting for her once she's up.

Put on a wash, make the sandwiches. Take the ashes from the sitting-room fireplace, clean the kitchen windows like she does every Friday. Dead-head and water the flowers in the window box, hang out the washing, head down to the village.

Drop the sandwiches to James, who opens the pub every morning at half eleven. Carry on to the supermarket with her list: milk, toothpaste, black pepper, biscuits, toilet rolls.

On the face of it, identical to scores of other Fridays since she married Hugh and moved to Roone – but like every day that has passed since Ellie's disappearance, it's coloured differently. Everyone feels it. They wake up with what has happened, they carry it around with them. It's the first topic of conversation between friends and neighbours: faces are searched for news before a word is exchanged.

Ellie, they call her, as if they know her, when all they know is what she's left behind: parents who are named Martha and Vincent, an older brother called Gary, a younger one called Ruairi. A plump grandmother in a powder-pink twinset who spoke tearfully on the news one evening, who pleaded with people to *pray for our little angel's safe return* as her red-cheeked husband stared mutely into the camera, the arm that was draped around her shoulders looking awkward, as if it had been placed there by someone else.

Marian has rung from Westport every day since Monday.

'I can't say I'm that surprised, Imelda – there's some awful funny characters around now. It's drugs I blame, they turn people into animals. Vernon is very worried about you – he's saying would you not think about coming home till this lunatic is caught?'

And Imelda assures her sister that she's quite safe, and reminds her there's no evidence to suggest that anyone kidnapped the little girl. She doesn't add that in the year and a half she's lived on the island the only drugs she's encountered have been alcohol and tobacco, or that Roone is her home now, and that she's perfectly happy to stay there. She doesn't say it because she'd be wasting her time: once Marian's mind is made up about something, there's no persuading her otherwise.

'But surely that child would have been found by now if she'd just wandered off – aren't there divers in the sea every day, and hasn't the whole island been well searched? No, someone took her, you can be sure of that. I wouldn't be surprised if it was one of those paedophiles – they're everywhere nowadays.'

The idea of someone using an innocent child to fulfil some

perverted desire is so awful that Imelda refuses to consider the possibility. Where is the poor little girl, though? Why hasn't she been found? How can a child simply disappear?

She pushes back the blankets – heavier than a duvet, but Hugh prefers them – and gets out of bed. She takes off her nightdress and stands under the shower, whose temperamental behaviour – trickling one minute, whooshing out the next, going from hot to cool without warning – makes using hair conditioner an exercise in optimism. No matter: there are bigger things to worry about, and her hair will never be remarkable, with or without the help of conditioner.

In the kitchen she poaches one of the eggs Gavin delivered on Thursday – deep orange yolk from their clutch of contented hens – and eats it on a toasted slice of Nell's poppy-seed bread. So lovely to be able to eat food that's locally produced.

She remembers the jar of honey that was waiting for them on a shelf in Nell's kitchen when Marian and Vernon persuaded Imelda to accompany them on a holiday to Roone two summers ago. *Lavender honey*, the label said, in beautiful copperplate handwriting. She found out later that it had been produced by bees belonging to Walter, the man in the house next door who had died the day before they arrived.

She looks around the kitchen that had belonged to Hugh's parents, and to his grandparents before them. The house is old, one of the oldest on the island. 'It's yours now,' Hugh had told her. 'Make what changes you want, put your mark on it.'

But even though it could have done with plenty of modernising, Imelda has changed as little as possible. It pleases her to think of past generations of Fitzpatricks sitting down to eat in this room every morning, sleeping in the same bedroom that she now shares with Hugh. It makes her happy to think she's part of that family, even if she joined it too late at fifty-four to add another generation.

She's replaced the dark kitchen cabinet doors with light oak ones and switched the patterned vinyl floor covering to plain white. Apart from that, things in the kitchen are pretty much as she found them. The heavy pine table, scored with the marks of previous knives and ringed with long-ago cups and glasses, still stands in the centre of the room. The clock that Hugh's father was presented with on his retirement from the island creamery hangs on the wall by the dresser, its gilt roman numerals faded but its brass pendulum swinging to and fro on its chain as steadily as ever.

She's left undisturbed Hugh's grandmother's collection of Hummel figurines, the little cowlick-headed boys and rosy-cheeked girls arranged so carefully on the dresser's shelf. They were surely cherished possessions: who is Imelda to come in and decide they've had their day?

They remind her of the glass animals her mother loved, the owls and hedgehogs and squirrels on the side table in the sitting room that were dusted faithfully each week. They remained undisturbed for years after her death, the dusting carried on by Imelda who hadn't cared for them in the least, but how could she not look after them? They sit even now in a box on top of the wardrobe in Imelda and Hugh's spare room – destined, it seems, to be in Imelda's care forever.

In addition to making as few changes as possible to her new home, Imelda has managed to reclaim something that had been lost. 'My father was the one with the green fingers,' Hugh told her. 'When he died our house plants struggled on for a while, but eventually they gave up.' So Imelda has reinstated them, placing a potted red geranium into each of the two deep windowsills in the kitchen, adding bits of greenery to the other rooms, filling vases with sprigs of fuchsia and sprays of montbretia as soon as the plants burst into bloom on every roadside in Roone, and yellow roses from the three bushes Moira gave them as a wedding present.

'I always wanted a sister,' she told Imelda. 'I'm so glad you met Hugh – I'd nearly given up hope of him finding anyone.'

Able to be happy for her younger brother, despite her own marriage having been destroyed by her husband. But now Moira is gone, taken from them without warning, the way these things happen sometimes.

Imelda finishes her breakfast and brings her dishes to the sink. She goes upstairs for the laundry hamper, fills the washing machine – a wedding present from Marian and Vernon to replace Hugh's ancient one – and switches it on.

She cleans her hands and assembles the sandwich fillings on the table – salmon, chicken, ham, cheese, tomatoes – and begins to butter bread. The sandwiches were her idea, something to offer the pub customers at lunchtime besides crisps and peanuts.

Hugh was dubious when she suggested it. 'I wouldn't want to upset the cafés. I wouldn't want to take custom from them.'

'It would just be a bit of healthy competition. I'm sure there's plenty of business to go around, especially in the summer.'

So he agreed to a set number of sandwiches in the pub from May to September when the village is crowded with holidaymakers, and for the rest of the year the island's three cafés rotate their opening days as they've always done to feed the small scatter of off-season customers in turn, and everyone is happy.

She picks up a tomato, smiling. Still unable to believe sometimes how perfectly her life has turned out. Going on holiday at fifty-three, having long since given up hope of finding romance. Accompanying Marian and Vernon to a little island off the Kerry coast that was only a name to her, simply because she was unable to think of a good enough reason not to. Meeting Hugh here, warming to him within five minutes of their very first encounter. Slowly realising, to her utter astonishment and joy, that it's never too late.

And if all goes well, there might be more happiness in store for them.

Following your initial interviews, garda clearance, home inspection and subsequent completion of our training course, the Board is happy to place you on its list of approved Foster Carers. When a case presents itself that accommodates your preferences, you will be notified.

Terribly formal and stilted, but still telling them exactly what they wanted to hear: they've been deemed suitable foster-carer material. Some time in the future, all going well, the phone will ring and they'll be told about a child who needs them. Imelda loves the bit about accommodating their preferences – they don't have any: they left their choices wide open, not wanting to rule anyone out.

A girl or a boy, it doesn't matter. Or maybe a pair of siblings, a brother and sister whose parents can't cope. She and Hugh will be happy to take them in, whoever they are, happy to offer a home for a while to some lost little soul or souls.

Imelda imagines bedtime stories, visits to the beach, plasters on grazed knees. Sausages for breakfast, or maybe pancakes. Something lovely anyway, something that will have them looking forward to getting up. She'll have to improve her flipping skills – her pancakes last Shrove Tuesday ended up as a pile of mush. Poor Hugh still cleared his plate, bless the man.

She lays tomato slices on top of ham, half an ear to the radio, glancing up every now and again when a car passes outside the window. So different in the winter here, when nothing might go by for an hour or more: these days the roads are full of vehicles with number plates from Cork and Limerick and Galway and beyond, all converging on Roone for a week or two of enjoyment.

Like the family of five who came from Tipperary a week ago, two boys and a girl with their parents, little knowing that three days after their arrival they'd be thrown into a nightmare.

According to the island grapevine – and of course Hugh hears it all in the pub – the Ryans are still in the house they were taken to after Ellie's disappearance. She assumes the boys will go home soon: normal life, or as normal as it can be, will have to resume for them. But the parents will surely stay here for another while: they'll want to hang on until there's some finding, however terrible.

What if that never happens, though? What if Ellie is never found, like scores of other people who've walked out of their houses, said goodbye to a husband or a wife, told a mother they'd see them soon, and vanished forever? Oh, it's too heartbreaking to think about – and yet it's never far from Imelda's mind.

She wraps the sandwiches in clear plastic and labels them carefully. She packs them into the cool box and sets it by the back door. She clears the ashes from the sitting-room fireplace and goes to the shed for a bucket of water to clean the window. When she comes back into the house the phone in the hall is ringing.

'Mrs Fitzpatrick?' The voice is unfamiliar.

'Speaking.' Still a small thrill when someone calls her by her married name.

'This is Jan Cleary from the Fostering Services Agency in Tralee. You and your husband have been put on our list of foster carers.'

Imelda sits down abruptly on the velvet-covered stool attached to the phone table. 'We have, yes.' Her smile stuck, her heart picking up speed.

'I'm ringing to tell you that a case has come up, a girl in need of respite foster care, and we thought you might be suitable.'

'Oh—'

Imelda has no idea what respite foster care means. Presumably it was explained to them during the course, but she has no recollection of it. She wishes Hugh was here so she could hand the phone to him and let him ask all the right questions.

'Just to remind you, respite care is a service we offer to our long-term foster families to give them a break from their duties. In this case, the break would start when the girl gets holidays from school.'

'I see.'

School-going age, so at least four or five. Not a baby or a toddler, which is probably better. More independent, no nappy-changing or bottle-feeding.

'School finishes on the fourth of June, so she'd be coming to you on Wednesday the fifth and staying till the end of August.'

'Right . . .'

The fifth of June – how far away is that? Imelda can't for the life of her recall how much of May has already gone by.

'It would be about twelve weeks in total.'

'OK.'

Twelve weeks. She'll be living with them for twelve weeks. The smile blooms again on Imelda's face. She wants to shout something out loud, something happy like *Hurrah* or *Yippee*, but of course she doesn't.

'Would you and your husband be interested? If you would, we'd need you both to come to Tralee and meet her, preferably some time in the next week.'

'Yes, yes, that would be wonderful. We can come anytime, anytime at all, thank you so much.'

'In that case, maybe we can settle provisionally on this day week. That would be the seventeenth – say around three o'clock? Do you need to check with your husband, and see if that day suits him?'

'Yes, I will. I'll do that. He's not here just now but I can call him, and I'll ring you back right away.' Imelda casts around in her distracted head for questions and finds one. 'Can you tell me her name? Am I allowed to ask that?'

'Eve.'

'Oh, that's—'

'You'll be given all the relevant information, her background and so on, if you decide you'd like to go ahead.'

'Oh, we would, I mean we do want to go ahead. Definitely, yes.'

The relevant information, such a clinical way of putting it. A young child's life, whatever dreadful circumstances have led her to live with a family that's not the one she was born into. All the sad details of it typed up and stored in a manila folder and slotted into an agency's filing cabinet.

Imelda thinks of another question. 'And her age? How old is she?'

'Fifteen. Actually, her sixteenth birthday is at the end of June, so if you take her she'll be with you for that.'

Imelda's heart stops. The smile slides slowly off her face. 'She's fifteen?'

'Yes. You didn't specify a preferred age, Mrs Fitzpatrick.'

'No, no, that's fine, fifteen is fine. It's just … I assumed – *we* assumed we'd be given someone younger, but of course it's fine.'

A teenager, not a little girl who can be tucked into bed at

night, or brought to the cinema in Tralee to watch whatever children's film is showing. A teenager, like the groups of young people who gather on the pier in the summer evenings, or sit huddled around tables in Lelia's after school.

Baggy clothing, long hair, eye makeup, earrings on odd parts of their faces. Looking past Imelda, who is too old and too nondescript to be of any interest to them.

'Mrs Fitzpatrick? Are you still there?'

'Yes, sorry, I'm still here.'

If they say no to this one they mightn't be offered another. And it's true they didn't specify an age, not wanting to limit their chances of being accepted.

'Is there a problem?'

'No, no, not at all … Er, I'm sorry, your name again?'

'It's Jan Cleary. Thank you, Mrs Fitzpatrick. I'll wait to hear from you then.'

'Yes, yes, I'll ring you back as soon as I talk to my—'

But the line has gone dead. Imelda replaces the receiver slowly and sits staring at the opposite wall. A teenager. A girl called Eve. She likes the name, which is a start. It's just that she doesn't know any teenagers personally – apart from Andy, of course, and he's fine, isn't he? Not the most talkative, it's true … In fact, now that Imelda thinks about it, she can't recall ever having had a proper conversation with him. What do you talk to young people about?

A child would be easy. In Imelda's experience, children are pretty black and white. And you know where you are with adults too, most of the time. But teenagers exist in an in-between place

– no longer innocent, not yet mature. They're half-formed adults, an unknown quantity, and Imelda and Hugh are going to take one in and be completely responsible for her for twelve weeks.

They will say yes, despite Imelda's misgivings, because she knows that Hugh will leave it up to her. 'If you're happy about it,' he'll say, like he says about most things, 'let's do it.' And Imelda will tell him she's happy about it because they can't say no to their very first chance to foster.

So they'll ring the agency and tell Jan Cleary that they want to take Eve, and they'll travel to Tralee next week to meet her. And if everything works out they'll install her in the second bedroom on the fifth of June.

She returns to the kitchen and goes to the calendar that hangs on the back door. She counts the days that are left in May and gets twenty-one, and five more in June makes twenty-six. In twenty-six days she and Hugh are going to become foster carers for the first time. The thought is both terrifying and … nothing else, just terrifying.

They haven't a clue. They won't know how to handle her. Imelda will be useless. She'll do everything wrong. And they're too old anyway, Hugh fifty-two and Imelda fifty-five. What in God's name were they thinking, looking to become foster carers in their fifties? No, what was Imelda thinking, because it was all her idea?

Eve will probably ask to go back to Tralee after a day with them. Or she might run away, go missing like Ellie Ryan.

No. Stop that.

She turns away from the calendar, cross with herself. She's just got the call she was praying for, and here she is falling to pieces because it isn't precisely what she expected. So Eve is a few years older – so what? They *chose* to do this; nobody forced it on them. They attended the course, they did all they were asked to do. A man visited them a few weeks ago and deemed their house suitable, and they were accepted. Someone believes they can do it, and they're right. She and Hugh will manage: they're intelligent and caring people. They'll find a way to make it work.

She looks at the bucket that sits on the floor by her feet and can't for the life of her think what it's doing there. She sits at the table, picks up her mobile phone and calls Hugh.

'I have news,' she says when he answers.

✳

It is Joe's sixteenth birthday. Joe is Claire and Paddy Geoghegan's middle child, and the reason why Claire is still married.

'He's Down's syndrome,' she'd told Denis, right after 'I'm married', and 'I have three children', and 'There's something you need to know about Joe.'

Joe is why she won't leave her husband, why she has to meet Denis in secret. Denis is in competition with a sixteen-year-old boy who is Down's syndrome, which means there is no competition.

'He needs the two of us – he needs the security of both of his parents around him. I couldn't do it to him. I don't want to do it to him.'

Denis doesn't know where the family lives. He's never asked and Claire has never said. When they meet it's in his house – or rather, the house he's been renting since he walked away from his marriage. The best thing about it is its isolation, so nobody sees the woman in the brown car pulling up outside it every Wednesday around four o'clock, nobody except the man who waits for her.

He's kept count, he's that pathetic. Since he moved into the house just over twenty-one months ago, Claire has come to him eighty-five times. A yoga class is what she told her husband, knowing he wouldn't question it. Two hours they have every week, less twenty minutes for her journey to and from Tralee. One hundred precious minutes every seven days, not counting the occasional weeks she's missed, for various reasons.

And each time she leaves, after he's watched her car disappear around the bend at the end of his laneway, to reappear briefly three times as it winds its way through the landscape back to Tralee, becoming depressingly smaller with every viewing, Denis experiences the same dull despondency that every one of her departures causes.

When she's finally out of sight he turns back to the house and climbs the stairs to the bedroom that smells of her perfume. He lies on sheets that are still warm from her body and pushes his face into the pillow that has cradled her head. He closes his eyes and counts the days till her return.

It is no way to live – and yet how can it be otherwise, when the only alternative he can see is to let her go? Tormented as he is now at the thought of her returning each week to the house she shares with another man, how much more anguished would he feel at the prospect of never being with her again?

There are times in his abject misery when the pain of not seeing her every day, the agony of sharing nothing but the smallest part of his life with her, causes him to wish for the death of her son. He imagines a quick, painless passing that would leave her broken and grieving, and reaching out for Denis.

He smothers the image each time it occurs, horrified that he has allowed it to take shape. He pushes it from him, turns his mind away from it – but it worms its way back silently to poke at the edges of his consciousness. It catches him unawares, every now and again.

He daydreams about bringing Claire to Roone, the two of them living happily on the island he loves – but even as the pictures form in his head he knows they can never become reality. Roone was where he and Moira grew up; the island was hers as much as it was his. He and Claire would never be welcome there, even if some miracle allowed them to be together.

Moira's sudden death in December had left him shaken and saddened. Even though he'd walked out on her, even though their marriage had caused him to be lonelier with each passing year, there was a bond between them as Nell's parents which he accepted would always exist, and which he had no wish to dissolve. Their pasts were bound together, and if he hadn't been able to love Moira in the way she deserved to be loved, he felt a fondness for her that hadn't diminished after they'd parted.

When Imelda's call came in the afternoon of a bitterly cold December Tuesday, one week before Christmas, Denis was washing his solitary lunch plate, his single knife and fork, his water glass. He dried his hands on the tea towel before picking up the phone. His brother-in-law's name on the screen was a surprise: Hugh never phoned him, not any more.

It wasn't Hugh. 'I'm afraid there's bad news, Denis.' It had taken him a second to place Imelda's voice. 'It's about Moira.'

As he listened, Denis felt everything plummeting down inside him, everything thudding into his feet to leave him light-headed and hollow and unstable. He clutched the edge of the sink and held on to keep himself upright. He stammered out some kind of a response and hung up without saying goodbye, and made his way on shaking legs to a chair.

And for the rest of that awful day – the frozen sterility of the hospital morgue, an incoherent Nell sobbing in his arms, the journey back to Roone, Denis crawling behind James's car, the steady procession of sombre locals to Nell's house as the news had seeped throughout the island – while all that was happening, his overriding emotion was regret.

He shook hands with men and women he'd grown up with, aware that they'd come for Nell, not for him. He was the blackguard who'd abandoned his wife, who'd left his marriage behind without a backward glance. Now her death damned him further, he knew that. Nobody looked him in the eye as they told him they were sorry for his trouble: it was Nell's trouble they were sorry for, not his. And even though he felt genuine grief at Moira's death, Denis understood that he'd forfeited any right to their sympathy.

But stretched out later under the thick tangerine quilt in

Nell's spare bedroom – hours later, after the last of the callers had gone home and Nell had finally made her way, red-eyed and wrung out, to bed – a tiny voice inside Denis's head had whispered: *You're free.* And he recognised, with growing shame, beneath the sadness and the remorse and the guilt, an infinitesimal sense of relief.

You're free, the voice insisted. *Your wife is dead. You're no longer married.*

It was horrible. It was contemptible to feel anything but sorrow at the passing of the woman who had been the mother of his child. It was every bit as reprehensible as wishing a mentally disabled boy dead.

And any sense of relief was also misplaced, given that Denis's freedom was worthless: it had gained him nothing as long as Claire remained married. And she would, because of Joe.

'He's turning sixteen on Friday,' she told Denis. 'We're going out to dinner.' Lifting his hand directly afterwards, pressing it to her lips. Trying, he knew, to take the sting from her words, but of course he pictured them, the happy family group sitting around the table, a birthday cake in front of Joe. His loose grin as the candles burnt, as his parents and sisters sang to him.

'Tell me about the wedding,' she said, moving the subject away from Joe. 'Tell me what Nell wore.'

Claire knows about Nell. Denis has told her about his hairdresser daughter; he's described the salon above Hugh's pub in the middle of Roone's only village. Claire has heard about the broken engagement, about Nell beginning a relationship with her ex-fiancé's brother.

And of course she knows about the small child disappearing on Roone, like everyone in Ireland knows – practically everyone in the world must know at this stage. Denis had heard about it on a news bulletin as he drove home from Tralee on the day of Nell's wedding. Later that evening he'd spoken to Nell.

'Still no sign,' she told him. 'Everyone is searching. We're going out as soon as we've changed.'

And that was Monday, and this is Friday. Nell is married and Joe is sixteen, and Denis is on his way to Roone to have dinner with Nell and her new family, and the girl's parents have been without her for five days.

The ferry is packed, none of the faces familiar to Denis. Holidaymakers, he assumes, or people curious to see the island that has been mentioned on news reports all week. The bay holds more boats than usual, many of them bigger than the trawlers and fishing craft of the islanders. He spots Nell's yellow rowboat among those pulled up high on the pebbly shore.

As the ferry approaches the pier Denis notes the huddle of vans parked outside the hotel, each carrying a television- or radio-station logo. Not all Irish either, not even half of them Irish. Hoping for news, like everyone else. Gone soon no doubt if nothing develops, off to chase the next big disaster.

He drives off the ferry as the church bells ring out the Angelus. He waves at Dougie Fennessy passing in his taxi. Dougie's answering nod isn't accompanied by a smile, as it would have been in the past. Denis still hasn't been forgiven.

He turns left onto the coast road, away from the village, and covers the short distance to the house that has lain empty since

Moira's death. He's driven past it on his way to Nell's in the intervening months, but this will be his first time to stop, his first time in nearly two years to spend a night under its roof. He parks by the gate and sits in the car.

'I won't have a bed for you,' Nell said when she was saying goodbye to him on Monday, 'but I'd still love you to come.' Her spare room gone with James and Andy moving in, Denis's only choice from now on – not mentioned by Nell – to take the last ferry back to the mainland after dinner or stay in his own house.

His first instinct was to return to Tralee. The thought of revisiting the empty house, stirring up all the memories it held, was not something that appealed to him. But the more he thought about it, lying in bed on the intervening nights, the more foolish that notion seemed.

The house belongs to him; it's a far finer house than the one he currently lives in. Is he to drive past it for the rest of his life because he walked away from the woman he shared it with? Isn't he entitled to reclaim it now that she's gone, and to use it if and when the need arises?

So he has come back to it.

He takes his weekend bag from the passenger seat and gets out, drawing the familiar sea-sharp air into his lungs as he stands by the car, remembering the scene that had taken place on the morning he'd left, shortly before he'd pulled the front door closed for what he'd imagined would be the last time.

July the twenty-ninth, almost two years ago. Moira sitting at the kitchen table, her face changing slowly as he had begun to speak. Incomprehension replacing the smile she'd greeted him with when he'd come downstairs, a frown settling into the space between her eyes as understanding dawned.

Anger following, a tightness pleating the skin around her mouth, a narrowing of her eyes as he continued to say what had to be said. Her flat refusal to accept what she was hearing.

We've been married for over thirty years. You can't do this to me. You can't destroy what we have. You're not leaving me. I refuse to let you.

The words as clear and sharp as if she'd said them yesterday.

A pot of marmalade on the table, he could picture it clearly, some fancy stuff with a bit of gingham around the lid that she'd picked up at a market in Dingle the week before. Next to it the blue and white milk jug they'd had forever that didn't quite hold a pint.

A place set for Denis as usual. His outsize green cup, the one Nell had given him for a birthday because he'd remarked once that a refill of tea was never as satisfying as the first cup.

Everything the way it always was that morning, until he'd opened his mouth and changed it all.

He still has a key to the front door. It hangs on his key ring beside the ones for his car, for the rented house, for the school in Tralee that gave him a job. He takes his overnight bag from the back seat and walks up the path. He glances in through the sitting-room windows and sees the familiar suite of furniture within. He puts his key into the lock and turns it.

The hall is cool and smells like he remembers, the same mix of wood and polish that he always got on entering the house, ahead of any other scents – food, detergent, perfume – that were contained within. He runs a finger along the curlicues carved into the hallstand – has he ever seen it empty of coats before? – and it comes away grey with dust. The phone sits on its usual little table, but when he picks up the receiver there is only a blank silence.

He looks at the closed kitchen door, remembering all the times he opened it to find Moira inside, chopping carrots for his dinner or rolling out pastry for an apple tart, or sticking labels onto jars of homemade mayonnaise. Strange not to hear the radio floating out to the hall, always on when she was there – and she was nearly always there.

His footsteps sound too loud as he climbs the stairs, automatically stepping over the seventh – whose creak, he assumes, is still there. The banister's slightly knobbly surface feels sadly familiar under his palm. Guiding him countless times up to bed, or down to breakfast.

On the landing he pauses a moment outside the master bedroom before turning the knob and pushing the door open. He stands on the threshold and takes in the room.

The double bed has been made up, a pair of folded towels sitting on the duvet. On the dressing table the Tipperary crystal vase, his sixtieth-birthday present from the school staff, is stuffed with montbretia. The top half of the sash window has been pushed down six inches, the net curtain swaying gently in the air that wanders in.

He crosses the carpet to the wardrobe. It's empty, apart from a clutch of wooden hangers and a soft smell of must. The chest of drawers is empty too, its top freshly polished. He imagines

Nell here yesterday or the day before, shaking out sheets for him, stuffing pillows into cases, doing what she could to banish the feeling of disuse that more than four months of emptiness would have created.

It must have been hard for her: she must have thought of her mother. She must have remembered clearing the house of Moira's possessions, a month or so after her death.

'Do you want me to come?' Denis asked. 'I could help' – but Nell had said no, Imelda had already offered, they'd manage without him, so he was spared the ordeal of going through his late wife's effects, stuffing her clothing and shoes into black plastic bags, packing her books into boxes, everything a reminder of the life they'd shared.

He drops his holdall onto the floor and sits on the side of the bed, feeling utterly alone. Through the net curtain he can see the seagulls wheeling joyously in the sky as they have always done, uninterested in thwarted love or deceased spouses or vanished children.

He regards the bed, the curved wooden headboard, the two pillows encased in blue-and-white check, the matching duvet cover. He thinks back to all the nights he and Moira had slept there, side by side. All the times they'd been intimate, the mechanical coupling that had relieved him physically but left him lonelier than before.

He remembers Moira's announcement that she was pregnant, his happiness at the news tempered with the bleak realisation that becoming parents would bind the two of them more closely together.

Not that he didn't love his infant daughter: he did, instantly and unconditionally and forever. It was Nell who had kept the marriage intact, who had made it possible for him to live with his loneliness for years until at the age of sixty-one, Nell's rearing long since finished, he had attended an educational conference in Tralee and met Claire Geoghegan.

His phone rings, its call jumping into the silence, startling him. He sees Nell's name on the screen.

'Are you on the way?'

'I'm at the house, just dropping my bag.'

'Oh . . .'

In the small pause that follows, he imagines her digesting the fact that he's back there for the first time. 'You have the place looking nice,' he says. 'I won't be long.'

'I hope it's not cold. I opened your bedroom window on my way to work, to air it out a bit.'

'No, it's fine. It feels just right.'

'The water's still cut off. I meant to switch it on and forgot.'

'I'll do it.'

'And turn on the immersion.'

He smiles. Looking after him, because there's nobody else. He remembers his one fear when he left Moira was that Nell might disown him, that in abandoning one he might lose them both. He remembers the leap his heart gave every time his phone rang, the hope that it was her at the other end. And when the call he'd prayed for finally came, it was short and terse.

I don't know why I rang, she said. *You really hurt me – you hurt both of us*. And hearing the pain in her voice, Denis cursed himself for putting her through it. But she'd made contact, she'd got in touch – and before hanging up she said she'd call again. It was a thread to clutch at.

Little did he realise that her second call, just two days later, would be to tell him that Walter had dropped dead. Little did he imagine that his return trip to Roone would happen far, far earlier than he'd anticipated, and that his next encounter with Nell would be across Walter's freshly dug grave, a week to the day since he'd packed up and gone.

But they'd survived the upheaval and sadness, they'd come through it all. Nell had forgiven him, he wasn't disowned, and for that he was immensely grateful.

He rises and crosses the room to the window. He reaches up and unhooks the net curtain's covered wire. He pulls the fabric off and lets it crumple onto the floor. He's always hated net curtains, the way they diffuse a room's light, the way they blur and filter the view outside.

In the bathroom he opens the valve under the sink and hears the gurgle of pipes being refilled. He splashes his face with cold water and brushes his teeth, avoiding the mirror. Sixty-three since February, no good news to be had from a mirror any more. The best he can do these days is keep his hair trimmed and his jaw shaved.

'You have a gentle face,' Claire tells him, which is probably the most positive thing she can think of. He's never been handsome, with his beaky nose and jutting chin, and hair that in his youth insisted on springing from his head in an untameable brown shock. Now there's much less of it, and what there is has become butterscotch-coloured and listless. The joys of impending old age.

Back in the bedroom he pushes the window up until an inch of a gap remains. He lifts a small bag of groceries from his holdall and goes downstairs. In the kitchen he plugs in the empty fridge and deposits milk and butter there, leaving the rest – tea, bread, marmalade, apples – on the worktop.

Moira's copper pots and pans still hang where they have always hung, in the alcove between the sink and the cooker. Her collection of cookery books sits on the shelf beneath, her food processor – he has never once used it – on the worktop, next to the knife rack.

He regards the chair that was always hers, directly across the table from the one that was always his. He looks out of the window above the sink and sees the shrubs that she planted and nurtured. For the first time since he entered the house he feels her presence acutely. He fancies he catches a drift of her rose-scented perfume – but when he turns from the window it's gone.

He leaves the kitchen, closing the door softly behind him. He lets himself out of the house and sets off to walk the half a mile of coast road to his daughter's house, turning up the collar of his raincoat.

He pulls his key from the door and hangs his damp umbrella on the row of hooks. He sniffs and smiles. Nell's roast chicken, redolent with rosemary and bay leaf and lemon – and something sharper, overlaying the food aroma.

He walks down the hall to his son's bedroom. The door is open, a sheet covering the portion of wooden floor that's visible. Andy is barefoot, halfway up a stepladder, sweeping a paint roller back and forth along the opposite wall. From his iPod on the windowsill Emeli Sandé sings about a clown behind the glass.

'Looking good,' James says.

Andy turns. 'Hi.' His black T-shirt and his face are speckled with paint. There's a streak on the front of his hair, and a drop on his left instep. He climbs down and reloads the roller from the tray at his feet.

The shade he opted for, much to their relief, falls somewhere between duck-egg blue and turquoise, Marine something or other on the can, the first coat almost finished. The colour gives the room an altogether different feel, cooler and more airy than the flower-sprigged wallpaper Nell had originally chosen. More to James's taste too, a fact that he decides to keep to himself.

'Nearly dinnertime,' he says.

'I'll stop in a minute.'

Andy hasn't mentioned Ellie since they spoke with the detective at Manning's on Tuesday morning, but he's watched the news with them every evening since then, something he never did before. James stands for another minute, watching the sweep of the roller, ribbons of blue-green banishing the flowers, before turning and heading for the kitchen.

Nell glances up from the open oven door, her cheeks lightly flushed. 'There you are – thought I heard you coming in.' She closes the door, moves to lower the volume on the radio. 'I hope you're hungry.'

'Starving.' James crosses the room and pulls her into an embrace, feeling her arms slide around him. They stand locked together, a perfect fit, his face pressed to her hair, a hand cupping her head as he drinks her in, as he feels her warmth and softness against him. *This*, he thinks. *Just this*.

He moves his head, finds her mouth, feels his body begin to respond as they kiss. She eases out of his arms, laughing.

'My father's on the way – he'll be here in a few minutes. You can set the table.'

James takes side plates from the rack. 'You think he's OK about staying in the old house?'

'Hope so.' She tumbles broccoli into boiling water. 'I'm glad he decided to stay. Might mean he'll spend more time here over the summer.'

James makes no comment as he places knives and forks on the table. She's been coaxing her father back to Roone since Moira's death, tempting him with chicken and fillet steaks and fish pies – wanting, understandably, to draw her remaining parent closer, but James is doubtful of the reception Denis would get if he were to spend more prolonged periods on the island.

From working behind the counter at Fitz's, James is well aware of the antipathy among the older Roone locals towards a man who abandoned his wife without warning – and Moira's death, even though Denis can't possibly be blamed for it, has only served to harden their hearts further against him.

'I checked on the painting,' he says. 'Looks good.'

She stoops to lift the roasting dish from the oven, pushes the door closed with her hip. 'It's lovely, isn't it? He chose well.'

He watches her untie the twine that binds the bird's legs, peel a strand of hair from her damp cheek, reach for the half-full glass of water on the worktop. He watches her tip her head back, sees the muscles in her throat expand and contract as she drinks. She lowers the glass and catches his eye as she wipes a drop of water from the corner of her mouth with the back of her hand.

She smiles. 'Mr Baker,' she says softly.

As he's on the point of grabbing her again, the doorbell rings.

✳

A child's garment has been found. The news flies around the island: it's carried within minutes in hushed, rapid tones from café to bar to supermarket. It lands on the counter of Fitz's at twenty to eight.

'A vest,' Willie Buckley tells them. 'A vest or a T-shirt. Turned up in Charlie O'Reilly's net about an hour ago.'

The garment has been brought to Manning's. It's been presented to the detective on duty. No more is known, but plenty have opinions.

'There was no mention of a vest on the poster, or a T-shirt.'

'Well, there wouldn't be, would there? If it was a vest, I mean.'

'It said a cardigan, not a T-shirt. And a dress.'

'It might be a cardigan – Charlie wouldn't know the difference.'

'He'd know a cardigan with the buttons. He's not stupid.'

'Did he say anything about buttons?'

Behind the counter Hugh Fitzpatrick pulls pints, opens bottles, slices lemons, refills the ice bucket. He is probably the only person in the bar not thinking about Ellie Ryan, and the possibility of one of her garments having been located.

'Her name is Eve,' Imelda had said on the phone. 'They want us to go and meet her this day week. She's fifteen.' The sentences blurting out of her, the excitement evident in her voice.

'What do you think?' she asked, and what could Hugh say? Only that he was happy to go ahead, if she was. The yearning in her confessed to him early on, a few weeks into their marriage. 'It's something I'd love to do,' she'd told him. 'I don't know how you'd feel about it.'

Hugh isn't sure even yet how he feels about the notion of accepting someone else's child into their house, but he seems genetically incapable of doing anything that might take from his wife's happiness, so he found himself telling her it was something he'd be willing to think about. And to give Imelda her due, she'd waited a good few weeks before bringing it up again.

'We could do the course,' she said. 'It wouldn't tie us to anything.' And he saw the hunger in her face and said yes to the course. And now here they are, with someone waiting for them to claim her.

But fifteen. He knows bugger-all about fifteen-year-old girls. He's turned a few of them away from here, painting their faces to try to look eighteen when they ask him for vodka and orange, staring at him brazenly, daring him to say no. Or sending the boyfriends up to the counter, trying to hide at a corner table.

Still, if it's what Imelda wants he'll go along with it. She'll have more to do with the girl than he will, with the bar taking him out of the house most days. They'll get on fine, he's sure. Imelda gets on with everyone.

Just before ten o'clock, more information comes.

'It's not Ellie's,' Dougie Fennessy announces. 'They showed it to the parents. Definitely not hers' – and even though nobody really thought it might be, there's a collective slump among the gathered drinkers, a sense of disappointment that stops the talk for a while.

Hugh imagines the mother and father hearing that a child's article of clothing has been found in the sea. What kind of news is that for any parent to get? He pictures them being handed the garment – dripping, ripped maybe – and realising that it's wrong, it's not their daughter's. The mixture of despair and renewed hope the discovery must have caused – for if it isn't Ellie's, doesn't that mean she might not be in the water, that it's still possible she can be found alive? Clinging to hope, turning a wrong vest, or whatever it was, into a positive.

'I'll have a pint,' Dougie Fennessy tells him, and Hugh reaches for a glass and holds it under the Guinness tap.

FRIDAY, 17 MAY

'Here we go – one scrambled egg and one full Irish. Can I get you anything else? More toast?'

'It's the other way round, hon,' Cheryl from Texas says. 'I asked for the full Irish, Max wanted the eggs.'

'Oops, so you did. Here we go.'

'And Cheryl said no tomato,' Max adds, eyeing his wife's plate as the switch is made. 'She's allergic.'

'Oh dear – silly me, only half awake.' Laura deposits the tomato slices in an empty cereal bowl, thinking that Cheryl's rather generously proportioned figure would benefit more from hanging on to the tomatoes and ditching the rest. 'Now, is that everything?'

'I guess so.' Max picks up his fork and pokes at the mound of scrambled egg on his plate. 'Sounds like there's plenty activity out there this morning.'

'Yes, sorry about that. Caesar got out again last night.'

'Caesar?'

'Our pig. Every so often he breaks out of his sty and causes a bit of havoc in the garden.'

'Oh, my,' Cheryl murmurs, scattering salt on her sausages. 'Did he do much damage this time?'

'Not really. Trampled a few heads of lettuce, knocked over some of the runner-bean frames, helped himself to a bit of the broccoli. Could have been worse – last time he ruined about half of the rhubarb and made himself sick with far too many windfall apples. Poor thing doesn't know when to stop eating.'

'Oh, my . . .' Cheryl pops half a sausage into her red-lipped mouth.

'My partner – Gavin – is repairing the sty gate now, that's the hammering you hear. Not that it'll do much good – he's not exactly a handyman, which is why Caesar keeps escaping.'

Max butters a slice of soda bread, reaches for the apple jelly. 'I take it you're raising this pig so you can eat it. That the idea?'

'God, no – my boys would kill me, they're mad about Caesar. We won him in the church raffle at Christmas – he was the star prize.'

'My word,' Cheryl says, her heavy gold bracelets clacking together as she shakes ketchup onto the remainder of her breakfast. Not allergic to that form of tomato, then. 'I guess you folks had to learn how to look after him real quick, right?'

'Not really – Gavin worked in a zoo before we moved to Roone, so he knows a lot about animals. I did wonder if he'd rigged the raffle though – he wanted to open a zoo here. I thought I'd talked him out of it, but I'm beginning to suspect he's planning to fill the place with animals slowly and hope that I don't notice.'

'What could I do?' Gav had asked, the night he'd arrived home with a juvenile Caesar snuffling around in a wooden crate. 'I thought it would be rude to refuse to take him.'

'You could have swapped with whoever won the turkey or the ham, or Betty Buckley's Christmas cake. What are we going to do with a *pig*?'

'I'll look after him. You won't have to do a thing. He'll eat leftovers so he won't cost anything. And he'll be company for George.'

Because they already had George VI, Walter's little grey donkey that had trotted around the field with Seamus and Ben on his back when they'd holidayed at Nell's. As soon as they'd moved into Walter's house the twins had asked about the donkey.

'I remember him,' Gav told them. 'I used to talk to him all the time over the wall.'

'We put one of Mum's bras on him,' Seamus said.

'Yeah, we hung it off his ears. It was real fun.'

'It was not real fun,' their mother corrected sternly, winking at Gav above their heads. 'Poor Mr Thompson was terribly embarrassed.'

A discussion about George's future had ensued, during which Laura was seriously outnumbered.

'This is his home,' Gav pointed out. 'He should be back here. He'd be no bother, donkeys need hardly any minding, and he'd keep the grass down. And we could offer donkey rides in the summer, make a few extra bob.'

And Laura eventually gave in because she felt a tiny bit guilty about vetoing the zoo idea, and George was reclaimed from the farmer who'd taken him in after Walter's death. So now they have a donkey, a pot-bellied pig with a voracious appetite – getting bigger, literally, by the day – and twenty-eight hens that in theory are looked after by the twins. In reality, Ben and Seamus are sporadic farmers, and it's often left to Laura or Gav to collect the eggs and sweep out the henhouse. Still no regrets, though.

'We moved here from Dublin last year,' she tells Cheryl and Max. 'Complete change of scene for all of us.'

She remembers the twins settling into life on the island, making friends in Roone Primary School while Gav was resurrecting the vegetable plot and Laura was doing what she could with workmen around the place, scrubbing and painting as soon as a room was ready for it, hanging freshly laundered curtains and choosing the best positions for Walter's quaint old furniture, which had all been left behind in the house.

'Hadn't you run a bed and breakfast business before?' Cheryl with the tomato allergy enquires. As if she needs to ask.

'Nope – all new to me.'

Cheryl nods in the direction of Laura's abdomen. 'Hope you don't mind my mentioning it, hon, but I'm gonna guess you have a little bun in the oven.'

'Two little buns,' Laura tells her. 'Due the middle of August. My second set of twins.'

'Oh, isn't that just darling? Did you hear that, hon? Two little babies on the way!'

Max nods politely as he chews his bread, keeping his gaze well clear of Laura's mid-section. 'What's this poster we been seeing? Some child gone missing from around here?' he asks suddenly, and Laura's heart sinks.

She gives them an account of the incident, as brief as she can make it. 'It's unheard of, nothing like this has ever happened here before. Everyone is completely shocked.'

Ellie's disappearance has unsettled them all – the twins ask about her constantly, she's included in their night-time prayers. All they can do, all they must do, is look on her disappearance as a terrible aberration, and keep reminding themselves that they're living in one of the safest parts of Ireland.

After all eight guests have breakfasted and moved off, Laura goes upstairs, strips beds, gathers towels and facecloths and stuffs the lot into their hardworking industrial-strength washing machine, one of the few new appliances they'd invested in.

She makes tea and brings a mug out to the field, along with the empty egg basket and a bowl of leftovers for Caesar.

'How's it going?'

Gav straightens, a hand to the small of his back. 'Nearly there.'

As he sips the tea, Laura regards the patched-together sty door doubtfully. Hard to see a kitten being contained for long behind it, let alone a determined and increasingly tubby pig. It's in keeping with the rest of the sty, which took Gav, God love him, three days of hard labour to construct, using whatever old planks and poles he could scrounge from various neighbours. The whole affair looks to Laura as if it might have trouble surviving the next serious storm.

But she says nothing. He's doing his best – and Caesar probably loves his little bit of freedom every now and again.

As she crosses the field towards the henhouse that Andy repaints each year, George ambles over to butt his shaggy head into her hand. 'Morning, George,' she murmurs, pausing to scratch the rough hair between his eyes. 'Sorry about the hammering, it'll stop soon.'

She glances up at the sky. A spell of warm weather promised, according to this morning's forecast. Not much sign of it yet, cool and grey with dark clouds gathering on the horizon, not a lot of drying today for her sheets. Typical Irish summer, keeping you guessing from one day to the next. Not that she cares, happy to ignore the rain and make the most of the sun when it appears. Only sensible option.

In the henhouse she collects the eggs – a good day, twenty-two, and probably a few more this evening – and on her way back to the kitchen she gathers windfall apples from the grass beneath the tree in the little orchard that bears ripe fruit every year from September right through to June.

As she peels the apples under a running kitchen tap she becomes aware that Walter has wandered in.

'There you are,' she says. 'I was wondering where you'd got to.' She cuts the apples into chunks. 'See? Your tree is still going strong. I'm making a bit of apple sauce to go with the stuffed pork steak Gav is doing tonight – he just about trusts me to do that. The man thought he couldn't cook until he met me.'

She tosses the chunks into a pot, adds a splash of water and a handful of sugar and lights the gas ring under it. She gathers the peel into a basin and sets it on the table. 'Caesar's lunch – no such thing as leftovers with that animal around. The boys are on a mission to find something he won't eat. Last week Ben gave him porridge with mustard. No bother to him.'

She sloshes water around the sink, watches it swirl away. 'Walter, I'm afraid we have some bad news. A little girl has gone missing from the island – can you believe it? Just disappeared, nearly two weeks ago. She's only five.'

She wipes down the draining board and reaches for the towel. 'The family's not local – they were on holidays here. Her brothers have gone home but the parents are staying on at the hotel. Henry's given them a room there. They rarely come out, nobody's met them apart from the guards and Father William. Can't imagine how they're feeling.'

She lowers the gas flame under the saucepan and sinks wearily into a pine chair. 'Look at the size of me, Walter – I'm like a house. God knows what I'll be like in August, waddling around like an elephant.' She rubs her belly absently. 'Nobody knows what to do, Walter. We all feel so helpless. The whole island's been searched at least twice over, and divers are still working in the sea. I think we're all assuming she won't turn up alive at this stage, although nobody wants to say it out loud. It's such a horrible thing to happen. It's in my head all the time, and I'm guessing everyone feels the same.'

Walter makes no comment, of course. He can't: he's dead. But he's there, he's in the room with her, back in the house he called home all his life. Unwilling, she supposes, to cut his ties completely with it yet, taken from it as suddenly as he was.

'We aren't changing much,' she had assured him, during the renovations. 'I know it looks a mess, but it's more about fixing the bits that need fixing. We had to replace a lot of the floorboards because there was some dry rot, and we're adding insulation, putting in damp-proofing, and making the guest bedrooms en-suite because everyone expects that in a B&B now. But I promise we're keeping it as close to the way you had it as we can.'

She adores the house. She loves the old smell of it, the echo of its grandeur in every generously proportioned room, every ceiling rose, every picture rail. Her favourite place is the drawing room with its big fireplace and floor-to-ceiling bookshelves and beautiful bay window.

Nell told her it was the room where Walter was laid out and waked. Laura is charmed by the idea of the people who loved him watching over him all night before saying their last goodbyes.

She loves the old books that had been left on the shelves, a wonderful moving-in gift, all the skilfully bound and richly scented volumes of Dickens and Thackeray, Brontë and Waugh that beg to be opened, pressed to her face and inhaled. If she could bottle the scent she'd make a million. She's never been much of a reader, but Gav is happily working his way through them.

'You must always consider this house as much yours as ours,' Laura had told Walter. 'More yours, really. And we're naming the B&B after you. I hope you're flattered.'

She's not psychic. She never had visions growing up, never had any experience that led her to believe that she could commune with things beyond the confines of the natural world. After Aaron had died she'd yearned to see him again: for weeks she'd willed him back to her, unable to believe he was really gone forever. Desperately trying to convince herself, each time she woke from whatever fitful sleep she managed, that his suicide was just some horrible nightmare, that he'd walk back in at any minute and laugh at the state of her.

But he didn't reappear. He never walked back in. To her great despair she never once got the smallest sense of his presence, and she finally had to accept the agonising reality of his death.

And life moved on, and she's met Gav, and he's caring and exasperating and generous and clumsy and endearing and soft-hearted and hopeless, and what she feels for him will never come close to the overwhelming emotions Aaron stirred in her, but it's more than she'd expected to come her way, and he'll do her nicely for now.

And last summer, just a few weeks after they'd moved to the island, she was on her own in the little orchard at the side of the house, Gav having taken the boys to the village for ice-cream. She was stretched out on the grass, bathed in dappled light and looking up at the patches of blue through the leaves and marvelling that they'd achieved their wish to come and live on Roone.

And she'd gradually become aware of a stirring, a gentle displacement in the air around her. She sat up slowly and looked around. No Gav, no boys back from the village, nobody dropping by to say hello, no sign at all of anyone there. She was quite alone.

Except that she wasn't.

'Walter,' she breathed – because it was him, it was definitely him. She had no idea how she knew that, but she did. And she felt no fear, not a bit. How could anyone be afraid of such a kindly old soul?

His features were still vivid in her memory. The balding head, usually covered with a cap, the watery blue eyes, the patches of pink in his cheeks, the suggestion of an uptilt to the end of his nose that lent his sixty-something-year-old face a touchingly boyish air.

And the chivalrous way he had about him, the way he'd lift his cap an inch or two off his head when he met you, the way he'd hold a door open for you, so lovely to see it. His blush when Laura had invited him to come and hear her play guitar at Fitz's, the hesitant way he'd invited them to dinner, despite the boys being right little monkeys.

She recalled her sadness when Nell had emailed to tell her of his death. She imagined him dying all alone, and hoped it had happened too quickly for him to have been aware of it. She remembered Gav mooting the idea of buying the house, how enticing the notion had become, how impatiently she'd waited for Gav's house to be sold. She recalled how her delight when they eventually moved in had been tempered with sorrow that Walter wasn't part of Roone any more.

But now he had returned: he was right there, in the garden that had belonged to him all his life. 'We did it,' she told him. 'We came back to Roone, like you said we would. And we're getting George the Sixth back, and we're buying new hens, and Gav is going to try and get the vegetable garden going again. And we're planning to open a B&B next year.'

He never comes when the others are around. She's never

told anyone about him, not even Gav. She thinks it better not to mention it, in case it worries him.

She's happy Walter came back, happy that she's the one he chose to revisit. She likes the idea that she's the only one he comes to. She and Walter had a soft spot for one another in the two weeks they spent living as neighbours, despite the twins nearly running him over on their bicycles the first time they all met. They never got a chance to say goodbye when they left Roone. Laura had rung his doorbell on their last morning: she'd gone over with the boys to thank him for his kindness during their stay and to buy some eggs and honey to bring back to Dublin, but he never appeared. Little did they imagine that he was already lying dead on his landing, waiting to be discovered by Andy just minutes later.

She gets up and pokes at the softening apple chunks. 'Imelda and Hugh are going to be foster carers. Pity you never met Imelda – I think you would have liked one another. They're going to meet their first foster child this afternoon. Nell says they're a bit anxious, but I know they'll be fine. Those two were born to be parents.'

Nell has filled her in on Walter's story. Laura has heard about his wife dying in childbirth a long time ago, their only baby stillborn. He hadn't ever remarried, hadn't ever found another love. The awful tragedy he carried around with him for nearly forty years, and you'd never have known it from him. Maybe he's happy now that Laura is filling the house with the children he wasn't blessed with.

'Caesar escaped again,' she tells him, slotting the eggs into boxes. 'Never a dull moment. That sty is held up by the grace of God, Walter – I'm only waiting for the day it comes crashing down. I just hope poor Caesar is on one of his rambles when it happens.'

It's lovely to be able to chat. The fact that she's doing all the talking is a little sad, of course, but Walter is the perfect listener, and there aren't too many of those around. She turns off the gas ring, reaches for the brush and begins to sweep the kitchen floor.

'Nell is hoping her father will spend time on the island over the summer – now that his house is empty, I mean. I wonder what you thought of him leaving his wife. I suppose you were your usual tactful self and made no comment.'

There's a sound outside just then, and Walter drifts away like he always does. Gavin appears and drops his mug into the sink. 'Give me that,' he says, taking the brush from her.

Laura leans against the worktop and watches him sweeping. She wonders what he'd say if she told him she'd just had a gentleman caller.

'Eve takes a while to feel comfortable around new people,' the social worker tells them as they sit waiting in her office. 'Don't worry if she's not that responsive at first.'

There's an underlying smell of onions in her oddly shaped little office. One wall slants quite sharply inwards, causing the end wall to be a good two feet narrower than the one it faces. The lower half of the room's single window, which is set into the short wall, is covered by a tall brown filing cabinet, on top of which a stack of pale green folders perches precariously. With half its natural light source shut off, the office is dark enough, in the middle of a grey May afternoon, to need the salmon-coloured gooseneck lamp on the social worker's desk to be switched on.

Beyond the window Imelda can see a patch of mottled sky, a church spire and a pair of tall factory chimneys. On the wall above the window hangs a digital clock, the kind with numbers on plastic rectangles that flip down into place with a sharp little click each time a new minute is announced.

The slanting wall holds several framed certificates and is painted the same dull apricot as the others. To Imelda's left, a brown metal shelving unit, the filing cabinet's match, is crammed with thick box files and volumes of fat, hard-backed notebooks, some blue, some red.

The awkward little room, after the wide-open spaciousness of Roone, feels depressingly claustrophobic. Imelda can't imagine spending her working day there, sitting behind the chipped pale wood desk that has barely enough room to walk around it, having her minutes clicked out one after another until it's time to put on her coat and go home.

The social worker, not the one who had inspected their house, or the one who had spoken to Imelda on the phone – 'I'm Anita,' she said when they met, 'Eve's Fostering Link worker' – has dark hair pulled into a bunch so tight that the outer corners of her pale eyes are dragged upwards, and a face whose chin slopes towards the collar of her white pinstriped blouse, and cheeks scribbled with needle-thin red lines, and nails that are bitten as ragged as a child's.

Every so often her glance flicks to Hugh's missing forearm, to the jacket sleeve that's folded back on itself and pinned to the shoulder, but she makes no comment. Everybody looks; nobody ever mentions it.

Click! Eighteen minutes past three.

Anita is filling them in on Eve's story. 'Her mother – her birth mother – has had a serious methadone addiction for several years, heroin before that. Eve and her younger brother were taken into care five years ago, after Eve's school contacted us with concerns.'

'What about the father?' Hugh asks.

'Fathers – two different men, neither of whom, as far as we can gather, was ever in a relationship with the mother. We eventually traced Keith's father, who has some contact with him now, although Keith is still being fostered. We've been unable to trace Eve's father. Her mother … doesn't seem all that sure who he was.'

There's a short silence in the little room. From somewhere, piano music plays faintly. An engine revs, tyres screech as a vehicle speeds off. A horn toots sharply, twice.

'And where's the mother now?' Hugh, again.

Anita rubs the bridge of her nose with thumb and index finger. 'I'm afraid we're not permitted to give out that information. I *can* tell you that neither child has had contact with her for over three years.' A biscuit-coloured folder sits untouched and unopened on the desk before her.

Click!

'And are the children with the same foster family?'

'No. Unfortunately we weren't able to place them together. Eve is here in Tralee and Keith is in Dingle.'

'Do they meet up much?'

'We arrange a meeting three times a year, and of course they can write to one another anytime they want.'

Three times a year they meet, every four months. Four months is a long time not to see someone: in a child's mind it must feel like forever. Imelda sits on the rickety bentwood chair, listening to the conversation. Her wine trousers, the bottom half of her best suit, feel uncomfortably tight. On the way to Tralee, too late to do anything about it, she remembered wearing it to Nell's wedding and feeling it tight then too.

She tries to imagine having a mother who is a drug addict and a father who might be anyone and doesn't know you exist. Could the odds be stacked any less in your favour?

Imelda and Marian had lost their own mother early: she'd died of cancer when Imelda was just seven and Marian nine, but Dad was always there for them. He coped as best he could, as well as any man left with two young daughters would – and both grandmothers helped out too. Compared to Eve, Imelda had been lucky.

'Are there no other family members?' she asks. 'Grandparents, aunts or uncles?'

'Well, they exist, but the family appears to have disowned the children's mother a long time ago. She's originally from Cork – we're not sure how long she was living in Kerry before she came to our attention. We tracked down her family and contacted them, but they didn't really want to get involved.'

Two innocent children, punished for their mother's actions. It seems so cruel – but without knowing the full story, who is Imelda to judge?

'Eve is a quiet girl. She wouldn't be one for the books either – but you won't have to concern yourselves with that since you'll only have her for the holidays.' The social worker glances at the oversized watch that's wrapped around the cuff of her blouse. 'Now, if you have no more questions . . .'

Hugh and Imelda exchange a look. His left eyelid droops slightly, always a sign of tiredness. His face is paler than it should be. Imelda isn't the only nervous one. She has a lot more questions – she wants to ask more about Eve's full-time foster family – but Anita is already pushing back her chair so she remains silent.

'Let's go and meet her then,' the social worker says, easing her way out from behind her desk. The room is so cramped that Hugh and Imelda have to walk ahead of her out of the room. She ushers them down the corridor and into another room, only slightly larger than the office. It contains just a scatter of mismatched armchairs huddled around a low table.

There's an overpowering smell of damp in the room, undisguised by the chemical scent of air freshener someone must have sprayed not long before. The single small window, high up on the opposite wall, looks like it hasn't been opened in years.

'Have a seat,' Anita says. 'I won't be long.'

She leaves the door ajar. They listen to the click of her footsteps fading down the corridor. Hugh puts a hand lightly on Imelda's hip. 'OK?'

She nods, drawing him to a chair. She sits beside him and rubs her hands together, although the day isn't at all cold. 'Remind me to take in the washing when we get back,' she says. Never needing a reminder, but wanting now to pull the security of home around them with an image of sheets and shirts and pillowcases flapping on the line.

They sit silently side by side in the dreary little room as the minutes pass by. No clicking clock on this wall, no clock of any description. Imelda finds Hugh's hand and holds it loosely in both of hers, absently stroking his palm with her thumb. Inhaling the clammy air slowly, trying to calm the fluttering beats of her heart. A dentist's waiting room it feels like, the same jittery nervousness within her.

People hurry by in the corridor; shoes tap and shuffle and stomp past the door. Voices murmur, the piano music is abruptly shut off and replaced, seconds later, with what sounds like a racing commentary. A church bell peals somewhere, reminding Imelda of a distantly read Dickens story in which the rhythm of Sunday-morning church bells sounds to a listener as if they're chanting, *Come* to church, *come* to church, *come* to church. This one, a single repeated doleful beat, is more suggestive to Imelda of a funeral bell that simply states, *Dead, dead, dead*, over and over.

Finally, a new set of footsteps is heard in the corridor. Imelda thinks she recognises Anita's voice, although the words are indistinct. She tenses, releasing her hold on Hugh's hand to brush non-existent crumbs from her lap.

'... just in here.'

The door is pushed open. Imelda and Hugh rise to their feet, Imelda fixing what she hopes is a warm smile on her face, but which feels, dismayingly, more like a stiff stretched empty grimace, as she takes in the girl who enters.

Tall, an inch or two taller than Imelda. Long dark red hair that falls in flat sheets on either side of her unsmiling face. Small light brown freckles splattered across the biggish nose, sulky tilt to the mouth. Eyes green or grey, some pale colour anyway – hard to know from the flash Imelda gets before the lids are lowered, the gaze directed downwards.

Navy school uniform, skirt skimming the thin calves. Black socks bunched about her ankles, scuffed black thick-soled shoes that appear too big for her. Olive green rucksack slung over one shoulder. A sweetish apple scent wafting into the room with her.

Lots of thick black eyeliner, an upward flick to the outer edges, like that singer with the piled-up hair who died young. Shiny brown lipstick, salmon-coloured blusher smudged along her cheekbones. More makeup than Imelda ever uses. At fifteen, Imelda wouldn't have known what to do with eyeliner. Hard to imagine any school allowing it; maybe times have changed. Or maybe it was applied afterwards, on her way here.

'Eve, say hello to Mr and Mrs Fitzpatrick.'

No reaction, no sign that she's heard, gaze still fixed on the floor.

In the few seconds of tight silence that follows, Imelda feels compelled to take action. She advances a step towards the girl. 'Hello, Eve,' she says, in a voice she hardly recognises. 'You can call me Imelda if you like.'

Too bright, too false, the tone you'd use to jolly up a terminally ill relative. She wonders belatedly if she should have mentioned her Christian name – maybe it's not the done thing with foster children, maybe you're not encouraged to be too familiar. If they were told that somewhere along the line, she's forgotten. Maybe Anita is mentally scoring a black mark against them.

'We've been looking forward to meeting you,' she goes on, when the girl continues to ignore them. She keeps her arms by her sides, afraid to offer her hand in case it's ignored too.

'Hi there,' Hugh puts in. 'My name's Hugh. Nice to meet you.' Imelda and Hugh, two black marks.

Still nothing. It's as if they haven't spoken, or Eve hasn't heard. Imelda looks at the social worker, wondering if she has any notion of intervening.

'Eve,' Anita says quietly, 'Mr and Mrs Fitzpatrick have travelled here especially to get to know you a bit. The least you could do is be nice to them.'

The narrow shoulders lift slightly underneath the navy school jumper.

'Please say hello, Eve,' Anita says, in a less friendly tone.

'Hello.'

Mimicking the social worker's voice exactly. Giving them a lightning head-to-toe inspection, her gaze returning briefly to Hugh's right arm before falling away again. Another shrug to pull the rucksack higher up on her shoulder.

Anita draws in a breath, lets it puff out between her lips. She throws Imelda and Hugh an apologetic glance. In the ensuing few seconds of silence, tension builds in the little room. Imelda again feels obliged to say something.

'Eve, we'd really like you to come and stay with us for the summer.' Her voice sounds much too loud. 'We live on the island of Roone – I don't know if you've ever been there.'

Another shrug, accompanied by a twist of the shiny brown lips. Looking now in the direction of Hugh's shoes.

'It's really lovely. I only moved there a year and a half ago, but I couldn't imagine living anywhere else now. And the people are so nice.'

Nothing.

Imelda ploughs on: 'Hugh was brought up there, so he knows everyone. There are only about three hundred and fifty people living full time on the island, so it's very different from Tralee.' On and on she talks, saying whatever comes into her head. 'It's quiet in the winter, but it gets very busy in the summer. Lots of people come there on holidays.'

Eve lifts her head then and looks directly at Imelda. 'It was on the news,' she says flatly. 'A girl was kidnapped off it.' Holding Imelda's gaze now, hostility in her stare, it seems to Imelda. A confrontational edge to it.

Imelda opens her mouth to respond, but Anita gets there first.

'She may not have been kidnapped, Eve. Nobody knows what happened to her. I'm sure everyone on the island is very upset about it. Why don't you tell the Fitzpatricks a bit about yourself?'

The girl's face closes down immediately. Her lips press together, her eyes slide back to the floor.

She's fifteen, Imelda thinks. *She's being shunted from one house to another. She's about to spend several weeks in a place where she knows nobody. Of course she's not going to be happy about it.* 'It's alright,' she says. 'We'll have plenty of time to get to know each other when Eve comes to stay.' She turns to Hugh. 'Won't we?'

He could help her out. He could say something, instead of standing there like a mute.

He nods, smiling. Big help. Imelda feels a dart of irritation.

'Well,' Anita checks her watch again, 'in that case, we'd better let you two get on – I'm sure you've got lots to do.' She turns to Eve. 'We'll see them to the door, OK?'

The short journey is eternal. Making her way along the corridor between Hugh and Eve, Anita walking slightly ahead of them, Imelda feels brittle with tension. Out of the corner of her eye she can see the girl's white-knuckled hand wrapped around the rucksack strap. The rubber soles of her shoes drag squeakily along the floor with each step.

She must try again. She searches for a topic, and settles on the first that comes to mind.

'Do you like school, Eve?'

The question comes out of nowhere, regretted as soon as it's uttered. The kind of inane question childless adults ask small children, almost as lame as 'What do you want to be when you grow up?'

Eve glances at her with an expression of such complete scorn that Imelda's insides twist with dismay. She feels her face getting hot.

'I think we can take that as a no,' Hugh puts in.

Imelda turns and he grins at her, doing his best now to lighten the tension, but for the life of her she can't summon up an answering smile. Anita continues to walk silently ahead, even though she can't have missed the comment. Pretending she isn't with them, dying for them to get lost.

Imelda wants to slap her. You'd think she'd make some effort to break the ice between them. Hugh and Imelda have come here of their own accord to help her out – and it's her job, for God's sake.

They reach the reception area. The same elderly security guard they had encountered on their way in holds the door open for them.

'Wait here,' Anita says to Eve, stepping outside with the other two and pulling the door closed behind her. 'Sorry about that,' she says, her voice lowered. 'I know you didn't get a very good first impression. She'll take a while to get used to you, that's all.'

She pauses, no doubt waiting for them to assure her that they understand, that it's perfectly fine. Neither of them speaks.

She looks from one to the other. 'D'you think you're happy to go ahead with it?'

Imelda is acutely conscious of Eve staring at them openly now through the plate-glass window. Waiting to be rid of them too, no doubt. Or trying to lip-read, see what they thought of her.

'What do you think?' Hugh asks. 'Do you want to give it a go?' Throwing the ball into her court, as usual.

Twelve weeks, eighty-four days of sharing their lives with a young girl they've just met, a girl who has made no effort to be civil to them, who looked defiant and sulky the entire time they were with her. Twelve weeks of having complete responsibility for a teenage girl who's plenty old enough to demand some independence. Are they mad?

But this is what they signed up for. This is why Imelda scrubbed floors and washed windows and polished everything that didn't move when the man was coming to check out the house. If they walk away from it now they'll never know how it might have turned out. Nell has promised to help, and others surely will too. And who knows? Eve and Andy might well take to one another, and become friends.

'Why don't you both sleep on it?' Anita asks. 'I'll ring you in the morning and you can let me know then.'

'I'm happy to give it a try,' Imelda says, turning to smile through the window at Eve, telling herself not to mind when the girl immediately looks away, her dour expression unchanged. It will just take time. They'll persevere until they win her over.

'I'm going to paint the spare bedroom,' she tells Hugh, on the way home. 'It could do with it anyway.'

'I'll do it if you want.'

'I can manage. I've more free time than you. And I'll get new bed linen, something bright. And maybe a few pictures for the walls.'

'OK.'

Silence falls between them. The miles pass as Hugh drives along the country road that leads to the ferry port. She won't say anything negative. She won't say that he could have made more of an effort. There's nothing to be gained from it, and they need to work together to make this a success. She reaches forward and turns on the radio, although she doesn't much care for the afternoon programmes.

Twelve weeks, she thinks. In the grand scheme of things, that's nothing at all.

✳

The strawberries are watery and disappointing. Beautiful to look at, plump and rosy, but holding none of the lush sweetness of Irish-grown ones. Serves him right for trying to impress her.

'They're lovely,' she insists, pushing one into his mouth, licking a drop of juice from his chin. 'You're too fussy, Denis Mulcahy.'

His name on her lips always delights him. He puts the strawberries aside and begins to ease the sheet from her body, hungry for the sight of her. Wanting to memorise every bit of her, so preciously short is their time together.

She smiles, clamping her hands on her breasts as the sheet drops away. 'Dirty old man,' she says, spreading her fingers to tease him with glimpses, 'corrupting poor innocent Claire Geoghegan every week,' her breathing slowing and deepening as he continues to pull the sheet lower, inching his way down, feasting his eyes on her. 'Dragging her off to his bed every week,' she murmurs, stretching her arms above her head now, showing him all there is to see, arching her body towards him, 'feeding her strawberries and having his wicked, wicked way with her.'

As the sheet moves past her thighs she rolls away from him,

laughing, knowing he'll follow. Loving his wicked, wicked way every bit as much as he does.

This encounter is doubly precious, an unexpected, miraculous treat. It's Friday, not Wednesday, and Claire is here.

I can come today, her text read this morning. *Are you free at the usual time?*

Denis had stared at the screen. Today? Today was Friday. He never saw her on Friday. Since they'd met, once a week had been his lot. *YES*, he typed, the single capitalised word flying back to her. His head full of her for the rest of the day, scattering school business to the winds.

He'd bought the strawberries on his way home. He'd straightened his bedclothes, flung open the windows, stood under the shower, as giddy as a three-day-old lamb. When she'd arrived he'd shushed her explanation – something about Joe going to cousins, or cousins coming to Joe – with a kiss. He didn't care why she was there, didn't want to hear Joe's name uttered today.

They didn't make it to the bed right away. They got halfway up the stairs, with Claire's laughing protestations – '*Mis*ter Mul*cab*y!' – as he unzipped and unbuttoned her, as he shed his own clothing, as he kissed and nibbled and stroked and had his unexpected fill of her.

'Boy,' she breathed against his throat, when they were both limp and satiated, 'I should change my day to Friday.'

Sex hadn't been a big part of his marriage. Moira had never once initiated it; they'd never deviated from the missionary position or tried it anywhere other than in bed. It wasn't something that was discussed between them, and they hadn't talked during the act.

Denis had tried to make it enjoyable for Moira, but his limited knowledge, coupled with her lack of encouragement, had made it difficult for him to know if she was taking any pleasure from his earnest probing fingers, his amateurish stroking and pressing. Their lovemaking had been physically satisfying – for him anyway – but mentally saddening.

With Claire it's completely different. She lets him know what she likes, quite without shame, and is happy to discover what pleases him. She talks during sex, she laughs and gasps and cries out, using words he's never heard issuing from a woman's mouth, words that shock and delight and arouse him.

They've had sex in every room in the house. One sunny afternoon they went outside, stark naked, and did what came naturally on the lawn in front of the house, clearly visible to any car that might pass on the road, or any walker who might happen that way. Denis Mulcahy, he thought, respectable school principal, fornicating in broad daylight. Not so respectable that day.

He imagined someone photographing them, his exposed rear end splashed blurrily across the front page of the local paper. *Disgraced principal sacked*, or maybe simply *Sex education*. The dangerous possibility of that – of being caught, literally, with his pants down – only heightened his pleasure.

Only afterwards, when he considered Nell seeing such a photo and reading an account of her father's amorous adventures, did he feel chastened, and the al fresco exercise wasn't repeated.

Sometimes he finds bruises on his knees, on his hips and

elbows. His muscles ache after the unaccustomed exercise her visits provide. It's fun and exhilarating and wonderful. It has awakened him. It has brought him back to life.

He tries not to think about her having sex with her husband, but of course he does. He torments himself with images of her doing the same things with another man. Is he younger than Denis? Is he more handsome, more athletic, better endowed?

He knows nothing about Paddy Geoghegan, other than what Claire told him early on. A factory foreman from Castleisland who impregnated her four times – one miscarriage – over the course of their marriage. A recovering alcoholic who'd gone on the wagon nine years earlier, long after he'd destroyed any feelings she'd had for him.

'The only reason I'm still there is Joe,' she's told Denis more than once. But the images of her with her husband persist in Denis's mind. She's still married: the foreman is still entitled to demand his conjugal rights.

He watches her getting dressed, pulling on her skirt, buttoning her blouse. Sitting on the side of the bed to ease legs into stockings, to slip feet into shoes. Bending to press her mouth to his, whispering that she can see herself out, as if that ever happened.

He stands in the doorway long after her car has disappeared, feeling the cool May air on his skin, sniffing the rain that is to come. He presses his hands to his face, inhaling her smell, remembering where his fingers have been. He hears the song of a cuckoo from across the fields.

Eventually he turns and goes back inside.

✳

Half of his arm is missing. It freaked her out when she saw it. His jacket sleeve pinned up so you couldn't miss it. She hopes he never wears short sleeves – she'd vomit if she saw the end of it. If he ever comes near her in short sleeves she'll run a mile.

And the woman asking do you like school: Eve nearly laughed in her face when she said that. And living on the island where the girl was kidnapped. Eve has never been to an island; she's never been on a boat.

She's been to the sea a few times, but not for years. And she's never been in it, not even for a paddle. All that water stretching out as far as you can see, rushing towards you on a beach as if it's trying to grab you. She's not at all sure that she wants to live someplace where it's all around you, hemming you in. She imagines it lapping at the edge of every road, waiting on the other side of every garden wall. No escape from it.

'You could have been a bit friendlier,' Anita tells her when she's driving her back to the Garveys'. 'They went to the trouble of coming to see you. You could have talked to them.'

Eve doesn't bother answering. Anita doesn't care whether she talks or not. All Anita cares about is shoving the names on her list into houses. Once she has Eve in a house she'll forget all about her and move on to the next name.

Anita always says, *Ring if you have any problems*, but whenever Eve had rung she wasn't there, and she never got back when Eve left a message, so after a while Eve had stopped ringing. All that's worrying Anita now is that the people might change their minds because Eve didn't talk to them, and then she'll have to spend time finding another house to shove Eve into.

Eve doesn't much care if they change their minds. They said they were happy to meet her, but they didn't really look like they wanted her. Maybe they need the money, or maybe they just want someone to clean their house for the summer.

She doesn't care where she goes. Wherever it is, she'll only be there for the summer, and then she'll have to go back to the Garveys', like she does every year. Like she'll have to keep doing until she's eighteen, and free.

She doesn't think the man with the missing arm is like Derek. He didn't look at her the way Derek does. The only good thing she can think of to say about them is that they're keeping her away from him for the whole summer.

'Feet down,' Anita says, and Eve lets her feet slide slowly from the dashboard.

She wonders what Anita would say if she told her about Derek. Nothing, probably – or else something like *Stay out of his way. Make sure you're not on your own with him.*

Anita just wants an easy life. Anita hasn't a clue.

✳

'Bridie O'Callaghan was in today. Her dog had pups yesterday.'

'Yeah?'

'She showed me photos on her phone. They're adorable. Half setter, half Lab.'

They're on the beach. Not warm enough to sit, a stiffish breeze whipping the tops of the waves into peaks, but fine if what you want is to walk on the damp sand along by the shore. James pauses to skim a stone every now and again. John Silver bounds ahead, barking at the water.

Other walkers are scattered along the beach, everyone rain-jacketed, like Nell and James. All day the showers have been sudden and heavy but now, on the cusp of twilight, the sky is finally clearing.

The bay is clearing too, after twelve days of intense activity. The helicopter is gone, and most of the searcher boats. How terribly sad, Nell thinks, to take the decision to stop looking, to decide that there is no hope any more of finding Ellie, alive or dead. Of course, it had to be done – there are other searches to be carried out, newer dramas to attend to – but heartbreaking all the same.

James aims another stone at the water. 'Meant to tell you,' he says, watching it hop once, twice, three times. 'Tim phoned today.'

Nell hears the studied casual note in his voice. 'Did he? Everything OK?'

'Everything's fine.' He turns back to her. 'He was wondering if he and Katy could stay in the house.'

She stoops to pick up a piece of driftwood. 'Which house?' But she knows which house.

'Mine, now that it's free. He thought they might come down here for a week, maybe next month.'

The piece of wood is a foot long, about the depth of a spade handle, its surfaces ragged and eaten. Perfect for a game of catch. She whistles for John Silver and he comes dashing back.

'Would you be OK with that?' James asks.

'Of course I'd be OK,' she says. 'Why wouldn't I?'

It comes out a little sharper than she'd intended. She flings the stick, throwing all her weight behind it, and John Silver streaks off, barking deliriously.

'Your mother might come with them,' she says, wiping her hands on her jeans as James hops another stone across the water. 'She hasn't been to Roone in ages.'

Not since December, when she'd made the difficult journey down with Tim for the funeral. Katy, heavily pregnant, had stayed in Dublin but sent Nell a letter by Tim.

Desperately sorry to hear, she wrote, *wish I could be there. My thoughts and prayers are with you.*

James puts his hands on her shoulders. His cheeks are pink from the breeze. 'Are you sure it wouldn't bother you if they came?'

'Of course I am,' she replies. 'Andy should see more of his only cousin. And Katy's never been here, and she's heard so much about it. I'm sure she'd love to see it.'

John Silver hurtles back, sand skidding under his paws as he pulls up in front of them. He drops the stick at Nell's feet and looks up hopefully.

She stoops and grabs it, leaving James's hands holding nothing. 'Tell them to come,' she says, and flings the stick far.

SUNDAY, 26 MAY

A sharp rap on the car window makes him start. He lowers the book he's been pretending to read and turns to see a youngish foxy-haired man in a navy uniform and peaked cap peering in at him, face screwed up questioningly. He slides down the window.

'Can I help you there?' the man asks. His tone just short of aggressive. A whitehead, ripe for the squeezing, nestles beside the flare of a nostril.

Denis shakes his head, summoning a polite smile. 'Thank you, I'm fine. Just waiting for someone.'

'At the pool, is it?' His head tilting in its direction on the word.

'That's right.'

Is he a security man of some kind, or just a uniformed busybody who has decided he doesn't like the look of Denis? There's a logo on the jacket's breast pocket – three initials around a yellow triangle – that rings no bells. Maybe he's a local eccentric who dresses up in something he found in a charity shop and patrols the streets, pretending to have some authority.

But he could be legit, employed by the pool owners, maybe. Told to keep an eye out for men hanging around on their own, or anyone who seems to have an interest in the stringy-haired children emerging intermittently from the building across the street that houses the town's public pool.

'My granddaughter,' Denis tells him. 'She's in the gala today. Great little swimmer.' There, that should keep him happy.

Not entirely. 'You didn't go in to see her?'

'My daughter asked me not to: the little one gets nervous if she knows there are too many of us watching.' The lies flowing out of him as he lifts a shoulder and gives the man a what-can-you-do look – raised eyebrows, crooked half-smile. 'My job is to wait for the news when they come out, then take them somewhere nice for a bite to eat.'

Move off, he says silently, hating how he's forced into this false camaraderie. *Leave me alone. Go and stick your nose into someone else's business. Don't assume I'm a pervert just because I'm sitting across the road from a swimming pool.* Wanting to turn and watch the door again, in case he misses them coming out.

'Deirdre's in a swimming gala on Sunday,' Claire told him on Wednesday. 'We're all going to see her.' Not imagining for a second that Denis might decide to tag along, not dreaming that he'd look up the local paper and get the information he needed. The thought never crossing her mind, Denis was sure, that he would get into his car, drive to the pool and sit across the road, waiting for them to come out.

Whatever masochistic instinct is at work here, whatever compulsion has taken him over, he feels a clamouring desire to see the man who has what Denis doesn't. He has no plan to approach him, nothing like that. He just wants to put a face to him, make him real. He doesn't know why his need has become so urgent – what good will it do, seeing the features of his rival? But here he is all the same.

'Well ...' The uniformed man is clearly not convinced of Denis's innocence, but short of accusing him of paedophilia, there isn't much more he can do. Denis turns his head and sets his gaze once more on the pool door, and eventually he hears the man moving away.

Maybe he's planning to keep him under observation. For all Denis knows he may already have taken note of his registration number, all set to pass it on to the guards if no granddaughter materialises. Maybe Denis should have come clean and told him he was waiting to spy on his married lover: maybe the man would have taken pity on him and left him alone.

The minutes tick by. He checks his rear-view and wing mirrors and finds no sign of the man in uniform. Children and adults continue to enter and leave the pool building. Deirdre is fourteen and in second year: that's all he knows about her. She's fourteen and her brother Joe has just turned sixteen and Niamh—

And suddenly there she is, there's Claire. His heart flips over as she emerges from the building. The red coat, the red and black silk scarf that he's often removed. Her arm linked with that of the stocky dark-haired youth who walks beside her – and even from across the road Denis can make out the slanted deep-set eyes and slightly lumbering gait that mark him out as different.

And directly behind them comes a girl with a red sports bag slung across one shoulder. Deirdre, the swimmer. Dressed in navy tracksuit, white runners, long fair hair pulled into a high ponytail. Taller than her older sister, who wears jeans and a black jacket, a wide red band or scarf keeping her shoulder-length darker hair off her face.

And between the girls, the factory foreman. Denis fixes his attention on Paddy Geoghegan as they walk past the front of the building towards the car park at the rear. Average height, average build. Pale hair receding at his temples. Short neat beard, dark-rimmed glasses, grey jeans beneath a blue anorak. Younger-looking than Denis by a few years, but not enough to be significant.

Unremarkable, the kind of man you'd nod at on passing in the street and instantly forget. The man standing ahead of you in the supermarket checkout queue, or reaching for a book down the aisle from you at the library, if he ever saw the inside of a library.

Paddy Geoghegan, the perfectly ordinary recovering alcoholic who has fathered three children with Claire, the woman he's been married to for almost twenty years.

'I don't love him,' Claire tells Denis, over and over. 'I did when we got married, but not any more, not for a very long time. I love *you*.'

But she lives with Paddy, not with Denis. She shares a house with Paddy, while Denis gets a visit once a week. She sits across the dinner table from Paddy each evening, surrounded by their children. She and Denis have never eaten a proper meal together. She goes to swimming galas with Paddy while Denis watches from across the road. She goes upstairs with Paddy every night.

'We haven't had sex in years,' she insists. 'Not since long before I met you.' But even if that's true, what good is it?

The five of them walk around the side of the building. Just before they disappear Claire turns her head, smiling, towards the trio behind her. Her mouth opens, but the words are lost to Denis. He's not part of the conversation, and never will be.

After they've gone he sits on, his book lying open in his lap. A few minutes later a dark grey Volvo emerges from the car park, and he sees Claire sitting in the front passenger seat beside her husband. She doesn't look in Denis's direction, neither of them does, as the car swings right and moves off.

Denis watches it disappear into the stream of traffic. Heading home to put on the dinner, or maybe eating out to celebrate Deirdre's performance, acting out the fabricated scenario Denis presented to the security guard, or whatever he was. Doing something together anyway, the five of them. The Geoghegan family.

And as he sits there, Denis understands why he's come. He's made the husband real because a real man will make it impossible for him to keep doing what he's been doing with Claire.

After a few minutes he starts his car. He makes his way through the town and turns left at the outskirts, onto the same coast road that Claire takes every Wednesday when she comes to him. He drives the five miles that lead to the cheaply furnished, carelessly insulated little house that has been his home since he left Roone.

He lets himself in and makes straight for the kitchen. He pours a measure of brandy into a tumbler and drinks it down like water, standing at the sink that still holds his lunch crockery. He puts the glass on the draining board, throat burning, goes to sit at the table and sinks his head into his hands.

He can't do it. He must do it.

✳

The poster is ragged around the edges, its ink faded after twenty days of showers and sea breezes and sun. Have you seen Ellie? it still asks, above the picture of the smiling little girl with her ice-cream, but nobody at all has seen Ellie.

The search is officially over. The bay holds nothing more than the usual mix of fishing trawlers and pleasure craft for this time of year. Most of the reporters and TV crews packed up and went home at the end of the first week, and the rest have drifted away in the days since then.

The crowds of curious day-trippers pouring off the morning ferries have dwindled – nothing happening, nothing to see – and visitor figures have returned to Roone's normal early-summer quota.

The guards who were drafted in from Tralee and Killarney and Dingle have all returned to base, leaving the case in the care of Sergeant Fox, who has never encountered anything more challenging in his twenty years on the island than a few over-enthusiastic revellers on a Saturday night, or occasional pilfering of temporarily unattended beach bags.

And most tellingly of all, the house Ellie's family originally rented, the house from where she disappeared – owned by a man from Galway, according to local reports – is occupied again. It had remained vacant for a fortnight after the family were moved out, and even Lelia Doherty was unable to discover whether the next group had cancelled or been allocated a different property, or whether it had been booked at all for that period.

But now it's let again.

'James saw a car parked outside when he went around to check on his place,' Nell told Laura the previous evening, over the stone wall. 'A Wexford registration. I wonder if they know it's the house she disappeared from.'

The incident seems to be fading from the collective memory: no mention of it on the evening news any more, nothing in the national papers. Could people be forgetting about Ellie? Have they simply moved on, like the reporters, to the next drama?

Roone hasn't forgotten. The subject mightn't be discussed as earnestly as before but it's still there: she's still in everyone's thoughts. There's a restrained feel about the place, a dampening of spirits. The island has been stunned and subdued by what has taken place.

The little girl's parents remain at the hotel, her father joining in the searches up to the last, her mother venturing out of their room only to wander disconsolately in the hotel's rear gardens in the company of various strangers – family members, everyone presumes – who come and go from the island.

'They take all their meals in the room,' Lelia reports. 'Henry brought them up a bottle of brandy when they moved in, but he says they haven't touched it. All they asked him for was an internet connection and Father William's phone number. Sergeant Fox checks in with them every day, not that he has anything new to tell them. Poor creatures, I don't know how they haven't gone dotty.'

It is not yet seven o'clock on Sunday morning. Laura woke early with her stomach clenching uncomfortably. She slid out of bed and crept from the house to see if half an hour of sea air would make things any better. In the ten minutes or so she's been walking along the coast road towards the village she hasn't met a soul.

Nearly three months still to go, and she looks as if she could pop at any moment. Under a pink fleece jacket that doesn't nearly go around her she wears one of Gavin's shirts, which falls almost to her knees, and a pair of navy XXL leggings, the only things she feels comfortable in these days. Just as well living on Roone usually requires no dressing up whatsoever.

The morning is crisp – she's glad of the jacket, despite its limited coverage – but the day is promised good, with a clear sky and a faint haze hovering over the distant fields. Maybe the fine spell everyone's been waiting for is on the way at last.

She approaches the apricot façade of the hotel, rubbing absently at her still-cramping abdomen, and glances up at its double row of cream-shuttered windows. She wonders which room Ellie's parents have been occupying, and how much sleep they get each night between Henry's crisp white sheets as they wait to find out if their little daughter, or what remains of her, will be found.

She walks on towards the church, fifty yards beyond the hotel. Directly across the road from it stands a woman, still as a statue, legs braced and slightly parted, her back to Laura as she faces out to sea. Green knee-length skirt or dress, grey top above it, white-sandalled feet. One arm crosses her chest, its hand tucked into the opposite armpit. Her other arm hangs by her side, a cigarette stuck between the fingers.

The pose, if you didn't study it closely, has a languid feel to it. She could be someone simply looking out to sea, an early-rising holidaymaker admiring the morning view. But as her steps bring her closer Laura fancies she sees a rigid set to the shoulders, a clenched look to the calves, a suggestion of tension about the entire figure – and suspicion dawns that the woman is in fact Martha Ryan, Ellie's mother.

Laura hasn't encountered her in the flesh, but she's seen numerous replays of the haunted face of the woman at the press conference, and it was framed by hair just that dark brown colour, and that length. And who else would be standing alone here at this hour? It's surely her – it must be her.

Laura slows her pace, uncertain as to whether she should acknowledge the woman. She can hardly pretend not to have noticed her, even if she's on the other side of the road – and the woman has to have heard Laura's footsteps. But maybe she'd prefer to be left alone, maybe the last thing she wants—

Just then she turns her head abruptly and looks directly at Laura, and any doubts Laura might have had as to her identity are banished. There is such utter defeat and devastation in her white, exhausted face that the only thing for Laura to do is hurry across the road to her.

'Hello,' she says, as she approaches. 'I live here – my name's Laura. I'm so sorry this awful thing has happened to you.' Resting a hand briefly on the woman's shoulder, feeling the thin cloth of her creased grey cardigan, the coolness of the skin beneath. 'I'm so terribly sorry.'

The woman nods once, not the smallest part of her expression altering. Deep shadows beneath her eyes, no makeup, hair uncombed, pale lips tinged with blue from the sharp early-morning air. Her free hand, the one not holding the cigarette, moves to pull the edges of the cardigan together, the left side of which is stained with something pink. Her whole body, Laura notices, is trembling.

'You're cold,' she says, beginning to take off her fleece jacket – but the woman shakes her head, almost angrily, and takes a step back. She raises the half-smoked cigarette and peers at it.

'I'd given them up,' she says, the words jerking out of her, voice low and husky. 'First time I was pregnant. Never went back … till now. Can't get enough of them now. Eating them up.'

She puts it to her mouth and the tip glows fiercely as she closes her lips around it. The corner of a cigarette box pokes from one of the cardigan's pockets. There's a musky, unwashed odour from her. Everyone on Roone knows her name is Martha, everyone in Ireland and beyond. Martha and Vincent, both in their mid-thirties.

How do you bear it? Laura wants to ask. *How can you stand here talking calmly about smoking? How are you not driven out of your mind by what's happened?*

She searches for something to offer, some way she can help. 'Is there anything you need?' she asks. 'Any … clothes or, I don't know – toiletries, or books or something?' Books, when her child is missing – God almighty. As if all the woman needs is the latest bestseller.

Martha makes no response. It's as if Laura hasn't spoken. She looks out to sea again. 'She's not there,' she murmurs, so quietly that Laura almost misses it. 'I can't feel her there. I can't *sense* her in the—'

She breaks off, jamming the cigarette quickly between her lips again, dragging deeply on it once more, the hand that holds it trembling violently. Laura stands helplessly by, unable to think of anything else to say.

Martha turns back to her abruptly. 'You think she's dead, don't you?' A sharpness in the voice as her eyes search Laura's face, smoke stuttering out with the words. 'That's what you're all thinking, isn't it?'

'No, of course I—'

'You *are*. I know you are. Everyone is. They stopped looking for her – why else would they stop looking? You think we should go home, we should just forget about her. You don't want us here, in case we keep the tourists away. You'd prefer us to leave you alone.'

'Of *course* not. Nobody thinks that. We can't imagine what it must be like for you.'

'No, you can't. Nobody can. Nobody can *possibly*—' She bites off the end of the sentence again, takes another deep drag on the cigarette. Drops the butt and grinds it angrily under her sandal. 'She's not dead,' she says fiercely, her sandal mashing the butt into the grass. 'She's *not* dead.' Her toenails have been painted a deep burgundy but the varnish is badly chipped. 'I'd know if she was dead.'

'We're all praying—'

'I lost my mother when I was thirteen,' she says, glaring at Laura. 'When my daughter was born, do you know the first thing I thought?'

Laura shakes her head.

'I thought, *I hope I don't die until she's all grown up.*' She shakes her head from side to side, hands shoved now into her cardigan pockets. 'That's a good one, isn't it?' Biting down hard on her lower lip.

Laura watches her dumbly, wishing there was something to say that would offer her a grain of comfort. Knowing there isn't.

'Do you have children?' Martha demands suddenly.

'Yes, two boys.' Laura's hand goes instinctively to cradle her abdomen.

Martha glances down, and Laura realises that she hadn't noticed her pregnancy up to now. She watches the woman's face change, watches her press her palms to her face, sees her body begin to heave with ragged sobs. When Laura, close to tears herself, attempts to embrace her she stumbles out of her reach, warding her off.

'*Ellie*,' she wails, hands tearing at her hair now, ripping out a sizeable hank that tumbles to the ground, tears streaming down the face that has become ugly and distorted with grief. 'Where *are* you, child? Where have you *gone*?'

'Please—' Laura says, reaching towards her again but she pushes her away and moves blindly across the road, back in the direction of the hotel. Sobbing wildly, shoulders heaving, sandals flapping with every staggered step, looking as if she might fold and crash to the ground at any second. Thankfully, no car was coming: she appears completely oblivious to her surroundings.

Laura fishes a tissue from her pocket, dabs her eyes and blows her nose as she watches the woman stumble past the hotel gateposts, the awful sounds that issue from her fading as the distance between them increases. When she finally disappears from view Laura turns back to the sea, lapping gently against the harbour wall, looking so calm and harmless.

Has it taken Ellie? Did the child go alone to the little beach near the holiday homes? Did she clamber onto the rocks that bordered it, unobserved by anyone? Did she slip and fall in, and sink below the water? Will they ever find out?

She looks down at the strands of ripped-out hair that lie scattered across the grass. She rubs her hands together to warm them, checks her watch and begins to retrace her steps towards the B&B, turning her thoughts to the eight breakfasts she will shortly have to cook, glad for once of the routine of rashers and sausages and eggs on a frying pan.

✳

Imelda stands back and regards the rough butter-yellow rectangle. Not quite as fresh a colour as she had anticipated – you really can't go by the bit on the front of the tin – but she thinks it might do. The bedroom is south-facing, so it gets the best of the light. She tries to picture the walls all yellow, lit up by the afternoon sun … Yes, it's definitely the best of them. It'll brighten up the place and give the room a nice warm feel.

Hugh thinks she's daft, she knows he does. Of course he says nothing, but she can see it in his face. What does the colour of the walls matter? his expression asked, as Imelda ignored him and chewed her lip and contemplated the sample pots in the Tralee paint shop the other day, picking them up one after another and coming home in the end with five.

But the pale grey is too cold, the camel and cream too insipid, and while she loves the apricot, she feels it might be too strong for the size of the room. So yellow it is or, rather, Tuscan Gold. The names they put on paint colours: somebody getting paid, she presumes, to sit there and think them up. Nice work if you can get it.

Tomorrow she'll take the ferry across again, go back to the shop and buy a can, and she'll bring it to a department store, pick up a bed linen set to tone in and a couple of cushions to throw on the bed. What else?

A nice lamp to replace the old-fashioned brass one sitting on the locker, and a bedside rug in a plain colour instead of that tatty old patterned thing that should have been thrown out years ago. And a picture or two, something with a seaside theme.

She lays her brush carefully on top of the little tin and wipes her hands with a damp facecloth. Will Eve notice the effort they're making for her? Will she care? Impossible to know – and unfair to judge her from that one meeting.

She wonders if the girl has her own room in her real foster home, or if she shares with one of the other children. The parents have three of their own, the social worker had told them, a boy and a girl still at home and the eldest girl working as a nurse in New Zealand. Eve has been living with the family since she and her brother were taken away from their mother.

Five years she's been sharing their house, since she was ten. No doubt she's formed some kind of bond with them. But why is she being farmed out for the summer? Does it happen every year, and if it does, is Eve sent somewhere different each time?

So many things Imelda would like to know, but she's reluctant to lift the phone and bother Anita. It's just background information anyway, more to satisfy Imelda's curiosity than anything else. They'd have been told, surely, if any of it was relevant.

In the bathroom Imelda washes the paintbrush under a running tap and thinks about Hugh's birthday next month, and how she still has to decide on a present for him. Last year she gave books: a new story from a detective writer she knew he liked, a collection of American poetry, a biography of Franco. This year she's thinking of music, or something to wear.

The phone rings in the hall. She dries her hands and goes downstairs to answer it.

'Imelda,' her sister says. 'I can't believe you're actually at home. The number of times I get no answer when I ring, and no machine to leave a message.'

Marian has got it into her head that mobile phones are bad for your health. She's never owned one herself, and appears to think that even calling someone else's from a landline might do her some harm.

'I'm here now,' Imelda says. 'Everything alright?'

'Well, Vernon has a bit of a tickly throat, but he will go out without a scarf, so what can he expect?'

'He'd hardly need his scarf now, would he? It's nearly June.'

'That's what he says, but you know as well as I do that you can't depend on the weather in Ireland, no matter what the calendar says.'

Imelda scratches at a mark on the dado rail beside her. 'That's true enough … So, any other news?'

'Yes – we're thinking of coming to Roone for a week or two, maybe early July. We were talking about it last night, and we thought it might be nice, especially as we haven't been back there since your wedding.'

'Oh.' Eve will still be with them in July, sleeping in their one and only spare room: where on earth are they to fit Marian and Vernon? 'Holiday time already,' she says, casting about rapidly. 'Imagine.'

'You don't sound very happy at the prospect of seeing us.'

'No, no, of course I'd be delighted, we both would. It's just that we only have the two bedrooms – well, there is a third, but it's tiny, not much more than a box room, really – and you know we're getting the foster.'

'Imelda, will you stop? We weren't thinking of staying in *your* house. We wouldn't dream of barging in with you and Hugh, especially when you'll have your visitor.'

Visitor. Marian has made no secret of the fact that the idea of Hugh and Imelda wanting to become foster carers bemuses her. *Why would you draw that on yourself, Imelda? Who knows what problems you might be bringing into your home? Why not make a donation to a children's charity if you want to help? I'm only looking out for you, dear, you know that.*

Imelda does know that. Marian is always well-intentioned, even if Imelda is sometimes tempted to put a gag on her. If Eve proves difficult to manage, Marian will take great pleasure from reminding Imelda that she told her so, and Imelda will have to grit her teeth yet again. But by July Eve will surely have settled in with them, will be bound to have made a few friends.

'We're thinking we'll book into a B&B this time,' Marian goes on. 'Nice to have the breakfast served up to you in the morning, and we'd be going out anyway to eat in the evenings – you know Vernon won't hear of me cooking dinner when we're on holidays.'

'Well, there are lots of nice B&Bs here – in fact, a friend of ours opened one recently. I could make a booking there for you, if you like.'

She has no idea what kind of a B&B Walter's Place is. Going by Laura's bubbly but slightly chaotic personality, she suspects the day-to-day running of the operation might be a little slapdash – but she can hardly pass her by if she's booking a place for Marian and Vernon, not with Laura an immediate neighbour of Nell's.

And who knows? It could be lovely. The house, what she's seen of it, is certainly impressive.

'It's right next door to Nell's,' she tells Marian, 'where we stayed when we came, remember? So you'd find it easily.'

'Right next door? Wasn't that where the old man died, the day before we arrived?'

Trust Marian to remember that. 'Yes, that's the one. The new owners stayed in Nell's house too, funnily enough. They were there before us.'

'What – they rented Nell's, then bought the house next door? Did they know beforehand that the poor man was sick?'

'Walter wasn't sick. He dropped dead. And Gavin and Laura didn't know one another when they stayed in Nell's. They were there at different times. They only met when they were both back in Dublin.'

Small pause. 'They just happened to meet in Dublin, after staying in the same holiday home at the other side of the country?'

Imelda was beginning to wish she hadn't mentioned it. 'Not exactly. Gavin left a book behind him in the house, and Laura took his address from Nell and looked him up when she got home, to give him back the book.'

'And now they're living on the island together?'

'Yes. They're a couple now, and they bought Walter's house last year.' She almost added, *And Laura already had two little boys, and there are two more babies on the way*, but caught herself in time. That would take another lengthy explanation. 'I'll fill you in on all the details when you get here.'

'Right then, that's settled. I'll ask Vernon about dates and you can book us in. By the way, has that whole unpleasant business with the missing child died down yet?'

Imelda closes her eyes. Unpleasant business, like someone caught with a hand in the till or cheating on a test, rather than a family ripped asunder, never to be the same. Marian's heart is in the right place but Lord, sensitivity will never be her strong suit.

'The parents are still here. Laura, the woman with the B&B, met the little girl's mother this morning.'

'And what did she have to say for herself?'

'Nothing much. She was very upset.' *In bits* was how Laura had put it, according to Nell.

'Of course she was. She'd be better off back home, if you ask me, than hanging around Roone where no good news can come now.'

'I suppose … but it must be so hard for them to leave.'

'No doubt, no doubt. Well, I'd better go and get the dinner on for Vernon. He says he's not hungry but I know if I do him a bit of a mixed grill he won't say no. He loves a lamb cutlet.'

'Give him my best.' Her brother-in-law is well looked after, whatever about Marian's tactlessness.

As she hangs up she hears the back door opening. She returns to the kitchen and there's Hugh.

'Well?' he said, coming over to kiss her cheek, smelling of the pub where he's spent the last several hours. 'Good day?'

'Good day,' she tells him. 'Bedroom colour has been chosen. Yellow it is.'

'Glad to hear it.' He sits and shrugs off his shoes, yawning.

'I went for a walk earlier,' she says, 'over by the lighthouse.'

'Fine day for it.'

'Yes … I was thinking we might go to the beach on Thursday if the weather holds. Bring a picnic.'

'That'd be good.'

Thursday is his full day off. The beach is the small pebble one on the south of the island where they met, little more than a twenty-foot-wide strip of stones running along the bottom of the cliffs for a hundred yards or so before it turns into big flat slabs of rock. Not in the least popular, an awkward scramble down a lane to get to it, most of the sunlight blocked by the cliffs. No big waves there, too short for a decent beach walk. Nothing, on the face of it, to recommend it.

But catch it on a calm dry day, when the only sounds are the soft comforting *lap lap* of water on stones and the plaintive cries of the gulls in the sky above, and you couldn't find a more peaceful place. They go there often, separately and alone – and every time Imelda turns the corner at the bottom of the gravelly lane that leads down to it she's reminded of her first visit there.

The surprise she felt at the abrupt sight of the sea before her, followed almost immediately by the alarming realisation that a man was sitting on the pebbles not three yards away from her.

So accidental, their first meeting – and so miraculous that it happened at all. If Walter hadn't died, Hugh wouldn't have been sitting up all night at his wake. If it had been raining in the morning he mightn't have stopped the car on his way home and gone down to the beach, feeling the need for some time alone with his thoughts.

And even with Hugh in the right place at the right time, they still wouldn't have met if Imelda had turned left instead of right at Nell's gate when she'd gone for a walk that morning, or if she'd passed by the little unmarked lane instead of deciding on impulse to see where it led her.

And none of that would have happened if Vernon and Marian had chosen a different location for their holiday, and never travelled to Roone at all. The quirks and vagaries of chance that had brought Hugh and Imelda together and changed her life utterly.

'Bridie O'Callaghan's dog had six pups, couple of weeks ago,' Hugh says.

'Did she?'

'Gavin was telling me. Half setter, half something else.'

'Lovely.'

He has told her about a dog he used to have that died a few years before they met. She remembers being relieved that he hadn't replaced it – she's a bit nervous of dogs, never trusts them not to turn on you out of the blue.

She opens the fridge and takes out the salmon cutlets she got from the pier that morning, after delivering the sandwiches to the pub. She brushes them with oil, sprinkles black pepper, adds a dab of butter. She turns on the grill, gets carrots from a shelf in the pantry and begins to peel them.

Hugh pushes his shoes aside and gets to his feet. 'Fancy a glass of wine?'

'I will so … There's a bottle open in the fridge.'

She remembers calling into his pub, a few days after meeting him on the beach. She was with Vernon and Marian, and she'd had no idea he owned a pub. She remembers how the sight of him behind the counter, so unexpected, made the blood rush to her face, how she regretted not taking more care with her appearance. Her hair all windswept, her lipstick completely worn off since she'd put it on that morning.

She takes the glass from him, sips the cold white wine. He brings home lovely bottles from the wholesale off-licence. She hasn't a clue about wine, drinks anything she's given, but you'd know the ones he chooses are good. Or maybe she's biased.

She puts the carrots on to boil, lays the salmon on the hot grill pan. She slices cold cooked potatoes, left over from the previous day's dinner, and brushes them with oil and arranges them around the fish. She's not much of a cook – better at baking, by far – but Hugh eats whatever she puts in front of him, and he makes dinner on his day off, or takes her out to Lelia's.

She wipes her hands and goes to sit on his lap. He grins. 'What's this now?'

'Your wife wants a cuddle,' she tells him, and he obliges.

✳

'They're all coming,' Nell says. 'Colette and Tim and Katy and Lily. Some time next month, for a week. They'll stay in James's house. It'll be good to have someone using it. We should have put it up for rent, but we never got around to it.'

It's an hour before nightfall. James is at work in the pub and Andy has taken the ferry with friends to the cinema in Tralee. The evening is warm, bringing out the midges. She sees them swarming by the hedge, feels them tickling her scalp.

'It'll be nice to have them here,' she says, scratching. 'It'll be different, of course. It'll be a little strange.'

Tim back on Roone, living with someone who's not her. Different, but not in a bad way. They've all moved on.

'I'm dying to see Lily again,' she says. 'We haven't seen her since the christening. She was so tiny.'

They'd driven up to Dublin from Roone in February, a week after she was born. They have a photo of Andy sitting on Tim and Katy's leather couch, holding his new cousin in his arms, and one of Tim changing his daughter's nappy. And a few at the church, everyone in their finery, Lily wearing the lace gown Colette was christened in.

'Remember,' Nell says, 'all the plans we had, Tim and I. We wanted at least four children – well, I did anyway.'

She used to imagine herself as Mrs Baker, with rosy cheeks and a gingham apron. The impossibly twee picture she had in her head, making gooseberry tarts and turning crab apples into jam for her perfect family. All sorted.

And she did become Mrs Baker, only it was a different one.

'I still want lots of children,' she says. 'I still have lots of time.'

Andy is sixteen. James had his first child sixteen years ago, when Nell was nineteen. She and James will have been married three weeks tomorrow.

'Will you wait?' she'd asked him, and he'd said yes, so they didn't sleep together until after they were married. Partly because of Tim, partly because of Andy. And then, after December, partly because of her mother.

Did James resent her asking it, knowing that Nell had shared a bed with his brother every weekend for well over a year? Does he ever wonder if she compares them now? Some things remain unsaid between them, and maybe it's as well.

'Fingers crossed,' she says, 'it'll happen soon. I'd be over the moon.'

Katy must have got pregnant on their honeymoon in Italy, Lily born barely nine months after the unexpected wedding. Nell might be pregnant now too. The thought of holding her own baby causes a pull somewhere deep inside her, an elemental tug that feels like an ache.

'Did you feel it too, when you thought about having children?' she asks – but the question is too sad to bear, since it can never be answered. She turns from her mother's grave – no headstone yet, just a wooden cross at the top of a mound of earth that's covered with a first sprinkling of bright green grass – and makes her way out of the cemetery as the light continues to seep from the sky, and the midges dart silently about.

'Six,' Francis O'Callaghan says gloomily. 'And so far only two homes got.'

James gives a final top-up to Francis's newly pulled Guinness and places it before him. 'You've time enough, haven't you? They're only a week old yet.'

'Ten days – but the longer they stay unclaimed, the more attached Bridie and the kids will get. I'll have a battle on my hands to give them away if it goes on much longer.'

'And who's taking the first two?'

'Henry Manning – his collie died last year, remember – and Leo Considine.'

'So you have four to go.'

'That's right.'

James recalls Nell mentioning the pups when they were walking on the beach over a week ago. 'I'll spread the word,' he promises Francis. 'I might find you a few takers.'

'Do that, good man.'

As Francis dips his head towards the Guinness, James is signalled by another customer. Sunday nights from May to September are busy in Fitz's, but he doesn't mind. Better to be kept on the move than twiddling your thumbs and watching the clock go around.

At the end of the evening, when the takings have been stored in the safe, the used glasses assembled on the counter and the table tops wiped, he and Sean Carmody lock up and James sets off to walk the fifteen minutes home. He could sit in with Sean, who's driving two miles further in the same direction – and if it's spilling down he's glad of the lift – but on warm, dry nights like this the stroll is the perfect end to a busy evening in the pub.

It's ten past midnight when he reaches the end of the village street and turns right onto the coast road. He passes the church in darkness and the hotel still lit up – and further on the house where Nell had spent her childhood.

Across a field to his left the sea moves gently, its surface shimmering with a million points of light. He looks up at a night sky that's pierced with stars and inhales the pure air and thinks again about the topic that's been occupying his head for the past ten days.

'Only if it's OK with you and Nell,' Tim said. 'I know Katy would love to see the island.'

And when he'd told her about the phone call, Nell had sounded put out. Understandable if she doesn't feel entirely comfortable with them coming. Her ex-fiancé returning with his wife to the place where he and Nell had got together and been a couple and fallen in love and become engaged.

I picked the wrong brother, she'd told James. He keeps going back to that, keeps reminding himself that he's the one she married, not Tim. And yet … he's not entirely comfortable himself with the notion of Tim and Katy coming to stay. But he could hardly say no, with the house lying vacant, and no real reason for not wanting them other than his own foolish insecurities. So he'd said yes, and now they're coming.

His mother is coming too, which he regards as a good thing. She and Nell have always got on, even if she was temporarily thrown by the whole broken engagement and subsequent surprises. And hopefully she'll be an antidote to any awkwardness that might manifest itself within the group.

'You and Nell will be very happy,' she'd said to James on his wedding day. 'You're kindred spirits.' Bidding him farewell on the path outside the restaurant in Ennistymon, draping her lilac shawl across her shoulders. 'And Andy is fond of her, which is important.'

He knows the unease he feels is unfounded. He has nothing to worry about. He and Nell were meant to be together, even if she chose Tim first. And Tim is married with a family, his relationship with Nell long over. A week will go quickly; a week is nothing.

But despite all his reasoned arguments the unease persists, and there's nothing he can do about it.

He walks past Walter's old house, the metal sign he painted for the B&B swinging gently in the soft breeze. A light still burns in one of the guest bedrooms. He wouldn't fancy living in a B&B, strangers in your home every night, paying to sleep in your sheets, use your facilities. Not his cup of tea.

He approaches Nell's house – *their* house. Their home. He walks up the garden path, fishing in his pocket for his key. Before he can reach it the front door opens and Nell stands there, in pyjamas and bare feet.

'Heard you coming,' she whispers. 'Couldn't sleep.'

He's not the only one with things on his mind. He drops a kiss on her head. 'Mug of cocoa?'

She considers. 'Glass of wine?'

'Sounds good.'

They go inside.

WEDNESDAY, 5 JUNE

One calendar month after their only daughter's disappearance from Roone, Martha and Vincent Ryan pack their bags and move out of the hotel room in which they've been living for twenty-three days and nights.

The only witnesses to their early-morning departure are hotel owner Henry Manning and Maria Fennessy, taxi driver Dougie's eldest daughter, who happens to be on duty behind the reception desk at the time.

The Ryans drive the hundred yards or so to the pier and board the ferry, remaining in their car for the brief duration of the trip to the mainland. Vincent leafs through the newspaper that was waiting for them as usual by the door of their hotel room. Martha sits with half-closed eyes hidden behind oversized sunglasses, fingers twined loosely in her lap. Nobody approaches the couple apart from ticket collector Leo Considine, who gives no sign that he recognises them as he issues their ticket and makes change.

As soon as Henry returns to his office at the rear of the reception area, Maria phones her parents to tell them the news. Dougie passes it on to Lelia Doherty when he calls into the café at ten for the takeaway coffee and bran muffin he indulges in each weekday morning. His wife Ita mentions it to Gavin Connolly when he delivers eggs, cabbages and onions to her house soon after that.

From the ferry port on the mainland the Ryans drive non-stop to Mallow, a journey of a little over two hours. Here they stop at a small café for breakfast, neither of them having eaten before leaving Roone, despite Henry's urging. Vincent orders a plain omelette, Martha asks for wholegrain toast. Not a word is exchanged as they eat without any apparent sign of pleasure. The waitress who serves them is struck by their silence, and remarks to a colleague that they must have had a row.

When he returns home from his deliveries Gavin tells Laura Dolittle the news. Laura phones Nell Mulcahy, who has already heard it from Lelia. Imelda Fitzpatrick gets it from the cashier in the supermarket whose cousin is engaged to Leo Considine, who had belatedly identified his early-morning passengers.

By noon, as the Ryans are pulling up in the driveway of their Tipperary home, practically the entire population of Roone has been made aware of their departure from the island. The item is carried on the community-radio news bulletin at three o'clock that afternoon, and by five Henry Manning has taken half a dozen phone calls from national media employees.

When Martha and Vincent Ryan turn on the main evening news at nine, having put their two sons to bed and sent home the grandparents who were looking after them, it is to be confronted with the familiar smiling photograph of their daughter Ellie, whom by now both of them privately, and separately, assume to be dead.

Martha lets out a wail of anguish, burying her face in her hands. A few seconds later the phone rings in the hall.

'Ignore it,' Vincent says immediately, reaching for the remote control and realising, with a thump of despair, that their nightmare will never, ever be over.

He stands by his office window and listens to the bell ringing. Less than a minute later the first of the children emerge from the building's front entrance, making their way in an untidy straggle across the school yard with bags slung over shoulders, coats trailing behind them. He watches the younger ones finding parents at the gate and climbing into cars, the older ones walking off in small groups.

He remains at the window as the school empties, as the last of the classes are released for the day. He sees the teachers following shortly afterwards, all eleven of them making their way in ones and twos towards the car park, nobody hanging around any longer than is absolutely necessary. He watches them getting into their cars and driving off, glad to be finished for the day. Glad to be getting away from him.

It didn't take him long to realise that his presence in the school was unwelcome. He sensed the antipathy each time he walked into the staffroom: he saw how their eyes slid away from him, how conversations stopped when he approached. How no information was forthcoming unless he looked for it.

His vice principal was no different from the rest of the staff, perfectly civil but not in the least friendly or welcoming. Within a week Denis realised that the man must have felt hard done by. Thirteen years the second in command, no doubt fully expecting to step into the boss's position once it became vacant, but for whatever reason, Denis had been deemed the better candidate. Not by the rest of the staff though – going by their attitude, most if not all agreed that the wrong man had got the job.

In almost two years at the school Denis hasn't made a single friend, never been asked on Monday what he'd done over the weekend, never been invited to meet up with any of them outside school hours. The fact that he was ignorant of the circumstances surrounding his employment, the fact that it was a board-of-management decision to award him the job, seems to count for nothing. Someone has to be made to feel bad, and Denis is an easy target.

He's never gone out socially with them. Two Christmases have come and gone with no talk of a party. There was no suggestion last June of an end-of-year night out, and so far there's been no mention of one this year. When Denis brought up the subject with his vice principal he was told that they generally didn't bother with that sort of thing.

He suspects this to be an untruth. As far as he can see, they get along with one another well enough – why wouldn't they opt for a night out at Christmas, or at the end of a school year? He thinks the parties might be happening without him, but far from being upset at this notion, he feels only relief at being spared the ordeal of trying to make small talk all evening with people who patently dislike him.

He won't miss them. He won't cast them another thought when he leaves, and he doubts that his departure will cause any of them a single sleepless night. He knows they'll think he's been hounded out, and is content to leave them with this misapprehension. He presumes that the vice principal will try his luck again when the top position becomes vacant once more. Maybe this time he'll be appointed, or maybe he'll be passed over for the second time. Either way, Denis couldn't care less.

He drafted his letter of resignation on Sunday night and posted it on his way to work this morning. The chairperson will have it tomorrow, the rest of the board will be informed most likely before the week is out. He'll make an official announcement at the next staff meeting, but it'll be a formality because Jackie Fenton, the third-class teacher who sits on the board, will no doubt take great pleasure in telling them all at her earliest convenience.

He's going to resign. He's going to retire from teaching. He's worked the requisite number of years to be eligible for a full pension – but even if he hadn't, he'd have little hope of being offered a new job at sixty-three. Not that he particularly wants a new job.

He's had forty years of working, of being woken by a persistent beep every weekday morning. Forty years of trying to keep a class of energetic youngsters motivated and challenged, or a school functioning in the face of the tide of obstacles that rushes to meet him each day. He won't be sorry to be finished with all that.

But of course it's not the job he's running from. He could go on coping with a sulky staff, with belligerent parents and unruly children and paperwork that never ends. He could handle all of that for another two years if he had to.

He checks the clock on the wall above his desk and sees that it's ten minutes to four. He's never here at this time on Wednesday; for the past two years Wednesday has been the day he's left the school as eagerly as the children, rushing home to spruce himself up, expectant as a three-year-old for Christmas as he stood under the shower, humming.

Not today. Never again. The thought fills him with a clammy misery. She's on her way to him right now, but for the first time he won't be there to meet her. Instead she'll find a letter taped to the front door, saying goodbye.

Please don't get in touch, he'd written, the words dragged from him onto the page. *I'm sorry*, he'd continued, the understatement shouting out at him. *Please know that this is the hardest thing I have ever had to do. I will miss you every day until I die. You will be deeply loved until I die.*

'You're quiet,' she said last Wednesday. 'What's up with you, Mr Mulcahy?' Teasing him, pulling at the sparse hairs on his chest, tweaking his nipples, running her nails across his abdomen. 'Tell me. *Tell* me.'

But he'd said nothing, he'd taken the coward's way out again. He'd written a letter telling Claire goodbye instead of saying it face to face, just like he had with Nell when he'd left her mother.

It's the husband, it's Paddy – but it isn't just him. It's the two blonde daughters, it's the disabled son. It's seeing Claire with them, and realising that she's happy with them. Happy with her family.

And despite the profound joy that meeting her has brought to Denis's life, despite the pleasure her visits provide, and the preciousness of their time together, the fact remains that their affair isn't making him happy. On the contrary, he's never felt as lonely and sad as he does when they're apart. And guilty too, now that he's seen the other life she leads.

And though it pains him to admit it, though the passion he feels for Claire is stronger than he ever felt for Moira, the truth is they don't know one another, not in the way a couple should. How can you possibly claim to know someone when all you share is a brief physical encounter once a week or so? Maybe they wouldn't have lasted in the real world, maybe an everyday routine wouldn't have suited them at all – but how he would have loved the opportunity to find out. How he would have loved to take her out on a date.

I can't come between you and your family any more. I want to, more than anything, but I can't. I can't do it to you, or to them. And I can't accept what it makes me.

Claire never pretended with him. She'd never hidden the fact that she was married with children and wasn't prepared to change that. 'I won't live with you,' she said. 'I can't get a divorce. I can't leave Joe or the girls.' And what good is that? What good is a part of her, when he wants it all?

He had to put a stop to it. It was eating him up, it was destroying him. And even though the thought of never seeing her again makes him want to weep, he knows it's the right thing to do, and his only hope of ever being at peace with himself again. And so he had written his goodbye and taped it to his front door, unable to post it to her home and unwilling to send it to her school.

He looks at the clock again. She's there now, she's reading his letter – or maybe she's finished and is on her way back to Tralee. He draws his phone from the pocket of the jacket slung over the back of his chair. Nothing. No missed calls, no texts.

He scrolls through his contacts until he comes to her name. He stares at it on the screen. He could ring her now: he could say it was a mistake, he hadn't meant it. He could persuade her to come back to him, even if she was angry. They could meet as usual next Wednesday, they could keep on doing that until one of them died.

He presses the delete key. *Delete this contact?* his phone asks, and he selects *yes* before he can think about it. He watches her vanishing from his screen. He scrolls through the list again and she's gone.

She's gone. He's alone. He's a sixty-three-year-old widower with an extremely broken heart.

But he has Nell. He's not completely alone. She's married now, with a husband and a stepson, and she's made no secret of her desire to have her own children. But he's still her father, and he will always be able to lay claim to that precious title.

In the autumn he might take a trip somewhere. Tuscany –

he always wanted to go there – or Provence, maybe. He'll eat peasant food and sit in the shade and count his blessings. He will heal himself, and time will help him.

And he will return to Roone, of course. He'll give his landlord notice. He'll keep the house till the end of August and over the summer he'll ease his way back to the island. He'll give people time to get used to him again before moving back fully. He'll give them time to accept the idea of his return.

Eventually his old life will be restored – only of course it won't be his old life: it will be completely different. The memory of what he did to Moira and to his marriage, and the sadness of Claire's absence, will always be there. Over the past two years he's been utterly changed, and his life can never be the same.

It might not turn out well, going back to Roone. He might find it impossible to fit in again, after smashing apart the life he had carved out for himself there. He might not be welcomed back, no matter how much time passes. He might never be forgiven.

But to grow old on Roone, to walk the roads he knows as well as the lines on his palms, to inhale the unsullied, seaweed-scented air he grew up with, to come full circle in the only place that truly feels like home to him – that is worth more than anything, and he will do his utmost to make it happen.

He takes his jacket from the chair and pulls it on. He locks the office and heads for the back door. On the way he meets the caretaker mopping the corridor.

Gerard nods at him, pushing his bucket to the side to allow Denis to pass. 'Mind your step there.' The only member of staff who doesn't appear to harbour a grudge against him, the only one who doesn't seem to have been put out by his appointment. 'Turned out not too bad.'

'Not too bad,' Denis agrees, picking his way across the wet tiles. 'See you in the morning, Gerard.'

He lets himself out and gets into his car. He drives to a cinema and buys a ticket. He sits in front of the screen until he's sure any danger of meeting her on the road has passed.

Back home, the only sign that she called is the absence of his letter from the front door. He lets himself in and goes upstairs and removes his clothes. He stands under the shower and wonders, not without some element of fear, how exactly the rest of his life is going to go.

'Well,' Anita says, getting to her feet after what has seemed to Imelda like an eternity of struggling small talk, 'I'd better be making tracks, or they'll think I've been kidnapped.'

Immediately the words are out her face begins to redden, a tide that washes up slowly from her neck. Imelda pushes back her chair, throwing a glance at Hugh.

He takes his cue. 'Will you find your way back to the ferry,' he asks, 'or would you like me to drive ahead of you?'

'No, no, it's quite straightforward. I'll be fine, couldn't get lost if I tried, really.' She fumbles in her bag, head bent. 'Lovely little island, lovely and scenic. I can't believe I've never been here before, and it so close. Must be just lovely to live here all the time.'

Still mortified, poor thing, over a silly slip of the tongue that has offended nobody. Pulling out a tissue that she doesn't need, dabbing at the nose that isn't running.

'Will you take a slice of cake with you?' Imelda asks.

Anita pats her stomach, hidden beneath layers of jacket and blouse. 'Oh no, thank you very much, better not.' She turns to Eve, still seated at the table. 'You have my number if you need it. Call me anytime, OK?'

And Imelda hears, *Call me if they don't treat you well. Call me if you decide after a day that you don't want to stay in this old-fashioned house with a couple who should have got themselves a dog if they wanted company. Call me if you need to be relocated with people who know how to look after you.*

She pushes the voice from her head and shows the social worker to the front door, agreeing with her that they're getting a lovely dry spell, yes, about time. She thanks Anita for her help, tells her she hopes the traffic won't be too heavy on the road back to Tralee.

Imagine if she prevented the woman from leaving the house. Imagine if she planted herself in front of the door and said, *Take her back. We've changed our minds, we've made a huge mistake. She clearly doesn't want to be here, and we don't want her either. We have no idea how to handle her – we don't even know how to talk to her. Please take her away.*

They shake hands. 'Any problems, any issues, give me a shout,' Anita says, back in control, and Imelda smiles and nods and thanks her again in the over-bright voice that must by now be grating on the woman's nerves. She stands in the doorway until the little white car that delivered Eve to them is out of sight, and then she returns to the kitchen to rescue Hugh, her insides clenching.

They sit exactly where she left them, directly across from one another, Hugh calmly eating cake as if it's just another Wednesday. Has he even tried to talk to her?

Eve looks older without her school uniform, baggy orange top failing to disguise the surprisingly developed chest. At fifteen Imelda was still in vests, nothing needing to be supported underneath. Marian had bought her her first bra at sixteen, more of a gesture towards womanhood than an actual working mechanism. But Eve is definitely wearing a bra, the outline of the straps on her shoulders clearly visible under the thin material of the top.

The dark red hair is pulled into a loose low ponytail at the back of her neck, twin sections falling free on either side of her face that Imelda assumes have been deliberately left there. Her eyes are framed again in deepest black, eyelashes stiff with mascara, mouth painted chocolate brown.

She might be quite pretty if she smiled, and maybe used a little less makeup. Imelda tries to imagine her looking in the least bit happy: she'd be transformed. Give her a few days, let Roone work its charm on her. She'll bloom like a flower if she gives it half a chance.

And a haircut from Nell would help too – the long straight hair gives her a dragged-down look. A nice shoulder-length bob maybe, or a short crop for the summer. Eve will be meeting Nell on Friday evening: she and Imelda have been invited to dinner.

She mustn't be hungry. She hasn't touched the slice of cake – lemon, Hugh's favourite – that Imelda cut for her, and she barely sipped her orange juice. She slumps in her chair now, arms folded under her chest, gaze fixed on the tablecloth.

The little white car had arrived on the two o'clock ferry, met by Hugh who drove ahead of it back to the house where Imelda was waiting with damp palms and dry mouth. She instinctively offered her hand to Eve when the girl stepped from the car, and Eve placed her cool, lifeless one in Imelda's for a second, refusing to meet her eye or respond to the welcome she got.

Her luggage was pitifully small for a stay of twelve weeks: one shiny red holdall, about the size Imelda would use for a weekend away, and a badly scuffed brown satchel slung diagonally across her body. She followed silently as Imelda showed her and Anita the room that was to be hers, the room that Imelda had spent a week preparing. She looked impassively into the bathroom, made no comment on the view from the landing window, or the swallows' nest under the eaves outside.

'Isn't it nice, Eve?' Anita would ask every so often, and each time the girl nodded dumbly, and looked bored.

She's bored by them. How foolish all Imelda's preparations seem now, how pathetic her deliberations about the paint colour. She could have painted the room black, Eve would hardly have noticed – or maybe she'd have preferred it.

'You won't have a little bit of cake?' Imelda asks her now.

Eve shifts in her chair. 'I'm not hungry.'

Hugh finishes his slice, brushes crumbs from his hands. 'Would you care for a bit of a walk around the island, just to get your bearings? It's a lovely day for it.' His afternoon cleared specially, a shift swapped with James.

But Eve shakes her head, unfolding her arms to scratch at a spot below her left elbow. 'Can I go to my room?' she asks, without looking at either of them.

A beat passes. 'Of course you can,' Hugh replies. 'Come down whenever you want. Would you like to bring the cake up with you? You might feel like it later.'

'No … thanks.'

She stands and slouches to the door in faded jeans that trail on the floor and look much too big in the hips for her – Imelda can't imagine what's keeping them up. She leaves the room and they listen to her feet clumping up the stairs, and the bedroom door opening and closing.

Hugh looks at Imelda. 'Fresh cup?'

As if nothing at all is wrong. How can he be so casual? How can he not see how badly this is going? Imelda sinks into the chair that Eve vacated. 'What a disaster.' She rubs at the creases in her forehead. 'She hates it, she hates being here. She hates us.'

'Don't be daft – of course she doesn't hate us. She doesn't know us enough to hate us. She just needs time to settle in, that's all.'

'How can you be so sure?' Imelda demands, even though that's what she's been telling herself. 'How do you know she'll settle?' Hearing how hysterical she sounds, but unable to shake the fear that they're going to fail horribly in their first fostering mission. 'What if she's like this for the whole twelve weeks?'

Hugh regards her calmly. 'In that case,' he says, 'we'll make sure she's fed and looked after, and when she goes back we'll ask for someone friendlier next time.'

He's humouring her, or trying to. Imelda doesn't smile, not in the mood to be humoured. 'She didn't touch the cake, not a single bite. Why would she not eat it? Was she trying to make a point, trying to tell us she doesn't want to be here?'

'I'm sure it's not as complicated as that,' he says. 'Maybe she hasn't got a sweet tooth. Or she might be on a diet. Aren't young girls always on a diet?' He puts out a hand. 'Here, pass it over.'

He's doing his best. Imelda gives him a small, reluctant smile as she hands over the plate. 'That's your third slice. You'll ruin your dinner.'

'I most certainly will not. Have you ever known me not to eat my dinner?' He picks up the cake and bites into it. 'Bet she's dying for some now,' he says, his mouth full, crumbs scattering on the table. 'Bet she's lying on that bed wishing she'd taken it up with her.'

Imelda's smile fades as the image takes form in her head. Eve stretched out on a strange bed, hands behind her head, staring up at an unfamiliar ceiling. Wondering what they're saying about her maybe. Or maybe not caring. Wondering how soon she can phone Anita to come and get her.

Hugh finishes the cake and reaches for her hand. 'Sweetheart, don't worry. This is the worst bit. She doesn't know us and she's in a strange place. Of course she's going to take some time to relax and fit in. We'll just have to have patience.'

Imelda searches his face for further reassurance. 'You really think that's all it is?'

'Of course I do – what could she have against us, when we're only trying to help her? Look, we'll have dinner in a while, and after that she might watch a bit of telly, or one of those DVDs you got, and then it'll be bedtime. So that's the first day over. And after that we'll keep doing the best we can until she realises we're not the enemy, and she's lucky to have us looking after her.'

Lucky – with a mother too addled with drugs to be capable of being a parent, and a father she's never known. Lucky never to have experienced the security of her own loving family. Lucky to be packed up like a household pet and farmed out for the summer.

But they have to remain positive, and Hugh is putting Imelda to shame. 'Sorry,' she says. 'I'm just terrified we'll mess up.'

'We'll do our best, and we won't mess up. It's what we wanted, remember?'

She loves him for the *we*, when the whole notion of fostering was hers, definitely hers. He hadn't been that hard to persuade, though.

'We'll get through it,' he says, squeezing her hand. 'Don't you worry. And we'll have plenty of help. You know everyone is behind us on this. Aren't you taking her to Nell's on Friday? And if it's fine tomorrow you could bring her to the beach after lunch – she might like a swim.'

'Yes, she might.'

He gathers plates and brings them to the sink. She watches

him rinsing them off, and hopes to God Eve likes shepherd's pie.

By the time dinner is ready, three hours later, she hasn't reappeared. Hugh mounts the stairs to call her. Standing in the hall, Imelda hears his soft tap on the spare-room door, the sound of his voice. When Eve slouches into the kitchen a few minutes later she wears the same shapeless clothes, the same dour expression. What has she been doing, stuck in her room all afternoon?

Despite their best efforts, she remains unresponsive throughout the meal. She clears her plate without comment and mumbles the briefest possible response to any questions. Eventually they give up trying to include her in the conversation, but Imelda imagines her to be inwardly sniggering at everything they say to one another.

After the apple-tart dessert Hugh gets to his feet. 'Well,' he declares, 'someone's got to work in this house.'

Eve doesn't react. She continues to stare at the table, somewhere between the sugar bowl and the jug of custard. Hugh grins at Imelda, not at all put out. 'See you later, love.'

He bends to kiss her lips as he always does, but self-consciousness makes Imelda present her cheek to him instead, a gesture she instantly regrets. Eve isn't even looking, for God's sake. She smiles an apology but Hugh is already halfway to the hall.

She listens to the click of the front door closing behind him. The silence when he's gone seems immense, broken only by the tick of his father's retirement clock on the wall. Imelda glances up and see that it's just past seven – how in God's name are they to get through the rest of the evening?

She pushes back her chair: better to be doing something. 'Typical man, left us with the washing up,' she says, smiling uselessly at the girl who still refuses to look anywhere in her direction. 'Do you want to wash or dry?'

Eve glances up then, and for an instant Imelda is convinced that she's going to refuse to do either. The seconds tick by, their eyes locked together. Imelda's skin prickles, the smile frozen on her face. She can't look away. To look away would be wrong.

'Dry,' Eve says.

Relief floods through Imelda. She hands her the tea towel and runs water into the sink, searching for a topic of conversation to get them through the next few minutes. Not the weather, she can't talk about the weather. That's nearly as bad as asking Eve if she likes school.

'What happened his arm?'

The question takes Imelda by surprise. For an instant it makes no sense to her. 'What?'

Eve regards her impassively. 'His arm. What happened it?'

Ah, his arm. Imelda squirts washing-up liquid into the sink, riffles the water to make bubbles. 'Nothing happened to it,' she answers lightly. 'Hugh was born like that. His mother took a drug called Thalidomide when she was pregnant and it—'

'She was on *drugs*?'

Imelda turns off the hot tap. 'Not the kind of drugs criminals sell,' she says, remembering as soon as the words are out that Eve's mother is an addict. 'I didn't mean—' she says, flustered, breaking off because she doesn't know what she didn't mean. Eve's blank expression stays unaltered. Maybe she missed the blunder.

Imelda wonders suddenly if the girl is a little slow – that might explain the lack of reaction. Or maybe she's under the influence of something herself: maybe the mother isn't the only addict in the family. Lord, what have they taken on?

She begins again. 'Thalidomide was a prescription drug. A lot of women were given it by their doctors for morning sickness. It was new, and nobody realised how harmful it was until babies like Hugh started being born.'

No response. In the short silence that follows, Imelda takes glasses from the table and brings them to the sink.

'How does he write things? How can he write stuff with no hand?'

'Hugh writes with his left hand,' Imelda replies evenly, irritation beginning to nudge at her edges. Does the girl have to be so blunt? Not a scrap of feeling in her voice – she might be asking about a robot.

She forces a smile onto her face as she puts a glass on the draining board. 'What would you like to do tomorrow, Eve? Anything in particular?'

'No.' She picks up the glass.

'I have to go out around eleven,' Imelda says. 'I make sandwiches for Hugh's pub – did we mention he owns a pub in the village?'

'No.'

'Well, he does, and I deliver sandwiches there every morning. You could come with me and see a bit of the place, if you're up by eleven.'

A shrug.

'And I thought we might go to the beach in the afternoon if it's nice. There are some lovely beaches on the island. Did you bring swimming togs?'

'No. I can't swim. I got no togs.'

'Oh … well, we can get you one if you like. I'm sure we could borrow one, or buy one.'

Another shrug. Imelda gives up, turning her attention to the radio, and the rest of the washing-up is conducted without another word. Early days, Imelda tells herself. Patience.

When they've finished she takes off her apron. 'Would you like to watch television?' she asks. The evening is lovely, calm and still bright, but she's darned if she's going to make a second offer of a walk. 'Or there are some DVDs you might like.'

'I'd like to go to my room.'

It's half past seven, nowhere near any kind of bedtime. But if her room is what she wants, Imelda is more than happy to go along with it.

'Of course you can. Do you have everything you need?'

'Yeah.'

'I showed you where the towels are, didn't I?'

'Yeah.'

'Goodnight then. See you in the morning.'

Eve slouches out of the room. Imelda leans against the dresser, taking up a Hummel figurine and fingering it absently, feeling the tension draining out of her.

One day down, eighty-three to go. They'll never feel it.

*

'I like that one.'

They study James's latest work in progress, resting on the easel at the far side of the patio. 'It's lovely, isn't it? I've been at him for ages to do the creamery.'

'Wish I could paint.' Laura yawns. 'God, I could sleep for Ireland these days. So I take it you're enjoying married life?'

Nell smiles. 'I am.'

Less sad, Laura thinks. Maybe not entirely happy yet, but less sad than before. 'James is behaving himself then.'

'He is.'

'And Andy?'

'He's great too. We're exactly the same as we were before, except that we're living under the one roof now, and technically I'm his stepmother.'

'Is he house-trained? Does he clean up after himself?'

'He does, as much as any teenager. I don't go into his room: James says it's safer that way.'

'Wish I had that option. If I never went into the twins' room it would self-destruct within a week.'

'Ah, they're only small ... By the way, will you come to dinner on Friday?'

'Don't see why not – what's the occasion?'

'I've invited Imelda and her foster girl. You know she was arriving today.'

'I'd forgotten. Did she come? Have you heard?'

'No, but I'm assuming she did. I'll ring in the morning, give them a chance to settle her in.'

Laura had been surprised to hear that Imelda and Hugh were

interested in fostering. She wouldn't have imagined they'd want anyone disturbing their cosy little marriage – and she'd have thought them too old, both in their fifties, to be considered as foster carers. Wrong on both counts, it would seem. Interesting to see how they get on.

'Count me in. I'll leave Gav tucking up the guests.'

'Good. You can chat to her if she's a bit shy.'

Silence falls. The light is fading but the air is still warm and smelling pleasantly of woodsmoke, and someone's barbecued steak. They sit on Nell's patio with a jug of cloudy apple juice on the table between them, and a bowl of fat green olives from Marks & Spencer that had travelled down from Dublin with Laura's stepmother on her last visit, along with several other delicacies.

John Silver dozes at Nell's feet, head on his paws. A swarm of midges hovers by the stone wall. Something chirps in the lawn. Laura can hear the distant cluck of the hens as they settle to roost in the henhouse at the top of the field on the other side of the wall. No sound issues from behind the twins' open bedroom window, just visible above the apple trees in the little orchard that was planted by Walter's grandfather. All is well.

'Would you think of it yourself?' Nell asks.

Laura adjusts the cushion at her back. 'Would I think of what?'

'Getting married. To Gavin, obviously.'

Laura reaches for her glass and runs a finger around its rim, making it sing. She's made no mention of his two proposals to Nell, or to anyone.

'Ah no,' she says. 'I've had my wedding. Not sure the magic would be there this time round, to be honest.'

'No?'

'No. Gav is lovely, he's the best in the world, but . . .'

Nell refills their glasses. 'But you're happy with him, aren't you?'

'Of course I am. He's a sweetheart.'

'He certainly is.'

Another pause. Laura swats at a fly circling the olive bowl.

'Andy was thrilled when you asked him to be in charge of the donkey rides,' Nell says. 'He can't wait for them to start.'

'Neither can the boys. I'm hoping to have as little as possible to do with them. I should warn you that Gav is planning to get James to design a poster.'

'I'm sure he'll be happy to do it.'

Laura sips juice, shifts in her seat again. 'Is your father coming over at the weekend?' She knows the story of Nell's father, everyone on Roone does. The disgraced school principal, running off with another woman.

'Hope so. He wasn't sure when I rang. I thought he sounded tired.'

'He'll be glad of the holidays. He might spend some time here over the summer.'

'Oh yes, I imagine he will.'

Hasn't been discussed between them then.

Nell takes another olive. John Silver lifts his head suddenly, ears cocked. A second later they hear a car go by on the road. He drifts down again, closes his eyes.

Nell places a bare foot on his back. He grunts, tail swishing once across the flagstones. 'I do believe he's missing Andy.'

He and James had left for Dublin earlier in the day: Karen's sixth anniversary tomorrow. They'll stay tonight with Colette in Dalkey and meet up in the morning with Karen's parents, who are travelling over from Wales to visit their daughter's grave.

'Did you not fancy going with them?' Laura asks.

'Ah no … James did suggest it, but I'd have felt a bit of an intruder, to be honest.' She sips her apple juice. 'And they're having dinner this evening with Tim and Katy.'

'So what? That's all over. Weren't you fine with them at the wedding?'

'I was. It's not really them … Well, it is and it isn't.'

'You'll have to get over that, Nell.'

'I know. I know I will.'

Laura tips back her head and watches a bird swooping over the apple trees next door. Heading home to bed. The hens must have nodded off, no sound from them now.

'Actually, they're coming here,' Nell says. 'Did I mention?'

Laura turns back to her. 'Who?'

'Tim and Katy, and Lily. And Colette. They're all coming, in about a fortnight.'

'Are they? For a holiday?'

'Yes. They invited themselves – well, Tim did. He rang James and asked if they could use his house.'

Laura laughs. 'Did he? That's gas. Tim back on Roone.' She takes an olive, pops it into her mouth. 'Bet she'll love it here.'

'Katy?'

'Yeah. She's a country girl, isn't she? Bet she'll want to move here. They could buy James's place.'

Nell smiles. 'Ah, stop.'

In the brief silence that follows, John Silver lifts his head and yawns. He gets up and potters to the shrubbery and cocks his leg.

'Nice,' Laura tells him. 'In the presence of two ladies. Very nice.'

'You won't feel it now till the next lot of twins,' Nell says. 'How long more, about two and a half months?'

'Don't remind me. Middle of August – Jesus, is that only two and a half months?' She pulls the cushion out from behind her and thumps it. 'I've forgotten what a comfortable position feels like.'

'Poor you. And you're still convinced you're having girls?'

'Sure of it. I'm thinking Emma and Pearl. Gav wants Gladys, after his mother. I think he's only saying it to scare me.'

'I'm dying to meet Gladys. Why don't you invite her down? She might be a help to you in the B&B.'

Laura shudders. 'Don't even joke about it. She's the classic Irish mammy – her boy can do no wrong. I'm the hussy who tempted poor innocent Gav to live in sin. She's scandalised that I'm expecting. Thank God she didn't turn up to the official opening. I nearly killed him when he said he'd invited her.'

'Ah, poor Gladys.'

'Poor Gladys my foot. I'm praying she won't come to the christening.'

They sit on, drinking apple juice and eating olives as the day comes softly to a close. And for the first time since it happened, no mention is made of Ellie's disappearance.

✳

From the bedroom window she can see the back garden, which has yellow roses growing by a patio of big grey slabs with cement between them. A path made of pieces of broken slabs curves its way through the lawn past a clothes line – empty now of the sheets and shirts and towels that hung on it earlier – and a shed with a tin roof that's spotted with rust, all the way down to a shoulder-high wall at the end that's so covered in ivy you can only make out tiny bits of the stone.

Everything about this house feels old, as if it's been here forever. All those little ornaments on the dresser in the kitchen – no prizes for guessing who collects those – and that clock on the wall, like something you'd see in a museum. Even the round knobs on the doors look ancient. It's about as different as you could get from the Garveys' house, which is fine by her.

Beyond the wall is a field that has something tall and yellow growing in straight rows, and past that field are more fields, some with cows or sheep in them, and a few scattered houses with red or grey roofs, and not very high hills that are patched in green and purple and brown, and a lot of sky, which is mostly pale blue.

She can't see the sea, the window faces in the wrong direction, but she can smell it. The breeze is full of it, sharp and tangy. She feels it in the back of her throat every time she breathes in. And when she licks her lips she tastes salt.

The smell reminds her of the periwinkles people sell on the streets of Tralee, little white paper bags of them that come with a pin to yank them out of their shells. She used to love them when she was small, but now the sight of their curled-up slimy little grey-brown bodies repulses her, and the thought of eating one is too disgusting to contemplate.

She still likes the smell though. She'll leave her window open while she's staying here.

She presses her palms to the cool glass and pictures a small dead girl somewhere out there, stuffed under a bush or curled up at the bottom of a well. Or maybe the murderer threw her into the sea – maybe she'll be pulled out of it in a net some day, half of her eaten away by fish. Or maybe she'll never be found, like that little kid who disappeared in Portugal.

She turns away from the window and inspects the room that is hers. A room to herself – she rarely gets that – and not full of junk either. There's a faint smell of paint mixed in with the sea smell, and the rug on the floor looks brand new, the ends still curling under a bit. They painted a room for her, and bought a new rug.

She crosses to the bed and sits on the side of it. She pushes her hand between the two pillows, feels the softness there. She takes off her shoes and lies on her side. She closes her eyes and inhales the clean smell of the pillowcase, and imagines it hanging on the clothes line, flapping in the breeze that brings the sea with it.

After a while she opens her eyes. Her red bag, the one Valerie Garvey was throwing out, is on the chair where the wife left it.

It feels too weird to call her Imelda, even in her head. Eve won't call her anything, or him either. It's safer that way.

'Here,' the wife said, 'let me take that bag.' Reaching for it while the husband was hanging Eve's jacket on the hallstand with his one hand. 'Come up and I'll show you your room,' the wife said, walking ahead of them to the stairs, 'and then you can see the rest of the house.'

Still horribly queasy, Eve could hardly take in what she was seeing. She followed Anita and the wife, making an effort to look interested so Anita would stop giving her looks, but all she wanted to do was sit somewhere with her head down and not have to talk to anyone.

Her first ever boat trip hadn't gone well. Within a minute of Anita driving onto the ferry, as soon as the solid ground was replaced with the tilt and bob of the water, Eve's insides had begun to dip and fall along with it, and before another minute had gone by a dull ache had started up in her head.

'I feel sick,' she told Anita, who said she probably needed air, but it had been no better when Eve got out of the car. She stood by the open door, trying not to think of the water underneath, nothing keeping them up but water. Trying to ignore the awful lurch and tumble that was still happening inside her.

When it became worse she made her unsteady way to the ferry's tiny little toilet and stuck her fingers down her throat and vomited up the marmalade sandwich she'd had for breakfast. It didn't make her feel much better. When she got back into the car Anita asked if she was OK and she nodded and watched the island getting bigger.

She was still feeling queasy at the end of the grand tour, when the wife had led them into the kitchen and produced cake. She couldn't look at the slice that was put in front of her, and when she took a sip of the juice it nearly came up again, so she was afraid to have any more even though her throat felt horribly dry.

As soon as Anita left she made her escape. She could hear their voices downstairs – the kitchen is directly underneath her room – and guessed they were talking about her, about how ungrateful she was not to eat the cake, or go for a walk with the husband. Let them say what they liked. She rubbed her stomach and burped a bit, and gradually the sick feeling went away.

By the time the shepherd's pie was ready she was starving. She could feel them watching her as she tried not to eat it too quickly. And they had dessert: she couldn't remember the last time she'd had apple tart, or any dessert.

And she didn't have to do all the washing-up, just the drying; that was another surprise. Put her foot in it though, asking about your man's arm. It was the only thing she could think of to say, but you could see the wife didn't like it. Better keep quiet in future, stick to answering questions.

It's still bright outside and much too early to go to bed but she likes being on her own – she's best on her own. It's so quiet here, much quieter than at the Garveys'. It'll be hard to sleep tonight, none of the usual noises to keep her company.

She'll have to find a way to get out of going to the beach with the wife tomorrow. She'll have to find a way to escape again. She'll think of something.

Offering to buy her swimming togs though. Just buy her something brand new, without her even asking.

She gets up, unzips the red bag and upends it on the bed. Out spill her blue top, her other jeans, three pairs of knickers, a bra, some socks and her envelope. She slides the envelope under the mattress without opening it and puts the clothes away in the top drawer of the dressing table.

She stores the red bag in the empty wardrobe and takes her makeup out of the satchel someone left on top of a recycling bin in the shopping-centre car park. It amazes her what people throw out.

She sits in front of the dressing-table mirror and sticks out her tongue. She puts it back in and tries making a smile but it looks like something she's being forced to do so she stops. She examines the thick border of black around her eyes. Her disguise, so they won't see her.

There's no sound from downstairs. She thought she'd heard a door opening and closing a while back, but nothing since then. She doesn't know if the wife is still in the house, but she thinks she probably is. They won't leave Eve on her own: they don't know yet if she'll burn the place down when their backs are turned.

She sits with her face propped in her hands and looks at her reflection and thinks of spending the summer in this old house, with people who might have no hidden agenda at all. The prospect makes her feel vaguely afraid.

SATURDAY, 8 JUNE

'Andy!'

He swings around just in time to deflect the ball with a swipe of his palm. It hurtles off to the left, well away from the danger zone. Less than twenty seconds later, before the opposition has time to launch another serious attack on the goal, Bugs Deasy, today's ref, blows his full-time whistle.

Clive Mason, red-faced and damp with sweat, sprints up to Andy. 'Jesus, you were miles away – they nearly scored.'

Andy swings a fist in his direction. 'They didn't though.'

Clive ducks, aims a return punch that catches Andy under the ribs. 'That's because you're one lucky bastard.' He grabs Andy in a headlock and checks the road beside the field, to the right of the goalpost. 'Hey,' he says, 'who's your one?'

Andy struggles free, shoves Clive backwards, is careful not to look towards the retreating figure on the road. 'Haven't a clue,' he says, dodging another swipe.

He has a clue. He recognised her the minute she came

into view, even though she hardly looked at him last night. He watched her stride past the field without a glance towards the football match, her pace fast enough to lift the long red hair an inch from her shoulders with every step.

He remembers her name.

'Eve,' Imelda had said when she introduced them. 'She'll be with us for the summer.'

'Hey,' Andy said to her, and she echoed his greeting and met his eyes for a nanosecond before looking away and pretty much ignoring him – ignoring everyone apart from John Silver – for the rest of the evening.

Her eyes were ringed with black, like Amy Winehouse's. Her mouth was dark brown. She didn't smile once.

Her blue top was loose, but still her chest pushed against it. Her top is orange today, and he was trying to see if he could make out her shape behind it when the ball came flying towards him.

She's here for the whole summer, staying in Imelda's house.

He likes her hair. He likes long hair on girls, and he likes that deep red shade.

He wonders where she's going. He wonders what she looks like under the orange top.

'She's fit,' Clive says, staring after her. 'I'd give her one.'

Andy dives for his knees, and brings him down.

✳

'You heard Francis O'Callaghan has pups,' James says, pulling a pint. 'He's looking for homes for them.'

Hugh continues to slice lemons on the little platform he's constructed to accommodate his shorter arm. 'Is he now.'

'Yeah. Setter and Lab, I think he said.' James skims the foam off and sets the glass in front of the waiting customer. 'You should put your name on one – didn't you have a dog before?'

'I did. I'd take one flying, but Imelda isn't that keen.'

'Ah.'

It's early afternoon; the lunchtime rush is over. Nell has gone back upstairs after an egg-salad sandwich.

'How's your girl settling in?' James asks.

Hugh sweeps the lemon slices into a bowl. 'Good enough,' he says. 'She's quiet, likes her own space.'

She hardly opened her mouth at dinner, Nell told James when he got home from the pub last night. *Even Laura couldn't coax much chat out of her. I could see poor Imelda felt embarrassed that she wasn't making more of an effort to be friendly.*

What about Andy? James asked. *Did she talk to him?*

Not a word.

'Early days,' he says to Hugh. 'It's tough being the new person. She'll come round.'

'That's what I tell Imelda. She's taking it a bit personally, thinks Eve doesn't like us.'

'That's a pity. Hopefully she'll settle in soon.'

'She will, I'm sure … I hear Tim's coming back to see us.'

From a table in the corner a customer raises an almost-empty pint. James acknowledges the signal and starts a fresh one. 'He is – they're all coming, my mother too. Week after next.'

'Good that you can all get along, that there's no awkwardness, I mean.'

'No awkwardness,' James replies lightly, his eye on the golden liquid as it pours from the tap into the tilted glass. 'All in the past.'

'That's good. I take it they'll be staying in your house.'

'They will – might as well have someone in it.'

The afternoon moves along, a steady flow of visitors to the bar – cyclists and walkers in need of refreshment, day trippers passing an hour, holidaymakers on their way home from the beach. At half past four Sean Carmody arrives to begin his shift, and James becomes officially off duty.

He calls up to the salon, where he's told not to wait. 'I'll be another half-hour here at least,' Nell says, undoing one of Maisie Kiely's rollers. 'Take the clothes in if they're dry.'

On the way home he passes the waste ground beside the creamery that Andy and his pals use for football matches. It's empty now apart from a few scattered orange rinds: must have been a game earlier. James gathers them up and throws them into the bin by the roadside. Keep Roone beautiful.

On the telegraph pole beside the waste ground hangs a poster, ragged around the edges and so weathered and worn that its image is almost invisible. Underneath the faded lettering of *Have you seen Ellie?* someone has written *No!* in stark black marker. James removes the poster and folds it into a small square and slides it into his back pocket.

He reaches the house and lets himself in. He stands in the hall and listens, and hears nothing.

'Andy?'

Silence. In the kitchen the sink holds a bowl and a mug, fragments of Andy's Weetabix crusted in the bowl. James scrubs it clean and lays it on the draining board. He walks out to the patio and regards his half-finished painting, and realises that something is missing.

He changes into his old jeans and T-shirt. He picks up a thin brush and loads it with a mix of ochre and cream and white, and carefully adds a ragged poster to the telegraph pole that stands to the left of the creamery.

It's the third day, if you don't count Wednesday. Three days that feel like three weeks to Imelda.

Eve has as little to do with them as possible. She eats the food that's placed before her; she speaks only when a question forces her to respond; she does exactly what's asked of her. After that, they might as well be living on different planets. Imelda can almost see the wall she's built around herself. She's made it as plain as she can without actually saying it out loud: she doesn't want to be there.

She was asleep, or pretending to be, when Imelda was leaving with the sandwiches the morning after she arrived. No answer from her room, no response to Imelda's repeated taps on the door.

'Leave her,' Hugh said, making out his list for the cash-and-carry. 'I'll be here till you get back. I'll give her breakfast when she gets up.'

But she didn't eat breakfast. By the time she finally put in an appearance at half past twelve – seventeen hours since she'd gone upstairs – Imelda had been back over an hour, and Hugh had left. She slouched into the kitchen in the same clothes she'd worn the day before, hair tumbling around her face, eyes as black-ringed as ever. Had she cleaned it off and reapplied it, or was it yesterday's, still in place?

'Well – you had a good sleep,' Imelda said cheerfully. 'You must be hungry. How about some scrambled egg?'

'OK.'

And an excruciating half an hour followed, during which Eve was prevailed upon to set the table while Imelda scrambled eggs and toasted bread, and kept up a desperate one-sided chatter before finally giving up and switching on the radio, and busying herself with non-existent jobs – wiping worktops, cleaning the window ledge, dusting the Hummel figurines – while Eve ate silently.

The day was fine, no rain expected. Imelda recalled her offer the day before of an afternoon on the beach, and wondered how in Heaven's name they'd get through several hours together if Eve continued to be so uncommunicative. Magazines, she supposed. Lots of magazines.

As she was filling the kettle for coffee she didn't want, having run out of anything else to do, Eve brought her plate and glass to the sink and washed them up without being asked, which was something. Imelda spooned coffee into a mug.

'You want anything else?' she asked. 'A piece of fruit or a biscuit?'

Eve shook her head. 'Can I go for a walk?'

She must have forgotten about the beach offer – but at least she wasn't scurrying up to her room again. 'Of course you can. That would be lovely,' Imelda replied. 'Give me a minute to freshen up.'

'I can go on my own,' Eve said, draping the tea towel back on its hook. 'You don't have to come. I can find my way around.'

A beat passed. Imelda felt her face getting hot. 'Well, fine, if you'd rather that.'

Was it fine though? Letting her out on her own, not having any idea of the lie of the land? Mind you, there was little chance of her getting lost on Roone, the coast road going round in a circle, the only other road cutting straight through the centre of the island, every byway and lane in between linking the two. And a relief, if Imelda was honest, not to have to accompany her.

She gave Eve a tourist map, and an umbrella when the girl didn't produce one of her own. She pointed out the attractions, warned her about the cliffs and walked her out to the gate. 'Be back by dinnertime,' she joked, dinner a whole five hours away.

When Eve was completely out of sight Imelda went straight upstairs. She pushed open the girl's bedroom door and walked cautiously inside. The room was in semi-darkness, the curtains closed and billowing gently inwards, the paint smell, despite Imelda's best efforts, still hovering faintly in the air. Had Eve noticed?

Imelda crossed the floor and pulled the curtains apart. The window was fully open: trying to banish the smell of paint? She smoothed the sheet and pulled the covers up on the unmade bed, removing a single long red strand of hair from the pillow and noting as she did the black smudges that dotted the pillowcase. She looked around for a nightdress or pyjamas but found none, and no sign of slippers either.

A pair of damp grey knickers hung on the back of the chair. She must have forgotten about the laundry hamper Imelda had pointed out in the bathroom the day before.

A supermarket plastic bag sat on the dressing table. Imelda peered inside and saw a jumble of well-used tubes and pots and jars and brushes and mascara wands. Clinique, she read, and Yves St Laurent and Mac. Brands she wouldn't buy herself, the cost of them.

She left the room, closing the door quietly behind her. In her own room she changed into her gardening trousers, and for the following hour or so she weeded the flowerbeds, enjoying the warmth of the sun each time it slipped out from behind the clouds. Would have made a nice day for the beach.

Hugh was right, she told herself. The first week or so was bound to be tricky. Once Eve got to know a few people she'd be fine. And tomorrow evening they were going to Nell's, so she'd make a start on meeting the locals.

The afternoon wore on. Imelda cleaned out the fridge, humming Adele's James Bond song. She mopped the kitchen floor, washed the sitting-room windows inside and out. When Eve was still not back at four, she phoned Hugh at the pub.

'She's been gone nearly three hours.'

'I wouldn't worry. The day is dry, the fresh air will do her good. She'll be grand.'

At five o'clock Imelda peeled potatoes and cut cabbage and lit the gas under the bacon joint, her stomach clenching with anxiety. What had she been thinking, letting Eve off on her own? Those clumpy shoes she wore were all wrong for walking. What if she'd gone clambering over rocks and twisted her ankle – or worse, fallen into the sea? What if she'd gone too near the cliff edge and toppled over, or been knocked down by a car coming too fast around a bend? Some of those tourists drove like maniacs.

A mobile phone – it suddenly struck Imelda that she should have asked Eve for her number. All teenagers had them, didn't they? If she could afford expensive makeup she surely had a phone. Stupid not to have thought of it: if Imelda had her number now there'd be no problem.

It was no good, she'd have to go and look for her. She snapped off the gas and took her car keys from their hook. She pulled open the back door – and almost collided with Eve coming in.

'*There* you are,' she said, relief flooding through her. 'I was just about to try and find you.'

Eve shrugged – and the by now familiar gesture sent a surge of irritation through Imelda.

'Eve, I was worried about you,' she said, trying to keep the annoyance out of her voice. How could the girl not get that? 'You've been gone over four hours, and you don't know your way around the island. I thought you might have got lost.'

'I wasn't lost,' Eve muttered, sounding sulky. 'I had the map.'

Imelda stepped back to let her in, biting back another sharp response. *Ignore it*, she told herself. *No harm done, she's able to look after herself.* 'Well, I'm just putting the dinner on – bacon and cabbage, hope you like it.' She relit the gas ring and tumbled the potatoes into the steamer, the effort of hiding her impatience nearly killing her. 'So where did you go anyway? You must have seen loads.'

Eve deposited Imelda's umbrella on the worktop. 'Just around.'

Hopeless. Blood from a stone. Was she like this with her regular foster carers, or was it reserved for Hugh and Imelda? What on earth had they done to deserve this sullen treatment?

But sullen or not, they were still responsible for her. She suddenly remembered the phone. 'Eve, can you let me have the number of your mobile phone? I thought we should have it, just in case.'

'I haven't got one.'

'Oh . . .'

No phone – could that be true? That age group all seemed to have them. They'd be glued to them in Lelia's, tapping away at them or huddled together, laughing at something on a screen.

Then again, phones cost money. A new and alarming thought struck Imelda – were she and Hugh supposed to be providing pocket money? The notion hadn't crossed her mind till this minute. Surely to goodness the social worker should have mentioned it.

She'd better ask. 'Eve, do you need some money? Anita didn't say anything to us about pocket money, but if you want some, please let me know.'

An expression she couldn't read flashed across the girl's face. 'Yeah,' she mumbled. 'I could do with some.'

Imelda reached into the handbag that sat on the worktop and found two twenty-euro notes inside. She handed one to Eve. 'Here, take that, and let me know if you need more, OK?' Was twenty euro enough? What kind of pocket money did teenagers get? Oh, Imelda hadn't a clue, they were so ill-prepared.

Eve took the money and stuffed it into her jeans pocket, muttering thanks. Surely to goodness she could muster up a smile – but none came.

'Can I have some water?'

'Of course you can, you don't have to ask. Or there's juice in the fridge if you'd prefer it.'

'Water's OK.' She took a glass and filled it at the sink and drank it down. Thirsty work, walking for four hours.

Imelda thought of something else. 'Eve, I was in your room while you were gone, just doing a little tidy-up, and I happened to notice that you'd rinsed out your underwear. You know you're welcome to leave anything in the laundry hamper in the bathroom.'

A beat passed while Eve rinsed the glass and set it on the draining board. 'I can wash my own stuff,' she said. 'And I can clean my room. You don't have to do it.'

Imelda felt her face getting hot. *Keep out* was what she'd heard. And maybe Eve was right: maybe Imelda should have asked before going into her room – but God, she could be nicer about it. She saw Eve reaching for the tea towel.

'Leave it,' she said sharply, unable to stop the words flying out. Eve jumped as if she'd been stung. Imelda could have bitten her tongue off.

'Sorry,' she said. 'It'll dry by itself. That's all I meant.'

Eve scratched her elbow, another gesture Imelda was becoming familiar with. 'Can I have a shower?' she asked.

'Of course you can. Eve, I didn't mean to snap at you—' But she was gone, and didn't reappear till Imelda called up the stairs that dinner was ready. And after a dismal silent meal, Hugh filling in at the pub for Sean, who was gone to a wedding, Imelda washed the dishes and Eve dried them, and then she went straight back upstairs, presumably to bed.

And that was Thursday, two days ago. And yesterday, when she surfaced again at lunchtime, Imelda told her that they were going to Hugh's niece's house for dinner, and Eve nodded and headed out for more solitary wandering.

And far from being pleased to be meeting new people at Nell's, she showed no interest whatsoever in any of them. Even Laura, who could probably manage a conversation with a slug, was defeated, and Imelda couldn't wait for the night to be over so they could go home.

And now it's the afternoon of day three and Eve has made her escape again, walking the roads or lying on some beach, or maybe climbing one of the hills. Imelda has no idea.

And Hugh has no idea either.

'You're doing fine,' he tells Imelda, even though he can't possibly know how she's doing, because since Eve arrived he's hardly laid eyes on her.

'She spends about sixteen hours in bed,' Imelda tells him.

'Teenagers sleep a lot,' he replies. 'It's a well-known fact.'

'She's wandering around the island on her own every afternoon. She could be anywhere, with anyone. She's our responsibility.'

'She's nearly sixteen, old enough to be out and about by herself.'

'She could have an accident – she could fall into the sea.'

'Well, if she insists on going out alone, I suppose that's a chance we'll have to take.'

'She won't talk to me. She barely answers my questions.'

'I wouldn't worry, love. It's just her way, don't take it personally. You said she didn't talk to anyone at Nell's either.'

It makes Imelda want to scream. *You're not here*, she shouts at him in her head. *You don't understand what it's like*. She knows she's not being fair – he has to go to work, he has a business to run, it's not his fault that he doesn't see much of Eve – but Imelda still wants to hit him when he bats away her concerns.

She looks down at the ball of pastry sitting on the worktop, waiting to be rolled flat and lifted carefully into the greased pie tin, battered and ancient, that used to belong to Hugh's mother, and God knows how many Fitzpatrick women before her. Rhubarb tart she's making for this evening's dessert, still doing her best to please an ungrateful brat.

Ungrateful brat: the phrase comes out of nowhere, and shocks her. Even to have thought it is unforgivable. It's something Marian would say without thinking. Eve isn't a brat, of course she isn't. She's just difficult to figure out.

Imelda takes a deep breath, and then another. One, two,

three, she counts silently, and continues until she gets to ten. She'll try something else. She'll think of some way to get through to her.

She reaches for her rolling pin and begins to flatten the pastry, humming determinedly along to the song on the radio.

✳

'You're tired,' Nell had told him last night.

'I suppose I am, a bit.'

'You won't be sorry to get holidays.'

'I won't really.'

They sat on Nell's patio, with its view of Roone's hummocky hills that was shared by all the houses on that stretch of the coast road, Denis's own included. John Silver pattered about the garden, sniffing under shrubs, sitting to scratch vigorously behind an ear, cocking his leg by the stone wall. James's latest painting, a fine view of the creamery, stood drying on its easel.

Now was the time, with Andy nowhere to be seen and James at work, and her other visitors not yet arrived.

'Nell,' he began, 'there's something I wanted to tell you. Well, two things really.'

A wariness right away in her face, a little parting of the lips, a tiny narrowing of the eyes. Hardly surprising, given that his last revelation had been that he was leaving her mother.

'I've come to a decision,' he said. He uncrossed his ankles, straightened one trouser leg. Looked at, but didn't touch, the glass of cider she'd poured for him. 'I've handed in my notice at the school.'

Her mouth opened a little wider. 'You're *leaving*? But you've only been there two years.'

'I know. To be honest, it's not something I had planned to do.' He hesitated, unsure how to word the next part. 'The thing is, Nell, my—'

He came to another halt. My what? My relationship? My affair? Neither seemed possible.

He began again. 'The thing is, I've parted company with Claire.' He'd never said her name to Nell – or to anyone, he realised suddenly. Never uttered her name aloud, except when he'd been with her. 'We're not … together any more, and I thought it might be best to get a complete break. You understand?'

'Oh, Dad …'

Instantly concerned, her face full of sympathy. Able to feel sorry for him, despite the upheaval his now defunct romance had caused her.

'It's alright,' he said. 'It's for the best, love. A clean break.'

'But … are you OK? I mean—'

She broke off. Of course she broke off. What daughter wants to be discussing her father's love life?

'I'm fine,' he said. 'I'm totally fine.' What was a little white lie – or a big white lie – if it comforted her? 'I'm not entirely sure what I'll do next, but there's no rush in deciding.'

'Will you look for another job?'

'No, I don't think I'll do that. I'd hardly get one at my age – and I don't particularly want another, to be honest. I'm only two years away from retirement, so I'm just going to push the clock forward on that.'

'You're retiring.' He watched her digesting it. 'Will you come back to live here?'

'I'd like that. I'll spend more time here over the summer, see how it goes.'

'Great,' she replied – but he saw the anxiety in her face. She lived here, she knew what they all thought of him.

'Don't worry about me, Nell. There's nothing for you to worry about.'

She gave a small smile. 'I'm your daughter. It's my job to worry about you.'

He laughed, his heart lifting for the first time in a fortnight. 'I think you've got that the wrong way around, pet.'

John Silver took his head out of the shrubs just then, ears pricked – and seconds later the doorbell rang, the sound coming to them through the open back door, and for the rest of the evening they weren't alone again.

The meal passed off pleasantly, as meals hosted by Nell generally did. Even Andy, whose conversational skills couldn't always be counted on, was in good spirits, and seemed to be enjoying himself. The only guest who appeared ill at ease was Imelda's foster girl, whose eyes were ringed with what looked like black ink. She addressed nobody, barely responded to questions and seemed far more interested in Nell's dog than in any of them, so eventually they all took the hint and left her alone.

Waiting for sleep later, Denis decided to go for a walk in the morning if the day was as fine as promised. There was nothing taking him back to Tralee, and Roone was made for walking.

When he woke, surprisingly late, it was dry and calm. Not much blue in the sky, but not looking as if the heavens were planning to open. He dressed and went downstairs, and ate pear chunks stirred into yogurt standing at the kitchen window, looking out on flowerbeds neglected since Moira's death, weeds claiming space alongside the perennials.

He visualised her bent over the beds as she so often was, easing out the long dandelion roots and depositing them in her old plastic basin. Looking up when he would rap on the window, waving in at him.

He rinsed out his bowl and put on the walking boots that lived in the boot of his car and set off at a few minutes past eleven, his head full of memories of other walks from that house. Walks to try to fill the emptiness before Claire had come along. Walks to calm his racing thoughts after they'd met. Walks to the school in the evenings to phone her in peace, walks to plan his escape.

He decided on one of his favourite routes, a challenging three-hour circle from his house that took in the westernmost cliffs. He had always loved the cliffs, loved to hike along the path just inside the safety fence, a few feet only from the cliff edge, loved the wide-open view of the wild sea it presented. He would clear his mind and drink in the majesty, and it would soothe and calm him like it always did, and help his healing to begin.

He quickly fell into the familiar rhythm, tapping his stout blackthorn stick on the ground as he walked. Quite a few cars passed along the road, most of them unfamiliar. He waved to the drivers like all Roone residents did; some returned his salute and more looked straight ahead, unable to cope with a stranger waving at them.

He recognised Jim Barnes, who raised a finger to tap his temple when he saw Denis, and Betty Buckley, who flapped a hand at him as she sped by in her dented Toyota. He wasn't being ignored, which was a start.

Along the way he encountered other pedestrians. Hikers with rucksacks, alone or in small groups, a couple hand in hand, the woman a good six inches taller than the man, another woman with an empty buggy and two small children who raced ahead of her. He passed a few faded posters still hanging on their telegraph poles. That poor little girl.

It took him the best part of an hour to get to the base of the cliffs. The sun struggled to break through the solid sheet of white cloud that the sky had now become, but the air continued balmy and still. He began his ascent, leaning slightly into the slope, taking his time. He remembered running up as a youngster, racing friends to the top. He broke into a laughably slow jog and was breathless within seconds.

He recalled lines from T. S. Eliot, an old man rolling up the bottoms of his white flannel trousers to walk along a beach. A haunting feel to the poem, a loss of love colouring its verses, a loneliness and a poignancy running through it.

The old man was him, except for the white trousers. Pottering about the place, looking for mermaids who wouldn't bother singing to him. Never again to feel such an emotional response to a woman, he was sure: Claire had been his quota. Less than two years of the happiest times he had known, diluted with pretty much equal parts of jealousy and guilt. Not much of a bargain, when you thought about it.

He got to the top of the cliffs, hot and weary, and made his way to the spot locally considered to have the best view of the island's western shore. He leant against the metal safety fence, enthralled as always by the panorama that was spread out before him.

The sea straight ahead stretching as far as America, white and pale green and dark turquoise and black, dotted here and there with the coloured smudges of sailboats. The waves closest to the land rushing in below him to throw foam onto shiny black rocky slabs before slithering away again.

In the far distance to his right, barely visible, was the dark strip of the south Kerry coastline. Above him the wide, wide sky, still bumpy with cloud, the sun whitening a patch but failing yet to penetrate it.

He regarded the rusting metal sign beyond the safety fence, embedded deep in the soil and pointing straight out to sea. *The Statue of Liberty: 3,000 miles.* He thought about travelling to America, standing in a lift that climbed up through the giant statue, maybe managing to get all the way to the top of her torch: a very different view from there. Maybe next year.

He walked on, past a little copse of trees, along by the stone wall on his right that kept Tony Seymour's sheep from wandering. The path was well peopled, not one familiar face among them. Good that the holidaymakers were still coming to the island after the child going missing, quite a few Roone businesses depending on what tourists spent there during the summer months.

He sat to rest on one of the heavy wooden seats facing out to sea that the council had provided in the days when councils had money. He looked at the view again and thought about applying for volunteer work in Africa. Would they take someone his age?

Or maybe he could correct examination papers, or set them. Proofread theses? Write a textbook? There had to be something he could do, some use that could be made of him. He was hardly on the scrapheap, even if he couldn't run up a hill any more.

Eventually he moved on, making his way over familiar paths and tracks and laneways, taking a more roundabout route back to the coast road. He was still a mile or so from his house when he turned down a grassy lane. It led to the small pebble beach that Hugh and Imelda liked but that attracted very few others. He'd take off his shoes and socks and dip his aching feet into the salt water: ages since he had a paddle.

After a steep enough descent the lane opened onto one end of the beach. At the other, a hundred yards away, the pebbles met large rocky slabs. As far as Denis could see, the place was completely deserted. He would sit on the pebbles for a while and catch his breath.

And now it's three o'clock, and he's been here for half an hour, and nobody else has come. He decides it's time for his paddle. He clambers to his feet and crunches across the stones until he reaches the first rocky slab, and leans against it to shed his footwear.

As he straightens up, barefoot, trousers rolled to his knees, he becomes abruptly aware that a figure is stretched out on one of the rocks, no more than the length of a swimming pool away

from him. Orange top, blue jeans, black shoes. Lying perfectly
still, limbs splayed starfish-like, facing the sky. Must have been
lying there all the time.

A girl, a young woman. Obvious from the curves beneath
her top.

It's Imelda's girl from last night, he's almost sure. Wearing
a different top, but the red hair tumbling over the rocks is
unmistakable. He wonders if she's feeling chilly, lying there
without a jacket, the breeze coming off the sea stiff enough now.

She's not moving. Nothing stirs apart from her hair, strands
lifted every so often by the breeze. Denis strains to make out if
her eyes are open, but she's too far away.

Should he call, make sure she's alright? But why wouldn't
she be? She's just lying on the rocks. Still, he'd be happier if
she moved. He remembers her near-silence of the night before,
and guesses that she wouldn't welcome interruption. He has no
wish to disturb her, provided she's OK.

He waits. The seconds tick by, and still she remains
motionless. As he's on the point of calling out she lifts a hand
to brush hair from her face. Denis relaxes, and makes his way
gingerly over the pebbles to the water's edge.

She must be aware of his presence. There's no way she could
have missed the rattle of his approaching footsteps, not from
that short distance. Clearly not looking for company, pretending
she hasn't noticed him.

The deliciously cold water makes him draw in his breath.
The Atlantic, always bracing. He remembers swimming in the
bay as a child, jumping off the pier with his friends on summer

evenings after school. Could his childhood possibly have been as idyllic as it seems now? Does everyone remember the good times and scrub away the bad?

He stands ankle-deep, letting the small waves lap over his feet, conscious all the time of his silent companion. He wonders what her story is. All Nell had told him was that she was already in foster care, and coming to Hugh and Imelda just for the summer.

Is she an orphan then? Did she ever know her parents? Are there siblings? Being a teenager can be tough even if you're surrounded by a loving family. Small wonder she isn't full of the joys.

The cold begins to crawl up his legs. He risks a glance across and sees that she hasn't moved. He turns, leaves the water and goes back to where he left his things, coughing and clearing his throat and generally making as much noise as he can, and she doesn't even twitch. He dries his feet with a sock, rubbing hard to get the blood flowing.

He ties his shoelaces and looks across again. Shame she has no friends here. Maybe she and Andy will find some shared interests – although judging from their non-communication last evening, that doesn't seem very likely.

He scans the little beach, still completely deserted apart from the girl. Chosen deliberately, he suspects, for its seclusion. It feels wrong to be leaving her alone there, but what can he do other than join her, which he's sure wouldn't be appreciated – and which, to be honest, doesn't appeal to him particularly – or stay where he is, babysitting her until she leaves?

How old is she – fifteen? Sixteen? Old enough to be out alone, or Imelda would be with her. He brushes his hands on his trousers and leaves the beach, feet tingling pleasantly, stomach reminding him that he hasn't fed it in a good while.

He wonders if Imelda and Hugh are aware of her whereabouts. Even if they are, there's not a lot they can do about it, other than to warn her about the unpredictability of the sea. They can hardly insist that she stay off the beaches, when Roone is literally surrounded by them.

Sad though, to think of her all on her own like that.

He'll say nothing to them: he's only fussing. Back at the house he eats two bananas and follows them with half a dozen digestive biscuits and a cup of black tea, having forgotten to bring milk with him. The sooner he's settled back here the better: it's as much as he can do to keep one house properly stocked with food.

Standing on the ferry's deck half an hour later he strains to see down to the beach, but he'd need binoculars to make her out. Hopefully she's gone by now, back to Hugh and Imelda's to warm up.

He turns to look towards the mainland as it looms to meet him, and sees in his mind's eye the little house five miles outside Tralee that's waiting to receive him, the house that he has filled with memories of Claire. He needs to leave it, as soon as he can.

He turns back and watches the island getting smaller as he's taken away from it, and he thinks about his imminent return there.

✳

She sits up and watches the ferry getting smaller, remembering how sick its movement made her feel on the way to Roone, and already dreading the thought of having to board it again. She hugs her knees tightly; it helps her to stop shivering. She should have worn her anorak – the beach is always windy – but she forgot it today.

The sound of someone else's footsteps was shocking, another person on the beach. The fact that it's deserted is the best thing about it, and why she comes back to it every afternoon, after discovering it on her first day.

She likes the pebbles, less messy than sand. She likes how the water rushes up and rattles away, washing them clean again and again. She likes the giant black shiny slabs of rock, loves lying out on them, letting every part of her sink into them. She loves closing her eyes and listening to the quiet rumble of the sea and thinking about nothing.

It feels a bit like she's moving away, like she's leaving all the bad stuff behind and going somewhere else where nothing wants to hurt her. She thinks she could get to like the sea, as long as she didn't have to be in it – or in a boat anyway.

So the footsteps were a shock. She opened her eyes, turned her head slowly and saw a man, an oldish man, at the far end of the beach. She watched as he lowered himself onto the pebbles and then just sat there looking out to sea. She was pretty sure he hadn't seen her.

She closed her eyes again and tried to relax, tried to shut him out, but he remained an unnerving presence at the edge of her consciousness. For a long time he didn't move, and she had almost managed to forget about him when she heard him rattle his way to his feet again.

Good – he was leaving. But the footsteps, when they came, didn't fade away, and she realised with increasing dread that he was walking towards her. He'd seen her, and he was coming for her. They were all alone – there was nobody around to help her.

She tensed, eyes squeezed shut, listening as his shoes banged across the stones, getting louder and louder. He was going to attack her – he was going to overpower her. He was going to do what Derek did. What Derek does.

She made a frantic silent plan. She'd hear when he began to pull himself up onto the rocks – you couldn't do that quietly. She'd jump to her feet and dash across and kick him in the face as he was clambering up, and hopefully stun him. She'd jump down and make her escape and race away, and he'd never catch up with her.

She waited, heart fluttering, every muscle stiff with tension, poised to leap into action. The footsteps approached the rocks, she drew in her breath – and abruptly they stopped, and she heard nothing more.

She held her indrawn breath, afraid to let it out in case she missed something. Maybe he was sneaking around, trying to find an easier way to get up to her – but she'd hear him moving about on the pebbles, impossible not to. And she heard nothing, apart from some shuffling sounds over by the edge of the rocks.

She risked turning her head a few inches, opened one eye

a fraction and squinted through it – and saw his hand braced against the rock as he bent forwards to carry out some task. But what?

She let out her breath slowly, quietly, and continued to watch him. And then he lifted his head and glanced around, and she turned away quickly and tensed up all over again, waiting once more for him to make his move.

But he didn't.

She watched the sky, seeing his shape out of the corner of her eye, ready to put her plan into action if he moved. A breeze flipped a lock of hair into her face, blocking him from her view, and she brushed it away. And then she heard him on the pebbles again, and when she dared to look over, he was paddling in the water.

He was paddling. He'd walked across to the rocks so he'd have something to lean against while he took off his shoes and socks.

The relief washed over her like a wave. It flooded through her and left her drained. It brought tears to her eyes that she had to blink away. She felt them rolling warmly down the sides of her face. They trickled into her ears.

He paddled for about five minutes. She heard the soft splash of his feet as they sloshed through the water. She heard him moving back up the pebbles as he approached the rocks again, but the fear of him was gone. When he'd replaced his shoes and socks he turned and walked back across the beach and disappeared, and she was alone again.

Did he see her? She doesn't know, but she thinks he probably did. She wonders if he recognised her. She'd realised who he was when he went paddling. She hadn't said much to him at the dinner, or to anyone else.

They'd all tried to get her to talk – especially the pregnant one, whose name Eve has forgotten. She kept saying stuff that made the others laugh, kept trying to include Eve in the conversation. Eve caught the wife watching her a few times – she'd known she was mad at her for not trying harder.

The wife is getting tired of her, she can see that. The wife is disappointed in her going off on her own every day; she doesn't like the way Eve won't talk to her, or let her wash her clothes or go into her room.

She feels bad about it, especially when she thinks of the wife opening her bag and handing over twenty euro, just like that. It would be easier if the wife wasn't so nice to her.

She gets up, stamping her feet to get the feeling back into them. She walks to the edge of the rocks and looks down, wrapping her arms around her chest. The sea is dark green, she can't see the bottom of it. She saw a fish in there yesterday, his fat silvery body flicking its way through the sea. She imagined jumping in and swimming after him, moving silently through the dark green like a mermaid.

Only she can't swim. They tried to teach her in primary school: she was taken to the pool along with the rest of her classmates, everyone piling onto the bus every Tuesday morning. But she hated the smell of the chlorine, and she was too frightened to let go of her float when the others did, and she saw the way Cathy Payne and her friends sniggered at the togs Mam had bought her in the charity shop. And finally the instructor had got fed up with her and left her alone.

Everyone leaves her alone eventually, except Derek.

The tips of her fingers are already numb. She'll have to move soon or she'll be stuck there, frozen solid.

The wife must be dying to know where she goes every afternoon. Eve wonders if she knows about this little beach. The husband probably does, since he was born and bred here.

The dog last night was nice. He reminded her a bit of Scooter. She wished it was just her and the dog – and the dinner, which she'd loved. Some kind of a fish pie with mash on top, and strawberry mousse after. Nell is a good cook, better than the wife, although the wife's apple tarts are lovely.

Nell's stepson had three helpings of the fish pie. Andy, his name is. He's the same height as her. She likes the colour of his eyes.

She saw him today, playing football with his friends. She saw him watching her.

MONDAY, 17 JUNE

Andy sinks lower in his seat, pulling his hat down over his forehead, doing his best to become invisible. He wishes his father didn't feel he had to kiss Nell goodbye every time they part. Anyone would think he wasn't going to see her for a week instead of just a few hours. And right outside Fitz's too, where everyone can see them. Deeply mortifying.

Nell gets back into the car. 'Sorry you had to witness that,' she says, grinning at him. 'We're disgraceful, aren't we? In broad daylight too.'

He has to smile. She gets him, which is the cool thing about her. She doesn't treat him like a kid the way some adults still do. Her lipstick is a bit smudged, but he's not going to say anything about that.

'Come and sit beside me,' she says, reaching across to flip the back of the passenger seat forward so he can manoeuvre his way out. He settles into the front seat and Nell pulls away from the kerb, tooting the Beetle's horn once as Andy's dad waves them off.

They're going to the old house. Andy is helping Nell to clean it up for Gran and the others who are arriving from Dublin on Saturday, the same day the donkey rides are due to start at Walter's Place.

She drives to the end of the street. 'Looking forward to Hugh's party?'

Andy glances at her but she's not smirking.

'Not really,' he says, feeling his face become warm as he turns away to look out of the side window. 'It'll be full of old people.'

'Cheek of you. Anyway, it won't. Laura's boys are coming, and Eve will be there too.'

He watches Willie Buckley hauling crates from his boat by the pier. 'She doesn't talk to anyone.'

'She's just shy. It must be awful to be sent from one foster home to another like that, to a place where you don't know anyone. She probably feels a bit like you did when you came here first.'

He wonders if this is true. She certainly gives the impression of not wanting to make friends, not wanting anyone to notice her, or speak to her. Exactly the way he'd felt when he came to Roone.

'I told Hugh to use the boat anytime they want. I thought you and I might join them sometime, just so she'd have someone her own age there.'

'Maybe,' he says, watching a group of colourfully clad cyclists approaching from the opposite direction. Doing his best to sound as if it's not something he'd particularly choose to do, but something he might consider as a favour to Nell.

She's been to their house for dinner twice. The second time was two nights ago, and again she'd hardly spoken to them. She wore the orange top he'd seen on her the day after the first dinner. It looks like she only brought two tops to the island, the orange and the blue, because in the six times he's seen her she's been wearing one or other of them.

Six times. Twice at their house, once while he was playing in the match, once when she walked past Laura and Gavin's place as he was painting the henhouse, once when he and his dad passed her in the car, once when she passed him in Imelda's car. Imelda waved out to Andy but the girl just stared at him through the window, unsmiling.

The girl. Eve.

He'd caught her eye once at the second dinner, or he thinks he did. He'd glanced in her direction as Nell served the cheesecake she'd made for dessert, and it seemed as if her black-rimmed eyes met his for an instant before she looked away. He'd got the impression she'd been watching him. The thought is interesting.

'Actually,' Nell says, 'if we finish up early in the house we could take the boat out for an hour today. Party's not till five, we've got piles of time. And the sea will be like glass.'

Andy regards her warily. 'Just us?'

'Just us – unless you'd like me to swing by and collect Eve.' She flashes him a grin.

'No,' he says, 'you're OK.'

They drive past the holy well, a group of people clustered around it, their bicycles leaning against the hedgerow. More cyclists.

Nell says, 'The donkey rides will be fun, won't they?'

'Yeah, should be a laugh.'

They approach a sharp bend in the road.

'I'll have to call round and see you in action. I still think you should wear a T-shirt like the boys.'

'No way.'

'Aw, but you'd look—'

And that's all she says, because that's when the car hits them.

✳

'Ta-*dah*.'

Laura straightens up and inspects her sons. 'Lovely. You look very smart, both of you.'

Two redheads, identical cowlicks cocking out from the freckly foreheads. Two pairs of blue eyes, two upturned noses. Different grins – one minus a front tooth (Ben), the other with a full dental complement (so far). Grey shorts, navy sandals.

And above the shorts, two bright yellow T-shirts that James had delivered less than five minutes ago.

Walter's Place Donkey Rides, they announce, below an image of a fat saddle-wearing broadly beaming donkey. The donkey also features on a poster that Roone Primary School's secretary photocopied for them twenty times, in exchange for two bottles of apple juice for each member of staff. The posters have already been distributed around the various business premises of Roone for window display.

The rides are kicking off at the end of the week – and Ben and Seamus have been charged with the tasks of collecting money and issuing tickets, a responsibility they're taking very seriously.

'Andy is your boss,' Laura has told them, 'and you must do what he tells you, or you'll get the sack.'

'We can't offer you a salary,' she's said to Andy, 'but you get to keep ten per cent of the takings, if you're interested.' And he was, so that was that.

She doesn't imagine the rides will turn into a big money-spinner. They'll be weather-dependent for a start, and aimed at under-eights only. And at just three euros a ride, they'd need a constant queue of mini customers to make it pay. But output is minimal, and if their profit covers the twins' birthday presents in November — fishing rods, they're both looking for — and some of the new babies' expenses, it'll be worth it.

They're all set. A rough circuit has been marked out in the field: starting and finishing in front of the vegetable plot, looping around Caesar's sty, skirting the orchard and the henhouse, which got its annual coat of paint last week from Andy. Jim Barnes, whose youngest daughter is in Ben and Seamus's class at school, has loaned them a saddle and a bridle for George.

'Hold on to the riders all the time,' Laura has warned Andy. 'Don't let George speed up, keep him nice and slow.' With no special insurance taken out — the expense would make the whole scheme useless — the last thing they need is a fall, followed by a lawsuit. But George is gentle, and can be relied on. She hopes.

'Keep an eye on them,' she's told Walter. 'Just in case.'

Although she can't for the life of her see what good Walter

would be in the event of a donkey-ride emergency. Even Roone's magic has its limitations.

'Can we go with Andy to deliver the leaflets?' Ben asks. 'He says it's OK if you say we can.'

Two hundred leaflets, typed up by Andy on his laptop and printed out by Henry at the hotel, the first fifty scheduled for door-to-door distribution on Thursday afternoon, two days before the grand opening. Not too soon in advance, or half of them will have forgotten.

Laura tucks in a corner of a sheet. 'You can if you stay with him all the time. Promise me you won't wander off, even for a tiny minute. Cross your hearts.'

Because a little girl is still missing, and for all they know someone might be to blame for that, and might still be on the island. It isn't something Laura dwells on – you can't live like that, suspecting every stranger you meet – but it does no harm to be careful.

The image of Ellie's mother's devastated face has remained with her. How long before that woman, that family, can get back to anything remotely resembling normal life? Will it ever happen, with one member unaccounted for? Is it better or worse, now that they're back home?

She imagines the mother walking into Ellie's bedroom, seeing the familiar cuddly toys and clothes and books. Torturing herself with photograph albums, unable to remove dog-eared paintings stuck with magnets to the fridge door. Walking down the street and meeting Ellie's classmates, whose mothers don't know how to talk to her any more.

But being here must have felt like a nightmare too. Living in the place where they last saw her, a place that they will forever associate with the catastrophe. Surrounded by strangers, any one of whom might be responsible. The sound of the sea in their ears wherever they go, no way of turning it off, the thought always there that she might be lying at the bottom of it.

Six weeks today since her disappearance. No more discussion of it among the islanders when they meet, nothing on the news in the evenings. The case still open, with no outcome to close it, but barring any fresh discovery or new evidence it will remain dormant until its first anniversary, when no doubt there will be an appeal for information in case anyone's conscience has been troubling them for a year.

But what happened on Roone that day won't leave Laura alone. It sits in her head, silently counting the days and weeks since the little girl was last seen alive. And even though Nell was married on the same day, and Laura was there to witness it, she finds herself using Ellie's disappearance rather than Nell's wedding as her marker for May the sixth.

Is it because she's pregnant with daughters of her own? Is that the reason it preys on her mind so much? Will she remember Ellie in years to come? Will she cross Laura's mind every time she looks at her own girls?

The twins have long since stopped asking about her. At some stage her name dropped out of their bedtime prayers, and Laura let it go: no need to keep reminding them. She wonders if they'll ever think of the little girl who disappeared when they were children too, or if the incident will be erased completely as they get older.

Maybe they'll remember. Laura still sees the skinny gap-toothed face of a boy growing up a few streets away from her – Eddie? Eamon? Blond thatch of hair, ears that stuck out beneath it. Two or three years older than Laura, their social circles rarely intersecting. Knocked off his bicycle and killed by a van when Laura was eight or nine. His mother, supported by relatives, blindly following his coffin out of the church, not looking left or right to see the guard of honour the whole school had formed. Maybe they'll remember.

The summer is moving on. Each day the ferry brings new families and groups, driving or cycling or walking off to spend time on Roone. Every night the B&B is filled to capacity, eight hungry mouths to feed each morning. Thankfully, Gav does his own thing before heading off on his morning rounds, and the twins have more or less mastered the knack of fending for themselves too.

Think of the money, Laura tells herself as she lumbers from kitchen to dining room with plates of food that still make her want to retch. Think of living on Roone all year round, think of leaving the rat race behind. Except that sometimes it feels like she's brought the rat race with her, stuffed it into her suitcase along with her dresses and shoes and hairdryer, so hectic have her days become.

And two months from now, all going well, her new arrivals will put paid to any feet-up time for the foreseeable future.

'I'm not complaining,' she tells Walter. 'I still love that we're here, and I'm happy about the babies. It's just that I'm getting more massive every day and my energy is flagging and I'm going to need help soon if the B&B is to stay open, except that we can't afford to pay anyone, but if we close it we'll find it really hard to make ends meet. And Gav does his bit with the garden and the animals, but I'm better at meeting the guests and settling them in and making the breakfasts and cleaning the rooms. And it all gets a bit overwhelming sometimes, you know?'

He knows. Walter understands.

Gav appears at the bedroom door. 'Come on, you two – time to give Mum a rest. Let's collect the eggs and feed Caesar and the hens, and do a few practice runs with George for Saturday.'

Laura looks at him gratefully. Pity he's not more of a businessman – he's practically giving away the eggs and vegetables. But he's wonderful with the boys, as good a father to them as if they were his, and she knows what matters more.

She plumps the pillows and folds down the blankets. 'Give me an hour,' she tells him, 'at the very least.'

She listens to the sound of their feet thumping down the stairs. When all is quiet she walks from the guest room to the one next door that she shares with Gav. She draws the curtains and kicks off her shoes and stretches out on the bed with a deep sigh. The window is open: the boys' chirrupy voices carry faintly up to her from the field, but their words get lost on the way.

She closes her eyes, letting her thoughts drift. Four new lots of guests due this evening, all the rooms ready for them. Hugh's birthday party at five, Laura and the boys invited purely because Imelda wants to make a bit of a fuss with the silent foster girl there. Poor Imelda, feeling the strain of dealing with an uncooperative teen, still trying to be the perfect foster mother.

Laura feels her thoughts becoming sluggish. With any luck Gav will manage to keep the boys amused for a couple of hours. She drifts off.

Twenty minutes later she's shaken gently awake.

'Something's happened,' Gav tells her, his smile missing – and the first thing that jumps into Laura's head is that Ellie's body has finally been found.

✳

Imelda watches Eve filling a glass at the sink.

'Eve, I don't think I mentioned that Nell has a little boat, and she's said we can use it anytime we like. I was thinking we could go on Thursday when Hugh is free, if the weather's fine.'

Eve turns off the tap. 'I get sick on boats.'

Once again, her efforts are thrown back at her. She tamps down her annoyance, laughs lightly. 'Oh, but this is only a little rowboat – it doesn't have an engine or anything. It would just be Hugh rowing.'

'I still don't want to.'

Imelda's smile fades. She turns back to the washing machine, prickling with irritation. 'Fine,' she says. 'Nell just thought you'd like it, that's all.' Useless, everything she tries is useless. She pulls clothes out of the drum in silence and piles them into the laundry basket, listening to the tap running again, the clink of the glass on the draining board.

''Bye,' Eve says, opening the back door, clearly dying to be gone. Off on her daily wanderings.

'Be sure you're back at five for the party.'

'OK.'

The party Imelda has been getting ready for all morning, the worktop covered with sausage rolls and cheese biscuits and chicken wings and a lemon cake. No comment, of course, from Eve when she came downstairs for lunch. She's probably dreading it: pity about her.

Imelda takes the clothes outside and pegs them on the line, even though the grass is still damp from the last shower and the sky looks heavy with the next. As she pulls a pillowcase from the basket she thinks of the present she gave Hugh that morning, the hurriedly bought sweater in Tralee on Friday, watching the clock to be back in time to put on the dinner.

She should have asked Eve to go with her. If Eve had gone they could have eaten out, or bought a takeaway to have on the ferry. Hugh was working till late – there would have been no rush to get home.

But Imelda had found herself unable to suggest it to Eve, unwilling to spend the afternoon with the girl trailing around glumly after her. She'd chosen to head off on her own as soon as Eve left the house, which had given her less than an hour in Tralee. And the navy sweater has every sign of being a rushed purchase.

'It's perfect,' Hugh told her – and the fit is fine because she knows his size, but it's safe and dull, and not one she would have picked out if she'd taken her time and tried a few more shops.

And she can't blame Eve for it, but still she feels resentful.

Back in the house she phones Nell to tell her that her boat won't be required, but Nell's phone must be switched off because all Imelda gets is somebody's recorded voice telling her to try again later.

And about half an hour after that, as she's in the middle of piping *Happy Birthday Hugh* on top of the cake, her phone rings.

'There's been an accident,' Hugh says, and Imelda's heart swoops in her chest.

Denis clears his throat. 'Before you all go,' he says, 'there's something I want to tell you. It's not on the agenda.'

In the act of pushing back chairs and putting away notebooks, they stop. He's aware of a communal alertness, an unspoken *Here it comes* in their quick exchange of glances. They all know: this is not news to them.

Jackie Fenton, board member and undoubted bearer of the glad tidings, has the grace to flush. Cathal O'Neill, who teaches fourth class and who has never, as far as Denis can remember, initiated a conversation with him, purses his mouth and examines his fingernails. The vice principal, seated across the table from him, looks somewhere to the left of Denis's ear, his face carefully vacant.

'I've handed in my resignation,' Denis says, his gaze sweeping around the table, nobody's eyes there to meet his. 'I'm leaving at the end of August.'

Dead silence. Nobody says a word. Nobody, to give them their due, pretends to be surprised. Feet are shuffled. Somebody clears a throat, quietly.

'The job will, of course, be advertised in the usual way, in case any of you are interested in applying.' The vice principal appears fascinated now by a spot on the wall above Denis's head. Spellbound by it.

'I'd just like to thank you all for making me feel welcome when I came to work here,' Denis says into the continuing silence. 'I'd like you to know that it didn't go unnoticed.'

It's childish; it's beneath him. But it gives him a small kick of satisfaction, and they deserve it. He lets another few seconds go by, lets their discomfiture play out a little longer.

'That's it,' he says eventually. 'You're free to go. See you all in the morning.'

Not a word from them. Not a single remark, not one good wish. They gather their things in silence and exit the room in an untidy, rushed huddle, nobody wanting to be left behind with him.

Denis sits on, waiting until the last car door has slammed in the yard outside, until the sound of the last engine has died away as they escape one by one. Plenty to be said out of his earshot, he's sure. Meeting up somewhere even now, probably, to pull his news to pieces, to wonder and speculate.

Does anyone have the grace, he wonders, to feel privately ashamed? Will any of them lie in bed tonight and wish they'd behaved differently towards him? Will their consciences trouble them at all, or will they convince themselves that they did nothing wrong, that they were perfectly polite to him and did all that was expected of them?

He looks down at the typed agenda before him. *Staff meeting, 17 June*. Hugh's birthday: fifty-three, or is it fifty-four? Moira used to have him over to dinner every year, bake him a cake when he had nobody else to do it. Now Hugh has Imelda, and Denis isn't part of his celebrations any more.

He slips the agenda – his last – into the spiral-bound notebook he uses for the meetings and gets stiffly to his feet. He spent much of yesterday tramping along country roads outside Tralee, taking random turns, going where his feet led him. He walked until his soles burnt and his calf muscles ached with every step, and then he sat on a low stone bridge – nothing but a dried-up stream bed underneath – and ate the sandwich and drank the carton of juice he'd brought along.

He spoke to nobody. He encountered a number of fellow hikers, travelling mostly in pairs, and a troop of half a dozen cyclists who sped past, and a young woman pushing a buggy that held a solemn-faced toddler. A few farmers buzzed around their fields in tractors, raising an arm when they spotted him.

A man sitting on a garden seat outside an old house stared at Denis as he walked by. Greying hair in need of a cut, oversized green tweed jacket, brown trousers, black shoes with missing laces. Something in the face, some vacancy, some slackness about the mouth, that hinted at mental deficiency. Denis smiled at him, and the man stared on. Or maybe he wasn't looking at Denis at all, but at something inside his head.

Denis walked so far he lost his bearings. There was an

unnerving mid-afternoon hour when nothing at all looked familiar, no landmarks guided him, and the prospect of being stranded by nightfall began to seem alarmingly possible. He was about to call into a farmhouse for directions when he rounded a bend and saw a main road ahead of him, and by the side of it a sign that pointed him back to familiar territory.

And today he's paying for it. A tightness in his thighs and calves, an ache in his chest every time he fills his lungs. Nothing that won't fix itself in a day or two.

He lifts his jacket from the back of the chair. Nine more days of school to go, more than enough. He'll be in and out of the building over the summer, things to see to after the teaching stops, but with any luck he won't encounter anyone except Gerard, who's been charged with painting the classrooms while they're vacant.

He lets himself out of the back door of the school and there is the caretaker, cleaning windows. When he sees Denis approaching, he climbs down from his stepladder and drops his yellow sponge into the bucket beside him.

'They tell me you're leaving,' he says, wiping his hands on his grey trousers. 'I'm sorry to hear it.'

Denis takes in the thin, honest face before him. Gerard, mid-forties, widowed young with three children to bring up. His mother living with them. That, he realises, is the sum total of what he knows about Gerard, the one person who has shown him any kindness since he joined the school.

He puts out his hand. Gerard's, when he clasps it, is warm and still damp.

'Thank you,' Denis says. 'I appreciate that. Don't stay too long.'

'Nearly done here,' Gerard tells him, climbing back onto his ladder. 'Five minutes I'll be off.'

As Denis opens his car door his phone rings. He sees Hugh's name on the display.

He presses *call answer*. 'Happy birthday,' he says.

'Denis,' Hugh says – and just that single word, the quiet way it's spoken, causes the smile to slide off Denis's face.

'The Bianchis stayed with us last night,' Laura says. 'I reminded him to drive on the left when they were leaving this morning. I knew he wasn't listening.'

'There should be a road sign about driving on the left,' Gavin says. 'There should be one down at the ferry port. We should put one up ourselves if the council won't.'

'It was only a matter of time,' Laura says. 'That bend is lethal, it's so sharp. Thank God he wasn't going too fast.'

'He was going fast enough,' Gavin says. 'Both cars are written off.'

'Oh, don't,' Imelda says. 'It doesn't bear thinking about.'

James says nothing at all.

It was a head-on collision. Paolo Bianchi, who looks about eighteen, and who was driving a new rental car on the wrong side of the road, walked away with a bumped knee and a few scratches. His wife, whose name James heard and promptly forgot, escaped almost as lightly – minor bruising, various cuts that didn't need stitching, a single broken finger.

Nell, behind the wheel of her ancient, pre-airbag Volkswagen Beetle (and unprotected by a seatbelt), cracked three ribs and sustained severe bruising to her chest when she slammed into the steering wheel. She also suffered a hairline fracture to her wrist ('Her radius, to be exact,' the hospital doctor told James) and cuts to her face and hands from flying glass.

Andy, sitting in the passenger seat (and also minus a seatbelt), sprained his ankle and received a bang to the head that knocked him out briefly, and narrowly missed being blinded in his left eye by a shard of windscreen glass that sliced into his cheek an inch beneath the eye.

'They were in an accident,' Dr Jack said on the phone, the words causing a damp icy wave to pass through James. 'They're OK, they're both OK, but I've sent them to Tralee hospital for treatment. Dougie's taken them over – he came on the scene just ahead of me.'

He hardly remembers his journey from the pub to the pier, barely recalls Leo Considine ushering his car onto the ferry ahead of the others, having already carried Nell and Andy over in Dougie Fennessy's taxi. The road to Tralee seemed to take forever, James following signs for the hospital once he reached the town, his brain refusing to remind him where it was, although he'd been there more than a few times before.

His heart hammering every inch of the way, the echo in his head of another race, two years earlier, the day Walter died and Andy was the one who found him, and James had got a similar phone call. Andy in tears that day, Walter's death unlocking something in him that had been bottled up since Karen had been taken from them.

Why did she have to go? He'd wept in his father's arms. *Why did she have to die like that? It wasn't fair.* Crying for his dead mother, Walter's passing somehow giving him licence to let his sadness flow out.

'Hey,' Andy said today, 'don't look so worried. I'm OK.'

Sitting up in bed by the time James got to the hospital, his face criss-crossed with cuts, a dark red bruise on one temple, an obscene line of stitches running from under his eye almost to his chin. More cuts on the backs of his hands, an ankle heavily bandaged, his jeans taken off him with a scissors, his shoes (a single terrifying splotch of red on one) sitting on the floor by his bed. An unasked-for cup of tea handed to James by a cheerful nurse – who saw, no doubt, that the patient's father was in a considerably worse state than the patient.

'We'll hang on to him for the night, just to keep an eye on him – we always do that with a head injury,' she told James. 'You can bring him home tomorrow, all going well. Your wife is through here,' she went on, leading him from Andy's room to another down the corridor. 'She's a bit shaken up but you can take her home and put her to bed.'

Nell was alone in a kind of anteroom. No beds, just three trolleys. She lay on one by the window, eyes closed, a blue blanket tucked around her lower half. Her face, like Andy's, was speckled with cuts, some little more than red dots, others longer. Her injured left arm rested on the blanket, a plaster cast going from her knuckles halfway to her elbow, the rest of the arm blotched with red and purple bruising.

James stood looking down at his wife of less than two months. He reached out and touched the fingertips of her injured arm – and instantly she opened her eyes.

And instantly they filled with tears.

'How is he?' Her voice lower than a whisper, barely audible even in the silent room.

'He's fine, sitting up in bed.' James reached for her good hand and enclosed it in his. 'Don't cry, my love.'

'I could have killed him.' The tears, despite his plea, running down her face, tumbling over one another on their way to her chin. 'I got him to sit in the front, I didn't make him wear a seatbelt, I never—'

'Stop that,' he ordered, thumbing the tears away. Reaching down to press his lips to her hot, clammy forehead. 'Nobody on Roone wears seatbelts, myself included, you know that. We're all as careless as hell. This wasn't your fault. None of it was your fault.'

Denis arrived just then, looking as frantic as James felt, the sight of her father's stricken face only serving to make Nell even more distraught.

'I'm alright,' she wept – clearly not alright, and James wondered if the occasion was reminding father and daughter of Moira's accident, and their heartbroken visit to the hospital morgue.

And Paolo Bianchi's chalk-white pallor, his stuttering apology to James when they met in the corridor, his hand shaking as he extended it. 'I do mistake,' he kept repeating. 'I do big mistake. I am very sorry, sir. I hope your family is OK. I hope they is OK.'

And now it's evening and Nell is home and has been put to bed with painkillers and a sleeping tablet. When they left Andy he was watching television and eating the cream doughnut James had found in the hospital shop. Imelda and Laura and Gavin have gathered in Nell and James's house as James attempts to come to terms with the day's drama, a barely tasted glass of brandy that someone gave him cradled in his hands.

He should ring Tim. He should call off their trip to the island, or at least postpone it. Or should he? Will it make any difference if they're here? He can't think straight. He'll ring his mother tomorrow and talk to her, let her make the decision. He should have rung already to tell her, but he can't face the inevitable questions. Tomorrow will do.

He raises the brandy glass to his lips – and lowers it without touching a drop.

He could have lost them. He could have lost both of them, like he lost Karen. He might have been widowed for the second time – he might have had to bury his son. Try as he might, he can't stop this horrifying possibility replaying itself in his head. They could have been snatched away from him. He might have been visiting their—

He feels a hand on his shoulder. He looks up.

'They're OK,' Laura tells him, replacing the brandy with tea. 'They'll be fine, they'll be as right as rain. Don't be crucifying yourself.'

Easier said than done. He sips the tea – much too sweet –

and looks out of the window at the pink and orange sky, and tries to stop feeling terrified.

✳

'There was an accident,' the wife said.

Eve knew about the accident already: she'd walked past the cars on her way back to the house. The front of the yellow one all bashed in, a real mess, the silver one not as bad but still pretty smashed up. Nell had a yellow car like that – Eve had seen it outside the house when she and the wife had gone to dinner. She remembered thinking it looked like the one Noddy drove in the books a teacher had read to them years ago.

A man in a Day-Glo jacket was sweeping the broken glass to the side of the road; another was directing traffic around the two cars. A few people stood about in clusters, watching them. Eve saw the front part of a mobile phone being swept up along with the glass. Two hub caps, surprisingly intact, leant side by side against the hedge.

'Nell was driving,' the wife said, 'and Andy was with her.'

His name made Eve's skin twitch. He was in the yellow car?

'Thank God they're not badly injured,' the wife said, 'but they've been taken to Tralee hospital. Andy is being kept in for observation, but Nell is coming home later, and I wanted to drop over and see them. Will you be alright on your own for an hour or so?'

Which was funny when you thought about it. Eve was always alright on her own: it was when other people came along that she stopped being alright.

The birthday party had fallen flat on its face, the food still sitting on plates on the worktop, *Happy Bir* written in chocolate letters on the white icing of the cake.

'Hugh had to stay on in the pub, with James gone,' the wife said. 'Not that we'd be having a party under the circumstances. Help yourself – that's the dinner tonight' – so Eve had got a plate and taken chicken wings and sausage rolls, wanting to ask more about the accident but saying nothing. She'd see him around; she often saw him around.

'I'm not hungry,' the wife said. 'I might have something later.' Turning on the radio and putting up the ironing board, leaving Eve to sit alone at the table, letting her know that she'd succeeded in pushing the wife away. The thought gave Eve no satisfaction at all.

When she'd finished eating the wife was still ironing. Eve washed her single plate and dried it. She hung the tea towel and pushed down her sleeves.

'Goodnight,' she said to the wife, turning for the door.

'You don't have to go upstairs so early every night,' the wife said. 'You can go into the sitting room and watch television, or a DVD. I won't bother you.'

Something in her voice, a coolness that hadn't been there before. Finished trying to be nice, because it was getting her nowhere.

Eve opened her mouth – and closed it again. She wouldn't understand, none of them would. 'I'm OK upstairs,' she said, her hand on the door handle.

'You're sure you don't mind being left on your own?'

'No.'

'I'm just waiting for Laura to call to let me know when they're back.'

'OK. Goodnight.'

Upstairs Eve pulled the chair to the window and sat looking out at the pink sky until she heard the wife's phone ringing. She waited until the sound of her car crunching over the gravel had died away completely and then she made her way back downstairs.

In the kitchen she saw that the party food had disappeared, apart from about a third of the cake, which still bore the half-written message. Eve cut off a slice – the *r* and the dot of the *i* – and ate it, and tidied up the crumbs she'd scattered. She opened the fridge and took out a carton of juice and filled a glass.

And now she's back in her room, alone in the silent house. She pulls the chair over to the dressing table and sits in front of it. She removes her makeup, wipes away the fancy foundation and blusher and eyeliner and lipstick she slips into her pocket when the snooty girls behind the counter aren't looking. They're only testers she takes – it's not like she's stealing anything.

When her face is clean she crosses to the bed, slides her hand under the mattress and pulls out the envelope.

She's opened it just once since she got here, to slip in the twenty euro the wife gave her. She hadn't planned on looking at the other stuff inside, just wanted to have it with her while she was here – but now she lifts the flap and lets everything tumble out onto the duvet.

She puts the money back in and lays the envelope on her

pillow. She picks up a photo and looks at her brother aged eight, a few months after he was taken away from Mam and given to the Begleys.

The photo isn't a proper one: it was taken on a mobile phone and printed out on ordinary paper, like all the others. It's in black-and-white, but Eve can remember the real colours. Keith is dressed in a grey jumper and the jeans that Mam had burnt one time she was high as a kite. The shape of the iron was stamped on the front of the thigh in brown, but Keith had flatly refused to give them up when Mrs Begley tried to coax him into another pair.

In the photo, which was taken by Mrs Begley, Keith sits stiffly upright beside Eve on a green couch, looking like he's waiting for the dentist. Too small to understand why he'd been sent to live with strangers, and why his sister hadn't been allowed to go with him.

'We didn't manage to find a place for both of you,' a woman in the fostering agency had told Eve when she'd asked to stay with Keith. The woman was the fattest person Eve had ever seen, and her breath stank of coffee all the time, and her name was Kate.

'I'm your social worker,' she told Eve, but all Eve wanted was her family back.

'Where's our mam?' she asked, and *Getting better* was all she was told, which made no sense to Eve. Mam wasn't sick: she just went funny when she took stuff.

'Can I go and visit Keith?' Eve asked.

'Of course, as soon as I can arrange it.'

But it took her eleven weeks to arrange it. Her car was far too small for her – she spilt out of the driver's seat in all directions – and it smelt horribly of some kind of animal. Eve had to breathe through her mouth for the half-hour it took them to drive to the Begleys' house. She wanted to open the window but Kate wouldn't let her – 'It's freezing out there.'

It was two days before Christmas. Kate went back to sit in her car after Mrs Begley opened the door to them, dressed in a pink tracksuit and navy slippers. The house was stuffy and there was a smell of dinner cooking that made Eve's stomach rumble.

'He's a quiet boy, isn't he?' Mrs Begley said, leading Eve down the hall to the sitting room with the green couch. 'He won't wear the lovely new trousers I got him. Maybe you'd have a word.'

Keith sat on the green couch in his burnt jeans and grey jumper, his thumb stuck in his mouth, something he hadn't done in years. He turned his head when the door opened, regarded his sister mutely.

'Hi,' Eve said, walking towards him, conscious of Mrs Begley standing in the doorway. She took a seat beside him. 'Hi, you,' she said, punching his arm lightly.

'Don't move,' Mrs Begley said, and they sat still until she reappeared with a mobile phone. 'Thumb out, Keith,' she said, and he slid it out with a soft pop. 'Cheese,' she said, clicking, and they both blinked.

As soon as the door closed Keith turned to Eve. 'Why can't I come to live in your house?' he asked. 'When can we go home? Where's Mam gone?' The questions fell out of him, and all Eve could do was rub his sleeve and tell him she didn't know. She was ten then, there were a lot of things she didn't know – and anyone she asked didn't seem to know either, or pretended they didn't.

She gave Keith a pack of markers she'd found on a windowsill in the school hall. The yellow one was missing, but he didn't seem to notice.

'D'you like it here?' she asked him, lowering her voice in case Mrs Begley had her ear pressed to the door. 'Are they nice?'

His thumb crept back into his mouth as he nodded. His hair was cut shorter than usual. There was a small almost-healed wound on the tip of the ear that was closest to her. She wondered how he'd got it, and if it had hurt. The idea that she couldn't protect him from things now was unbearable.

'Are they nice to you?' she repeated, and again his head dipped once, and she had to be content with that.

'What's your school like?'

'OK.'

'Have you friends?'

'Mm.'

'Did you get my letters?'

Another nod.

She wondered if anyone had read them to him: when they were in the same school he had gone to the slow teacher; he wouldn't manage them on his own. But it didn't matter if nobody read them: what mattered was that he knew she wasn't forgetting about him.

'Where's Mam gone?' he asked again, the words coming out

funny with his thumb in the way, and for the second time she told him she didn't know, and he sucked on.

After a while the door opened and Mrs Begley came in with plastic cups of lemonade and a plate with two Jammie Dodger biscuits on it. 'You can eat mine,' Eve told Keith when they were alone again, although her mouth watered at the sight of them.

He cried, abruptly and unexpectedly, when she left. He tried to pull open her car door, and Mrs Begley had to hold his arms down until they drove off. Eve couldn't hear him over Kate's revving of the engine but she saw his gaping mouth, his screwed-up eyes, his red cheeks.

She wanted to wave goodbye but it felt wrong to do it while he was crying so she turned away and looked straight ahead instead, the photo Mrs Begley had printed out for her clutched in her hand, biting her cheek hard to keep anything stupid from happening.

'Aw, poor little thing,' Kate said, 'he's upset,' and Eve wanted to punch her in the face. He was upset because they'd taken him away from his home and forced him to live with strangers. If they hadn't come poking their noses in he'd be fine: Eve would have gone on looking after him, like she'd done for as long as she could remember.

She kept up the letters to him every Friday, like she'd been doing since they were separated, even though she couldn't spell to save her life, and there was so little she could tell him. There was plenty going on but nothing she wanted him to hear, so she made up other stuff.

I went to the sinima, she wrote. *I went to a partey in my frends house. I went for a walk and got cot in the rain.* Useless letters, full of lies, but she never missed a week. *Hope your OK*, she'd write at the end of each one, but he never wrote back to tell her if he was or not.

She wrote the letters on pages torn from her copies and put them into envelopes that the school secretary gave her. She dropped the letters into the fostering agency on her way home from school.

She asked Kate repeatedly if she could go back to see him, but each time Kate just said, *Leave it with me*, and nothing ever happened. One day when she dropped in her letter she was told that Kate wasn't working there any more, and that Sue would be dealing with her from then on.

'You get four visits a year,' Sue told her. Sue was tall and thin and wore black clothes, and you could see the pink of her head where she parted her hair. 'Your next visit is scheduled for the end of March.'

In March Keith's hair was a bit longer and he wasn't wearing the burnt jeans. Eve gave him the bundle of comics she'd found in a bag outside the door of a charity shop. They sat in the same room as before, on the green couch that was covered now with a purple blanket.

It was hard to find things to talk to him about. He said very little, just answered the questions she asked. They had different lives now, different houses, different families. 'Remember Scooter?' she said, a neighbour's dog they used to throw sticks for, and he nodded without smiling, although he'd loved Scooter.

He didn't ask if he could go and live with her, and he made

no mention of Mam. She let him have her Jaffa Cake when Mrs Begley appeared with the tray. She put an arm around his shoulders when Mrs Begley aimed her phone at them and said cheese.

She tossed his hair when she left, and he pulled his head out from under her hand. He stood on the path as Sue drove away, no sign of tears this time, no answering wave when Eve lifted her hand. She looked back before the car was at the end of the road, but he had already gone inside.

In June he wasn't at the house when Eve arrived. 'I don't know what's keeping him,' Mrs Begley said. 'He knew you were coming.' He turned up ten minutes later, red-faced and sweating, a football under his arm. 'Look who's here,' Mrs Begley said, and he sniffed and looked at Eve, and for a horrible moment she thought he'd forgotten her.

She flicks through the photos Mrs Begley has given her over the years. Keith standing red-cheeked with a few others beside a lopsided snowman. Keith blowing out nine candles stuck into the top of a swiss roll. Keith dressed as a vampire for Hallowe'en, red lines running from plastic fangs down to his chin. Keith wearing a too-big brown jacket and cream trousers, palms pressed together on his confirmation day. Keith running on some beach in a pair of blue togs she's never seen.

'Write back to me,' Eve tells him each time they meet, but nothing ever comes from him. She unfolds a newspaper cutting Mrs Begley sent two summers ago. It shows a picture of Keith and two of his friends standing beside an ice-cream van on one of the few good days they'd had. *Thought you might like this,*

Mrs Begley wrote, but Eve had already seen it, and what she would have liked was a letter from her brother.

With each visit she can feel him drifting further away from her. They have so little in common now, nothing to hold them to one another except a fading memory of growing up together in a house shared with a mother who wanted drugs more than she wanted children, and a series of men who were best avoided.

She sifts through the rest of the photos, watching her brother's face grow leaner, his limbs longer with the passing years. He's thirteen now, and very different from the frightened little boy who'd tried to clamber into the car beside her five Christmases ago.

He's nearly as tall as her, shot up in the past year. 'I can't keep him fed,' Mrs Begley tells her. 'I don't know where he puts it – I'm broke from him.' She makes it sound like Keith is eating just to annoy her.

His voice is different too, dark and deep like a man's. Eve got a shock the first time she heard it last Christmas. It makes him sound like someone she doesn't know. He's turning into someone she doesn't know.

But she remembers when he crept into her bed as a toddler, she remembers holding him until he fell asleep, his skinny little pee-smelling body warm against hers. She remembers the two of them huddled in the shed, where they often hid until Mam's friends would leave and it was safe to go back into the house.

She remembers him helping her to put Mam to bed, and she remembers how awful it felt every time he cried with hunger and she had nothing to give him.

She picks up the last photo, the only properly developed one of the lot. It's old now, about eight years old. It shows the three of them, the only one she has with Mam in it.

It was taken by Sarah's mother at a school sports day, the only one Mam ever turned up for. Keith, who was in Junior Infants, is wearing a medal on a red ribbon that he won for running. His face is nearly as red as the ribbon, and two of his teeth are missing. Eve and Mam are standing on either side of him.

Mam is wearing a grey dress with long sleeves that hide the needle marks, and long black boots even though you can see that it's a sunny day. Her smile looks crooked, as if her face was drawn by a small child who hadn't figured out how to do mouths. Her hand rests on Keith's shoulder.

Eve has seen her once in the last five years. It didn't go well.

She returns the photos to their envelope and slides it back under the mattress. She sits on the chair in the room that she keeps to as much as possible when she's in the house, so they can't get to know her.

She can't let them get to know her. She can't let any of them in. It's safer that way.

SATURDAY, 22 JUNE

'Denis.'

So softly he hardly hears it above the hum of the bustling shopping centre. Instinctively he turns, realising who it is in the few milliseconds it takes to move his head.

Three and a half weeks since they've met, three Wednesdays endured without her. The loneliness still heavy in him, her face, her voice drifting regularly into his head. The pillowcase unchanged where she'd rested her head on her last visit to his bed.

She's alone. She carries a supermarket bag in each hand. She wears a pale pink mac that he doesn't remember seeing before. There's a nervous smile on her face that kills him to see.

'How are you?' she asks, in the same tender voice that she used to say his name when he was inside her. 'How are you keeping?'

The sight of her almost undoes him. He nods, beyond words. The longing to touch her is as physical as an ache, to pull her towards him and wrap his arms around her, like he did every time she came to him. Embracing before a single word had been spoken between them, hanging on tightly to one another as if their existence depended on it.

He finds his voice. 'You? How're things?'

'Miserable,' she replies, her sad smile still in place. 'Lonely beyond words. Missing you like you wouldn't believe. But I can't blame you.'

This is unbearable. He makes a move to turn away.

'Please don't go,' she says quickly. 'Just talk to me, just for a minute. I won't look for anything else, I swear.'

So easy, so tempting to start it all up again with her. Coming face to face in a place the size of Tralee was a possibility that he'd hungered for and dreaded in equal measure. Dying to see her, but aware of the feelings the sight of her would unpack. He stands speechless.

'Have you been to Roone?' she asks, searching his face. The collar of her mac is twisted on one side. He will not reach out to straighten it.

'Nell was in a car accident,' he says, watching her expression change. 'She's alright, she's home again. Her car was written off.'

'She's OK?'

'She's getting better. She'll be off work for a while.'

'Oh …. poor thing.'

'I've resigned,' he says, the information slipping out without warning. 'I'm leaving the school and moving back to Roone.'

She nods slowly. He sees her eyes fill with tears.

'I'm taking early retirement.'

She blinks and the tears are pushed out and roll silently down her cheeks. She lifts an arm, still holding her shopping, and brushes a pink sleeve across her wet face.

'That's good,' she says, more tears spilling out. 'Nell will be glad to have you back.' Biting her bottom lip to stop the trembling that has begun. The pink sleeve streaked with her sadness.

Denis wheels abruptly and strides away, his errands forgotten. The exit doors slide open at his approach. He glances behind and sees her standing where he left her, still watching him mutely. Still begging him to come back to her, still breaking his heart. He turns away again and walks through the doors.

He crosses the tarmac to his car without looking back. His car softens into a grey blur and he wipes his eyes with the back of a hand, echoing her gesture exactly.

✳

Five days later she's still painfully conscious of every breath.

'That's the cracked ribs,' Dr Jack told her. 'It'll get better, give it another while. In the meantime, just take it easy.'

Take it easy – as if she has a choice. As if she'll be doing anything much for at least a month with a wrist out of action and a still-tender bruise that spreads all down her left side, slowly turning from pinkish red to yellowish purple, and painkillers that leave her woozy and forgetful. Even walking around the house and garden, which she's forcing herself to do every so often, sets her chest aching and brings her out in a light sweat.

Andy may be left with a scar on his face; they'll have to wait and see. She can't look at the line of stitches without blaming herself for them. If only she hadn't suggested he come with her, or if she'd left him in the back seat, or made him wear a seatbelt. Or if she'd bothered to wear one herself, given him the good example. So careless she'd been, careless and stupid.

But she must be positive. Andy is on the mend, they both are, and for that she's immeasurably grateful. Their cuts are healing, their bruises fading. Every day she can see an improvement in both of them. As soon as she can she'll go swimming, let the sea work its healing magic on her.

She thinks that maybe Mam was looking down on them, protecting them from worse harm. She thinks it's not at all outside the bounds of possibility.

From her seat on the patio she hears the buzz of voices from the field next door: sounds like the donkey rides are still going strong. George will be tired, plodding around all afternoon. And poor Andy is so disappointed to be missing them, but he'll take over as soon as he's able. Nell wonders how his replacement is managing; she'll call Laura later on the phone James got her to replace the one that was smashed up. All her numbers lost, only about half of them retrieved so far.

She checks her watch and sees that it's ten to six. Any minute they'll be here, if they got the half-five ferry that Tim was aiming for.

'You couldn't have put them off for a while?' she'd asked James, when he told her they were still coming.

'My mother's insisting. She wanted to come sooner but I said no.'

'But the house isn't ready for them – the beds aren't made, nothing's cleaned.'

'Don't worry about that, they'll manage. They're not expecting the Ritz.'

So they're on their way to a dusty house with unmade beds and windows badly in need of a shine. Let them, she thinks wearily. Let Tim fill a bucket and wash the windows. Let Katy make up the beds and sweep the floors. Let Colette stock the fridge with the milk and butter and eggs that Nell had been going to get in. Let them fend for themselves, they're well able.

It will be Katy's first trip to the island. *Can't wait to see it*, she'd written, a million years ago when Tim and Nell were getting married, and she was coming to their wedding on Roone. *Can't believe we're finally going to meet*.

Nell's wrist throbs, but it's too soon for another painkiller. She longs for her bed, but that's out of bounds until she's endured at least an hour of talking to the Bakers. She sighs, not too deeply.

'They won't stay long,' James says, leaning forward to tuck a strand of hair behind her ear. 'We'll give them a drink and send them on their way. Anyhow, they'll want to put Lily to bed.'

She's about to ask if he remembers Andy as a small baby when the doorbell rings, making her jump. She winces at the dull throb the movement causes in her damaged chest.

James gets to his feet. 'Stay put,' he orders, as if she had any intention of moving a muscle. He disappears, followed by John Silver, who insists on checking out all callers.

Nell closes her eyes, pressing cautious fingertips to her left thigh, feeling the tenderness there – and without warning she hears the awful shriek of brakes, the enormous bang that followed, feels the terrifying sensation of being flung forward to slam against the steering wheel with such force, the horror of seeing Andy slumped—

She jerks her eyes open with a gasp that causes her chest to clench again with pain. She lays a trembling palm on her racing heart, sees without seeing the shrubbery, the stone wall, the clothes line, the path to the little wooden shed.

'Nell.'

She turns, still shocked by the slap of the memory.

Tim crouches by her seat. 'You OK? You look like you've seen a ghost.'

She shakes her head, unable to speak.

He lays a hand gently on her bare arm, rests it there. 'Poor Nell,' he murmurs, his green eyes searching her face. She can smell his aftershave, so familiar. 'Ssh,' he says. 'Take it easy. Just breathe.'

His hand is warm. The touch comforts her.

'Were you remembering?' he asks. 'Was that it?'

She nods. 'I couldn't remember anything,' she says, her voice shaky, 'and just now it came back. I saw—' She breaks off, the words summoning up the fear again.

'Ssh,' he repeats, pressing gently on her arm. 'That can happen. I've heard of it happening. It must have been frightening.'

His voice is soothing. The exchange is oddly intimate, like a lovers' private conversation. She has a sudden feeling he's going to put a finger to her lips. They know one another so well, it would be the most natural—

'There you are.'

Nell starts, still jittery. Tim rises unhurriedly and steps back as his mother emerges from the house, prettily turned out as always in a mint green dress, open-toed cream patent shoes. She stoops and presses her cheek briefly to Nell's, giving no sign that she's seen anything untoward, leaving the delicate scent of face powder in her wake.

'Nell, look how pale you are, and your poor scratched face. We couldn't believe it when we heard. I wanted to come down straight away but James wouldn't hear of it – he can be very bossy when he wants.'

She takes the seat vacated by James and reaches out to cradle Nell's uninjured hand. 'How are you feeling, dear?' she asks.

'A bit stiff and sore,' Nell tells her. She holds up her plastered wrist. 'I'll be out of action in the salon for a while.'

'I can see that – and I've just met poor Andy inside with his crutches. Not to worry, we'll take good care of you both while we're around. I hope James is doing all he can.'

'He is, he's great.'

'Are you putting vitamin-E oil on those cuts?'

'I am, every day. The hospital recommended it.'

'That's good. It's marvellous to prevent scarring. I hope Andy is using it too.'

Nell is conscious of Tim observing them, arms folded, leaning against the stone wall. She wishes James would reappear. He must be talking to Katy in the kitchen, although she can't hear voices.

'How was the journey?' she asks Colette. 'I hope it wasn't too much for Lily.'

'Oh—' Her mother-in-law shoots a glance at Tim. 'They didn't come, Nell. Katy's mother is a bit unwell right now, so Katy went to Donegal with Lily instead.'

'Oh dear … I hope it's nothing serious.'

'Hopefully not. They think a chest infection.'

Tim has come to Roone without his wife and child. She considers the implications of this. Colette could have made the journey on her own, couldn't she? Not by car, she's not much of a driver, but she could easily have got the train to Tralee and someone would have met her. When Nell was working in Dublin she took the train home practically every weekend, and her father met her at the station in Tralee.

He could have met Colette today. He's not here this weekend – 'End-of-year stuff,' he'd told her on the phone, promising to come on Thursday as soon as the school closes for the summer – but he'd certainly have collected Colette at the station and driven her to the ferry point, and James would have met her at the other end.

But maybe Tim was anxious to see Andy, maybe he wasn't just chauffeuring his mother here. Or maybe Katy had persuaded him to go with Colette, feeling that three would be too many to descend on her sick mother.

Still, it strikes her as a bit strange.

'Here we go.'

James emerges from the kitchen with a tray, Andy hobbling after him. They take their seats and Nell sips the juice that's poured for her and does her best to join in the conversation.

She catches Tim's eye, just once. He smiles.

✳

On her way to the sitting room Laura pauses in the hall. It's pretty much as she remembers it the first time she and the boys called to buy eggs and honey from Walter, except that now the rather sombre wallpaper is gone, painstakingly scraped off one weekend by Gavin and James, and has been replaced by three coats of cream paint.

The small black-and-white floor tiles are the same, the worn but beautiful red-and-wine-and-cream-patterned carpet runner remains on the stairs. Walter's mahogany hallstand still occupies the space it did before, at the bottom of the stairs. A tweed cap Laura found on a shelf in the scullery hangs from one of its brass hooks, above the twins' yellow oilskins and Gav's awful army green anorak, and her few bits and pieces.

On the wall between the sitting room and kitchen doors hangs the portrait of Walter that James painted in the weeks following his death. Walter sits at his kitchen table, the remains of his bread-and-butter pudding in a blue-and-white bowl before him. Immaculate white shirt, dark green bow-tie, flushed cheeks, slightly tousled hair.

The painting is based on a photo James took at the dinner party Walter hosted two days before his death, the one Laura and the boys had attended. She can't look at it without feeling a lump in her throat. Two days he had left.

Laura's father has never seen the painting, or any other bit of the house. He's been invited but he's never shown up. Susan, of course, has visited several times. On her first trip she stayed a week, helping with the clear-up – the builders had just moved out – and insisting that Gavin and Laura had a few nights out while she was there.

'I want some quality time alone with my best boys,' she told them. 'We have lots of catching up to do, don't we?' And the twins were delighted, knowing they'd be allowed to stay up disgracefully late with Susan in charge.

The boys never mention Grandpa these days. They've probably forgotten what he looks like. Laura decided years ago that her birth must have been a complete accident – she couldn't imagine him ever agreeing to father a child. And in accepting his offer of marriage, Susan has probably forfeited her chance to have children. Love can be weird sometimes.

It's twins again, Laura emailed to Susan, as soon as Dr Jack had broken the news to her. *Might as well have two more while I'm at it*. Susan responded with a goody bag of Laura's favourite toiletries from Brown Thomas, along with a card full of excited congratulations, and a promise to visit as soon as she could. The card was signed by both of them: he'd taken the trouble to scrawl *Congratulations, Luke* in the distinctive hand that every art collector in Ireland was familiar with. Luke, never Dad.

She opens the drawing-room door and crosses to the enormous navy-and-white check couch – one of the few things they'd transported from Gav's house in Dublin – that fits beautifully in the generous bay window. She sinks into it, settling a lime green cushion at her back. Long day, she thinks. Good, though. Better than she'd been expecting.

Within a minute Gav appears, carrying a small glass. 'Medicinal,' he says, handing it over.

'Good lad.'

She raises the glass to her nose and inhales the rich fumes. She downs the brandy in one, the fierce burn of it coursing deliciously through her – easiest medicine in the world – and hands him back the glass.

He places it on the mantelpiece and takes a cherry red cushion from an armchair and sets it on the end of the couch. 'Lie down,' he orders, and Laura stretches out obediently, closing her eyes. 'Good call on the donkey rides,' he says, sitting on the other end, taking her feet into his lap and slipping off her shoes. 'I thought you'd lost it.'

She half opens her eyes and looks at him. He could do with a haircut. 'I know you did.'

He drops her shoes onto the carpet and begins to massage the balls of her feet with his thumbs. He's unexpectedly wonderful at massage. If massage was an Olympic event he'd get gold, no question. She pictures him standing on the podium, the Irish flag flapping behind him. If the B&B goes bankrupt he could set up as a masseur.

'I mean,' he says, 'she'd have been the last person I would have asked.'

'I know.'

Laura closes her eyes again, her hands resting on the substantial dome that shelters her unborn daughters. She feels them squirming around inside her – arguing, probably, about whose turn it is to kick Mammy.

Gav moves on to her toes, squeezing and pulling and circling each one gently in turn, taking his time with them. Bliss. She feels her neck and shoulders unclenching happily.

She supposes his wife taught him the art of massage. She doesn't ask.

'Made a tidy bit too,' he says.

'Sure did.'

A hundred and thirty-five euro, forty-five small customers in four hours. A fairly steady demand from the start, only one five-minute break for poor George from two o'clock to six but he took it all in his stride and behaved impeccably throughout the afternoon.

And Laura's spur-of-the-moment gamble has paid off. Who'd have guessed?

It started with Imelda's phone call on Thursday afternoon, just before the boys got home from school.

'I'd like to book a room for my sister and brother-in-law, if you have space. They'll be staying for two weeks. They're not coming till the beginning of July, but I wasn't sure how much notice you'd need.'

As organised as ever. Imelda would run an excellent B&B, never mix up a breakfast order, never leave someone without towels like Laura had done last week. Never skip mopping a bathroom floor in the hope that nobody would notice. (Nobody had – or if they did, they said nothing.)

'Let me have the dates,' Laura told her, 'and I'll check the bookings.'

The sister had been matron of honour at Imelda's wedding,

marching up the aisle ahead of the bride in a sensible navy jacket and skirt, looking like she wasn't at all sure about this business. Probably got the surprise of her life when Imelda told her she was getting married.

Laura hadn't spoken to her on the day, knew nothing about her and the husband except that they lived in Westport, and had stayed in Nell's house right after Laura and the boys. Would be interesting to see how like Imelda she was.

'How's your girl getting on?' Laura asked, when the booking had been safely made.

'She's ... fine.' A careful note in her voice. 'We don't see a lot of her actually. She likes to go off on her own a good bit.'

Not surprising. Hardly opened her mouth at Nell's, looked like she wanted to be anywhere else. Laura did catch her throwing a few sly glances in Andy's direction a couple of times, but that might have been because he was the only one her age there.

It could be shyness: she was at the age where social situations might feel like the worst form of torture. On the other hand, maybe she was just dying to see the back of Roone – it was hardly a laugh a minute at Hugh and Imelda's.

'She hasn't made any pals yet?'

'Well, no. Not that I'm aware of.'

And then the idea hopped out of nowhere into Laura's head – and jumped from there out of her mouth.

'She wouldn't fancy doing our donkey rides, would she? We had Andy lined up but obviously he's out of action for a while, and none of his pals seem keen to take over. Gav has offered to step in but I feel he has enough on his plate already. I'd rather we got someone else if we could.'

Even as the words were being spoken, Laura wondered what on earth had prompted the suggestion. But Eve looked capable enough – and you didn't have to be a talker to lead a donkey around a field. All you needed was a bit of sense. Right?

Silence at the other end of the line. And then, cautiously, 'Donkey rides?'

'Yes. They're scheduled to begin on Saturday. All she'd have to do would be to walk beside George, and hang on to whoever was on his back so they didn't fall off. It would be from two to six, Saturdays and Sundays to begin with, maybe more often if they go well, and payment would be on a commission-only basis – ten per cent of the takings. I thought it might be something for her to do.'

Another silence. Imelda was trying to think of a way to say no. And the more Laura thought about it, the dafter the notion seemed. Eve would be a disaster, she'd hate the prospect of putting herself out there in a crowd. She'd die rather than do it.

'Listen,' Laura said, 'don't worry about it, I just thought—'

'Oh, no,' Imelda said quickly. 'I think it's a wonderful idea. I'm just not sure if Eve … Can I talk to her and get back to you?'

'Absolutely. Tell her to give me a ring later on if she's interested.'

Hanging up, Laura was sure that that was the last she'd hear of it, and part of her – most of her – hoped she was right. Crazy idea, pregnancy hormones turning her batty again. They'd find someone else, or Gav would do it. They'd manage somehow.

But that evening her phone rang, and it was Eve.

'I'd like to do the donkey rides,' she said, her voice sounding small and distant, and Laura silently cursed her impetuousness as she arranged for Eve to come a bit early on Saturday so they could have a practice run with the boys. What else could she do, after offering the job?

Gav was surprised. Of course he was. 'You asked *her* to do the donkey rides? You said she didn't talk to anyone when you met her.'

'I know, but she's at a loose end, and I thought it might bring her out of herself a bit.'

And the look he gave her said *crazy pregnant woman*, and he had the sense not to say it aloud, even though she agreed wholeheartedly. And Laura woke in the middle of Friday night and thought, *What the hell have I done? She'll bankrupt us: someone will fall off and we'll be sued for everything we have, and plenty more. We'll have to leave Roone and go back to Dublin. We'll have to move in with Gladys.*

She prayed Eve would change her mind. She begged God to give her a dose of something non-life-threatening that would stop her coming. But Eve turned up on the dot of half one, by herself and on foot. And she took first Ben and then Seamus around the circuit on George's back, and she got the hang of the stepladder mounting and dismounting – Gavin's bright idea – right away.

'You're a natural,' Laura told her, and Eve blushed a bit and looked at her shoes, a hand resting casually on George's neck. They seemed to have taken to one another.

'Why is it all black around your eyes?' Ben asked, and Laura told him to shush, but Eve just said, 'Eyeliner', as if it was a perfectly logical question. More at ease, it appeared, with him and Seamus than with adults.

And from start to finish it all went swimmingly. And they made a hundred and thirty-five euro, and Eve earned thirteen euro fifty, which Laura bumped up to sixteen. A pittance for four hours' work, even if it was pretty undemanding stuff, but Eve seemed happy enough going home.

'See you tomorrow,' she said, tucking the money into her jeans and waving goodbye to the twins, who by the look of it thought she was pretty cool. Wonders would never cease.

Tomorrow Laura will offer her the navy top with the drawstring neckline. She'll say it doesn't fit her any more, which is quite true, and that she was looking for someone to give it to, which isn't true at all – she was expecting to be wearing it again by Hallowe'en – but she suspects Eve could use a few new bits and pieces.

And isn't her sixteenth birthday coming up? Didn't Nell say something about it the other day? Laura must talk to Imelda about that. The kid could do with having a bit of fun.

The pocket of her fleece begins to ring. She groans. Gavin pulls out her phone and looks at the display. 'Nell,' he says, and Laura holds out her hand.

'How did it go?' Nell asks.

Laura closes her eyes as Gav resumes the business of making her feet happy. 'Wait till you hear,' she replies.

✳

She didn't think anyone would want her to work for them. Laura must have been really stuck for someone.

She was wary of taking the job, wary of getting involved in anything here. But in the end she said yes because of the money, and because she likes little kids, and because she was getting a bit bored with the beach. She didn't have to get friendly with anyone; Laura probably wasn't interested in being friends anyway, after Eve doing her best to ignore them all when they'd met at Nell's house.

She'd turned up not really knowing what to expect. She'd never seen a donkey up close, and wasn't all that sure she wanted to. She had no idea what it would be like, leading him around a field all afternoon. What if he kicked her, or galloped off suddenly and she couldn't catch him?

But the minute she saw him she loved him. She loved him, with his big soft eyes and long nose and short legs. She loved the feel of his round warm body, and the way he gave a little shiver when she laid her palm on it. She loved how he stood so patiently beside the stepladder while she helped the children up and down. He wasn't a galloper, that was obvious.

'Good George,' she'd whisper every so often into his long ear, as he walked sedately beside her around the field. 'Best George' – and the ear would twitch and she'd know he was listening.

And she enjoyed the little kids, their excited faces when she put them up on the donkey. The questions they asked – what was his name, what did he eat, where did he sleep, did he have a mammy. Looking at her as if they were sure she knew all the answers. The trustful way the smaller ones held her hand, like Keith used to do.

And Laura's boys were gas in their yellow T-shirts. Sitting on the wooden bench beside the stepladder with their little leather money bag and roll of tickets, counting out change so carefully, taking their duties so seriously. Ben missing a tooth, so it was easy to tell them apart.

And Laura was nice. Laura *is* nice. Telling Eve she'd taken them out of a hole, telling her how delighted they were when she'd said yes to the job. Apologising for the sixteen euro, saying she hopes it'll be more tomorrow. Sixteen euro seems good enough reward for something you enjoyed doing, something that filled up your afternoon.

But she's only filling in until Andy is up to the job, however long that'll take. She'd thought he might be there today – just to check it out, seeing as how he lives right next door – but there was no sign of him. She hasn't laid eyes on him since the accident.

'How did you get on?' Imelda asked when she got back, when Gavin insisted on driving her back, saying she'd walked more than enough for one day. 'Did you like it?'

Eve told her she did.

'Was that Gavin driving off? I would have come and collected you if you'd rung.'

Eve said nothing.

'Are you tired now?'

Eve said, 'A bit.'

'Well, dinner will be about twenty minutes. You just have time for a shower if you want to freshen up.'

Eve said OK, and went upstairs.

In her room she adds the money she was given to the twenty she already has. Thirty-six euro now – and she'll get more every time she does the donkey rides. She'll have a decent bit to add to her savings when she goes back to Tralee.

She's looking forward to going back tomorrow. Not just because she'll see George and the twins, although that's good enough. She's looking forward to tomorrow because tomorrow he might call around, since he lives right next door.

You never know.

❋

If he puts a hand on either end of the cut and stretches the skin it helps a bit, forces the edges to come together, but when he's not doing that it looks pretty gruesome. The stitches are horrible, big black knotty things, twelve of them – and the thought of the thick thread snaking its way under his skin is gross. He's fairly sure they'll hurt coming out.

His ankle isn't throbbing any more and he's getting better on the crutches, but he can't play football or walk John Silver, so he's been housebound most of the time since he got home, surfing the net or reading, or writing a bit.

'Between us,' Nell says, 'we have three legs and three arms, which is practically an invincible force.' Trying to be cheerful about it, but he can see she's pretty fed up with not being able to work. They tried playing cards but all Nell knows is gin rummy, which Andy last played when he was nine or ten, and beggar my neighbour, which he'd never heard of but which sounded suspiciously childish, and snap, which he hates, and which Nell can't really manage anyway with her cast.

Uncle Tim brought him Call of Duty: Black Ops II, which will make him the envy of his pals, and a 4GB stick of RAM to make sure his laptop can cope, but what Andy really wants to do is get his stitches out, which should be happening next week, and fling away the crutches, which might take a bit longer, and have his face looking halfway decent again, which he hopes will happen eventually.

Laura's been in to see them every afternoon since they came home from the hospital. She's brought grapes and eggs and walnut whips, and get-well cards made by the boys.

'Eve is going to do the donkey rides,' she'd told Andy yesterday. 'Only until you're better, then you can take over.'

He can't imagine it. She'll glare at the children, ignore their parents. She'll be a disaster – she'll close down the rides after a day. Word will spread: people will stay away. There'll be no job to take over when he's better.

They didn't stay away today though. He could hear them, even from before two o'clock. Children's voices, lots of them. He imagined her leading George silently around, imagined the parents watching her, then looking at one another to see if everyone thought the same.

He wanted to peer over the stone wall – he was dying to see how it was going – but he stayed away. He couldn't be caught sneaking a look, not with his face the way it is.

He was in the sitting room a while ago when he heard Nell on her phone in the kitchen, after Tim and Gran had left.

'How did it go?' Nell asked, and he lowered the volume on his laptop, and from Nell's surprised reaction – 'Really?... I don't believe it ... *Was* she? ... That much, really? ... Well, that's good to hear' – he could gather that the donkey rides had, in fact, gone rather well.

He stands in front of his bedroom mirror now, leaning on his crutches as he examines his damaged face. 'Keep applying the vitamin-E oil,' Gran had told him. 'You'll see the difference eventually.'

'It gives you character,' his dad had said. 'All the girls will want to go out with Scarface.'

Andy doesn't imagine a scar will make him any more popular, but maybe the girls he knows will get used to it and not notice after a while. He'll just have to wait and see. In the meantime he'll lie low, and not even show his face next door.

Especially not next door.

THURSDAY, 27 JUNE

'The first time I met Nell,' Colette says, 'I warmed to her. There was a freshness about her that I found appealing. Of course, I've since realised it was Roone I saw in her, the legacy of being brought up on a small island. She seemed … *unsullied*, if that makes any sense.'

It doesn't make a lot of sense to Denis. It sounds like anyone who wasn't brought up on Roone must be sullied. But he smiles and says nothing as the ferry ploughs its usual furrow through the sea to the island.

They stand at the rail, as he's stood so often. How many times, he wonders, has he made this journey? Thousands, tens of thousands? He remembers crossing the sea to secondary school every day as a teen with the handful of other scholars. No car ferry then, just a few enterprising fishermen coming together in an informal sort of co-op to bring island people to and fro in their boats. No cars on the island till the early sixties – hard to believe now.

'I'm sure you're glad to be on holidays,' Colette says. 'No more alarm clocks.'

'Yes,' he says. 'That part will be very welcome.'

But the alarm didn't bother him: he never objected to getting up in the mornings. Except maybe in the depths of winter, with howling gales and rain pelting against the window, and only wet blackness when you pushed the curtains apart. But once the mornings got brighter it was a pleasure to open his eyes and see the light coming in, even if it was still raining.

He had never woken up with Claire. They had never fallen asleep together. He would have liked to, just once. He would have liked to watch her sleep, see her face with all its guards down.

'And no going back after the summer this time,' Colette says. 'That must be a little terrifying.'

Denis looks out over the sea. 'I might do some travelling.'

'Yes, good idea. Now that you have the time to go off-season, when things are quieter.'

But when he thinks of unpacking his solitary suitcase in some strange bedroom, he feels dubious. Standing at the Trevi fountain, surrounded by couples and families and groups of friends. Sitting alone before a breathtaking view or a marvellous sunset, thinking only of the one you yearn to share it with.

'I gave up my job when the boys came along,' Colette says, 'but of course that was different, with children to raise. I didn't have time to relish my freedom, or regret leaving the social life of work behind.'

Denis has no idea what work she did. He knows virtually

nothing about her, apart from the fact that she's Nell's mother-in-law, and a widow for the past dozen years or so. Nell never met her husband, dead before she and Tim got together. He wonders if Colette went back to work after he died, or if he'd left her financially secure enough not to have to.

She's undoubtedly attractive, and well turned out. And intelligent and educated and well spoken. He suspects that Nell is attempting some crude form of matchmaking by arranging for them to be travelling to Roone together today.

'She's going to Tralee in the morning,' Nell had told him on the phone. 'She wants to do some shopping – she's having us to dinner on Friday night. Tim isn't going – he's setting up a website for James's paintings – so Colette is getting a bus from the ferry port to Tralee. Since you're coming out anyway I thought she could get a lift back with you.'

'I'm not sure what time I'll be travelling,' Denis said. 'I could be held up a bit at the school.'

'Not a problem – she'll wander around the shops, she doesn't mind what time she comes back. Would I give you her number, and you could text and arrange to meet when it suited you?'

So he took the number – what else could he do? And he sent the text as promised, and picked her up outside the library, and here they are.

'I hope they gave you a good send-off,' she says, her pink scarf fluttering in the breeze that's coming off the sea.

'They did,' he says. 'I'm well and truly retired now.'

He couldn't say it had been excruciating, but it hadn't fallen very short. The whole school waiting for him when he'd walked into the hall, along with pretty much the entire board of management, the parish priest and what looked to him like at least half the parent body.

'A small affair' was how the vice principal had put it, following Denis to his office after the morning break. 'Half eleven in the hall,' he'd said, and Denis sat in his office and listened to the chatter of the classes, oblivious to their shushing teachers, as they passed his door one after another on their way to the hall to bid him goodbye.

Speeches from the priest and the vice principal, both thick with cliché; a rendition of the school song by the children; a presentation of flowers and a card from the boy and girl in sixth class who were picked for everything, by virtue of his father being a parent rep on the board and her having won the school a clatter of computers in a poetry competition the previous year.

A second presentation, this time from a blushing parent, of a beautiful piece of pottery, a ceramic rendition of a currach, complete with flat-capped boatman, created by a local artist. A gift, it turned out, from the entire parent body, putting the staff's miserable bouquet firmly in its place.

Denis thanked everyone, making no specific mentions. He told them he'd enjoyed his two years at the school, but now it was time to move on. He kept it short, conscious of the shuffling of small feet, the hot stale air of the hall. He wished them all a happy summer. They clapped their appreciation and trooped out, back to their classes to pack up and go home.

'I envy you, having been brought up here,' Colette says, as

the island draws closer. 'I would have loved growing up on Roone.'

So many times he's heard non-islanders express a similar sentiment. He wonders how many of them, given the chance of going back and reliving their youths in a place with no cinema, no disco or nightclub, no wine bars or theatres or fast-food outlets, would take up the opportunity.

How many would be happy with a library that arrived in the back of a lorry once a week and stayed for two hours, or a ferry that stopped operating at ten o'clock every summer evening, and earlier in the winter?

He drops Colette at James's old house, glancing at the one a few doors down, the one that every islander could identify. A colourful beach towel thrown over the garden seat in front, a black car parked in the driveway. He imagines a little girl walking away from it early one morning, and never coming back.

'Can I offer you a cup of tea?' Colette asks. 'Or you might prefer a glass of wine.'

Her scent is heady and sweetish. Claire wore a grapefruit perfume – he would nose out the places where she'd applied it. 'Here,' he'd say, 'and here.' Working his way around her body, pressing his face to her skin, lifting a foot to sniff an instep, parting her toes in turn as she lay pliant. Kissing his way back up to her mouth. Taking the scenic route.

'I won't delay,' he tells Colette. 'I'm anxious to see Nell – I missed her last weekend.'

'In that case I won't hold you. But I hope you'll join us for dinner tomorrow night.'

'Thank you. That would be lovely.'

She's not his type, too self-assured and polished for him; and he's fairly sure she hasn't the slightest interest in him. He imagines a little black book full of Dublin men's phone numbers, well-off widowers and divorcés who are lining up to take her out. And he's not looking for anyone new, definitely not.

When he reaches Nell's house the only one there is Andy. 'She's next door,' he tells Denis. 'There's a party on. She said she won't be long.'

'What's the occasion?'

'A birthday.'

He's not exactly a mine of information. 'Whose is it? Not the twins?'

Andy rubs his nose. 'No, just someone who's here for the summer. The one who's staying with Hugh and Imelda.'

Ah, the quiet girl from the beach. Denis wonders why Andy isn't there – surely he would have been invited. Didn't feel like showing his face maybe, with that nasty-looking cut slicing its way down one side. 'When are the stitches coming out?'

'Tomorrow.'

'That's good … and is your father around?'

'He's at work.'

'Fine. Well, I'll head over to my place and come back later, just for a chat. Tell Nell I'll do my own food.'

'OK.'

When he reaches his house Denis takes the ceramic currach from its box and makes room for it on the sitting-room mantelpiece. He arranges the staff's flowers in a vase and places it in the centre of the kitchen table. He slides the accompanying card from its envelope – and when he opens it a book token for €100 falls out.

With every good wish from the staff of St Brendan's, he reads, their signatures scattered underneath. He feels a fleeting guilt at having despised their stinginess before stowing the token in his wallet. He tears up their card – he's not that guilty – and deposits the pieces in the bin under the sink.

It feels good to put that part of his life behind him, good to think he won't be meeting them again, won't have to put on a professional face and pretend he's not aware of their rudeness.

He's on summer holidays, and it's looking like there's a distinct chance it won't rain non-stop for the next few months. He feels a lifting of his heart as he puts two eggs on to boil and unwraps the wedge of cheese Colette had insisted on giving him in return for the lift: *I hope you like it stinky*, she'd said, handing it over.

He does like it stinky. He lifts it to his nose and inhales its gloriously intense earthiness, its barnyard pungency. Probably cost her a fair bit in some fancy deli. He wonders if she was born into money or married it.

Tim has money. Plenty, by the look of it. A year-old BMW parked outside James's place, the one that had brought them to the wedding. A house recently purchased in the Dublin mountains. A full partner in the firm he joined just a few years ago.

Amazing that James is so different: no worldly goods to speak of, no obvious ambition to make his fortune. But in

Denis's opinion, money and happiness, if not exactly mutually exclusive, rarely make comfortable bedfellows. Nell and James have enough money to live the life they want – all the fortune anyone needs, surely.

He quarters a tomato, opens a jar of pickles and takes the lid off a tub of coleslaw. He cuts and butters a slice from a loaf of brown soda bread that was waiting for him on the worktop. When the eggs have boiled he shells and chops them, and arranges everything on a plate with a thick wedge of the cheese. He eats his dinner sitting on the step outside the back door, flapping at the flies when they wander over.

A dog, he thinks. He'll get himself a dog as soon as he's settled back here. He has an idea Nell mentioned someone's dog having pups not so long ago – was it the O'Callaghans'? He would have had a dog before this but Moira was more of a cat person, so they'd gone through a succession of cats ending with Felix, a demanding tabby that had died of peritonitis two months before Moira was knocked down.

He finishes his meal and checks the sky and finds no sign of rain for the rest of the evening. He'll shower and change and walk over to Nell's, and begin to settle into the gentler rhythms of summertime.

✳

Tim turns on his stool, doing a slow sweep of the pub, taking in the scattered afternoon drinkers, the empty fireplace, the collection of framed photographs of island life through the generations, all donated by customers. The large-scale map of

Roone on the far wall, tourist attractions, beaches and walking trails indicated. 'Nothing changes around here.'

James grins. 'You say that like it's a bad thing.'

'And you seem to think it's good.'

'I do.'

Tim gestures with his glass at the display of liqueurs behind the counter. 'Bet nobody looks for those.'

James leans against the shelves, folds his arms. 'You'd be surprised.'

'I would.' He sips his gin and tonic, yawns, cracks the knuckles of both hands in turn. 'Nell always hated me doing that.'

James keeps his smile in place. 'And what does Katy think?'

'Doesn't even notice.'

James scoops ice from its bucket into a glass, drops in a lemon slice. He tops up the glass with water from the tap and drinks.

'Website pretty much there,' Tim remarks. 'Few tweaks and it's done.'

James runs a sleeve past his mouth. 'Thanks for that.'

'No problem.'

He hadn't asked for a website – he's happy to offer his paintings to the galleries he's always dealt with, happy to let them find customers – but Tim offered to design one. 'You'd sell direct, have no commission to pay,' he said, and it seemed churlish to refuse, although James figures he'd probably charge a lot less than the galleries if someone offered to buy direct from him, so he could well end up losing money. He plans to ignore the site once it's set up, and Tim will be none the wiser.

A man signals from one of the tables. James nods and begins to fill a pint glass with cider.

'Something to run by you,' Tim says.

'What's that then?'

'I was thinking of staying on here for a bit.'

James glances up. 'Staying on Roone?'

'Yeah, if there's nobody waiting to use the house.'

'Hang on.' James delivers the drink and returns. 'Fine by me,' he says, ringing in the purchase on the till. 'What about Ma, though? Does she not want to get back to Dublin?' Their mother's social life was far busier than James's, with frequent trips to the theatre and concert hall, book-club meetings – she was a member of at least two – and midweek hotel breaks with various groups.

'She'll go back on Saturday as planned. I can run her to the station in Tralee.'

Sounds like it's all arranged. 'Is Katy coming down with Lily?'

'Maybe. It'll depend on her mother.'

James wipes down the counter. 'You've got more holidays coming to you?'

'I'm a partner,' Tim says. 'I can set my own holidays.' A small edge in his tone that doesn't escape James. 'And I can work from here if I want. I can work anywhere.'

I can work from here: the irony hits James immediately. It was Tim's insistence, once he was made a partner, that Nell move to Dublin after they were married that had ultimately caused her to call off the wedding. And now he's back on the island, and working from Roone isn't a problem any more.

Without his wife and child.

'So how long would you be staying?'

Tim shrugs. 'Dunno yet … Another week, maybe a bit longer. Unless you have a problem with my being here.' He raises his glass and drains it.

James waits until he lowers it again. He waits for eye contact. 'Of course not. The house is empty. You're welcome to it.'

Tim smiles, rattling the remaining ice cubes in his glass. 'Thanks, bro. I'll try not to trash the place.'

'I'd appreciate that.'

Her name isn't mentioned again by either of them.

✳

It couldn't have worked out better.

'I'm delighted with how she's doing,' Laura had said on the phone on Sunday night. 'She's so careful with the little kiddies, and my boys think she's cool even though she doesn't say a lot – maybe that's why. Anyway, I wanted to thank her, since she's working for such a pittance, and I thought a surprise party here might be nice.'

'A party?'

'Yes, for her birthday. Nell says it's this Thursday. Did she get that right?'

'She did, it is—'

'So my plan was to ask her to come over on Thursday afternoon to deliver leaflets door to door about the donkey rides. That'll keep her busy for about an hour, and when she gets back we'll make a bit of a fuss. What do you think? Or had you anything planned yourself?'

All Imelda had planned was a cake for dessert that evening, maybe with a few candles pushed in. No fuss: Eve would hate a fuss. No party with everyone invited, like she'd been planning before Eve's arrival, before she discovered how much the girl resisted any friendly overture. But if Laura was willing to take the chance on having her efforts thrown back in her face, who was Imelda to stop her?

'I hadn't much planned really,' she told Laura. 'I could bake a cake for it, if you like.'

'I was hoping you'd say that. And you'll come, of course, and Nell says she and Andy will drop in. And Thursday is Hugh's day off, isn't it? Bring him along and we can pretend it's his party too, for the one he missed.'

And just like that, Imelda's anxieties about practically ignoring Eve's sixteenth birthday were washed away. 'It sounds great,' she said. 'Thank you so much. Are you sure you don't mind the extra work?'

'What work? All I'm doing is taking a few sausage rolls and chicken wings from the freezer and putting them into the oven, and making a bit of jelly. Nell said she'll bring ice-cream, and you're making the cake – and get Hugh to rob a few bags of crisps and peanuts from the pub. *Voilà* – we have a party. It'll be a laugh.'

So like Laura to magic a party out of nowhere. Imelda hoped Eve wouldn't seem too ungrateful. So hard to know how she'd react: a surprise party could go in any direction. But she's doing alright, by the sound of it, with the donkey rides, which is wonderful. Maybe she gets on better with Laura. Maybe a younger woman would be able to connect more with her.

And look at her now, dressed in a very nice navy top Imelda hasn't seen up to this – she must have been saving it for her birthday. The neckline a little low, but never mind. And she actually appears … if not exactly happy, at least not as sullen as she usually does.

Taken aback, certainly, to find them all waiting for her when she returned from her leaflet deliveries with the twins. She stopped dead, mouth open in surprise at the sight of everyone gathered around the patio table where everything had been laid out – for an awful moment Imelda was afraid she was about to turn and run.

But then Laura, maybe fearful of the very same thing, took her by the arm and steered her to the empty chair between Nell and Hugh.

'It's nothing much,' she said, 'just a little surprise to wish you a happy birthday. We couldn't let sweet sixteen go by, now could we?'

They sang 'Happy Birthday', and then they sang it a second time for Hugh, and a tiny hint of a smile finally appeared on Eve's face as the twins demanded that she blow out her candles and make a wish. Imelda wondered what she wished for, and then decided she was probably better off not knowing.

And now she's eating cake and looking fairly relaxed, even if she's still not saying very much to anyone apart from the twins, who do seem to have taken a fancy to her. A little pile of opened presents sits by her plate – a trio of pretty hair slides from Laura, a toy donkey from the twins, a pair of green flip-flops from Nell (how on earth did she know her shoe size?).

Imelda and Hugh have already given their gift. Imelda handed over a card with thirty euro tucked into it when Eve appeared in the kitchen at lunchtime as usual. Money seemed like the safest gift to Imelda, even if it was horribly impersonal.

'Happy birthday,' she said, 'from both of us.'

Eve took the card and thanked her, and slipped it into her jeans pocket without opening it. Presumably she investigated it as soon as she went upstairs after lunch to get her jacket, but no further comment was made before she headed off to deliver the leaflets. Imelda didn't like her thinking they hadn't planned a party, but she couldn't very well tell her it was waiting for her at Laura's.

Eve has been living with them for a month, more or less. They're a third of the way there. They'll manage, now that Imelda has accepted that Eve isn't interested in making friends with them. They're doing like Hugh suggested at the start: looking after Eve as best they can, and hoping for someone more cheerful next time.

The party breaks up. Nell is the first to leave, telling them that her father is due, and also that she wants to check up on Andy, who didn't turn up after all – a stomach bug, according to Nell. Pity he wasn't there, someone Eve's own age instead of just two little children and a group of adults. He might have been ignored, of course, but still.

'Want a lift home?' she asks Eve as she and Hugh get ready to go – and Eve, as expected, replies that she'll walk.

✳

'He's staying on?'

'He is, another week or so.'

'Doesn't he have to get back to work?'

'Apparently not.'

'And what about Colette? Is she staying too?'

'No, she's getting the train home on Saturday. He's bringing her to Tralee.'

'And Katy and Lily? Are they coming down?'

'He doesn't know. He says it depends on how her mother is.'

Nell lies in the dark, digesting it. He's not going back to Dublin with his mother. He's staying on Roone. On *Roone*, which he never seemed to become attached to, even when he was spending every weekend here, and they were planning to spend the rest of their lives on the island.

Or maybe he'd never been planning that – maybe it had always been his intention that Nell would move to Dublin, and he had been biding his time until he could figure out a way to get her to agree to that.

'Nell? Are you awake?'

'Yes.'

'What do you think?'

She lets a few seconds pass as she considers her reply. 'I think it's strange,' she says slowly. 'Tim never got to love the island like you did. I kept hoping that would change, and that Roone would work its charm on him, like it did with you and Andy – and Laura and Gavin – but it never happened.'

'No . . .'

And now he's going to put his mother on a train and return

here alone. He's going to stay on Roone in James's house for a week or so, and Katy may or may not show up with Lily. All a bit peculiar.

She moves closer to James, places her good hand on his chest. Not something, she decides, that need bother her unduly. Her eyelids are heavy but she's wary of going to sleep. To sleep is to risk another flashback; a second one last evening as she was dropping off, four days after the first. Just as vivid, and every bit as disturbing. Jolting her from near-sleep, making her heart thump painfully in her chest, throwing her back into those horrifying seconds when the Italian couple's car loomed in front of her, and there wasn't a thing she could do to avoid it.

Don't think about that now, think about something else.

'Looked like Eve enjoyed her party today.'

James strokes her arm. 'That's good.'

'Pity Andy didn't come.'

He gives a soft laugh.

'What?'

'Nothing.'

'I'm not matchmaking, if that's what you think.'

'No, of course not. By the way, my mother thinks your father is just *dreamy*.'

She thumps him lightly on the chest. 'Shut up.'

He grabs her hand and brings it to his mouth – and that starts a whole new series of events.

She's still a little tender, but he's gentle, and they manage.

*

A birthday party, for her. A proper party, with wrapped-up presents, and a cake and candles. They sang 'Happy Birthday'. She blew out the candles and didn't cry, although she really, really wanted to. Not crying this afternoon was one of the hardest things she's ever had to do.

And she didn't make a wish. Look what had happened when she'd wished she could see Mam again, when she'd done everything she could to make her wish come true. Look how that had turned out.

'I don't want you back,' Mam told her, when the fostering agency had finally arranged a meeting, three years after Eve and Keith had been taken into care. 'I can't look after you, I can't look after myself.' Huddled into a too-big coat that smelt of fish, holding it closed with a shaking yellow-fingered bitten-nailed hand. 'Look at me, I'm a mess,' Mam told her, with a mouth of intermittent yellowy-brown teeth, scabby sores around her nose and defeated eyes. 'You're better off with the Garveys.'

Better off with the Garveys, when Derek does what he does, every chance he gets.

Don't tell, he said, when he did it for the first time. When Eve was ten and he was fifteen, two weeks after she'd moved in with them. *If you tell they won't believe you. I'll say you're making it up, and they'll take you out of here and put you into a loony bin for the rest of your life.* And the thought of that was so terrifying that she let him do it, and said nothing.

And he's still doing it, and she's still saying nothing, because she knows that what he says is true. Nobody will believe her. Not Mrs Garvey, who adores him, or his sister Valerie, who's nice to

Eve when they're at home with her parents but who tells her not to come near her in school, and who sniggers about Eve to her friends. And not Mr Garvey, who watches television most of the time, and who has never, as far as Eve remembers, used her name.

And she's too scared to say it to anyone in the agency in case the other part is true too, and they lock her up in a loony bin. So she's waiting until she's eighteen when nobody can stop her leaving the Garveys' house.

And in the meantime she's careful not to let anyone in, because if she lets someone in she might be tempted to tell them, and if they don't believe her she'll be carted off. So she pushes them all away, does everything she can to keep them from getting in. It's horrible to have nobody, it makes her feel lonely all the time, but it's safer.

When she's eighteen she'll get a job, maybe something with animals or children, but she'll take what she can get. She'll find a place to live, some flat big enough for two people – she's got over two hundred euro saved, not counting the money she's getting here – and then she'll take Keith out of the Begleys' house and bring him to live with her.

She turns over and closes her eyes and tries not to think about the boy who didn't bother coming to her birthday party today. He doesn't matter, he makes no difference. In eight more weeks she'll never see him again. It's good he didn't come today: she has a feeling he might be someone she'd be tempted to let in.

All she has to do is get through the next two years.

SATURDAY, 29 JUNE

'I get the impression she's terrified to let her guard down, poor creature. From what Nell tells me she's had it tough.' Laura tucks in a corner of the sheet. No more fitted: a pain to iron. Learning as she goes along.

'I did think asking her to do the donkey rides might bite me in the behind – sorry, Walter – but I have to say she worked out fine, and for some reason the boys have become her number one fans.' She gives a flick of her duster to the dressing table, the windowsill, the lockers. Checks the wardrobe and finds nothing.

'We had a surprise birthday party on Thursday for her. Nothing fancy. I hope she liked it. Hard to know with her. Sweet sixteen, I remember it well. I had two fellows after me, but I liked one of their older brothers – and didn't he announce about a week later that he was going into the priesthood. Gorgeous-looking, awful waste. I was in mourning until I met Aaron.'

She goes into the en-suite and gathers towels, facecloths,

bath mat. Place not too messy, thankfully. The Cotters hadn't looked the type to leave a mess. You can usually tell.

'Tim Baker is staying on here, sending mother back to Dublin on the train this afternoon. And wife and baby up in Donegal – what do you make of that? Good-looking man, I have to say – I can see what attracted Nell.'

She drops her bundle on top of the pile of sheets on the landing and moves into the next bedroom. Two walkers here, left at the crack of dawn – didn't want a cooked breakfast, praise the Lord, happy with the bread and cereals she put out for them last evening, with instructions to help themselves to yogurt from the fridge.

Left their dishes in a neat pile on the draining board, along with their rinsed-out yogurt pots. Her kind of guests.

'Isn't it lovely and quiet? The boys are gone with Gav on his rounds. They're on school holidays since yesterday, God help us all, but he's going to take them with him every morning – let's hope the novelty doesn't wear off. And from today we're doing the donkey rides every afternoon, weather permitting, so that'll keep them out of trouble.'

She lowers herself onto the end of a stripped bed. 'I don't mind telling you, Walter, that I will be damn glad – sorry – when these babies come out. I feel like I'm hefting a sack of potatoes around with me. Can't remember the boys being this much of a load, but I was nine years younger then. Or maybe girls weigh heavier, all those extra hormones.'

As she heaves herself to her feet, a clatter is heard on the stairs. 'Ah – they're back. End of our peace. Talk later, Walter.'

'Mum!' They burst into the room, faces alight. 'Guess what!'

'Don't kill me, I had nothing to do with it.' Gavin appears in the doorway. 'And I haven't said yes, I told them they had to ask you.'

Laura looks warily at the small eager faces. 'Ask me what.'

'Can we have a pup?'

Laura's mouth drops open. 'What? No.'

'Pleeeeeease, Mum!'

'No, absolutely not.' She glares at Gavin.

'They just saw them,' he says, 'when we went to O'Callaghan's. There was nothing I could do. I didn't say yes.'

Ben looks at him indignantly. 'You did – you said it was OK if Mum says yes.'

'Yeah – you said it could be our birthday present.'

'Birthday present?' Laura looks at Gavin incredulously. 'Their birthday isn't for months – and we are NOT getting a pup, no way.'

'Aw, Muuuuuuum.'

'Listen,' Laura says firmly, 'we have a donkey, a pig and twenty-eight hens – which are supposed to be looked after by you two, I might mention—'

'But we *do*!'

'You do *not* – I have to ask you every day to feed them or collect the eggs, and I *still* end up doing it myself half the time, or Gav does.' Gavin opens his mouth to speak, and she silences him with a look. 'If we got a pup, I know who'd have to look after it.'

'But Mum—'

'But Mum nothing. We are *not* getting a pup and that's final.'

Two dejected faces. She hardens her heart. 'We'll talk later,' she promises Gavin.

He looks as dejected as the boys. Pity about him. She indicates the bundle of laundry. 'Gather the stuff from the en-suite, and the rest is on the landing. And you two, go and check the field and see that everything is ready for the donkey rides.'

After they've trailed out she makes her way to the main bedroom, where she kicks off her shoes and stretches out on the bed.

She would have liked a dog growing up but her father was allergic – or so they'd told her. She remembers Norma Kelleher getting a pup for her birthday one year, remembers daydreaming about Norma dying in some horrible accident and her parents being so devastated they couldn't look at the pup and Laura taking it off their hands. The only pets she remembers having were goldfish, and they weren't exactly bursting with personality.

But a pup now, when the place is already crawling with animals, and she's six weeks away from taking possession of two infants – out of the question, abominable timing. Maybe in about five years' time, when she can run the B&B blindfold, and babies and all they bring with them are a distant memory.

As she feels her eyes closing she imagines she hears a faint yapping sound. Power of suggestion, she thinks, drifting off.

✳

Andy's face lights up like a Christmas tree. 'For me?'

'For you,' James replies. 'Thought you could use a treat, after what happened.'

'Brilliant – thanks, Dad.'

'Not sure John Silver's too happy, though.'

They regard the small reddish-brown pup, leaping excitedly around John Silver as the older dog, lying in his customary position by the stone wall, makes a valiant effort to ignore it.

'Does Nell know?' Andy asks.

'No, but she'll be fine.'

Dr Jack's removal of Andy's stitches has made a marked improvement to the appearance of his face. Maybe, James thinks, surgical stitches are deliberately made to look as if a small child put them in; maybe it's a cunning ploy to make the injury look radically better when they're not there any more.

Not that anyone looking at him would miss the scar, which is still very much in evidence. But hopefully time and the stuff he's rubbing into it every day will fade it, at least to the point where nobody remarks on it.

'How about a name?' James asks.

Andy considers, eyes still on the pup. 'Yeah, I'll think about that.' He whistles and extends a hand, and the little dog immediately turns and darts towards him, tail wagging frantically. Andy reaches down and takes him onto his lap, and the pup plants front paws on his chest and licks enthusiastically at his chin.

Instant bonding, James thinks. Should have got him a dog years ago when they'd moved to the island. Might have helped him in his grief . . . Might have managed to do what James hadn't.

'How long are they gone?' he asks. 'Nell and Gran.'

'About an hour.'

He gets to his feet. 'I'll go and meet them. You'll be OK with Buster?'

'Yeah – and it definitely won't be Buster.'

'Scamp. Rover. Patch. Spot.'

'Dad, just go.'

James grins and leaves the room.

✳

'Only sixty,' Colette says quietly.

'Yes.'

'Such a loss.'

'How old was your husband?' Nell asks.

'Fifty-five, four years older than me.'

'God.'

They stand in silence before Moira's grave. A couple of cars pass on the road. Rain begins to patter lightly, causing Nell to draw up the hood of her jacket and Colette to push open her pale yellow umbrella.

'Are you feeling alright?' Colette asks eventually. 'Not sorry we walked?'

'I'm fine, just sorry I'm so slow.'

'Don't be silly.'

Her energy levels mightn't have returned to normal yet, but twelve days after the accident her bruising has practically disappeared, a tiny residual tenderness all that remains. Her ribs have healed too, and the cuts to her face and arms. Her wrist is still out of action, with no hope of a return to work for two or three more weeks, according to Dr Jack. 'You'll need a bit of physio when the cast comes off,' he's told her, 'just a session or two to show you some exercises that will get it back to full strength. But you could do a bit of hairdressing straight away, go back part-time if you wanted.'

She mourns the loss of her car, the thirty-four-year-old Beetle she'd bought from a farmer's widow living outside Killarney a few months after moving back to Roone from Dublin. It was only twenty-six then, a year younger than Nell, and five hundred euros was all she paid for it. The colour of buttercups and not a mark on it, inside or out.

'Timmy wasn't allowed in with his wellingtons,' the woman had told Nell. 'I told him it was a lady's car.'

'We'll get you another one,' James has promised. 'When you're back to normal we'll have a look.'

It won't be the same, though. She loved that car, loved its round little body, its cheery colour.

'Nell,' Colette says, 'may I confide in you?'

'Of course.'

'I'm worried about Tim.'

It takes her by surprise. She waits for more, a small uneasiness flaring within her at the mention of his name.

Colette hesitates, a finger tapping lightly on the yellow base of the umbrella handle. 'Maybe worried is too strong, but I'm a bit concerned. I'm not sure why, really. There's nothing specific I can point to, it's just a feeling I have, a sort of … disquiet about him.'

A mother's intuition, not to be ignored. Nell is unsure how to respond. 'You haven't said anything to him?'

'Oh no … Like I say, I have nothing to go on. He just doesn't seem himself lately – he's a bit quieter than normal … Oh, I'm probably being fanciful, I hope I am. It's just, I wondered if he'd said anything to James.'

Nell shakes her head. 'If he has, James hasn't mentioned it to me.'

But he wouldn't, would he? The last thing James would do, she suspects, is share any problem of Tim's with her. She wonders what precisely is causing Colette's unease – because despite what she says, something must have triggered it. Is she afraid there's a more sinister reason for Katy's non-appearance on Roone? But Katy would never have pretended that her mother was sick – would she?

Maybe she hadn't pretended, though. Tim was the one who'd told them, not Katy. Maybe Colette had heard it from him too. Maybe Katy and Tim had had a row and Katy had gone off in a huff with Lily, and Tim had concocted the story of her mother's illness to save face.

She dismisses the thought as soon as it forms itself: who's being fanciful now? Surely he'd know there was a good chance that Colette would ring Katy to ask after her mother, and his lie would be exposed. No, he'd never be that reckless.

But there's still something not right about him staying on here, with Katy and Lily at the other end of the country. Nell can't deny that it's crossed her own mind.

'You know, it's probably all in my head, dear,' Colette says.

'Forget I said anything – and maybe we should be heading back. This rain doesn't look like it's going to ease up.'

And just like that the subject is dropped, and not spoken of again on the way back to Nell's house. But Nell ponders it silently – and by the time they meet James on the road an idea is forming in her head.

✳

The rain doesn't put them off. They stand patiently in line, plastic-raincoated, some in wellingtons, holding on to a parent's hand as they watch the donkey making his sedate way around and around the field. Some familiar faces, Eve is amused to see.

'You don't have to do it in this weather,' Laura told her. 'We can put up a sign to say it's cancelled' – but Eve said she didn't mind. What else would she be doing?

'If it gets too heavy I can stop,' she said, and Laura agreed, if Eve was sure.

'Oh, and I have another top, if you're interested. Don't feel you have to take it.'

It's bright green, a colour Eve wouldn't normally go for, but when she held it to her face she liked the contrast with her red hair. It's cut low in the front, like the navy one. There's a slit in the centre of the neckline, held together with a leather thong that you can loosen to show a bit more.

'You're well endowed, like me,' Laura said. 'I had the biggest chest in my class at school, got my first bra at twelve.'

Eve's first bra was bought by Mrs Garvey when Eve was

thirteen. 'You're getting to be a big girl,' Mrs Garvey said, staring at the front of Eve's school blouse. 'We'd better get you sorted.' She made Eve take off her blouse and stand in her vest while she got a tape measure. 'Thirty-six,' she said in a sour voice. 'Bigger than myself.'

Valerie Garvey is six months older than Eve and much smaller on top. She was still as flat as a boy at thirteen, but she badgered her mother until she got her own bra too. Eve saw it on the clothes line: two triangles, like a little girl's bikini top.

Derek made Eve show him her bra a few evenings after she got it. He put his hands inside it and squeezed. 'Titties,' he said, rubbing himself against her. 'Big juicy titties.'

Laura's chest is enormous. 'I'm not normally this huge,' she told Eve. 'It's because I'm pregnant. But I'm a big girl the rest of the time.' Her chest pushes out the shirts she wears; it makes the buttons pull away from their buttonholes. 'Gav will never be able to wear these shirts again,' she said to Eve with a wink. 'He'll look as if he has boobs.'

She's nice, it's hard not to like her. But Eve imagines telling her about the things Derek Garvey does to her, and makes her do to him, and sees the smile slipping off Laura's face. No more winking after that bit of news.

Every time Eve walks George past the stone wall that divides the field from the house next door she hears a dog yapping, but it doesn't sound like the dog that was there when she and Imelda went to dinner: it sounds like a smaller, younger dog. Maybe they got Andy a pup to cheer him up after the accident.

She'd glanced over the wall a while ago – she'd led the

donkey off his track a bit so she could see onto the patio – but nobody was there.

Her shoes are getting wet: she should have worn the flip-flops Nell gave her for her birthday. ('What size shoes do you take?' Laura had asked, the weekend before. 'I have a pair of boots ...' but anyone could see she had much smaller feet than Eve. Had she asked just to discover Eve's shoe size?)

As they round Caesar's sty she looks up towards the hen run and sees an old man in a tweedy jacket and grey trousers, and the kind of flat cap worn by countrymen. He's just standing there, next to the henhouse. Facing her, but too far away for her to make out his features clearly.

As she watches, wondering who he is, he bows his head slightly and lifts his cap an inch. She looks behind her to see if he's saluting someone else, but nobody is there – and when she turns back, he's gone.

She searches the field but sees no sign of him. Could he have made his way into the henhouse? Surely not – he'd have had to cross to the gate and open it, then get inside the little building, which would have taken far longer than the few seconds he had.

'Did you see a man over there?' she asks the little girl on George's back, but the child shakes her head.

She could have sworn he was there. Maybe she needs to get her eyes tested.

'It's a belated birthday present,' she tells him, enjoying the look on his face.

'You gave me my present. You got me a sweater, remember?'

'That was all wrong – I bought it in a rush. This is your proper present.'

They both regard the small creature in the cardboard box yapping up at them, minuscule tail pumping.

'Do you like her?' Imelda asks. She doesn't have to ask – it's quite obvious that he likes her – but she wants to draw out the moment.

'Of course I do,' he replies. 'She's wonderful. But I had the impression you weren't a big lover of dogs.'

'I'm just a bit wary of any I don't know. But I'll know this one.'

He tilts up her chin and kisses her. 'Thank you, love. It's the best present you could have got me.'

'I thought Eve might like it too while she's here. She seemed taken with Nell's dog, the few times we were over. She could bring it for walks maybe, when she's not doing the donkey rides.'

'Good idea.' He lifts out the pup and lowers it to the floor, where it immediately squats and produces a small puddle on the vinyl. 'Oh dear.'

Imelda laughs. 'Your first clean-up job,' she tells him, pulling sheets from the roll of kitchen paper. 'You can start the training tomorrow.'

She watches him mopping up, and thinks how lovely it would be if it was just the two of them like before, and immediately feels guilty. She scatters puppy food into the little stainless-steel bowl she'd bought and places it on top of a sheet of newspaper, and the little dog patters straight over and pushes her face into it, scattering pellets.

'Still raining,' Hugh remarks.

Imelda turns to watch it falling steadily and silently on the garden.

'She couldn't be doing donkey rides in this, could she?'

Imelda crosses to the sink, fills a chipped saucer with water. 'I suppose she must be, since she hasn't come home. I offered to drive her there, but she said she wanted to walk.'

'Hard to know, isn't it,' he says, 'what she thinks of us?'

Imelda places the saucer next to the bowl.

'You're not sorry we took her?' he asks.

She watches the little dog lapping noisily at the water. 'I don't think so,' she says eventually. 'But I'd like her to be nicer. And I know she's had it tough, but she could try, couldn't she, to like us?'

'Imelda—'

'She doesn't,' she says, turning back to him. 'She doesn't like us. She certainly doesn't like *me*.'

But she might like the dog. Imelda might, at least, have got one thing right.

✳

Katy

Hope all's well in Donegal. Shame you and Lily didn't make it to Roone this time. The accident was an awful shock but we're both well on the mend now, thank goodness. Give my regards to your parents.

Nell xx

TUESDAY, 2 JULY

Five days he's been on the island, the longest block of time he's spent here since his departure two years ago. After Moira's death he'd stayed just two nights in Nell's spare room before she'd persuaded him to return to Tralee.

'I have James,' she told him, 'and you need to get back to work.'

'I'll be over as soon as the holidays start,' Denis promised – but in the end she had come to him, unable to bear the thought of Christmas on Roone without her mother, and unwilling to travel with James and Andy to Dublin, as James had suggested.

And over the past five days, Denis has been left in little doubt that it will take a while longer for the islanders to accept his return.

Thursday was quiet, the day he'd travelled across on the ferry with Colette. He'd spent an hour with Nell before going back to his own house – he's not yet able to call it 'home' – to watch the nine o'clock news and read his book till bedtime.

Friday he'd spent in the garden, attempting to rid the flowerbeds of the weeds that had taken unchallenged possession of as much ground as they could; and on Friday evening, as planned, Colette had hosted a dinner party in James's house.

Sole on the bone, cooked perfectly in butter; tiny new potatoes and mangetout from Gavin's garden; spinach and rocket leaves tossed in a tangy dressing and scattered with olives, toasted pine nuts and curls of Parmesan cheese.

'Are you planning to spend much time here over the summer?' she asked Denis afterwards, as they drank coffee on the patio under a sky that was still not completely drained of light.

'I'll come and go,' Denis replied, helping himself to a wafer-thin mint from the dish before him, noting the colourful lanterns scattered about on the paving stones that he didn't imagine belonged to James. She'd thought of everything. If Denis married her he would be both Nell's father and her father-in-law. The ludicrousness of it made him smile.

If Colette noticed, she made no comment. 'There's a spare room in Dalkey, if you ever want to spend some time in Dublin.'

'Thank you,' he replied, hoping the remark had escaped Nell's notice – he'd never hear the end of it. He glanced across the table but she was preoccupied with Andy, much to his relief.

Tim and James had vanished after the meal, apparently putting some final touches to the website Tim had designed to showcase James's paintings. 'Don't spend long at that,' Colette had warned, and Tim had assured her it would take just a few minutes.

Difficult to know which son was her favourite – didn't all

parents have a favourite, even if they'd never admit it? Unless, of course, they'd had just the one, like him and Moira. He would have loved more, they both would, but it had never happened.

'So sad about that little girl,' Colette said then. 'James told me they were staying in this estate.'

'Yes, just a few doors up.'

She shook her head slowly. 'I cannot imagine how a family survives something like that.'

'No.'

'I had another child, you know,' she said then, so calmly and matter-of-factly that Denis wondered if he'd heard her correctly. Nell had never mentioned a third sibling.

'A daughter,' she went on. 'In between the two boys. Maria.' She gave a soft sigh, lifted her cup and sipped. Denis waited.

'She was born with a defective heart. She lived for two weeks. We never brought her home.'

'I'm so sorry.'

'James was just two. Of course he's aware of what happened – they both are – but I'm sure he has no memory of it.'

'No . . .'

Denis felt disconcerted at the turn their conversation had taken. He found himself wishing, selfishly, that she hadn't chosen to confide in him. They hardly knew one another, and he didn't know what to do with her tragedy. And yet he found himself touched by her dignity, her complete absence of self-pity.

She lifted her cup. 'But at least we had a grave, you see. It did help, somehow. It gave us a place to go. They have no place, those parents.'

'No. I see what you mean.'

She smiled then, unexpectedly, as if he had said the right thing. 'Would you like more coffee?' she asked – and the polished hostess was back, offering more coffee, telling Andy to go in and bring out those boys of hers before she boxed their ears.

On Saturday, despite a sky that threatened rain, Denis set off for a walk. He chose an old favourite route, taking in the holy well and the lighthouse, a seven-mile round trip that he spun out into three hours. On the way back he dropped into Nell's house, where he discovered Andy in possession of a new little dog, and James having gone to meet Nell and Colette, who had walked together to the cemetery.

He returned to his house and had a bath and ate his dinner, and decided afterwards, the rain having eased off, to stroll into the village for a drink at Fitz's, his first visit there in over two years. Don't make a big thing of it, he told himself. Just order a pint and make chat with whoever's there. Don't think too much about it.

James was behind the counter and greeted his father-in-law as cordially as he always did. The few locals Denis recognised nodded at him as if he'd never been away. He sat at the counter like he always had and listened to the conversations that carried on without him. After their initial salutes nobody looked his way, nobody made an effort to include him. He might as well have been invisible.

James, of course, spoke to him, in between pouring drinks and gathering glasses and cutting lemons. He made a point of speaking to him. Denis drank his pint and let on not to notice that he was being ignored by everyone else. It will take time, he reminded himself. You knew it would take time. You've started the ball rolling.

On Sunday morning he went to mass. Again the heads nodded, male and female, and again that was it. He walked up the aisle on his way to communion and he could feel their eyes on him. After mass he shuffled out with everyone else, looking straight ahead as he passed the little knots of people, and he kept going until he reached the cemetery.

'I'm paying the price,' he told Moira. 'I'm getting what I deserve.'

On Monday he called to Nell and they walked to the mobile library together. Her pace was still slower than normal; she leant on Denis's arm as they covered the three-quarters of a mile from her house to the place where the long white van parked, *County Kerry Mobile Library* in dark blue lettering along its side.

On the way they passed the pier, and the pebbly shore next to it where the islanders' boats were moored. Nell's *Jupiter* sat there along with all the others; no rowing or swimming for her since the accident.

'Remember when I fell into the sea as a baby,' she said, out of the blue – and Denis felt a diluted lance of the terror he'd experienced when she had tumbled from the friends' boat they were on and splashed into the water. Less than one year old, and at the stage where she was beginning to pull herself up to standing – and somehow, inexplicably, having strayed from their care that awful day.

'Your mother and I were the ones who nearly died.'

She gave a small laugh. 'I know – I was having a lovely time until you insisted on pulling me out.'

'You cried to go back in.'

'So you tell me.'

The white van sat on its usual grassy verge, a hundred yards ahead.

'You were in the pub on Saturday night,' Nell said then, the abrupt change of topic taking Denis by surprise. 'James told me.'

'I dropped in,' he agreed. It hadn't been mentioned yesterday when he'd joined them for a salad tea, and he thought James probably hadn't said anything to her. He waited for what was to come – but her next sentence jumped ahead to yet another subject.

'I'm getting flashbacks,' she said. 'Of the accident, I mean.'

'Are you?'

She nodded. 'It's happened a few times, usually when I'm nearly asleep.'

'That must be horrible.'

'It is. I hope they stop soon.'

'Are they affecting your sleep?'

'They are a bit.'

'Talk to Jack, he might be able to prescribe something.'

'… Maybe.'

And then they reached the library, where they encountered nobody at all, apart from Hugh and Imelda, and Tony the librarian who chatted away to them, and gave no sign that he knew or cared about anything Denis had done.

'How's Tralee treating you?' was all he asked, and Denis told him fine, and that was it.

On the way home Nell talked about how well Captain, the new pup, was settling in, and how James had got mackerel at the pier that morning for their dinner – 'You'll come, won't you?' – and how Imelda's sister and her husband were arriving for a fortnight and staying at Laura's B&B – 'which means that all my former tenants will be back on Roone, and all except one – Imelda – will be staying under the same roof. Isn't that weird?'

And now it's the afternoon of Tuesday, and Denis is packing his bag for Tralee. Five days is plenty long enough in a place where most of the people you've known your whole life aren't that bothered about talking to you.

He'll try again next week, or the one after it.

❋

'She's flying it,' Imelda says. 'Laura is delighted with her.'

'So I believe. And she's settled in alright at your house.'

'As settled as she'll be,' Imelda says briskly, and Nell leaves it alone and instead offers another slice of the fruit cake her mother-in-law had baked before she left.

'Colette got back alright to Dublin?'

'She did. She's off to Norway with her book club next week. They've just read some crime novel set there.'

'Well for some.'

'I know . . .'

'And how's your father getting on? I haven't seen him around.'

'Oh, fine. He's going back to Tralee this evening for a few

days. He still has the house there – he's kept it on till the end of the summer because he'll be in and out to the school, tying up loose ends and that.'

'Right.'

A short silence ensues. *He'll have to find a way back*, Hugh had told her, *they don't forget easily here*, and Imelda had realised there was a darker side to the island she'd come to love. Do wrong on Roone, whoever you are, and it's held against you.

'He finished with her, you know,' Nell says then. 'About a month ago.'

'Oh . . .'

Better not mention that she and Hugh had come to that conclusion on their own. Better not give any hint that they'd been discussing Nell's father's love life.

'So how are you feeling yourself these days?' she asks when the silence begins to stretch.

Nell looks tired. Shadowed crescents beneath her eyes, a washed-out pallor to her face. But the scratches are almost entirely gone, which is something.

'I'm alright. Dying to get this cast off so I can go back to work.'

Before Imelda has a chance to respond they hear a sudden scurry by the side of the house – and a few seconds later Captain erupts into view, blue leash trailing behind him as he speeds towards the women, yapping cheerfully.

'Here comes trouble.' Nell grins, bending to rub his head. 'How's your new lady getting on?'

'Oh, fine. Spoilt rotten, of course.'

'What did you call her?'

'Scooter. We told Eve she could name her, and that was what she picked.'

Nell laughs. 'Scooter? You did tell her it was a female, didn't you?'

'We did. But what harm, it doesn't bother us.'

And just then Andy appears around the corner, hobbling pretty nimbly on his one remaining crutch – and close on his heels comes Tim.

Imelda, rising to her feet, sees Nell's fading smile, the light flush that washes over her complexion at the sight of her ex. The constant reminder of a mistake almost made.

'Hello, ladies,' he says cheerily. 'I hope I'm not interrupting.' His glance skimming over Imelda to rest on Nell.

'Don't go,' Nell says, as Imelda pulls on her raincoat – and it isn't until a few minutes later, after the flurry of goodbyes, and she's lifting the latch on the little gate, that Imelda wonders if, in fact, Nell didn't want to be left alone with Tim.

But of course she's not alone: Andy is there.

✳

They're alone. Andy has deserted them, disappeared into the house with Captain and left her on her own with Tim, for the first time since he and Colette had come to Roone. No, before then: since the night, almost two years ago now, that he told her he'd been made a partner in the firm, which meant they'd have to live in Dublin after they were married, and she'd sat across from him in her favourite restaurant and realised that she wasn't, after all, going to marry him.

This was their first time alone since then, if you didn't count the curiously intimate handful of seconds they'd shared over a week ago. Right after her first flashback, and before Colette had followed him onto the patio. He had crouched by her chair and laid a hand on her arm. *Were you remembering?* he'd asked. *Take it easy,* he'd said. *Just breathe.*

'I've come,' he says now, sinking into the seat Imelda has just vacated, 'to check out the patients. Andy seems pretty much back to normal.'

'Pretty much,' she agrees, wondering again what holds him here, alone on an island he never seemed to care for. She imagines him working, sitting hunched over his computer in James's small house, heedless of the sea and sky, impervious to the beauty around him.

'Tea?' she asks – remembering, as soon as the word is out, that he never drinks it. 'Coffee,' she amends, 'or something stronger.' Feeling ill at ease in the company of the man who was once everything to her, wishing for someone else, anyone else, to join them.

Tim makes a dismissive gesture. 'I'll help myself if I want anything,' he says – and she thinks, as maybe she was supposed to think, of how at home he used to be in this house. No, not this house, but the one that predated it, the one that had gone up in flames shortly after their engagement had come to an end, taking her beautiful wedding dress with it. The house he had lived in every weekend for well over a year.

'James is at work till six,' she tells him, as if by mentioning his name she could magically conjure up her husband – or at least the spirit of him. But there are still two hours to go until six o'clock, and spirits aren't going to contribute much to the conversation.

'It's you I came to see,' Tim reminds her, fixing her with his green gaze. 'You and Andy.'

His eyes had been the first thing she'd noticed about him, the day he had walked into the Dublin salon where she worked. Not yet trusted with wielding scissors, Nell was given the task of washing his hair. She tucked a black towel around his neck and instructed him to lean back – noting, as she slid a hand under his neck to draw the longish muddy-blond hair into the basin, eyes that were the wonderful cleanly rinsed green of the water that she swam and floated in on sparkling summery Roone days. Thickly fringed with dark lashes, whites clear. Eyes you could easily lose yourself in, if you had a mind to.

His aftershave, or cologne, was gorgeous – and expensive, she'd bet, a blend of wood and spices – but it was the eyes that stayed with her, long after they'd finished their small talk, completely forgotten now, and he'd risen from the padded leather chair, shampooed and conditioned and damply tousled, a fresh warm towel draped around his shoulders, and Nell had moved on to her next customer.

'You're tired,' he says.

'A bit.'

He wears the same cologne now – she'd bought it for him a few times. French – Hermès – and just as expensive as she'd thought. It wafts across the wrought-iron table to her.

'Have you had more flashbacks?'

'I have,' she admits. 'Dr Jack's given me stronger sleeping tablets though.'

'How's the wrist?'

'It's OK, getting there.'

'And the ribs have healed?'

'Yes.'

Strange conversation. He could be her doctor.

'Any word from Donegal?' she asks.

There's an odd shift in his face – what looks like impatience, or annoyance, passes swiftly over it and is gone just as quickly.

'Much the same,' he says.

Katy will have got her postcard today. Maybe sending it was a mistake, an impulse she should have considered more carefully before acting on it. If Colette is worried about her son, let her do something about it – Nell is the last person who should be getting involved. If James knew, he would understandably wonder why on earth she was poking her nose in.

'So,' she says, 'are you finished—'

And at exactly the same moment, Tim says, 'Nell, the thing is—'

Both stop. She looks at him. They look at one another. A second passes, and another. All at once she feels certain that he's about to say something she doesn't want to hear. She glances towards the open patio door, willing Andy to reappear.

Tim follows her glance before leaning forward, placing his arms on the table. 'Nell,' he says, voice lowered, 'I need to tell you something.'

'Tim, I'm not sure—'

'The thing is . . .'

Oh, why won't the phone ring, or Captain rush out? Why doesn't anything happen to throw him off and stop the words?

'Look, you need to—'

'The thing is,' he begins for the third time, and she realises that he won't be stopped, and prepares to hear with resigned dread, 'I think I've made a big mistake, Nell.'

Her heart plunges to her toes. She shakes her head. 'Tim, please don't—'

'I've made a big mistake,' he insists, glancing again towards the patio door, then back to her. 'Nell,' he says, his voice low and urgent, 'I married the wrong—'

'No, I don't want to—'

'Nell, it's you I—'

'Stop,' she says fiercely, the force of the word sending a throb through her ribcage. 'Tim, I'm asking you to stop – just stop this. I don't want to hear any of it.' She puts a hand to her aching chest. Out of breath, out of words.

But he refuses to stop. 'I don't love her,' he says, leaning across the table. 'I thought I did, but I don't. She was just a rebound thing. You deserve to know this, Nell.'

'I don't want to. I have no—'

'I wasn't over you – I was far from over you. I shouldn't have got involved with anyone else, it wasn't fair to her. She deserves better than that.'

'Please, Tim, I'm begging you to—'

'And then,' he goes on, as if Nell's interruptions aren't

happening, 'she sort of grew on me, and before I knew it, we were getting married. It wasn't exactly planned, or certainly not something I had—'

'Hello, you two!'

Their heads swing in unison towards the voice – and here, miraculously, comes Laura, emerging through the sliding door with the waddling gait she's adopted lately, mountainous belly under its check cotton shirt leading the way, dwarfing even the enormous breasts that rise above it. Nell has never been so glad to see her.

'I'm not staying,' she goes on, seemingly impervious to the drama she's walked straight into, lowering herself into a chair between them. 'The donkey rides are still in full swing and I don't like to leave when they're on, although Eve is well able, only I've just had Imelda's lot booking in – do you remember them, Nell? I saw them at Imelda's wedding but I didn't talk to them at all as far as I remember – well, I felt a bit like a gatecrasher, I know you said come along, but still. Anyway, he's quiet enough but I get the feeling she might be a bit of work. I caught her running a finger along the windowsill when I showed them their room: all she needed was a white glove. Thank God I got Gav to do a bit of dusting there yesterday.'

She rattles on, looking from one to the other. 'Andy let me in. His face is getting so much better, isn't it? That vitamin-E oil is fabulous – I told him I was going to get it for my stretch marks and he didn't know where to look. He'll be ready to take over the donkey rides in no time, won't he? I hope Eve won't be upset, but I did make it clear from the start that she was just filling in.'

She stops and peers more closely at Nell. 'Are you OK? You're a bit pale. Do you want me to put the kettle on?'

Tim pushes back his chair abruptly and gets to his feet.

Laura looks at him in mild surprise. 'Don't go on my account, Tim – I'm not staying, honest.'

'I was on my way anyway,' he tells her, giving her a tight smile. He calls goodbye to Andy, and a distant response issues from somewhere within.

He turns to Nell. She can hardly bring herself to look at him. 'We'll talk again,' he says, and she nods mutely. He crosses the patio and disappears around the side of the house. As soon as the sound of his footsteps has faded completely Laura looks thoughtfully at Nell.

'Am I imagining it, or did I just walk into something?'

Nell leans back and closes her eyes. 'You could say that.'

✳

'You didn't mention that she's about to give birth.'

'Well, not exactly – she's got over a month to go.'

'She must be having an elephant then, the size of her. Vernon couldn't keep his eyes off her chest.'

'Hang on,' Vernon protests, but Marian pays him no heed as she helps herself to another of Imelda's almond slices. 'I have to say the bathroom floor didn't look a hundred per cent clean to me. And there was a right commotion in the field next door. *Donkey* rides she said when I asked.' The disapproval in her voice, as if they were conducting satanic rituals in Walter's field.

'Oh yes,' Imelda says. 'They started those a little while ago

– they're a great success.' She hovers the teapot over Vernon's cup; he nods and she pours.

'But Imelda, you wouldn't know what kind of a crowd they'd attract.'

Imelda smiles. 'On Roone? I don't think that needs to be—'

'And I hope they don't go on late into the night.'

Imelda imagines candlelit donkey rides, and hides a laugh with a cough. 'Not at all, they finish up around five or six. Eve is in charge of them actually – you might have noticed her. She leads the donkey around.'

Marian looks appalled, a piece of almond slice halfway to her mouth. 'Eve? *Your* girl?'

'Well, yes, if you want to call her that.'

'In charge of *donkey* rides?'

'Yes. She seems to enjoy it, and it gives her something to do.'

Marian looks at Vernon, who continues to stir sugar into his refilled teacup, oblivious. Clever Vernon, refusing to be drawn in.

'Well, I must say, I'm not sure I'd consider that an altogether wholesome—'

There's a brief and welcome interruption when Scooter attempts to scramble onto Marian's lap (tempted more, Imelda is sure, by the almond slice than by anything else) and is immediately banished to the kitchen, where she sets up an indignant yapping for all of ten seconds. When silence descends Imelda wonders warily what has distracted her, and decides to chance that it's nothing too destructive.

The pup was an instant hit with Eve – which Imelda belatedly realises is not a good thing.

'You got a *dog*?' she asked, crouching to gather the little pup into her arms, offering her face to the tiny pink tongue that began to lick it enthusiastically.

Finally, Imelda thought, something that makes her happy. 'You can give her a name, if you like,' she said – and without missing a beat, Eve said 'Scooter,' and then immediately afterwards, 'Can she sleep in my room?' – and Imelda, who firmly believes that dogs don't belong in bedrooms, found herself granting permission.

Eve and the pup are practically joined at the hip when Eve is in the house – she'd bring it with her in the afternoons, Imelda is sure, if she wasn't doing the donkey rides – and already Imelda is dreading the day when they must be separated. What was she thinking, introducing a dog into the household?

She wasn't thinking, of course, beyond the fact that Hugh would be pleased, and that she might finally coax a smile out of Eve. Foolish, impetuous gesture that can't be undone, and will only serve to make Eve miserable when she and Scooter have to part at the end of August.

'So how are you and Hugh coping with the child?' Marian asks, the question of the wholesomeness or otherwise of the donkey rides thankfully laid aside.

'Fine,' Imelda tells her. 'She's a quiet girl, doesn't have very much to say for herself, but she doesn't cause us any trouble.' All true, if leaving so much unsaid.

'The three of you will come out to dinner with us this evening, our treat.'

But Hugh is working up to closing time, so they settle instead on Thursday when he's off.

'Come to lunch tomorrow,' Imelda tells them, 'and you can meet Eve.'

She'll cook mushroom quiche, a favourite of Vernon's. Marian will do most of the talking, Eve will say as little as possible, and Vernon, Hugh and herself will fall somewhere in the middle.

It suddenly occurs to her that Eve might have been better off being fostered by Marian and Vernon. Marian needs listeners more than talkers around her – and whatever else you can say about Eve, she's certainly well able to listen.

✻

Nell sits alone at the kitchen table, a glass of water before her, filled and then ignored. The clock on the wall says four fifteen. The night is still black outside the window, no sign yet of the dawn.

You have to tell James, Laura had said, but she can't tell James. It would be setting brother against brother: it could cause a rift that might never be healed. It could destroy the family.

But isn't that exactly what Tim is trying to do? Confessing to his brother's wife that he still loves her, running the risk that Nell will tell James. Or is that exactly what he wants? Can he possibly think that Nell still has feelings for him too? Is he imagining them getting back together, leaving both their marriages in tatters?

And Katy, poor Katy. *A rebound thing* – wasn't that how he'd put it? *It wasn't fair to her*, he said. *She deserves better*. Wasn't that virtually word for word what Nell's father had said to her after he'd left her mother? *You didn't love her?* Nell asked him, and he replied, *Not in the way she deserved.* But her father had stayed married for over thirty years.

So is it better to admit your mistake as soon as you realise you've made it? Should Nell's father have left when Nell was still a child, given both her parents a second chance at love? And is Tim going to leave Katy and Lily now, with or without Nell?

She sinks her head into her hands – and lifts it immediately when she hears footsteps in the hall.

James enters, tousled and sleepy. 'What's up?'

'Couldn't sleep,' she tells him. 'I didn't want to wake you, tossing and turning.'

He crosses to the table, cradles her head in his hands. 'I wouldn't mind. Sure there's nothing wrong?'

She smiles up at him. 'I'm sure.' Hating the lie, but what else is she to say? 'Go back to bed. I'll be there soon.'

Alone again, she gets up and stands by the window, watching the dark beginning to wash slowly now from the sky, hearing the first trills and chirps from early-rising birds. Practically no night at this time of the year, the longest day just a fortnight ago.

If Tim had never visited Roone, or if she and James had got together before his arrival … Timing, she realises, has had everything to do with how her life has turned out. And isn't timing what determines everyone's story? Isn't it really as simple as being in the right place at the right time?

Don't I remember you? Nell had asked, at their first encounter on Roone, and at the same moment Tim had said, *I know your face from somewhere.* She remembers thinking, *He got the looks in the family.* Not that James is bad-looking, not at all. Blue eyes, regular features, lovely smile – but his are the kind of looks that grow on you over time. Tim is more immediately striking, with those startling eyes, that full bottom lip, the muddy-blond hair.

The truth was, she'd fallen in love with both of them. It had happened quickly with Tim – a couple of weekends in his company was all it had taken. So different with James, who'd already been her friend. Hard to know exactly when that had changed, when her fondness for him had blossomed into a deeper attachment.

She remembers her mother suggesting at some stage that they find a woman for James. *He's been on his own long enough*, Moira had said, and the thought had made Nell feel cross, even though she was engaged to Tim at the time. And when Laura had made a play for James while she was renting Nell's house, the thought of them together had felt all wrong to Nell.

She'd told herself she was just looking out for James, that she didn't want him to get hurt – but she must have been half in love with him even then.

I've loved you for ages, he'd told her, when Tim and Nell were in the past, and she finally acknowledged her feelings towards James. *I couldn't bear the thought of you marrying Tim, I didn't know how I was going to cope with it.*

She rubs her eyes, heavy with tiredness but sleep an impossibility with the thoughts that are galloping around in her head. *We'll talk again*, Tim had said as he was leaving, and it had sounded like a threat to her. What more is there for him to say? Hasn't he already revealed far too much?

I chose the right brother in the end, she thinks. James is the better man in every way; hard to remember now why she'd ever thought Tim could make her happy. But why did they have to be *brothers*, for Christ's sake? Why couldn't Tim have gone back to Dublin after their relationship had ended, never to be seen on Roone again?

The sky is streaked now with ribbons of gold and bronze and pink, beautiful to look at but not a good sign for the day ahead. She takes one of Dr Jack's sleeping pills from the press and washes it down with the water already poured. With any luck she'll be knocked out till mid-morning at least.

And when Tim comes back, because of course he will, she'll have to leave him in no doubt about where her heart lies. She dreads their next encounter, knowing how persistent he can be. He'll have to listen eventually. He'll have to accept that she's never going to love him again.

She makes her way back through the house and slips into bed beside her husband, who reaches out for her in his sleep.

FRIDAY, 5 JULY

Ben looks accusingly at his mother. 'You said a bad word.'

'No, I didn't. I was talking to the baby Jesus, so I used his name.'

'So what were you talking about?'

Laura flips rashers, her queasiness of the last eight months finally over. She could murder a rasher this morning. 'I was asking him to please help me make perfect breakfasts for all my lovely guests. Pass me over that plate.'

The milk is turned: that was this morning's complaint. Yesterday it was shell in the scrambled egg; the day before the toast was too dark. Does she lie in bed planning what to say, or does it come to her on the spot? And not a word out of the husband – not that he could get one in, with the non-stop moaning that comes out of her. Probably gave up trying years ago.

Two weeks they're booked in for, which means ten more breakfasts to endure, ten more complaints probably. Lumpy porridge: she hasn't used that one yet. Poached egg too soft or too hard. Not enough variety in the cereals. She'll find them.

The kitchen door opens and Gavin appears. 'Come on, Mister – your brother's waiting in the van.'

'Hens fed?' Laura asks.

'Fed and de-egged. The basket's in the scullery.'

'Thanks, love.'

He slides an arm around her waist. 'Quick,' he says to Ben, 'I'm going to kiss your mum.'

Ben makes a disgusted noise and vanishes. Laura is duly kissed.

'Feeling OK?'

She is not feeling OK. She is feeling tired and crotchety and grossly overweight. She is fighting a vague urge to burst into tears and another not so vague urge to eat everything in sight and a third almost overwhelming urge to lie down on the floor and go to sleep.

'I'm fine,' she says, cracking an egg into the pan. He doesn't have time for a baring of her soul: she'll offload on Walter later.

The paying guests are eventually fed, with no more complaints forthcoming. The overnighters depart and Marian and Vernon retire upstairs, as they do every morning for an hour or so. Hardly for a bit of how's-your-father – Laura would be willing to bet the entire donkey-ride profits that poor Vernon hasn't experienced the delights of the flesh for quite some time.

As she's slotting plates into the new dishwasher that's taken up residence beside the washing machine in the scullery – thank you, George – she hears some noise she can't define on the path outside. She straightens up and opens the back door.

'Hello,' she says. 'Have you come for a visit?'

He must have discovered the gap in the hedge, the one Gavin has been promising to shore up for over a month. She'll have to bring him back: they'll be looking for him.

But not just yet.

'Come in for a minute,' she says, stepping aside – and in he trots, snuffling around her ankles, standing on hind legs to poke his head into the washing machine's empty drum, sniffing at the basket of eggs.

'This way,' she tells him, and he follows her into the kitchen, where she takes a bundle of rasher rinds from the basin that's waiting to be brought out to Caesar, and scatters them on the floor.

'Don't tell,' she orders, as he wolfs the scraps and looks up hopefully for more.

She sits and pats what's left of her lap. 'Come here,' she says, and up he hops. 'You're pretty gorgeous,' she tells him. 'There's no denying it.'

He plants his forepaws on her bump and darts kisses at her face. 'Stop it,' she says, in a voice that tells him to keep going. This is not going to end well, she thinks, her hands cradling his warm, wriggling little body.

There are two left, Nell told her the other day. *Francis is still looking for homes.*

It's the last thing they need. Twenty-eight hens, a donkey and a pig makes thirty creatures to look after already.

But the donkey has turned into a nice little money-spinner, and they're making a tidy sum on the B&B. And Caesar eats mostly scraps. And the hens pay for themselves, more or less, with the eggs.

And the boys and Gav would love it.

And he's adorable, and his brother or sister would be just as gorgeous.

'Come on,' she says, tipping him back onto the floor and hauling herself upright. 'Let's get you home.'

She'll tell them as soon as they get back from the deliveries. She pictures their delighted faces, and checks the clock to see how long she has to wait to break the news.

She'll make them happy, which is all that ever really matters.

✳

He has to ring the bell twice. But the car is in James's driveway, so he waits. Eventually the door is opened.

Tim looks mildly surprised to see him. 'Hugh,' he says, making no move to invite him across the threshold.

'I was wondering,' Hugh says mildly, 'if we might have a little chat.'

The small smile stays in place. The door remains ajar. They've never got to know one another, not in any real way. They've sat at the same dinner table plenty of times, either at Nell's or in her parents' house. They've conversed whenever Tim dropped into the bar with Nell, but still Hugh knows next to nothing about the man she nearly married.

'We can do it here on the doorstep,' he says, 'or I can come in.' His voice neutral, no need for a confrontation unless it's looked for. He's never relished confrontation. A reasonable exchange between adults is what he's hoping for.

'Someone needs to talk to him,' Laura had said. 'I thought you might be willing.' So here he is, because he has always been very fond of Nell.

Tim stands back, holds the door open. Hugh steps inside, wipes non-existent dirt from his feet onto the mat. He follows Tim in silence into James's kitchen. A laptop sits on the table, its lid flipped up, the small hum of its motor audible, what looks like a chart set out on the screen.

'You're working,' Hugh says.

Tim pushes down the lid, crosses to the kettle. 'No worries – I can take a break.' He fills the kettle and plugs it in while Hugh remains standing in the centre of the room. 'So tell me,' he goes on, his back to Hugh while he takes out cups, milk, sugar, 'what did you want to talk about?'

'Nell,' Hugh replies simply. No bush-beating, no point in that. 'You visited her recently. She was a bit upset.'

Tim's face gives nothing away. He places everything on the table and leans against it, folding his arms, regarding Hugh impassively.

'So she asked you to come and have a word.'

'No, Nell didn't tell me about it. She doesn't know I'm here.'

Tim nods, unsurprised. 'Laura.'

'I think,' Hugh says in the same even voice, 'it would be best all round if you left.'

A grin then, with little amusement in it. 'Or what? You're

going to run me out of town?' The words accompanied by a darting glance, which Hugh doesn't miss, at the arm that finishes at the elbow. The cripple is threatening me.

I don't like him. The knowledge comes to Hugh. It slots into his consciousness like an envelope slipped through the mouth of a pillar box. He had never warmed to James's brother, never found common ground, never felt the camaraderie he enjoys with James.

He meets the younger man's gaze, aware that he would be easily defeated if Tim decided to throw a punch, imagining the two of them engaged in some kind of wrestling match, tumbling over one another on the tiled floor. But of course it won't come to that: Tim prefers to punch with words, and words have never worried Hugh unduly.

'Nell is happy with James,' he says. 'She made the right choice. You need to accept that and leave her alone now. Go back to your wife and child.'

Tim nods slowly, as if considering his suggestion, but Hugh can see the anger that narrows the green eyes. The kettle begins to hum, boiling water for drinks that neither of them wants.

'I think you should mind your own business.' The tone is light but the anger is there behind the words; it's there in the tightness of his face. It's there, hovering between them in the kitchen. 'This is between Nell and me. It's got nothing to do with you.'

Hugh stands his ground. 'She's married to your brother. Does that count for nothing with you? You had your chance with her, and you blew it. She's with James now. She's not interested in you any more – can't you see that?'

The kettle rumbles to a boil and clicks off. Tim steps away from the table and moves towards him – and for an instant Hugh is sure he's about to be hit. He braces his feet on the floor, he stiffens everything, wondering how he's going to explain a black eye to Imelda – but the blow he's expecting doesn't come.

Tim stops, no more than a foot away, and glares at him, all pretence gone. They're more or less the same height. Hugh sees the brownish stubble dotted on the chin and across the jaws. He smells the aftershave, feels the heat of Tim's breath on his face.

'You need to leave now,' Tim says, through lips that barely move. For a second, or half a dozen seconds, they remain standing there, eyeball to eyeball – and then Hugh turns and walks out to the hall. He counts the steps, seven, that take him to the front door, still not sure a blow isn't going to land on the back of his neck. He opens the door and lets himself out, and closes it softly behind him.

Driving to the pub to begin his shift – he'll be early, James will ask why – Hugh thinks about the twists and turns that wait to confront us through the years. Nell would have married him if Tim had been less focused on making money, or if she'd been less determined to stay on Roone. If circumstances had stepped sideways, how changed both their lives might have been. How changed James's life would have been, doomed to love his sister-in-law.

He feels the business unfinished, the situation unresolved – but what more could he have done? It is, as Tim said, none of his business. Could he have made things worse? Will Tim, enraged by his interfering, report their conversation to Nell and cause her further distress?

No way of knowing. All he can do is wait, and hope for the best.

✳

Willie Buckley is the one who finds it, lodged between rocks close to the pier. He reaches over the side of his boat and eases it up, his heart falling. A child's small sandal, bleached of colour, sole flapping, what's left of its buckle badly rusted.

It might not be hers, he thinks. It could have been shed by an eager little paddler, left too close to the water as he or she splashed about, its absence undiscovered until the tide had washed it away. It might be as innocent as that.

Word of the discovery spreads at its accustomed speed among the islanders. Before Sergeant Fox is halfway to Tipperary, the topic is being discussed throughout the village. By the time he rings the Ryans' doorbell, by the time Martha Ryan is handed the little sandal, by the time her face collapses at the sight of it, everyone on Roone is aware of what has been found.

And when Sergeant Fox arrives back on the island, one look at his face tells them all they need to know.

It's been over eight weeks. They each bury her silently, in their minds.

✳

James looks up as the pub door opens.

'Hello, stranger,' he says. 'You've been lying low.'

His brother walks to the counter. 'How're things?'

'OK. You?'

Tim shrugs. 'I just dropped in to say I'm heading off.'

James nods. 'Figured you'd have had enough of the quiet life around now.' He smiles, but it's not returned.

'I'll take a quick one for the road,' Tim says.

He's in a mood: that much is clear. Something has rattled him, the anger simmering beneath the surface. James says nothing as he holds a glass under the gin optic. If he wants to get it off his chest he will.

It's before noon, the pub empty of customers. Imelda has been in with the day's sandwiches. James gestures towards them but Tim shakes his head.

'Any news from Donegal?'

Tim pours tonic. 'Oh, you know. Same old, same old.'

'How's Katy's mother?'

He takes a swig. 'She's just grand. She's a grand wee woman.' His parody of a Donegal accent seems to James to have a cruel edge. 'And how's my ex?' he asks, watching James's face.

'She's doing OK,' James tells him, careful to keep his voice very cheerful. 'Hopes to be getting the cast off in the next week or so.'

'Good. That's good.' Tim nods, swirling the ice around in his glass. 'That's good,' he repeats, his eyes on the rattling cubes. 'I'm glad to hear it.'

He's tightly wound. James becomes aware of the ticking of

the clock on the wall behind him. Tim lifts his head then and looks directly at him again.

'The best man won,' he says. 'Hah?'

James meets his stare levelly. 'Tim,' he says, 'I don't know what's bugging you, but if you've got something to say, let's hear it.'

A beat passes. The clock ticks. The brothers stare at one another.

Tim lifts his glass abruptly and drains it. He sets it back down on the counter with a thump and gets up from his stool, drawing the back of his hand across his mouth. He reaches inside his jacket but James shakes his head.

'On the house.'

Tim ignores him, pulling a fiver from his wallet and slapping it on the counter. He puts out a hand to James, who takes it.

'So long, bro,' Tim says. 'See you back in Dublin some time. Look after the little lady. Tell her I'll see her soon.'

'See you,' James echoes, his hand smarting from the fierce clench. He doesn't suggest that Tim call by the house to say goodbye to Nell – or to his nephew, who didn't get a mention.

He won't ask Nell what occurred between them the other day that had her wide awake at four the following morning. He presumes whatever it was didn't go well between them, and is probably the reason why Tim is leaving now.

She'll tell him if she wants to – and if she figures he's better off not knowing, so be it.

✲

Nell

Lovely to hear from you. Everything's fine in Donegal. Mam was a bit poorly but she's much better now. Lily and I are heading back to Dublin on Saturday. Shame I missed Roone, next time for sure. I was glad Tim got to spend some time there – he's been working so hard lately we've hardly seen him, and by all accounts Roone is the perfect place to unwind. It'll be good to have him back though – he's been missed by his two ladies!

Take care,

Katy xx

✳

'Hey,' he says, coming out of his gate, taking her utterly by surprise. The sight of him sending a whoosh of something strange, but not unpleasant, through her.

She hasn't seen him since before the accident, well over two weeks. A thin red line runs down one side of his face, but apart from that he looks pretty much the same. She's glad she's wearing the lime green top: Laura had told her it's definitely her colour. *Perfect with your hair*, Laura had said. She catches him glancing at her chest, just for a second. She finds she doesn't mind.

'You OK?' she asks him, because now she's stopped, and one of them has to say something. 'After the car crash, I mean.'

He nods and points to the line on his cheek. 'Apart from this.'

It's noticeable, but it's not that bad. It's not something you couldn't look at. 'So you'll be doing the donkey rides soon.'

'Yeah … I need to build up my ankle a bit first.'

She looks down at the little pup sniffing at her jeans. The pup is attached to a blue leash that he's holding. She bends and pats the dog's head.

'Boy or girl?'

'Boy. Captain.'

'We have his sister,' she tells him. 'Well, Imelda and Hugh have.' Their names coming out naturally, the first time she's uttered them.

'What did they call her?'

'Scooter,' she says. 'I chose it.' Looking up to see if he laughs.

He doesn't laugh. 'Cool.'

She rises. 'Well … ' she says, unable to think of anything else.

'OK,' he says, as if she asked him something.

He moves off. She moves off.

She glances back, and catches him glancing back.

Eight weeks. She'll be gone in eight weeks.

She's only here for the summer.

Ten minutes he was waiting for her to show up, just hanging around inside the gate, pulling up daisies on the lawn. He hopes Nell wasn't watching from the house: she'd know well what he was doing.

She didn't seem too grossed out by the scar.

He likes her top – he likes the way it shows a bit more than the others. He hopes she didn't catch him looking. He didn't mean to: his eyes were pulled down there.

He likes her hair, the way it falls like a curtain on either side of her face. He wonders what she looks like without the makeup, without the black-ringed eyes and brown mouth. He thinks she'd look softer. He thinks he'd prefer it.

She looked back. They caught one another looking back. He wonders if she likes him. The thought makes his heart fold over pleasantly.

The only girl he'd liked, really liked, up to this was Jean Doherty. He'd walked home with her a few times after a group of them had spent an evening down at the pier or up at the lighthouse. He'd been working his way up to asking if she'd let him kiss her when she decided she liked Tony Barnes better.

And since then, over a year ago, he hasn't felt like that about any of the other girls in the group. He enjoys undressing them in his head, of course, and does it with unfailing regularity – and occasionally he imagines them undressing one another, which is interesting – but none of them has got under his skin in the way Jean did. He doesn't find himself seeking out any one of them in particular, like he did with her.

But this girl interests him. No, she intrigues him. He wants to pull her apart and see what she's made of. He wants to talk to her, find out stuff about her. And he wouldn't mind kissing her, lipstick or no lipstick, and maybe doing a bit more than kissing.

'Come on,' he says, and he and Captain lollop off together.

THURSDAY, 11 JULY

'Do you know what day today is?' he asks.

'Thursday.'

'No. I mean what's the significance of it?'

She thinks, leaning into him as they make their leisurely way along the road. 'It's the thirteenth, right?'

'Right.'

'The thirteenth of July. Is it someone's birthday?'

'Probably – but nobody we know.'

It's a little past ten o'clock in the morning. She's accompanying him to the village, where he's due at work. She'll visit the hair salon, check in with her stand-in Patrice, let her know, in the friendliest possible way, that her days as Roone's hairdresser are numbered.

'It's not St Swithin's Day, is it? That's some time in July.'

'No idea. Is he the one who brings the rain?'

'Yes, forty days. Anyway, I give up.'

'It's Tim and Katy's wedding anniversary.'

They pass the hotel. A clutch of cars parked in front, most with foreign licence plates. 'Oh … is it really?'

'It is really.'

'Because we didn't know, did we? The exact day, I mean, because they did it on holidays. We just knew the week – but I'd completely forgotten that as well. Their anniversary, imagine. A year already.'

She's gabbling. She stops. The relief she felt when James told her he'd left Roone. The first decent sleep she'd got that night, and no flashbacks since.

They walk on past the church. A man in a yellow raincoat studies the notices pinned up behind glass on the front wall of the building. His companion sits on the shallow stone steps that lead to the big carved wooden door, a map unfolded on his lap. A pair of bicycles huddles together against the steps' railings.

'How did you know?' Nell asks.

'My mother. I was talking to her yesterday. She's babysitting Lily tonight – they're going out to dinner.'

Out to dinner for their first wedding anniversary: so far, so normal. If her postcard was anything to go by, Katy had, or has, no idea that anything is wrong. *He was missed by both his girls.* Happily married, it sounds like, happy in her choice of partner.

'And they've asked Mam if she'll take Lily for a long weekend in the autumn, when she's weaned. They want to go back to Rome.'

'Oh … that's nice.'

Back to Rome, where they'd got married: probably the most romantic destination they could have chosen. And not till the autumn, so they're planning ahead as a couple. Tim is trying to make it work, he must be.

But if she had told him she'd made a mistake too, he would have left Katy and gone off with her, and to hell with all the broken lives they'd be creating.

She tucks her arm more firmly around James's waist as they approach the bend that will lead them onto the village street. 'We must get them a present,' she says.

He's still her brother-in-law, however much she might wish it otherwise.

✳

The morning is not promising. Clouds the colour of dough, and looking just as heavy, jostle for position in the sky. Still, Marian is determined.

'We can leave if the rain comes. Now, have we everything?'

Her shopping basket is packed with towels, swimsuits, magazines, hand wipes, sun cream (sun cream!) and a battery-operated transistor radio. In addition, Vernon's car boot holds Imelda and Hugh's blue-and-red check blanket, plastic-backed to survive exposure to the Irish beach picnic, and the wicker hamper Imelda had filled earlier with triangular ham sandwiches, cheese biscuits, slices of coffee cake and two large bottles of lemonade.

'Will she not come with us?' Marian asks, and again Imelda tells her that Eve is still asleep.

'Asleep – at nearly noon! Imelda, you're far too soft on her.'

Of course it's not true. Eve still rarely shows her face

downstairs before lunchtime, but Imelda has long since realised that she's simply staying out of their way for as long as she can. Since Scooter's arrival, the pup appears in the kitchen early each morning on her way to the back garden – and since Hugh's expert housetraining didn't include opening doors, Eve is clearly awake enough to let her out of the bedroom.

This morning in particular the girl is lying low until all danger of being dragged along on the picnic has passed – and for once Imelda can't blame her.

'What's *wrong* with the child?' Marian had demanded after their first lunch together. 'Hasn't she got a tongue in her head? The sulky face of her – and *plastered* in makeup, at her age! I'm surprised you allow it, Imelda.'

No, it's safe to say they didn't hit it off. The more taciturn Eve became during the lunch, the more Marian seemed to take it as a challenge to prise conversation out of her, and despite Hugh and Vernon's valiant efforts to ignore Marian's increasingly frustrated questioning and Eve's bare-minimum responses, the tension built to an almost unbearable degree, until Imelda felt a strong urge to knock both of their heads together.

Things didn't improve a jot at dinner the following evening. Thank God Marian and Vernon hadn't opted to venture further than Lelia's café, where Eve could make her escape straight after she'd cleared her plate, and head back to the house alone.

'Imelda, you must have the patience of Job,' Marian declared after she'd gone, and Imelda thought even Job would have been hard-pressed not to throw at least one of Lelia's pretty china dishes across the room.

In the few days since then, Imelda has managed to keep Eve and her sister apart, and she's determined to go on doing it for the rest of Marian's stay on Roone. A week down, another to go: at this stage Imelda is becoming well used to sticking it out until the allotted time has passed.

Their destination today is the pebble beach where Hugh and Imelda first met. Vernon and Marian have never seen it, and an excursion there today with a picnic lunch seemed like a good plan yesterday, when the sun was shining from a virtually cloudless sky. No matter: they'll make the best of it.

'Hard to believe we're here a week already,' Marian remarks as the four of them set off. 'Doesn't time fly?'

Imelda imagines Hugh, sitting up beside Vernon, thinking, *Not half fast enough*. She's fully aware that her husband tolerates his sister-in-law's company, no more – but unlike Eve, Hugh maintains an amiable front in her company. He gets on well with Vernon though. Everyone gets on well with poor Vernon.

'I hope you're enjoying your holiday,' she says to Marian.

'Oh yes, it's going very well. The B&B is a bit rough and ready, but I'm pointing out any little problems to the landlady. That's what you need when you're starting off, plenty of feedback so you'll get it right eventually. I had to have a word with her this morning about the biscuits in the room. We got the same custard creams three days in a row.'

'Oh dear ... ' Imelda will have to make it up to Laura, whom she hasn't seen since the birthday party. Poor woman, having to cope with Marian's 'feedback'. Probably fit to throttle her.

'But we've been lucky enough with the weather. Do you remember, Imelda, the awful weather we got the first time we came? Raining most days – I remember you arriving home drenched from your walks more than once.'

Imelda remembers slithering down the lane that led to the pebbly beach, her raincoat patched with damp, her trousers clinging to her calves, her socks sopping. She remembers the sight of Hugh waiting for her on the beach under his big black umbrella.

Their second encounter there, this one planned, or half planned. *The cut of you*, he said when he saw her, his eyes crinkling with merriment.

She smiles. The cut of her.

'So where's this famous beach then?' Vernon asks, and Hugh begins to issue directions as the clouds continue to block out the sky.

'I've got a stitch,' Gavin says, rubbing his side, the skin between his eyes crimped. 'I've had it all day.'

Laura spoons more spaghetti hoops onto Seamus's plate. 'Did you take anything for it?'

'No – what can you take for a stitch?'

'I've no idea. Ben, elbows down please. Seamus, take that knife out of your mouth.' She scans the floor. 'Where's Charlie gone? He'd better not be at that clothes line again.'

Ben scrambles from his seat. 'I know where he is.'

'Come back here – your tea will get cold.' But he's gone, out to the hall where dogs are decidedly *not* allowed. He reappears a minute later with Charlie in his arms.

'He just went out for a minute.'

'Hmm.' Laura regards the little dog, who wags his tail at her. 'It's not too late to send you back to O'Callaghan's house, you know.'

'*Mum!*'

But they know she doesn't mean it. She closes the door into the hall, a hand to the small of her back, a permanent ache there now. *Four weeks*, Dr Jack told her yesterday, *give or take*. The boys were a week late, so it's probably more like five. Give or take.

She fills her plate from the saucepan and sits at the table. 'Andy called over while you were out,' she says, dipping a toast finger into the sauce.

'Did he? Is he ready to do the rides?'

'He says he is, so I told him he could start on Friday. I thought I'd better give Eve a bit of notice.'

'Right.'

'So, anyway, I thought I might ask her to give me a hand in the house after that, just a couple of hours in the mornings. She could do the breakfast tidy-up, change the beds, that sort of thing. It'd only be for a fortnight or so, until I have to stop. And we're making enough on the donkey rides to afford it.'

'Good idea.'

She regards his plate. 'Why aren't you eating?'

He shrugs. 'Not really hungry.'

Not like him to be off his food – he eats like a horse normally.

God knows where he puts it. And he seems a bit pale too, under that farmer's tan.

'Any other aches and pains?'

'No.'

'Headache? Sore throat?'

'No.'

In the time she's known him he's never been sick, not so much as a tickly cough. Just her luck if he comes down with something now, when she's on the home stretch. Hopefully it's trapped wind, or something he ate earlier.

'Alka Seltzer,' she says. 'There's some in the bathroom cabinet. Or Milk of Magnesia. I think that's there too.'

'OK.'

Out of the corner of her eye she sees Charlie squatting on the tiles, a good foot from the spread-out newspaper they've been showing him for three days.

'Dog,' she says to Ben, who leaps from his chair like a rocket.

✳

He plays safe with his menu, serving up lamb chops, peas and mash, along with a bowl of lettuce, rocket and spinach leaves that he picked earlier from Gavin's vegetable plot.

'Take these,' Laura said, presenting him with a little bunch of nasturtiums held together with a rubber band. 'Throw in the flower heads after you've tossed your salad, they'll be dead impressed. And toast some pine nuts, if you have them, and sprinkle them on top.'

Denis doesn't bother with the croûtons or pine nuts. His

dessert is uncomplicated too: scoops of strawberry ice-cream topped with crumbled Flake bars. Keep it simple.

It's Nell's first meal in her family home since Moira's death. He's aware of how sad it must be: he hears it in the over-brightness of her voice, he sees it in the glances she casts every so often around the room, searching for something that can never be found. He's the wrong cook in this kitchen; but they need to move on, both of them.

James and Andy leave soon after dessert, Denis promising to accompany Nell on the quarter-mile journey in due course. They remain inside after the others have gone, the night too damp and gusty for the garden. He pours two small brandies to partner their coffees.

'So,' he says, their first opportunity to be alone all evening, 'how are you sleeping?'

'Much better now.'

'And the flashbacks?'

'Gone, hopefully. None for ages.'

'That's good. And the cast is coming off when did you say?'

'Next week, and then I have to have some physio.'

'You'll be back at work soon then.'

'I will. Not full time for a while, but I can do half-days.'

'And the Dublin visitors enjoyed themselves,' he goes on, careful to be busy with his coffee, stirring cream, spooning sugar. Careful not to mention Colette by name, in case Nell still harbours hope in that direction.

'They did … And you'll stay around awhile this time, will you?'

He lays down his spoon, crooks his finger into the cup handle. 'I will. I'll play it by ear.'

'Come around to us for dinner tomorrow,' she says, 'and maybe we could stroll to the village afterwards and drop into Fitz's. I haven't been in since the accident and I wouldn't mind a night out. James is off, so we can leave him at home.'

Protecting her father, not wanting him to sit alone all evening, at home or in a pub. Wanting everyone to see them together maybe, reminding them that he belongs here.

'That would be nice.'

The breeze rattles the leaves on the montbretia in the shrubbery outside the window. He hears them scratching gently against the glass.

'I forgot to tell you,' Nell says. 'Colette is in Norway.'

'Is that so?'

'She went yesterday, with her book club. They read books set in other countries, then visit them.'

He smiles. 'They must be well off.'

'Well, they choose the best times to go so they get good deals. She's been all over the place.'

He allows the silence to draw out. He hasn't pulled the curtains or switched on the lamps. The night is drawing in, the sky turned to shades of purple and pewter grey, the only remaining brightness a ragged slice of silver near the horizon. Denis can't tell if it comes from the sea or the sky or both.

'No stars tonight,' Nell says. 'Remember when Grandpa Will used to take me down to the beach at night to show me the stars?'

Denis had forgotten that. Doubtless he's forgotten so many things, the good along with the bad.

'Are you OK, Dad?'

He turns, surprised.

'Do you miss her?'

For a moment he's at a loss. He looks down at the disc of darkness in his cup. He smells the burnt-caramel scent of the coffee. He picks up his spoon and stirs, the tinkle it makes against the side of the cup loud in the room. 'Yes,' he says. 'I miss her.' He lifts the cup and sips.

Nell's quiet sigh is barely audible. 'Love has a lot to answer for,' she says softly. 'Doesn't it?'

They've both been scarred by love. His wound is still fresh, the pain of it raw and sharp. But Nell is happy now: her hurt has healed.

Hasn't it?

'Was it difficult,' he asks, 'having Tim around?'

His name was hardly mentioned at the meal. *He's gone back to Dublin*, James had said when Denis enquired, and no more was said.

Nell doesn't respond right away. He thinks she didn't hear, and decides not to repeat the question. None of his business.

'A bit,' she says eventually, lifting her brandy glass. He hears the small moist sound of her swallow. He waits for more words, but none come.

They sit on in the darkening room, drinking their coffees and brandies, content in their silence together, until at length

Nell gets to her feet. 'I'd better make tracks,' she says, 'let you get to bed.'

He walks her home, the wind catching hold of their jackets, whipping around their heads. He leaves her on the doorstep, hugging her goodnight.

'Sleep tight,' he tells her, waiting until she's opened the door and closed it. On his way back home the rain comes, a sudden heavy downpour that pelts at him for thirty seconds and disappears just as abruptly.

I'll get a dog, he thinks again later, towelling his hair dry in the bathroom, *if I come back to stay*. He's tired of loneliness, sick of his own sorry company. A dog would attach itself quickly; a dog would make him feel wanted again.

He'll get one, if he comes back to stay.

FRIDAY, 12 JULY

The alarm beeps her awake, as it does seven mornings a week. She reaches out to nudge Gav to knock it off – it's on his side – but all she finds is a cool smooth empty expanse of sheet. She opens her eyes and abruptly remembers, and hauls herself across the bed to silence the alarm.

So strange not to have him there. Since they moved to Roone they've had one night apart, when he travelled to Dublin to wish his mother a happy sixty-ninth birthday.

'Inflamed appendix,' Dr Jack said yesterday. 'Straight into hospital, that needs to come out.' So James had driven him to Tralee, and he's being operated on this morning to whip out a body part that doesn't do anything except cause trouble for a few unlucky individuals. Poor old Gav.

There's no way Laura will get in to see him, with the B&B and the boys and the animals and the donkey rides. But Nell has promised to drop in today: she and James are going to Tralee to look at second-hand cars – and barring complications

Gav should be home in four or five days. And there won't be complications, because they don't have time for those.

She'd have phoned Susan and asked her to come down for a few days, but wouldn't you know it, Susan and Laura's father are in Florence this week. It's a busman's holiday for Luke, of course, a trawl around the galleries the main purpose of the trip – everything revolves around him and his precious art – but hopefully Susan is getting some fun out of it too. Hopefully she's getting a trawl around the boutiques and craft shops.

Laura's never been to Florence. She imagines magnificent cobblestoned squares surrounded by colonnaded buildings made of old bricks weathered to the colour of ripe wheat, and beautiful arched bridges and narrow alleyways and balconies with tumbling jasmine. Probably all wrong.

She heaves her bulk out of bed, yawning. Standing in the shower she runs through the business of the day. Feed the overnighters, hold her tongue when Moaning Marian has her usual whine. Feed the boys, feed the creatures, collect the eggs.

James and Hugh are handling the café deliveries, bless them, while Gavin is out of commission. The householders who get door-to-door veg and eggs will have to fend for themselves for the next few days.

And Eve is starting the new regime this morning – talk about good timing. 'Come at ten,' Laura told her. 'Breakfasts will be finished by then, and we can start the tidy-up.'

Eve has been a godsend. Laura is so glad she took a chance on her. Still not a lot to say for herself, still giving the impression, most of the time, that she wishes everyone would leave her alone – but so capable with the donkey rides, so dependable and careful with the children. A nice decent girl under that shell, Laura is convinced.

It's seven forty-eight when she gets out of the shower. She pulls on a pink T-shirt, so grossly misshapen by her bump it'll only be fit for dusters when she's finished with it. She reaches down to take Gavin's shirt off the floor – the one she discarded last evening – and as she straightens up, a pain slices viciously through her back, the sensation so sharp it makes her cry out.

It's gone as quickly as it came, leaving a dull echo in its place. To be expected, pains and aches part of the fun and games at this stage. She stands still, a light, cool sweat breaking out on her face and neck, and waits to see if it returns. Nothing happens.

She finishes dressing, her movements cautious. She brushes her teeth and pins up her hair as best she can – the state of it – and makes her way out to the landing. Not a sound from behind other doors.

In the kitchen she puts on her apron, tying it with the length of elastic she's added to the belt. She takes her two frying pans from the press and sets them on the cooker. She opens the door to the scullery and Charlie patters in, sniffing at her ankles. 'Come on,' she says, pushing the back door open. 'Breakfast in a while.'

Sitting on the wooden garden seat outside the window, she inhales the cool, early-morning air as Charlie wanders about, reacquainting himself with the great outdoors. First thing every day she spends what time she can here if the weather allows, relishing the peace before anyone else gets up. Her soul food.

Looks promising today, the sky a clear washed blue, sun beginning to climb. She feels a ribbon of pain in her back, a diluted version of the earlier one. All she needs, backache in time for the breakfast rush.

'Walter,' she says – but he's not here today. She sits on until she hears a toilet flush somewhere in the house. She gets slowly to her feet and returns to the kitchen, her lower back throbbing steadily, Charlie at her heels.

✳

'Vernon.'

'Mm?'

'Vernon, wake up.'

Vernon opens an eye and sees his wife standing by the en-suite door, wrapped in a white bath towel.

'Vernon, there's a spider in the bathroom. I can't have my shower.'

He closes the eye. 'I'm sure he won't look, dear.'

'Vernon!'

He climbs out of bed, straightening his pyjama legs. The spider, hardly the size of a decent ladybird, is eventually located behind the cold tap in the sink. After some manoeuvring Vernon manages to capture it in a plastic cup and release it out of the window before clambering back into bed.

Ten minutes later, as he's drifting off again, a fragrant, damp Marian nudges his shoulder. 'The shower is free; in you go.'

He throws back the duvet and leaves the bed once more, knowing resistance is futile. As he scrubs the night away, Marian – usually at her liveliest in the morning – makes up her face at the sink.

'Vernon.'

'Mm?'

'I was thinking we could take up bridge in the autumn.'

Under cover of the running water Vernon allows himself a smile. Every autumn she settles on a new project. Last year it was oil painting, the year before that Italian cooking, before that French for beginners. He doesn't mind, although her enthusiasm rarely lasts beyond the first term, and sometimes falters long before that.

Creative writing was a bit of a disaster, and the less said about pottery the better. But he's quite enjoyed some of their experiences – and who knows? One day she might hit on the right class, and they might actually keep it up all year.

'Vernon.'

He rinses soap from his ears. 'Yes, dear?'

'I don't know if I dreamt it or not, but I thought I heard a scream earlier on.'

'What kind of a scream?'

'What do you mean, what kind of a scream? Just a scream. A woman.'

He turns off the water and steps out. 'You probably dreamt it, dear.'

He takes the drier of the two towels from the rail and wraps it around his waist as Marian leaves the bathroom, vacating the sink area just in time for his shave. He takes his razor and can of foam from the little mirrored press, humming something from *Oklahoma*.

Thirty-three years of marriage have left them pretty much perfectly in sync – and Vernon content enough with his lot, all things considered.

✳

'So you're off to Laura's this morning.'

'Yeah.'

No trouble getting up. No request to call her, she just appeared in the kitchen a few minutes after nine, Scooter pattering down the stairs with her.

Imelda lays tomato slices on the buttered bread laid out before her. 'These are the sandwiches,' she says, 'for the pub.'

Eve nods, filling a bowl with cornflakes.

'Today I'm doing cheese and tomato, egg mayonnaise, ham and cheese and chicken salad. I have to provide one or two vegetarian options every day.'

It's not so bad really. She just chats away, and Eve nods or shrugs or gives her one-word answers. There's no animosity, as far as Imelda can see; the disdain she'd thought she picked up on the first day they met had never materialised, thankfully. Eve simply keeps her distance, and Imelda makes no attempt to get closer.

'I could give you a lift to Laura's, if you like.' Still offering, because it would feel mean not to. 'It would be no trouble.'

'Thanks, but I can walk.'

'Right … Oh, and ask her if there's any news of poor Gavin, will you?'

'OK.'

Imelda tops shredded lettuce with cucumber and tomato and scattered chicken pieces. She adds a twist of black pepper and a shake of salt. She slicks mayonnaise onto the top slice of bread and lays it gently down.

The younger brother comes into her mind again. She's never tried to talk to Eve about him. His name – Keith, isn't it? – has never come up between them. Maybe she should have been less cautious at the start, less afraid of upsetting Eve. It might have drawn them closer if she'd shown more of an interest in Eve's family.

Maybe it's not too late.

'Eve,' she says, grating cheese. 'Can I ask about your brother – Keith, isn't that his name?'

A guarded look, one she knows well, comes immediately over the girl's face. 'What about him?' Her spoon halted in the bowl.

'Well … I'm just wondering do you see much of him?'

'No.' She raises the spoon to her mouth and crunches loudly. Imelda should probably leave it at that.

Or maybe she could venture a little further.

'He's younger, isn't he?'

A short nod.

'So he's what – about thirteen or fourteen, is it?'

Eve pushes back her chair abruptly, the legs scraping loudly on the tiles. 'Yeah,' she mutters, the word clipped off, bringing her bowl to the bin and tipping in the contents before Imelda can protest. Most of it uneaten, a few spoonfuls only.

'Eve, I didn't mean to—'

But she's already gone, flying back upstairs before any more interrogation can take place, Scooter abandoning her rubber bone to scurry after her new best friend.

Imelda halves the sandwiches, wraps them in clingfilm and labels them. Made it worse, she thinks. Tried to nudge open the door, got it slammed in my face.

Still, she tried. It's always worth trying.

✳

Keith.

His name, so unexpected, hitting her like a slap out of nowhere. What did she have to mention *Keith* for? The road ahead blurs; she dashes the tears away before they have a chance to fall. Everything was fine: what did she have to go and do that for?

A car passes. She's dimly aware of a hand lifted in greeting as it flashes by. Everyone trying to make friends with her, everyone refusing to leave her alone. Why can't they all just leave her alone?

She makes out the sign for 'Walter's Place B&B' ahead in the distance, swinging gently in the breeze that comes in from the sea. She looks towards the water, sees the coloured sails of the boats that bob in the bay, tries to swallow the lump that persists in her throat. He's having a good summer, she tells herself. He's OK. He's getting on OK.

She'll tell Laura today that she can't work for her any more. If she hadn't promised to come today she wouldn't. She'll go back to spending her afternoons on the beach. She'll have Scooter with her, it'll be fine. And if Imelda tells her they've been invited to dinner, or to anywhere, she'll tell her she doesn't want to go. She'll make them all leave her alone.

She passes the house with the red door, walking quickly, keeping her head down, hoping that nobody appears. He's the same as the others: he has to be kept away too. And stupidly, when nobody appears it makes her feel worse.

She approaches the B&B determinedly, blinking hard. 'Two hours,' Laura had said, 'ten till twelve' – which means she'll be gone long before he arrives to do the donkey rides. Just as well. She passes the field and sees George at the far end and smothers a pang. He's just a donkey, and Scooter's just a dog – but the thought of leaving Scooter at the end of the summer makes her feel like bawling out loud. Oh, why did they ever send her here?

Gavin's white van sits outside the gate, *Walter's Place Fresh Produce* in orange lettering on the side, above a cartoon of a basket holding carrots, onions and lettuce. She opens the gate and goes around to the side of the house, past the sty where the fat grunting pig lives – she won't be sorry to leave *that* behind – past the table and chairs where they gave her a birthday party she hadn't asked for.

At the far end of the field she makes out a quick movement behind the wire of the henhouse, and for a second she thinks it's the old man she saw before, back to tip his cap again at her

– but then the wire-covered gate opens and one of the twins emerges with a basket, followed moments later by his brother.

She turns towards the house before they can spot her – she's not in the mood for them today – and pushes open the back door that's never locked. Nobody seems to lock doors here, so different from the Garveys' house with its bolts and security chains and window locks. She walks through the scullery and into the kitchen.

Laura stands hunched over the table, one hand braced on its wooden surface, another pressed to her back. There's a clenched look to her face, the colour washed out of it. She makes a hissing sound through her teeth, the sound some people make when they're laughing. But she's not laughing.

The kitchen is a mess. Dishes are piled higgledy-piggledy on the table; frying pans and saucepans clutter the sink. The pup, Charlie, is lapping at a puddle of milk on the floor – and there's the dropped carton, still dribbling its contents out onto the tiles.

Eve takes in the scene, fear creeping over her. 'Laura – are you sick?'

Still bent forward, Laura takes her hand from the table and reaches it towards her – and not knowing what else to do, Eve steps forward and offers her own hand. Laura grabs onto it, her skin icy-cold. 'Hang on,' she says, the words as tight as her grip.

Eve's fear increases. This is wrong. This shouldn't be happening. She wants to move, to run for help, but she's trapped by Laura's vice-like grip. And then Laura lets out her breath with a whoosh, and releases Eve's hand. When she raises her head Eve sees a thin sheen of sweat on her forehead.

'Phew,' she says, dabbing her forehead with a crumpled serviette that she picks up from the table, looking up at the clock on the opposite wall. 'Seven minutes. We haven't got much time.' And before Eve can make sense of it, she adds, in a perfectly calm voice, 'It seems my babies have decided to come a bit early, Eve. Here's what I need you to do.'

✳

'Who on *earth* is that?' Marian mutters crossly, attempting to fasten her string of pearls. 'Vernon,' she calls, 'there's someone *hammering* at the door. Can you get it?'

'I'm on the toilet, dear.'

'*Lord*—' She lays the necklace down and crosses the room. 'I'm *coming*, I'm *coming*, no need to be so *loud*.'

She opens the door. At the sight of the girl her mouth drops open, her hand flies to her throat. 'Is it Imelda? What's happened? Tell me *quickly*.'

'Laura's having a baby, babies, she's having babies,' the girl says, the information galloping out so rapidly it sounds to Marian like one long unintelligible word: *laurashavinabaybeebaybees*. 'Down in the kitchen I rang the doctor but his phone is engaged and Nell is gone to Tralee with James and Gavin is in hospital there's no one else here all the other people are gone you need to come—'

'What? Stop – what? Slow down – what are you *saying*?'

Eve babbles on, her lightning delivery unaltered. 'She says your husband must take the boys somewhere I don't know some neighbour and she wants you to come down and help we have to *help* her.' The girl grabs Marian's cardigan sleeve. 'Please you must come *now* I don't know what to *do* the babies are coming—'

Marian gapes, horror blooming slowly in her face as understanding dawns. 'Jesus, Mary and holy St Joseph—*Vernon!*' she yells, having decided that the other three personages might not be of the most practical help. 'Come out here *now*!'

✳

Denis sits alone in his house, a poached egg cooling and stiffening on its slice of toast on the plate before him, the newspaper he walked to the supermarket for still folded by his elbow, its news unread, its crossword squares empty of letters.

What right do they have, he thinks angrily, to judge him? Which one of them has never made a mistake? Is he to be punished forever because he followed his heart?

Colm Daly was coming out of the supermarket when Denis approached. He nodded, gave a curt hello to Denis before moving on. Colm Daly, whose four children were taught by Denis, whose wife Mary played the piano every Christmas at the school concerts. Colm, who would have stopped for a ten-minute chat in days gone by, even if he and Denis had spent the previous evening, as they often had, on neighbouring barstools in Fitz's.

Give them time, Nell said. *They'll come round* – but why should Denis be forced to wait, forced to endure being ostracised, made to feel like some sort of pariah until they decide to let him back into their precious—

No. He cuts off the thought. He won't become bitter, he can't do that. He'll keep his dignity, he'll say nothing. He'll be patient, because he has no choice. He wants to stay on Roone, he wants to live out his days here, and he wants to be on cordial terms with everyone on the island. He won't allow them to change that.

Nell is right: they'll come round eventually. He opens the newspaper and scans the headlines before turning to the crossword page. He folds it open and picks up his knife and fork, pulling his plate towards him.

The doorbell rings.

He drops the cutlery and gets up, wondering who could be calling on him. Not Nell, gone to Tralee with James. Harry Jones maybe, looking to read the meter now that the house is inhabited again.

It isn't Harry Jones. It's Laura's two red-headed boys, accompanied by a man around Denis's own age, whom he's pretty sure he's never come across before.

'I'm terribly sorry to bother you,' the stranger says. 'You are Denis Mulcahy, yes?'

'I am.'

'Only I was asked to bring the boys to you, and ask if you'd keep an eye on them for a while. There's a –' he gives a small cough '– there's what you might call a small emergency at the bed and breakfast.'

'Mum is havin' a baby,' one of the boys puts in.

'She's havin' *two* babies,' the other corrects, 'not one.'

'Nell can't mind us 'cos she's gone to get a new car.'

'An' Gav is in hospital for a operation. He's gettin' his 'pendix out.'

Denis regards the two little boys, subdued by the drama of the occasion. He hasn't had much contact with them. He knows their names, but isn't sure which name goes with which boy.

'Can we watch television?' one of them asks.

A simple enough request. He stands aside and indicates the sitting-room door. 'The remote control is on the table.' He has yet to meet a child over six who can't operate a remote control.

They troop in, leaving Denis with their guardian. 'I didn't catch your name.'

The man extends his hand. 'Vernon McCarthy. My wife Marian is a sister of Imelda's. We rented your daughter's house two years ago.'

Ah, yes. Denis dimly remembers hearing of the trio, the last of Nell's tenants. He didn't meet them, having done his vanishing act from Roone a week or so before their arrival.

'We just happened to be staying in the bed and breakfast,' Vernon continues. 'We were about to go out when … all of this happened. Marian is with Mrs Dolittle – Laura – now.'

He looks bothered, as well he might. A woman in labour makes every man, unless he's a medic, feel very redundant.

'Have you called Dr Jack?'

'We can't get hold of him. We've left a message on his machine. We phoned Tralee hospital – they're trying to get someone out.'

Denis frowns. He had next month in his head for those babies: he must have got that wrong. 'So Laura is alone – apart from your wife, I mean.'

'Eve, the girl Imelda and Hugh are fostering, is there too. And Imelda's on her way, I just rang her.'

Three unqualified females, one hardly more than a child, attending what sounds like an unscheduled delivery – and two babies on the way, just to complicate matters.

'There's a midwife,' Denis says, 'Catherine Fahy. Her number should be in the book. Come in.'

As his caller steps inside, the sound of the television erupts from the sitting room.

✳

The pain comes in searing waves, lashing its way through her like a machete, making her bellow like an animal, making her curse like a navvy, covering her in tears and mucus and sweat, sweeping all logic and manners and modesty aside, and she wants Aaron – no, Gav, it's Gav, but he's not here, he's left her to bear this alone, the *bastard*.

In the dips between the pain, as she's whimpering with relief and bracing herself for the next attack, Laura is dimly aware of Imelda and Marian (*Marian???*) hovering around, laying cold cloths on her forehead, holding her hand – *Good girl*, they say, over and over, *you're doing fine, make as much noise as you want, the doctor is on his way, he'll be here any minute now, everything is going fine* – and every now and again Marian turns to snap something at someone Laura can't see – and now the pain is blazing back and it's blotting out everything else and it's all she can feel, dear sweet divine *Jesus*, it wasn't this bad with the boys, it couldn't have been anything like this bad, and all she wants is to die now, this very minute—

And then, somewhere in the dazzling, unbearable nightmare of it all, she feels Walter's presence – Walter is here, Walter has come. *Walter*, she sobs, *I can't do this* – and then he speaks to her. Walter *speaks*. His voice is little more than a whisper, but she hears it as clearly as if he had bent and put his lips to her ear. He tells her how strong she is, and that everything will be well, and that her babies will be born and will be perfect and will live – and she cries fresh tears, remembering the story Nell told her about his wife dying in childbirth all those years ago, along with their only daughter.

And when it feels like the pain is going to rip her apart, splice her clean down the middle, she begins to push because she must push, even though nobody has told her to – and she feels a dislodging at the white heart of the agony, a shifting within her, and Imelda looks petrified, and Marian looks like she's shouting something, but Laura's own sounds, her roars and grunts are drowning it out, and all she can do is push and push and push, and hope to God that it's the right thing to do.

※

When it's all over, when Imelda has gone to drive Laura, her baby girls and the midwife to the pier to meet the ambulance, when they've done what they can to tidy up, Marian and Eve regard one another warily across the kitchen.

'Tea?' Marian asks at length, and Eve nods, still too shocked by what has happened to do more.

'Well, put the kettle on then,' Marian says, taking a seat at the table, and Eve pushes herself away from the sink, fills the kettle and puts it on.

She tries to get her head around it. She saw *babies* being born, two babies slipping out one after the other, pushed out onto the bundle of towels they'd spread on the bed. And the stuff that had come out after them – Christ almighty, the thought of it now makes everything heave inside her.

From the start Marian was a bossy old cow, ordering Eve around like she was a servant. 'Take those two boys next door,' she told Eve. 'Tell whoever's there to hang on to them –' and Eve didn't have time to think about how she looked before she brought the twins to Nell's house, but it didn't matter because nobody was there, which didn't go down well with Marian.

'Keep them *outside* then,' she said crossly, as if it was Eve's fault, so Eve kept them in the field, put them onto the donkey's back and walked up and down with them until Marian's husband came out of the house, looking as scared as Eve felt. 'Imelda's on the way,' he told her, before taking the boys away and leaving Eve not knowing what to do.

She was tempted to make her getaway then, just slip off till all the fuss was over, but Laura had given her two tops and thrown a party for her, so she made herself go back inside, where she could hear the screaming before she got past the scullery.

For the past couple of hours she's been up and down the stairs like a yo-yo. She brought cold water and hot water, she found facecloths and towels, she answered the phone, she let Imelda in when she arrived.

But bossy as she was, Eve was glad Marian was there. It was good to feel that someone knew what to do, or at least acted like she did. Imelda wasn't much help, flapping around the place, telling Laura that everything was going to be fine, as if anyone believed that. Dabbing Laura's forehead and rubbing her back while Laura made enough noise to wake the dead – Eve would never have guessed she even knew half those words.

And when the babies finally came out, just before the midwife arrived, Eve and Imelda were given the job of wiping blood and other disgusting stuff from the tiny screwed-up faces with damp towels as Marian grimly cut her way with scissors (scalded by Eve) through the ropy greyish-pink cords that joined the babies to Laura – another thing that Eve can't recall without a lurch in her abdomen.

'I knew it!'

She turns. Marian stands at the open fridge door, holding up a carton of milk.

'I knew it was half-fat. She said it wasn't, but I knew well.'

Before Eve can respond – not that she can think of anything to say to that – the kettle boils. She searches for teabags and finds them stuffed into a cracked milk jug on the windowsill. She makes tea in silence and brings the pot to the table. She puts out mugs and spoons and sits wearily opposite Marian.

'You know,' Marian says, taking off the teapot lid and stirring the contents, 'it wouldn't kill you to be a bit friendlier. Imelda and Hugh have taken you into their home, they've bent over backwards to make you feel welcome, and all you do is sit there with a face as long as a wet week.'

Eve looks at her, and for a few seconds she makes no response. And then, God knows why – maybe because she wants to wipe the disapproving look off the old bat's face, maybe because the shock makes her careless, maybe because she's just sick and tired of keeping it all bottled up for so long – she opens her mouth and tells Marian exactly why she isn't a bit friendlier.

And as the words tumble out of her, as the horrible truth pours out of her, Marian listens in complete silence.

Monday, 15 July

Nell steps onto the side of the little boat and hovers for a second, finding her balance before springing off and diving cleanly into the water. She resurfaces a few seconds later, twenty yards away.

'It's perfect,' she calls, and Denis waves in acknowledgement before she swoops under again, as at home in the water as on dry ground. Her old spark returning, it would seem, after her months of mourning and weeks of convalescence.

'She's like a fish,' Vernon murmurs, seated at the boat's opposite end in a pair of rather startling wine-coloured trousers. 'Let's invite him along,' Nell had said, 'he's at a loose end, poor thing' – so the invitation had been issued and accepted.

The morning is warm and balmy, with a promise of more intense heat in the afternoon. On the whole, and despite a few recent wet days, this summer is turning out to be one of their better ones, after several that could best be described as falling somewhere between abysmal and mediocre.

Denis turns to the two remaining passengers, each engaged

in the serious business of fishing, with rods on loan from Lelia dangling over the far side of the boat.

'Any luck?'

'Nah.'

They respond simultaneously, which Denis has discovered is a frequent occurrence. But neither fisherman appears too bothered by his lack of success. They remind Denis of himself in days gone by, happily dipping a rod into the sea for hours, the possibility of a bite almost as good as the twitch on the line itself.

He hasn't fished in ages. He could take it up again – his rod must still be in the shed. The idea is appealing.

'You fish?' he asks Vernon.

Vernon shakes his head. 'Golf is more my thing. You play at all?'

'No. We don't have a course on the island.'

He could tell Vernon about the set of golf clubs he'd bought in a charity shop, a few weeks after meeting Claire. Forty euros he thinks he paid for them, his excuse to leave Roone every few days. Moira must have wondered why he'd suddenly taken up the game, but the question was never asked.

The clubs sat undisturbed in the boot of his car for months, until he left Roone and an excuse was no longer necessary. He eventually returned them to the charity shop, where they were accepted gratefully by the volunteer on duty.

No, he won't share that with Vernon.

'Can I have juice?' Ben asks, and Denis distributes cartons as Nell reappears, rosy-cheeked.

'We'd better head back soon – the donkey rides will be starting.'

It's business as usual at Walter's Place, despite the absence of both proprietors. Andy is handling the donkey rides with the twins – and, to everyone's surprise, Marian has taken it upon herself to keep the B&B up and running, with Eve as her assistant.

'Laura nearly fainted when I told her,' Nell reported yesterday after a visit to the hospital, 'but the more she thought about it, the more sense it made. She says Marian will have it spick and span – and even if she doesn't, nobody will dare complain about anything. I hope poor Eve is coping, though – I don't imagine Marian would be the easiest boss.'

Denis's sympathies lie more in Marian's direction: he can't picture the taciturn girl making any sort of a worthwhile assistant. Although it sounds like she made a fair fist of the donkey rides, so you never know.

The new babies are doing well, and scheduled to be out of their incubators in a few days. 'And Gav got to see them – they wheeled him down from his floor.'

All hospitalised parties ending up, happily, under the same roof – and all scheduled to be home in time for the Roone annual beach barbecue on Friday. The third barbecue in a row for which Denis is planning to be absent.

They make their way back to the pier, Denis and Vernon taking turns with the oars, Nell leading the fishermen in a fairly tuneful version of 'Row, Row, Row Your Boat'.

✳

Eve lies on the grass and looks up through dappled light at the smudges of deep blue sky that keep appearing and vanishing between the gently dipping and swaying greens and browns of the apple trees. No, not deep blue, pale blue – or maybe somewhere between deep and pale. She thinks what a wonderful thing it is to have nothing more important to worry about than the colour of the sky.

She's rolled her jeans up as far as they'll go, about six inches above her knees. The grass feels cool and soft beneath her calves. Tomorrow morning Imelda and Hugh are going to Tralee to talk to Anita at the fostering agency. Hugh rang and left a message on Anita's answering machine. Eve was upstairs on the landing, hands curled around the banisters, when he made the call.

'My wife and I will be in on Monday morning,' he said, 'to discuss an extremely urgent matter regarding Eve Mulhern, our foster child. We'll be arriving at ten o'clock.'

Eve liked the way he spoke, as if he wasn't even considering the possibility of being told that ten o'clock didn't suit. She liked the way he said *our foster child*, like she was someone they cared about. Thinking about it now makes her eyes sting a bit. She thinks what a wonderful thing it is to have someone say *our foster child* in just that way, about you.

She hears a soft snuffling sound and raises herself up on an elbow. 'This is the life,' she says, 'isn't it?' And Charlie and Scooter, tangled together in a sleepy huddle on the grass beside her, sigh happily and thump their tails in lazy agreement.

She lies back and again stares at the patches of sky. Ice blue.

No, that sounds too cold. Sea blue. Cornflower blue. Forget-me-not blue. Yes.

They believe her. They don't think she's making it up, they believe every single word that she's said. She thinks what a wonderful thing it is to be believed, after being afraid for years to tell anyone in case it made everything worse.

'Listen to me,' Imelda had said slowly and clearly. 'You will never go back to that house. Do you hear me? You will never set foot in that house again. I promise you that. Hugh and I will sort everything out.'

And Eve looked at the woman who had tried and tried to be her friend, the woman she'd pushed away again and again – and to her horror she found herself completely unable to stop the noisy, gulping sobs that *erupted* out of her. She cried loudly and messily, like a small child, and Imelda didn't try to hug her, she didn't say anything. She took the box of tissues from the worktop and placed it on the table and she let Eve cry for what seemed like a very long time. She just sat there. She was just there.

And when Eve, with eye-liner probably all over her face, and red puffy eyes and swollen lips, finally ran out of tears and sat head in hands taking deep shuddering breaths, Imelda got up and filled a glass with juice and cut a big slice of lemon meringue pie and set them before Eve. And for some reason, that set her off all over again.

She looks at the blue and green patchwork above her and thinks what a wonderful thing it is to have been sent to this place, to the house of two kind people who still want to help her, who refused to let her push them away.

They're going to arrange for a visit to Keith when they talk to the fostering agency tomorrow. They're not going to ask if it's OK, they're going to arrange a visit. 'We'll try and get Tuesday,' Imelda said. 'Some day this week anyway. We'll bring him out to lunch. And after we drop him back, you can do a bit of shopping.'

They've given her a hundred euro, on top of what they'd already given. She protested, but Imelda insisted. Imelda, Eve is discovering, can be just as bossy as her sister.

'You need summery bits and pieces,' she said, 'and a pair of sandals that you can walk in. You won't get much for a hundred euro.'

Laura's mobile phone, lying in the grass by her head, chirrups into life. She picks it up and takes the call, scribbling the details of the booking into the big notebook they found in a kitchen press. Eve's writing isn't half as neat as Marian's, but it does the job.

She likes running a B&B. She liked the two American couples who stayed last night, the wives exclaiming over her red hair, the husbands each giving her a ten-euro tip as they were leaving this morning.

She likes making the beds with sheets that smell like the sea, and coaxing the pillows into cases and arranging the towels neatly in the bathroom. She doesn't mind cleaning the bathrooms – most people only stay one or two nights, and there's only so much mess you can make in that time.

And even though she goes on a bit, Marian is fine once you keep nodding and agreeing. And she's not always bossy either.

'You'd be so much prettier,' she said, 'without all that muck on your face. You can hardly see your lovely eyes.' So this morning Eve put less eyeliner on, just for peace.

She might run her own B&B when she's older. She wouldn't rule it out. She closes her eyes, feeling in the grass until she finds a doggy body and resting her palm against its warm, breathing softness. She gets the sense they're not alone in the little orchard, but not in a scary way. It feels almost as if someone is watching over them. Watching over her.

She'll get shorts in Tralee, and a couple of T-shirts. And maybe a dress that floats around you when you walk. She's never owned a dress. And she'll get a swimsuit, a dark green one with a halter-neck, like one Kate Winslet was wearing in a photo. She'll go to Penneys, where you can get quite a lot for a hundred euro.

She feels emptied out of all the bad stuff. She feels ready to put some good stuff in. She thinks what a wonderful thing it is to let go of the bad stuff, to hand it over to someone else who's going to make it all go away.

And some time after that, as she drowses between sleep and wakefulness, footsteps approach.

'All done,' Andy says, and she opens her eyes and unrolls the legs of her jeans and packs notebook and phone into her bag. They put leashes on the two pups and set off down the road together.

FRIDAY, 19 JULY

'Our first Roone barbecue,' Laura says. 'We just missed it the year we were renting – remember? And last year we moved here a couple of weeks too late – typical.'

'You nearly missed it this year,' Nell points out, 'with your shenanigans.'

'That's true – but you know who to blame for that.' She indicates the two tiny infants, lying placidly on their blanket beneath the polka-dot sunshade, wearing matching striped T-shirts and not much else. 'Tweedledum and Tweedledee.'

'Oh, you've settled on names. How lovely.'

'Actually, we *have* settled on names. We're calling them Eve and Marian.'

Nell grins. 'You're not.'

'We are. How could we not, really, after them keeping us afloat for the last week – not to mention being there for all the gory details? I hope poor Eve wasn't traumatised.'

'Doesn't look too traumatised to me.'

They both turn to Eve, splashing in the water with Andy and his friends, and looking rather curvy in her green halter-neck swimsuit.

'I know – can you believe it? Talk about a transformation. She seems to have undergone a bit of a personality change. Running a business clearly agrees with her.'

'Not to mention having a boyfriend.'

'Is he? I wondered about that.'

'Well, I can't prise anything out of Andy – naturally – but it looks pretty obvious to me.'

'You're such a matchmaker. You know she's staying on as my assistant in the B&B till the end of August.'

'Yes, Imelda told me.'

'And we've asked herself and Marian to be godmothers, and they've said yes. Marian will be wonderful, she'll never forget a birthday. Eve might do OK if we asked Andy to be godfather.'

'I think that's a wonderful idea.'

The date of the annual barbecue was changed from the last to the third Friday in July as a mark of respect to Walter, whose death had occurred on the day of the barbecue two years earlier.

The change of date hasn't affected the favourable weather conditions that the Roone barbecue has always been blessed with. Even in the worst of summers islanders could always be confident of at least one sunny day, and in the eighty-odd years since the barbecue's inception they have never once been disappointed. Today is another fine day in a week-long heatwave that shows no sign of losing momentum.

It's late in the afternoon, the sun lower now in the sky. From where they sit Nell and Laura can smell the fish and meats that are being cooked over the coals in the half-dozen or so pits that were dug and lined earlier in the day.

'He used to bring potatoes,' Nell says, 'a big box of them, all wrapped in tinfoil.'

'Who?'

'Walter.'

'Ah … poor old Walter. He was there, you know,' she adds, 'when the girls were born. He spoke to me.'

Nell smiles. 'That's good.' Amazing the hallucinations childbirth must produce. Still, if it helped her to get through it, where was the harm?

'You're back to work next week then?' Laura asks.

'Yes. Mornings only for a week and hopefully full time after that.'

Ben and Seamus appear, covered with sand and freckles and demanding drinks, available from the large tent set up beyond the barbecue pits.

'Find Gav,' Laura instructs, 'and tell him to bring us some too. We'll have beer.'

'Can we have beer too?'

'Most certainly not.'

They watch them scampering across to the group of men that inevitably forms in close proximity to the drinks tent, which is currently being manned by Hugh and James.

'Shame your father isn't here,' Laura says. 'He probably hasn't missed many barbecues.'

'He missed the last two.' Nell recalls the only one she missed, stunned by her father's sudden disappearance and struggling with uncertainty about Tim. That was the one that Walter had missed too, dropping dead on his landing, his box of potatoes already wrapped in tinfoil on the kitchen table.

Her father should be here today, he has every right to enjoy it – but she can understand his decision to give it a miss. Too difficult for him to attend a gathering like this while his company is still largely unwelcome. They'll soften eventually, for her sake if not for his. She hopes it won't take too long.

She wonders what he's doing today. Probably out walking the roads if she knows him. Walking has always been his therapy.

Lonely for him, though. She hates to think of his loneliness.

✳

His feet are killing him, his own fault for wearing socks and walking boots on a day like this; nearly seven in the evening and the heat still intense. He limps past a house, then retraces his steps to hoist himself upwards to sit on the waist-high garden wall. If anyone comes out they'll surely take pity on him, maybe even offer him a cup of tea.

He vaguely remembers the house. He passed it on a walk some time in the past few months. He dimly recalls a man sitting on the garden seat outside the window. The seat is bare today, the windows all tightly closed despite the heat, nothing to be seen behind the net curtains. The dark green paint is peeling from the front door.

The wall isn't comfortable. Its knobbly, uneven top digs into his backside, but the discomfort is outweighed by the relief of being off his feet. He negotiates each foot carefully onto the wall to unlace and remove his boots and peel off his socks.

The air on his bare skin is wonderful. He sits and relishes the sensation, wriggling his toes and breathing in the sweet coconut scent of a nearby furze bush. Perfect weather for the Roone barbecue, as it always is. He pictures them all on the beach watching the sun going down; he sees the sunken pits giving off their tantalising scents of cooking food. Next year he'll be welcome.

After a while he eases the small rucksack off his back and drinks deeply from the water bottle within. The liquid is warm and plasticky from the heat of the day, but it's all he has. As he replaces the bottle he catches a movement out of the corner of his eye. He turns.

A small child of uncertain gender has emerged from around the side of the house. The pale-coloured hair is cut short; badly cut, as if someone did it with kitchen scissors. The child's face is streaked with what looks like dried mud – or maybe it's dried chocolate.

It wears beige trousers a little short in the leg, and a green woolly jumper – too warm, surely, for this sunny day. On its feet is a pair of lace-up brown shoes, again inappropriate for the weather. No socks. Whoever dressed this child was thinking about something else.

'Hello,' Denis says. 'Is this your house?'

The child regards him solemnly, in the way that youngsters can do, and makes no reply.

'Is your mammy inside?' He wonders if a parent is about to burst from the house and whisk the child away. The times they live in, where simply talking to a small child can get a man into trouble.

Again his little companion offers no response. Denis decides to give it one more try.

'What's your name?' he asks.

It opens its mouth. He waits.

'Ellie,' the child whispers.

'Ellie,' Denis repeats, hoisting a foot onto the wall, reaching for a sock. 'That's a nice name.'

Ellie. He pauses, the sock halfway on.

Ellie. He looks at the child, imagines curls instead of this butchered haircut.

A dripping ice-cream held in a pudgy little hand. *Have you seen—*

Ellie.

Dear sweet divine Jesus. He searches her face, his heart flapping, his hands suddenly cold despite the day. She gazes back at him impassively.

'Ellie what?' he asks, the smile frozen on his face, yanking on the sock. 'What's the other bit of your name, dear?' Fumbling for his boot, his eyes not leaving her face.

'Ryan.' A tiny whisper, so low he can barely hear it.

Christ almighty. Still smiling at her, one foot still bare, he reaches into his rucksack and pulls out his phone, hand trembling.

✳

'Are you sure I'm not pushing you into it?'

He smiles into the darkness. 'I'm sure.'

'I know I can be impulsive.'

He finds her hand and squeezes it. 'I love how impulsive you are.'

She turns and curls into him. 'He's nice though, isn't he?'

'Yes, he's nice.'

'I think he looks like her, even though they've got different fathers.'

'Mm, maybe a bit around the eyes.'

'Yes, there.'

They lie in silence for so long he thinks she's nodded off. He remembers how Anita's face changed when they dropped the bombshell on her at the fostering agency, how sharp her questioning became, how she pinched the skin on the back of her hand, pulling it up between thumb and forefinger as she listened to their answers.

He recalls their meeting with Keith the following day, the heartbreakingly awkward hug Eve gave him, the way she watched Hugh and Imelda as they were introduced. Wanting them to like him, Hugh thought, the way you'd want parents to take to a prospective fiancé.

He was touched by Keith's shyness, his tendency to tug at the hair above his ear when he spoke, the way he blushed when Eve reached across and wiped a smear of ketchup from his cheek. 'Messer,' she said, a fondness in her voice Hugh hadn't heard before.

He thinks how Eve has changed since the day of Laura's babies, when she told Marian, of all people, how she was being abused, had been abused for years, by the son of her foster carers. Such a thing to keep locked away. Small wonder she was so shut off from them.

It's not a transformation, it's small things. It's the rare smiles they see now; it's the remark that isn't a response to a question. It's the offer, some day during the week, to help Imelda with weeding. It's the packet of chocolate biscuits, diffidently produced, on her return from the B&B yesterday. It's the thought of her calling into the supermarket and picking them out for Hugh and Imelda.

He wonders how it will all play out, whether the Garvey boy will be investigated, or whether the agency will hush it up to save face. At fifty-three he doesn't have many illusions left. His thoughts become muddy with sleep.

The phone startles both of them. He fumbles for the lamp and switches it on, blinking. Twelve fifteen the clock radio says, in bright green numbers. Not the right time for a phone call.

He lifts the receiver, says hello, aware of Imelda watching his face anxiously.

'Hugh—'

It's Nell, at twelve fifteen. Let it not be a death, let someone not have died. What? Imelda mouths.

'They found her,' Nell says, her voice cracking, half crying, half laughing. 'Hugh, they found Ellie – Dad found her – and she's alive. Ellie Ryan, she's alive, Hugh.'

He lets out the breath he didn't know he was holding. 'That's great news,' he says, smiling at Imelda. 'That's the best news ever.'

THURSDAY, 1 AUGUST

The bunting is crooked, one end a good foot and a half lower than the other.

'It's not easy to hang it straight when you're depending on apple trees,' Gavin pointed out.

'I like it crooked,' Laura declared. 'It makes it a unique work of art. Anyone can hang bunting straight: where's the creativity in that?' – which earned her a heartfelt kiss from the father of her most recently arrived children.

'My ones are better than Ben's,' Seamus said, which earned him a slap on the arm from his mother.

The bunting is dual-purpose, images of birthday cakes and candles interspersed with baby bottles, rattles and cradles. Ben did the birthday ones, Seamus the christening.

Twenty-eight today, Laura thinks, waiting to see how it feels, which turns out to be not a whole lot different from twenty-seven. A mother of four at twenty-eight: not bad going.

'Happy birthday,' Gav had said that morning, presenting her

with the dress she'd ordered from a catalogue a month earlier. Size fourteen, in it by Hallowe'en, all going well.

'Happy birthday,' her sons chorused, presenting her with the bunting. 'And this,' they added, presenting her with the earrings she'd pointed out to Gav in the window of one of Roone's craft shops at least two months earlier. Good old Gav.

'Happy birthday,' Nell said, presenting her with the bracelet that went along with the earrings. Good old Gav.

'Happy birthday,' Eve said, presenting her with a framed photo of the boys sitting on George's back. Clever Eve.

'Happy birthday,' Susan said, handing her an envelope, 'from your father,' and a Brown Thomas bag containing the usual goodies and more. 'From me.'

'Happy birthday,' Imelda said, presenting her with the cake, as requested, and a card, which hadn't been.

'Happy christening,' Laura told her daughters, presenting them each with a full breast. They're twenty days old, much too young for presents. Anyway, milk is all they want, along with a fresh nappy every now and then.

She sits back and regards the faces gathered around her on the patio. Father William is on her right, having carried out his priestly duty and christened the new arrivals an hour earlier. Nell and James are seated next to him, whispering together like newly-weds. Or new parents-to-be, maybe: Nell is on orange juice and has a smugness about her. Laura certainly wouldn't rule it out.

Andy and Eve, freshly appointed godparents, are halfway down the table – both of them doing their best not to look like a couple, as if anyone is fooled. Marian and Vernon are across the way, the second set of godparents, back on Roone for the occasion. Marian in Sunday-best peach polyester, Vernon in his weddings, funerals and christenings suit.

Hugh and Imelda are beside them, beaming like Cheshire cats since hearing that Eve is to stay with them permanently – or at least until her eighteenth birthday. Not that it looks like she'll be going anywhere fast after that, not if young Andy Baker has any say in the matter. The fate of her brother is still undecided, but already he's been twice to Roone on day trips. Won't be long, it looks like, till he's installed here too.

She looks towards the far end of the table to Ben and Seamus, her firstborns and lights of her life, no less precious now than before their sisters came along and stole what was left of her heart. The babies in question are snoozing in the shade behind their brothers, an eye being kept on them by Susan, seated between the boys, who arrived yesterday from Dublin and is staying for a week. Step-grandmother to four, at the ripe old age of thirty-eight.

And next to Susan sits Denis Mulcahy, the man of the moment after discovering the whereabouts of Ellie Ryan, his miraculous find lifting the spirits of the whole island – of the whole country, if not the world. Moved back home for good as of last week, restored to favour on Roone, poor man.

But the tragedy of the middle-aged brother and sister who took Ellie off the island eleven weeks earlier, coaxing her away with promises of kittens, and brought her to the house they'd shared all their lives. Neither of them ever having had a job, the sister's life devoted to looking after her mentally slow brother since the deaths from cancer of both their parents before the siblings were out of their teens. A catalogue of heartbreak.

Their house isolated, no neighbours to call in for a chat and a cuppa, nobody to wonder about miniature items of clothing hanging on the line in the back garden, after the sister's stifled maternal instinct had flared into life at the sight of a small child standing alone by the roadside on one of the day trips around Kerry the pair took every few months in their battered old Ford. Their first trip to Roone, their first time to leave the Irish mainland.

An act of impulse, it would seem, no malice in it. An attempt to fill a yawning emptiness, no more. The little pink sandals thrown off the ferry, their only thought to make people stop looking for her, to keep her with them. Ellie cared for as best they could, clothed in charity-shop garments, fed each day and put to bed each night. Kept inside for fear of discovery, until the sister, alone in Tralee one day, suffered a stroke and was carted off to hospital, leaving her brother and his little charge to fend for themselves – and they muddled along for a few days until Ellie, momentarily unattended, wandered into the garden and met a man who was sitting on the wall.

The facts of the case were deeply moving, every aspect of the story bringing a lump to throats. Ellie's overjoyed parents embracing the little girl they'd never thought to see again; the brother's bewildered expression as he was led by police from the house; the sister lying in hospital, robbed of speech and movement.

The blurred photo that someone produced for the

newspapers and television screens, the two of them sitting side by side at some relative's wedding breakfast, staring solemnly into the camera. How could they be punished, despite the grief and desperation their actions had caused?

Laura regards Imelda's coffee walnut cake on the table before her, *Congratulations* the message on top, covering both occasions. So fortunate she is, living in a beautiful place with four healthy children and a man who loves her. Easy to forget that sometimes.

She looks down the table and finds Gav, seated across from the boys he's accepted as his own. Easy to forget how much she depends on him, until he isn't there any more. Hard to imagine him not being around. All kinds of love in the world, some you don't even realise are there, under your nose. She picks up a fork and taps it against her glass, and keeps tapping until the various conversations have halted, and everyone is looking in her direction.

She gets to her feet. 'A brief interruption,' she says, 'won't take long. I just wanted to put a question—'

She breaks off, unexpectedly nervous. What if it doesn't go as she planned? Is she being too cocky, assuming it'll turn out the way she wants it to?

She looks at the faces of her family and friends in turn, leaving Gav till last. She meets his eye. He winks at her. She smiles at him.

'I just wanted to put a question to you,' she tells him. 'I wanted to ask if you'll have me as your lawful wedded wife. Just if you felt like it.'

There's a second or two of dead silence. Gav doesn't move, nobody moves. She's made a mistake, possibly more enormous than any mistake that's gone before it, which is saying something.

Then his face breaks into a grin. 'Thought you'd never ask,' he says.

The table erupts in cheers. The babies jerk awake and burst into simultaneous, outraged wails. Their brothers, caught up in the drama, throw their plastic plates into the air, sending cocktail sausages flying. The two pups in attendance dive for the sausages before adding to the cacophony with wildly excited yips. Chaos reigns.

In the field George VI looks up and regards the madness briefly before moving off in search of quieter grass.

ACKNOWLEDGEMENTS

A big thank you to:

- my neighbour Thomas Bibby, for his computer games advice;
- my Facebook friend Clodagh Kavanagh, for guiding me through the fostering process;
- my nurse pals Ann Menzies and Nicola Quinn, for filling in the medical blanks;
- my editor Ciara Doorley, and all at Hachette Books Ireland;
- my copy-editor Hazel and proofreader Aonghus, for their invaluable help;
- you, for your support. I couldn't do it without you. Mwah.

One Summer
Roisin **MEANEY**

NUMBER ONE BESTSELLER

This summer on the island, anything is possible …

Nell Mulcahy grew up on the island – playing in the shallows and fishing with her father in his old red boat in the harbour. So when the stone cottage by the edge of the sea comes up for sale, the decision to move back from Dublin is easy. And where better to hold her upcoming wedding to Tim than on the island, surrounded by family and friends?

But when Nell decides to rent out her cottage for the summer to help finance the wedding, she sets in motion an unexpected series of events.

As deeply buried feelings rise to the surface, Nell's carefully laid plans for her wedding start to go awry and she is forced to make some tough decisions.

One thing's for sure, it's a summer on the island that nobody will ever forget.

Also available as an ebook

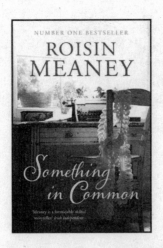

The friendship starts with a letter … from aspiring writer Sarah to blunt but witty journalist Helen, complaining about Helen's most recent book review. And there begins a correspondence that blossoms into a friendship which spans over two decades.

As the years pass, the women exchange details of loves lost and found, of family joys and upheavals. Sarah's letters filled with thoughts on her outwardly perfect marriage and her aching desire for children, and Helen's on the struggle of raising her young daughter alone.

But little do they realise that their story began long before Sarah penned that first letter – on one unforgettable afternoon where, during a distraught conversation on a bridge, Sarah changed the course of Helen's life forever.

This is the story of Helen and Sarah, and the friendship that was part of their destiny.

Also available as an ebook

Sometimes it's worth the effort …

One crisp September evening art teacher Audrey Matthews sits alone in room six at Carrickbawn Senior College, wondering if anyone is going to sign up for her Life Drawing for Beginners class.

By eight o'clock six people have arrived. Six strangers who will spend two hours together every week until Halloween, learning the fine art of life drawing.

Nobody could have predicted on that cold autumn day the profound effect the class would have on its students and their lives.

Least of all Audrey, the biggest beginner of all, who is to discover that once you keep an open mind, life – and love – can throw up more than a few surprises …

Also available as an ebook

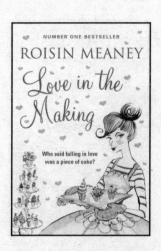

Happiness in life, and in love, is all in the making

Hannah Robinson is just about to open the doors to her new shop Cupcakes on the Corner when out of the blue her boyfriend Patrick announces that he's leaving her for another woman. Faced with starting a business on her own, Hannah begins to wonder if her life-long dream has just turned into a nightmare.

So her best friend Adam sets his birthday as a deadline – seven months to make her shop a success, or walk away from it all. And as Hannah immerses herself in early-morning icing, she soon discovers that she's too busy to think about Patrick and his now pregnant girlfriend … or to notice an increasingly regular customer who has recently developed a sweet tooth for all things cupcake …

Also available as an ebook

READING is so much more than the act of moving from page to page. It's the exploration of new worlds; the pursuit of adventure; the forging of friendships; the breaking of hearts; and the chance to begin to live through a new story each time the first sentence is devoured.

We at Hachette Ireland are very passionate about what we read, and what we publish. And we'd love to hear what you think about our books.

If you'd like to let us know, or to find out more about us and our titles, please visit www.hachette.ie or our Facebook page www.facebook.com/hachetteireland, or follow us on Twitter @HachetteIre.